ALICE IN WONDERLAND

AUTHORITATIVE TEXTS OF

ALICE'S ADVENTURES IN WONDERLAND

THROUGH THE LOOKING-GLASS

THE HUNTING OF THE SNARK

BACKGROUNDS

ESSAYS IN CRITICISM

Second Edition

A NORTON CRITICAL EDITION

LEWIS CARROLL

ALICE IN WONDERLAND

SECOND EDITION

AUTHORITATIVE TEXTS OF
ALICE'S ADVENTURES IN WONDERLAND
THROUGH THE LOOKING-GLASS
THE HUNTING OF THE SNARK

BACKGROUNDS

ESSAYS IN CRITICISM

Edited by

DONALD J. GRAY
INDIANA UNIVERSITY

W · W · NORTON & COMPANY

New York · London

Printed in the United States of America.

The text of this book is composed in Electra, with the display set in Deepdene.

Library of Congress Cataloging in Publication Data
Carroll, Lewis, 1832–1898.
    [Selections. 1992]
    Alice in Wonderland / Lewis Carroll ; authoritative texts of
Alice's adventures in Wonderland, Through the looking-glass, The
hunting of the snark, backgrounds, essays in criticism ; edited by
Donald J. Gray. — 2nd ed.
        p.   cm. — (Norton critical edition)
    Includes bibliographical references and index.
    1. Carroll, Lewis, 1832–1898—Criticism and interpretation.
    2. Children's literature, English—History and criticism.   I. Gray,
Donald J.   II. Title.
    PR4611.A4G7   1992
    823'.8—dc20   91-12533
ISBN 0-393-95804-3

W. W. Norton & Company, Inc., 500 Fifth Avenue, New York, N.Y. 10110
www.wwnorton.com

W. W. Norton & Company Ltd., Castle House, 75/76 Wells Street, London W1T 3QT

8 9 0

Contents

Essays in Criticism

Preface

In the second edition of the Norton Critical Edition of the *Alice* books, I have again included matter that suggests the important contexts out of which Lewis Carroll's best-known, and best, books were written. Principally, the *Alice* books, and even the mysteriously disturbing *The Hunting of the Snark*, are stories told to and written for children. Carroll mocked the conventions of nineteenth-century children's writing, and his books helped to change them. But for those very reasons, much of his playfulness depends for its point and effect on a familiarity with writing for children like that which Carroll's contemporaries, adults as well as children, would have brought to the reading and hearing of these stories. Carroll also appropriated some of the practices of popular comic entertainments of his time. He loved the theater, including the fairy-tale burlesque and fanciful transformations of theatrical pantomime, and all through his life he imitated, and eventually he greatly elevated, the verse parodies and language play that filled the mid-century comic magazines to which as a young Oxford tutor he occasionally contributed.

At Oxford, and as Charles Lutwidge Dodgson, Carroll was a tutor in mathematics, a kind of popular lecturer in logic, and a clergyman who never took the final step of ordination but who occasionally preached to university congregations. Both his mathematics and his religious beliefs were conventional, dogmatic, and out of touch with the most interesting speculations of his time. He was serious about using jokes and puzzles to teach logic to young people. But he seems not to have gotten past thinking of logic itself as a game, as a delightful demonstration of the treacheries of language and the procedures of thinking, and not as an instrument to refine them.

When Carroll took his religious convictions and his knowledge of mathematics and logic to the wonderlands of his writing for children, however, they all became freshly and profoundly interesting. Word and number games, and the amusing logic that moves with cool inexorability to nonsensical conclusions, become charms by which Carroll at once raises and holds at bay grave matters that deeply engaged his contemporaries: the predatory character of natural existence, the possibilities of extinction and of a void at the center of things, the impossibility of human reason and language ever to make satisfying sense. These are the themes that engage Carroll's twentieth-century adult readers, who are now probably most of his readers. But their resonance is most fully heard when they are listened to not just as anticipations of modernist skepticism and nihilism, but also as the night thoughts of a man whose intelligence and sensibility resided just as authentically in the axioms of Euclidean geometery and the charities of a providential deity.

To help readers hear that resonance, I have in this edition somewhat enlarged the selection from biographies and from Carroll's diaries and letters. I have also tried to mark the complications of his relationships with children, who were often warmed and dignified by his attentions, suspect as those attentions must be to our post-Freudian awareness. In my selection from the commentary on Carroll's writing, I have included some relatively recent essays that continue and extend the now orthodox interest of twentieth-century readers in the subversive and anarchic qualities of his writing (Auerbach and Rackin). I have also included parts of chapters from recent books that make his writing significant by placing it in the functions and concerns of nineteenth-century social comedy (Henkle) and in the generic meanings of comedy itself (Polhemus).

This second edition enables me to include "The Wasp in a Wig" episode, a recently discovered passage that Carroll excised from *Through the Looking-Glass* when he read the book in galley proof. His decision testifies to his judgment—the passage is not up to the standard of most of the rest of the book—and to the fact that Carroll did not treat the texts of his entertainments with the solemn deference accorded them by many of their critics and commentators.

I am grateful to the authors of the interpretative and biographical commentary reprinted in this edition for their permission to use their writing. As anyone must be who thinks or writes about Lewis Carroll, I am especially indebted to Roger Lancelyn Green for his edition of the *Diaries*, to Morton Cohen for his edition of the *Letters*, to the compilers of the several editions of *The Lewis Carroll Handbook*, and to the biographies of Derek Hudson and Anne Clark.

The texts of the two *Alice* books are those of an edition Dodgson prepared for publication in 1897. The text of *The Hunting of the Snark* is that of the first edition of 1876. The sources of the texts of other writing by Carroll reprinted here are indicated in the notes to each selection.

DONALD GRAY

The Text of

Alice's Adventures
in Wonderland

Alice's Adventures in Wonderland

All in the golden afternoon
    Full leisurely we glide;
For both our oars, with little skill,
    By little arms are plied,
While little hands make vain pretence
    Our wanderings to guide.

Ah, cruel Three![1] In such an hour,
    Beneath such dreamy weather,
To beg a tale of breath too weak
    To stir the tiniest feather!
Yet what can one poor voice avail
    Against three tongues together?

Imperious Prima flashes forth
    Her *edict* "to begin it": ~~command~~
In gentler tones Secunda hopes
    "There will be nonsense in it!"
While Tertia interrupts the tale
    Not more than once a minute.

Anon, to sudden silence won,
    In fancy they pursue
The dream-child moving through a land
    Of wonders wild and new,
In friendly chat with bird or beast—
    And half believe it true.

And ever, as the story drained
    The wells of fancy dry,
And faintly strove that weary one
    To put the subject by,
"The rest next time—" "It is next time!"
    The happy voices cry.

Thus grew the tale of Wonderland:
    Thus slowly, one by one,
Its quaint events were hammered out—
    And now the tale is done,

1. The three Liddell children, Lorina ("Prima"), Alice ("Secunda"), and Edith "Tertia"). Alice was ten when the expedition to Godstow during which the story was begun took place in 1862. She is seven in *Alice's Adventures in Wonderland*, which is set in May; and seven and a half in *Through the Looking-Glass*, which is set in November.

3

And home we steer, a merry crew,
  Beneath the setting sun.

Alice! A childish story take,
  And, with a gentle hand,
Lay it where Childhood's dreams are twined
  In Memory's mystic band.
Like pilgrim's wither'd wreath of flowers
  Pluck'd in a far-off land.

Christmas-Greetings

Lady dear, if Fairies may
    For a moment lay aside
Cunning tricks and elfish play,
    'Tis at happy Christmas-tide.

We have heard the children say—
    Gentle children, whom we love—
Long ago, on Christmas Day,
    Came a message from above.

Still, as Christmas-tide comes round,
    They remember it again—
Echo still the joyful sound
    "Peace on earth, good-will to men!"

Yet the hearts must childlike be
    Where such heavenly guests abide;
Unto children, in their glee,
    All the year is Christmas-tide!

Thus, forgetting tricks and play
    For a moment, Lady dear,
We would wish you, if we may,
    Merry Christmas, glad New Year!

Christmas, 1867

---

2. This poem was first printed in *Phantasmagoria* (1869). It was attached to the first Alice book when it was reprinted in the facsimile edition of *Alice's Adventures Under Ground* (1886), the manuscript book that Dodgson gave to Alice Liddell in November 1864.

Chapter I

DOWN THE RABBIT-HOLE

Alice was beginning to get very tired of sitting by her sister on the bank and of having nothing to do: once or twice she had peeped into the book her sister was reading, but it had no pictures or conversations in it, "and what is the use of a book," thought Alice, "without pictures or conversations?"

So she was considering, in her own mind (as well as she could, for the hot day made her feel very sleepy and stupid), whether the pleasure of making a daisy-chain would be worth the trouble of getting up and picking the daisies, when suddenly a White Rabbit with pink eyes ran close by her.

There was nothing so *very* remarkable in that; nor did Alice think it so *very* much out of the way to hear the Rabbit say to itself "Oh dear! Oh dear! I shall be too late!" (when she thought it over afterwards it occurred to her that she ought to have wondered at this, but at the time it all seemed quite natural); but, when the Rabbit actually *took a watch out of its waistcoat-pocket*, and looked at it, and then hurried on, Alice started to her feet, for it

7

flashed across her mind that she had never before seen a rabbit with either a waistcoat-pocket, or a watch to take out of it, and burning with curiosity, she ran across the field after it, and was just in time to see it pop down a large rabbit-hole under the hedge.

In another moment down went Alice after it, never once considering how in the world she was to get out again.

The rabbit-hole went straight on like a tunnel for some way, and then dipped suddenly down, so suddenly that Alice had not a moment to think about stopping herself before she found herself falling down what seemed to be a very deep well.

Either the well was very deep, or she fell very slowly, for she had plenty of time as she went down to look about her, and to wonder what was going to happen next. First, she tried to look down and make out what she was coming to, but it was too dark to see anything: then she looked at the sides of the well, and noticed that they were filled with cupboards and book-shelves: here and there she saw maps and pictures hung upon pegs. She took down a jar from one of the shelves as she passed: it was labeled "ORANGE MARMALADE," but to her great disappointment it was empty: she did not like to drop the jar, for fear of killing somebody underneath, so managed to put it into one of the cupboards as she fell past it.

"Well!" thought Alice to herself. "After such a fall as this, I shall think nothing of tumbling down-stairs! How brave they'll all think me at home! Why, I wouldn't say anything about it, even if I fell off the top of the house!" (Which was very likely true.)

Down, down, down. Would the fall *never* come to an end? "I wonder how many miles I've fallen by this time?" she said aloud. "I must be getting somewhere near the centre of the eartn. Let me see: that would be four thousand miles down, I think—" (for, you see, Alice had learnt several things of this sort in her lessons in the school-room, and though this was not a *very* good opportunity for showing off her knowledge, as there was no one to listen to her, still it was good practice to say it over) "—yes, that's about the right distance—but then I wonder what Latitude or Longitude I've got to?" (Alice had not the slightest idea what Latitude was, or Longitude either, but she thought they were nice grand words to say.)

Presently she began again. "I wonder if I shall fall right *through* the earth! How funny it'll seem to come out among the people that walk with their heads downwards! The antipathies, I think—" (she was rather glad there *was* no one listening, this time, as it didn't sound at all the right word) "—but I shall have to ask them what the name of the country is, you know. Please, Ma'am, is this New

Zealand? Or Australia?" (and she tried to curtsey as she spoke—fancy, *curtseying* as you're falling through the air! Do you think you could manage it?) "And what an ignorant little girl she'll think me for asking! No, it'll never do to ask: perhaps I shall see it written up somewhere."

Down, down, down. There was nothing else to do, so Alice soon began talking again. "Dinah'll miss me very much to-night, I should think!" (Dinah was the cat.[3]) "I hope they'll remember her saucer of milk at tea-time. Dinah, my dear! I wish you were down here with me! There are no mice in the air, I'm afraid, but you might catch a bat, and that's very like a mouse, you know. But do cats eat bats, I wonder?" And here Alice began to get rather sleepy, and went on saying to herself, in a dreamy sort of way, "Do cats eat bats? Do cats eat bats?" and sometimes "Do bats eat cats?" for, you see, as she couldn't answer either question, it didn't much matter which way she put it. She felt that she was dozing off, and had just begun to dream that she was walking hand in hand with Dinah, and was saying to her, very earnestly, "Now, Dinah, tell me the truth: did you ever eat a bat?" when suddenly, thump! thump! down she came upon a heap of sticks and dry leaves, and the fall was over.

Alice was not a bit hurt, and she jumped up on to her feet in a moment: she looked up, but it was all dark overhead: before her was another long passage, and the White Rabbit was still in sight, hurrying down it. There was not a moment to be lost: away went Alice like the wind, and was just in time to hear it say, as it turned a corner, "Oh my ears and whiskers, how late it's getting!" She was close behind it when she turned the corner, but the Rabbit was no longer to be seen: she found herself in a long, low hall, which was lit up by a row of lamps hanging from the roof.

There were doors all round the hall, but they were all locked; and when Alice had been all the way down one side and up the other, trying every door, she walked sadly down the middle, wondering how she was ever to get out again.

Suddenly she came upon a little three-legged table, all made of solid glass: there was nothing on it but a tiny golden key, and Alice's first idea was that this might belong to one of the doors of the hall; but, alas! either the locks were too large, or the key was too small, but at any rate it would not open any of them. However, on the second time round, she came upon a low curtain she had not noticed before, and behind it was a little door about fifteen

3. Dinah was also the name of the Liddells' cat, named, with her companion Villikens, after the characters in a popular midcentury dialect ballad.

inches high: she tried the little golden key in the lock, and to her great delight it fitted!

Alice opened the door and found that it led into a small passage, not much larger than a rat-hole: she knelt down and looked along the passage into the loveliest garden you ever saw. How she longed to get out of that dark hall, and wander about among those beds of bright flowers and those cool fountains, but she could not even get her head through the doorway; "and even if my head *would* go through," thought poor Alice, "it would be of very little use without my shoulders. Oh, how I wish I could shut up like a telescope! I think I could, if I only knew how to begin." For, you see, so many out-of-the-way things had happened lately, that Alice had begun to think that very few things indeed were really impossible.

There seemed to be no use in waiting by the little door, so she went back to the table, half hoping she might find another key on it, or at any rate a book of rules for shutting people up like telescopes: this time she found a little bottle on it ("which certainly was not here before," said Alice), and tied around the neck of the bottle was a paper label, with the words "DRINK ME" beautifully printed on it in large letters.

It was all very well to say "Drink me," but the wise little Alice was not going to do *that* in a hurry. "No, I'll look first," she said, "and see whether it's marked '*poison*' or not"; for she had read several nice little stories about children who had got burnt, and eaten up by wild beasts, and other unpleasant things, all because they *would* not remember the simple rules their friends had taught

[handwritten margin notes: "somehow this was supposed to happen to her—no accident" and "smart"]

them:[4] such as, that a red-hot poker will burn you if you hold it too long; and that, if you cut your finger *very* deeply with a knife, it usually bleeds; and she had never forgotten that, if you drink much from a bottle marked "poison," it is almost certain to disagree with you, sooner or later.

However, this bottle was *not* marked "poison," so Alice ventured to taste it, and, finding it very nice (it had, in fact, a sort of mixed flavour of cherry-tart, custard, pine-apple, roast turkey, toffy, and hot buttered toast), she very soon finished it off.

*   *   *   *

*   *   *

*   *   *   *

"What a curious feeling!" said Alice. "I must be shutting up *she is shrinking!* like a telescope!"

And so it was indeed: she was now only ten inches high, and her face brightened up at the thought that she was now the right size for going through the little door into that lovely garden. First, how-

4. This reference is a traditional kind of children's story, popular in the late eighteenth and early nineteenth centuries but beginning to seem old-fashioned by the time Dodgson told the Alice stories, in which clear lessons of obedience and prudence were enforced by visiting terrible calamities upon children who transgressed.

Dodgson placed asterisks after the paragraphs in which Alice drinks the contents of the bottle and, later in this chapter and again in chapter 5, eats the cake, in order to emphasize the abrupt changes characteristic of the strangely ordered experience of Wonderland.

ever, she waited for a few minutes to see if she was going to shrink any further: she felt a little nervous about this; "for it might end, you know," said Alice to herself, "in my going out altogether, like a candle. I wonder what I should be like then?" And she tried to fancy what the flame of a candle looks like after the candle is blown out, for she could not remember ever having seen such a thing.

After a while, finding that nothing more happened, she decided on going into the garden at once; but, alas for poor Alice! when she got to the door, she found she had forgotten the little golden key, and when she went back to the table for it, she found she could not possibly reach it: she could see it quite plainly through the glass, and she tried her best to climb up one of the legs of the table, but it was too slippery; and when she had tired herself out with trying, the poor little thing sat down and cried.

"Come, there's no use in crying like that!" said Alice to herself rather sharply. "I advise you to leave off this minute!" She generally gave herself very good advice (though she very seldom followed it), and sometimes she scolded herself so severely as to bring tears into her eyes; and once she remembered trying to box her own ears for having cheated herself in a game of croquet she was playing against herself, for this curious child was very fond of pretending to be two people. "But it's no use now," thought poor Alice, "to pretend to be two people! Why, there's hardly enough of me left to make *one* respectable person!"

Soon her eye fell on a little glass box that was lying under the table: she opened it, and found in it a very small cake, on which the words "EAT ME" were beautifully marked in currants. "Well, I'll eat it," said Alice, "and if it makes me grow larger, I can reach the key; and if it makes me grow smaller, I can creep under the door: so either way I'll get into the garden, and I don't care which happens!"

She ate a little bit, and said anxiously to herself "Which way? Which way?", holding her hand on the top of her head to feel which way it was growing; and she was quite surprised to find that she remained the same size. To be sure, this is what generally happens when one eats cake; but Alice had got so much into the way of expecting nothing but out-of-the-way things to happen, that it seemed quite dull and stupid for life to go on in the common way.

So she set to work, and very soon finished off the cake.

        *   *   *   *
           *   *   *
        *   *   *   *

Chapter II

THE POOL OF TEARS

"Curiouser and curiouser!" cried Alice (she was so much surprised, that for the moment she quite forgot how to speak good English). "Now I'm opening out like the largest telescope that ever was! Good-bye, feet!" (for when she looked down at her feet, they seemed to be almost out of sight, they were getting so far off).

She's getting taller!

"Oh, my poor little feet, I wonder who will put on your shoes and stockings for you now, dears? I'm sure I sha'n't be able! I shall be a great deal too far off to trouble myself about you: you must manage the best way you can—but I must be kind to them," thought Alice, "or perhaps they wo'n't walk the way I want to go! Let me see. I'll give them a new pair of boots every Christmas."

And she went on planning to herself how she would manage it. "They must go by the carrier," she thought; "and how funny it'll seem, sending presents to one's own feet! And how odd the directions will look!

> Alice's Right Foot, Esq.
> Hearthrug,
> near the Fender, [5]
> (with Alice's love).

Oh dear, what nonsense I'm talking!"

Just at this moment her head struck against the roof of the hall: in fact she was now rather more than nine feet high, and she at once took up the little golden key and hurried off to the garden door.

Poor Alice! It was as much as she could do, lying down on one side, to look through into the garden with one eye; but to get through was more hopeless than ever: she sat down and began to cry again.

"You ought to be ashamed of yourself," said Alice, "a great girl like you," (she might well say this), "to go on crying in this way! Stop this moment, I tell you!" But she went on all the same, shedding gallons of tears, until there was a large pool around her, about four inches deep, and reaching half down the hall.

After a time she heard a little pattering of feet in the distance, and she hastily dried her eyes to see what was coming. It was the White Rabbit returning, splendidly dressed, with a pair of white kid-gloves in one hand and a large fan in the other: he came trotting along in a great hurry, muttering to himself, as he came, "Oh! The Duchess, the Duchess! Oh! Wo'n't she be savage if I've kept her waiting!" Alice felt so desperate that she was ready to ask help of any one: so, when the Rabbit came near her, she began, in a low, timid voice, "If you please, Sir—" The Rabbit started violently, dropped the white kid-gloves and the fan, and scurried away into the darkness as hard as he could go.

Alice took up the fan and gloves, and, as the hall was very hot,

---

5. A fender is a low fence or screen whose purpose is to prevent ashes and coals from falling out of a fireplace.

she kept fanning herself all the time she went on talking. "Dear, dear! How queer everything is to-day! And yesterday things went on just as usual. I wonder if I've changed in the night? Let me think: *was* I the same when I got up this morning? I almost think I can remember feeling a little different. But if I'm not the same, the next question is 'Who in the world am I?' Ah, *that's* the great puzzle!" And she began thinking over all the children she knew that were of the same age as herself, to see if she could have been changed for any of them.

"I'm sure I'm not Ada," she said, "for her hair goes in such long ringlets, and mine doesn't go in ringlets at all; and I'm sure I ca'n't be Mabel, for I know all sorts of things, and she, oh, she knows such a very little! Besides, *she's* she, and *I'm* I, and—oh dear, how puzzling it all is! I'll try if I know all the things I used to know. Let me see: four times five is twelve, and four times six is thirteen, and four times seven is—oh dear! I shall never get to twenty at that rate![6] However, the Multiplication-Table doesn't signify: let's try Geography. London is the capital of Paris, and Paris is the capital of Rome, and Rome—no, *that's* all wrong, I'm certain! I must have been changed for Mabel! I'll try and say 'How doth the little—',", and she crossed her hands on her lap as if she were saying lessons, and began to repeat it, but her voice sounded hoarse and strange, and the words did not come the same as they used to do:—

> "How doth the little crocodile
> Improve his shining tail,
> And pour the waters of the Nile
> On every golden scale!
>
> "How cheerfully he seems to grin,
> How neatly spreads his claws,
> And welcomes little fishes in,
> With gently smiling jaws![7]

"I'm sure those are not the right words," said poor Alice, and her eyes filled with tears again as she went on, "I must be Mabel after all, and I shall have to go and live in that poky little house, and have next to no toys to play with, and oh, ever so many lessons to learn! No, I've made up my mind about it: if I'm Mabel, I'll stay down here. It'll be no use their putting their heads down and saying 'Come up again, dear!' I shall only look up and say 'Who am I, then? Tell me that first, and then, if I like being that person, I'll come up: if not, I'll stay down here till I'm somebody else'—but, oh dear!" cried Alice, with a sudden burst of tears, "I

6. Martin Gardner in *The Annotated Alice* (see Selected Bibliography) suggests that Alice will never reach 20 because the traditional multiplication table stops with multiples of 12, and in the system Alice is using, 4 times 12 will be 19 (p. 38).
7. A parody of Isaac Watts's "Against Idleness and Mischief," published in 1715 as one of his *Divine Songs for Children:*

How doth the little busy bee
  Improve each shining hour,
And gather honey all the day
  from every opening flower!

How skillfully she builds her cell!
  How neat she spreads the wax!
And labours hard to store it well
  With the sweet food she makes.

In works of labour or of skill,
  I would be busy too;
For Satan finds some mischief still
  For idle hands to do.

In books, or work, or healthful play,
  Let my first years be past, passed
That I may give for every day
  Some good account at last.

Watts was a very popular writer whose hymns and poems retained their popularity and authority through the nineteenth century. The best catalogue of Dodgson's parodies, in the Alice books and in his other writing, is the appendix (pp. 307–17) of *The Lewis Carroll Handbook*, by Sidney Herbert Williams and Falconer Madan, revised by Roger Lancelyn Green and further revised by Denis Crutch (see Selected Bibliography).

do wish they *would* put their heads down! I am so *very* tired of being all alone here!"

As she said this she looked down at her hands, and was surprised to see that she had put on one of the Rabbit's little white kid-gloves while she was talking. "How *can* I have done that?" she thought. "I must be growing small again." She got up and went to the table to measure herself by it, and found that, as nearly as she could guess, she was now about two feet high, and was going on shrinking rapidly: she soon found out that the cause of this was the fan she was holding, and she dropped it hastily, just in time to save herself from shrinking away altogether.

"That *was* a narrow escape!" said Alice, a good deal frightened at the sudden change, but very glad to find herself still in existence. "And now for the garden!" And she ran with all speed back to the little door; but, alas! the little door was shut again, and the little golden key was lying on the glass table as before, "and things are worse than ever," thought the poor child, "for I never was so small as this before, never! And I declare it's too bad, that it is!" *she forgot it again!*

As she said these words her foot slipped, and in another moment, splash! she was up to her chin in salt-water. Her first idea was that she had somehow fallen into the sea, "and in that case I can go back by railway," she said to herself. (Alice had been to the seaside once in her life, and had come to the general conclusion that wherever you go to on the English coast, you find a number of bathing-machines[8] in the sea, some children digging in the sand *her tears?*

8. A bathing machine was a portable shelter that was wheeled into the water before its occupants stepped out into the sea.

with wooden spades, then a row of lodging-houses, and behind them a railway station.) However, she soon made out that she was in the pool of tears which she had wept when she was nine feet high.

"I wish I hadn't cried so much!" said Alice, as she swam about, trying to find her way out. "I shall be punished for it now, I suppose, by being drowned in my own tears! That *will* be a queer thing, to be sure! However, everything is queer to-day."

Just then she heard something splashing about in the pool a little way off, and she swam nearer to make out what it was: at first she thought it must be a walrus or hippopotamus, but then she remembered how small she was now, and she soon made out that it was only a mouse, that had slipped in like herself.

"Would it be of any use, now," thought Alice, "to speak to this mouse? Everything is so out-of-the-way down here, that I should think very likely it can talk: at any rate, there's no harm in trying." So she began: "O Mouse, do you know the way out of this pool? I am very tired of swimming about here, O Mouse!" (Alice thought this must be the right way of speaking to a mouse: she had never done such a thing before, but she remembered having seen, in her brother's Latin Grammar, "A mouse—of a mouse—to a mouse—a mouse—O mouse!") The mouse looked at her rather inquisitively, and seemed to her to wink with one of its little eyes, but it said nothing.

"Perhaps it doesn't understand English," thought Alice. "I daresay it's a French mouse, come over with William the Conqueror." (For, with all her knowledge of history, Alice had no very clear notion how long ago anything had happened.) So she began again: "Où est ma chatte?" which was the first sentence in her French lesson-book. The Mouse gave a sudden leap out of the water, and seemed to quiver all over with fright. "Oh, I beg your pardon!" cried Alice hastily, afraid that she had hurt the poor animal's feelings. "I quite forgot you didn't like cats."

"Not like cats!" cried the Mouse in a shrill passionate voice. "Would *you* like cats, if you were me?"

"Well, perhaps not," said Alice in a soothing tone: "don't be angry about it. And yet I wish I could show you our cat Dinah. I think you'd take a fancy to cats, if you could only see her. She is such a dear quiet thing," Alice went on, half to herself, as she swam lazily about in the pool, "and she sits purring so nicely by the fire, licking her paws and washing her face—and she is such a nice soft thing to nurse—and she's such a capital one for catching mice—oh, I beg your pardon!" cried Alice again, for this time the

Mouse was bristling all over, and she felt certain it must be really offended. "We wo'n't talk about her any more, if you'd rather not."

"We, indeed!" cried the Mouse, who was trembling down to the end of its tail. "As if I would talk on such a subject! Our family always *hated* cats: nasty, low, vulgar things! Don't let me hear the name again!"

"I wo'n't indeed!" said Alice, in a great hurry to change the subject of conversation. "Are you—are you fond—of—of dogs?" The Mouse did not answer, so Alice went on eagerly: "There is such a nice little dog, near our house, I should like to show you! A little bright-eyed terrier, you know, with oh, such long curly brown hair! And it'll fetch things when you throw them, and it'll sit up and beg for its dinner, and all sorts of things—I ca'n't remember half of them—and it belongs to a farmer, you know, and he says it's so useful, it's worth a hundred pounds! He says it kills all the rats and—oh dear!" cried Alice in a sorrowful tone. "I'm afraid I've offended it again!" For the Mouse was swimming away from her as hard as it could go, and making quite a commotion in the pool as it went.

So she called softly after it, "Mouse dear! Do come back again, and we wo'n't talk about cats, or dogs either, if you don't like them!" When the Mouse heard this, it turned round and swam slowly back to her: its face was quite pale (with passion, Alice thought), and it said, in a low trembling voice, "Let us get to the shore, and then I'll tell you my history, and you'll understand why it is I hate cats and dogs."

It was high time to go, for the pool was getting quite crowded with the birds and animals that had fallen into it: there was a Duck and a Dodo, a Lory and an Eaglet,[9] and several other curious creatures. Alice led the way, and the whole party swam to the shore.

---

9. This passage is a relic from the original *Alice's Adventures Under Ground* which records an outing in which Canon Duckworth (the Duck), Dodgson (the Dodo), Lorina and Edith Liddell (the Lory—a parrot—and the Eaglet), and Alice were caught in rain. See Carroll's diary (p. 264 of this edition) and the passage reprinted from *Alice's Adventures Under Ground* on pp. 266–72 of this edition.

Chapter III

A CAUCUS-RACE AND A LONG TALE

They were indeed a queer-looking party that assembled on the bank—the birds with draggled feathers, the animals with their fur clinging close to them, and all dripping wet, cross, and uncomfortable.

The first question of course was, how to get dry again: they had a consultation about this, and after a few minutes it seemed quite natural to Alice to find herself talking familiarly with them, as if she had known them all her life. Indeed, she had quite a long argument with the Lory, who at last turned sulky, and would only say, "I'm older than you, and must know better." And this Alice would not allow, without knowing how old it was, and as the Lory positively refused to tell its age, there was no more to be said.

At last the Mouse, who seemed to be a person of some authority among them, called out "Sit down, all of you, and listen to me! *I'll* soon make you dry enough!" They all sat down at once, in a large ring, with the Mouse in the middle. Alice kept her eyes anxiously fixed on it, for she felt sure she would catch a bad cold if she did not get dry very soon.

"Ahem!" said the Mouse with an important air. "Are you all ready? This is the driest thing I know. Silence all round, if you please! 'William the Conqueror, whose cause was favoured by the pope, was soon submitted to by the English, who wanted leaders, and had been of late much accustomed to usurpation and conquest. Edwin and Morcar, the earls of Mercia and Northumbria——' "[1]

"Ugh!" said the Lory, with a shiver.

"I beg your pardon!" said the Mouse, frowning, but very politely. "Did you speak?"

"Not I!" said the Lory, hastily.

"I thought you did," said the Mouse. "I proceed. 'Edwin and Morcar, the earls of Mercia and Northumbria, declared for him; and even Stigand, the patriotic archbishop of Canterbury, found it advisable——' "

"Found *what?*" said the Duck.

"Found *it,*" the Mouse replied rather crossly: "of course you know what 'it' means."

"I know what 'it' means well enough, when I find a thing," said the Duck: "it's generally a frog, or a worm. The question is, what did the archbishop find?"

The Mouse did not notice this question, but hurriedly went on, " '——found it advisable to go with Edgar Atheling to meet William and offer him the crown. William's conduct at first was moderate. But the insolence of his Normans——' How are you getting on now, my dear?" it continued, turning to Alice as it spoke.

"As wet as ever," said Alice in a melancholy tone: "it doesn't seem to dry me at all."

"In that case," said the Dodo solemnly, rising to its feet, "I move that the meeting adjourn, for the immediate adoption of more energetic remedies——"

"Speak English!" said the Eaglet. "I don't know the meaning of half those long words, and, what's more, I don't believe you do either!" And the Eaglet bent down its head to hide a smile: some of the other birds tittered audibly.

"What I was going to say," said the Dodo in an offended tone, "was that the best thing to get us dry would be a Caucus-race."[2]

"What *is* a Caucus-race?" said Alice; not that she much wanted

---

1. In his edition of *The Diaries of Lewis Carroll* (see Selected Bibliography) Roger Lancelyn Green identifies this passage as a quotation from Haviland Chepmell's *Short Course of History* (1862) (p. 2).

2. The American word *caucus,* which is perhaps of American Indian origin, was still a strange word in mid-nineteenth-century En- gland. A political term referring to a private meeting of the members of a party or faction, it picked up opprobrious connotations in England. Dodgson often involved himself in the frantic tedium of university politics, and he seems to use the word here both for its strangeness and to suggest the fatuity of politics.

to know, but the Dodo had paused as if it thought that *somebody* ought to speak, and no one else seemed inclined to say anything.

"Why," said the Dodo, "the best way to explain it is to do it." (And, as you might like to try the thing yourself some winter-day, I will tell you how the Dodo managed it.)

First it marked out a race-course, in a sort of circle, ("the exact shape doesn't matter," it said,) and then all the party were placed along the course, here and there. There was no "One, two, three, and away!", but they began running when they liked, and left off when they liked, so that it was not easy to know when the race was over. However, when they had been running half an hour or so, and were quite dry again, the Dodo suddenly called out "The race is over!" and they all crowded round it, panting, and asking "But who has won?"

This question the Dodo could not answer without a great deal of thought, and it stood for a long time with one finger pressed upon its forehead (the position in which you usually see Shakespeare, in the pictures of him), while the rest waited in silence. At last the Dodo said "*Everybody* has won, and *all* must have prizes."

"But who is to give the prizes?" quite a chorus of voices asked.

"Why, *she*, of course," said the Dodo, pointing to Alice with one finger; and the whole party at once crowded round her, calling out, in a confused way, "Prizes! Prizes!"

Alice had no idea what to do, and in despair she put her hand in her pocket, and pulled out a box of comfits[3] (luckily the salt-water had not got into it), and handed them round as prizes. There was exactly one a-piece, all round.

"But she must have a prize herself, you know," said the Mouse.

"Of course," the Dodo replied very gravely. "What else have you got in your pocket?" it went on, turning to Alice.

"Only a thimble," said Alice sadly.

"Hand it over here," said the Dodo.

Then they all crowded round her once more, while the Dodo solemnly presented the thimble, saying "We beg your acceptance of this elegant thimble"; and, when it had finished this short speech, they all cheered.

Alice thought the whole thing very absurd, but they all looked so grave that she did not dare to laugh; and, as she could not think of anything to say, she simply bowed, and took the thimble, looking as solemn as she could.

The next thing was to eat the comfits: this caused some noise and confusion, as the large birds complained that they could not

---

3. Comfits are a confection made of preserved fruit, roots, or seeds coated in sugar.

taste theirs, and the small ones choked and had to be patted on the back. However, it was over at last, and they sat down again in a ring, and begged the Mouse to tell them something more.

"You promised to tell me your history, you know," said Alice, "and why it is you hate—C and D," she added in a whisper, half afraid that it would be offended again.

"Mine is a long and sad tale!" said the Mouse, turning to Alice, and sighing.

"It *is* a long tail, certainly," said Alice, looking down with wonder at the Mouse's tail; "but why do you call it sad?" And she kept on puzzling about it while the mouse was speaking, so that her idea of the tale was something like this:— 4

4. For an early version of this poem, see the passage from *Alice's Adventures Under Ground* reprinted on pp. 266–72 of this edition. In an essay written by two high-school students, Gary Graham and Jeffrey Maiden, and their teacher, Nancy Fox, the stanzas of "The Mouse's Tale" are printed in conventional form, revealing that each stanza has the shape of a mouse, with the last line as its tail.

Fury said to the mouse,
That he met in the house,
"Let us both go to law: I will prosecute you."

The authors note that the form of the stanza is that of a "tail-rhyme," a couplet followed by a single line of a different length. See *New York Times*, 1 May 1991 B1; and *Jabberwocky*.

"Fury said to
a mouse, That
he met in the
house, 'Let
us both go
to law: *I*
will prose-
cute *you.*—
Come, I'll
take no de-
nial: We
must have
the trial;
For really
this morn-
ing I've
nothing
to do.'
Said the
mouse to
the cur,
Such a
trial, dear
sir, With
no jury
or judge,
w o u l d
be wast-
ing our
breath.
'I'll be
judge,
I'll be
jury,'
said
cun-
ning
old
Fury:
'I ' l l
t r y
the
whole
cause,
a n d
con-
demn
you to
death.'

"You are not attending!" said the Mouse to Alice, severely. "What are you thinking of?"

"I beg your pardon," said Alice very humbly: "you had got to the fifth bend, I think?"

"I had *not!*" cried the Mouse, sharply and very angrily.

"A knot!" said Alice, always ready to make herself useful, and looking anxiously about her. "Oh, do let me help to undo it!"

"I shall do nothing of the sort," said the Mouse, getting up and walking away. "You insult me by talking such nonsense!"

"I didn't mean it!" pleaded poor Alice. "But you're so easily offended, you know!"

The Mouse only growled in reply.

"Please come back, and finish your story!" Alice called after it. And the others all joined in chorus "Yes, please do!" But the Mouse only shook its head impatiently, and walked a little quicker.

"What a pity it wouldn't stay!" sighed the Lory, as soon as it was quite out of sight. And an old Crab took the opportunity of saying to her daughter "Ah, my dear! Let this be a lesson to you never to lose *your* temper!" "Hold your tongue, Ma!" said the young Crab, a little snappishly. "You're enough to try the patience of an oyster!"

"I wish I had our Dinah here, I know I do!" said Alice aloud, addressing nobody in particular. *"She'd* soon fetch it back!"

"And who is Dinah, if I might venture to ask the question?" said the Lory.

Alice replied eagerly, for she was always ready to talk about her pet: "Dinah's our cat. And she's such a capital one for catching mice, you ca'n't think! And oh, I wish you could see her after the birds! Why, she'll eat a little bird as soon as look at it!"

This speech caused a remarkable sensation among the party. Some of the birds hurried off at once: one old Magpie began wrapping itself up very carefully, remarking "I really must be getting home: the night-air doesn't suit my throat!" And a Canary called out in a trembling voice, to its children, "Come away, my dears! It's high time you were all in bed!" On various pretexts they all moved off, and Alice was soon left alone.

"I wish I hadn't mentioned Dinah!" she said to herself in a melancholy tone. "Nobody seems to like her, down here, and I'm sure she's the best cat in the world! Oh, my dear Dinah! I wonder if I shall ever see you any more!" And here poor Alice began to cry again, for she felt very lonely and low-spirited. In a little while, however, she again heard a little pattering of footsteps in the distance, and she looked up eagerly, half hoping that the Mouse had changed his mind, and was coming back to finish his story.

Chapter IV

THE RABBIT SENDS IN A LITTLE BILL

It was the White Rabbit, trotting slowly back again, and looking anxiously about as it went, as if it had lost something; and she heard it muttering to itself, "The Duchess! The Duchess! Oh my dear paws! Oh my fur and whiskers! She'll get me executed, as sure as ferrets are ferrets! Where *can* I have dropped them, I wonder?" Alice guessed in a moment that it was looking for the fan and the pair of white kid-gloves, and she very good-naturedly began hunting about for them, but they were nowhere to be seen—everything seemed to have changed since her swim in the pool; and the great hall, with the glass table and the little door, had vanished completely.

Very soon the Rabbit noticed Alice, as she went hunting about, and called out to her, in an angry tone, "Why, Mary Ann, what *are* you doing out here? Run home this moment, and fetch me a pair of gloves and a fan! Quick, now!" And Alice was so much frightened that she ran off at once in the direction it pointed to, without trying to explain the mistake that it had made.

"He took me for his housemaid," she said to herself as she ran. "How surprised he'll be when he finds out who I am! But I'd better take him his fan and gloves—that is, if I can find them." As she said this, she came upon a neat little house, on the door of which was a bright brass plate with the name "W. RABBIT" engraved upon it. She went in without knocking, and hurried upstairs, in great fear lest she should meet the real Mary Ann, and be turned out of the house before she had found the fan and gloves.

"How queer it seems," Alice said to herself, "to be going messages for a rabbit! I suppose Dinah'll be sending me on messages next!" And she began fancying the sort of thing that would happen: " 'Miss Alice! Come here directly, and get ready for your walk!' 'Coming in a minute, nurse! But I've got to watch this mouse-hole till Dinah comes back, and see that the mouse doesn't get out.' Only I don't think," Alice went on, "that they'd let Dinah stop in the house if it began ordering people about like that!"

By this time she had found her way into a tidy little room with a table in the window, and on it (as she had hoped) a fan and two or three pairs of tiny white kid-gloves: she took up the fan and a pair of the gloves, and was just going to leave the room, when her eye fell upon a little bottle that stood near the looking-glass. There was no label this time with the words "DRINK ME," but nevertheless she uncorked it and put it to her lips. "I know _something_ interesting is sure to happen," she said to herself, "whenever I eat or drink anything: so I'll just see what this bottle does. I do hope it'll make me grow large again, for really I'm quite tired of being such a tiny little thing!"

She should be more cautious

It did so indeed, and much sooner than she had expected: before she had drunk half the bottle, she found her head pressing against the ceiling, and had to stoop to save her neck from being broken. She hastily put down the bottle, saying to herself "That's quite enough—I hope I sha'n't grow any more—As it is, I ca'n't get out at the door—I do wish I hadn't drunk quite so much!"

She's immature, doesn't want w/ deal w/ consequences of her actions

Alas! It was too late to wish that! She went on growing, and growing, and very soon had to kneel down on the floor: in another minute there was not even room for this, and she tried the effect of lying down with one elbow against the door, and the other arm curled round her head. Still she went on growing, and, as a last resource, she put one arm out of the window, and one foot up the chimney, and said to herself "Now I can do no more, whatever happens. What *will* become of me?"

Luckily for Alice, the little magic bottle had now had its full effect, and she grew no larger: still it was very uncomfortable, and, as there seemed to be no sort of chance of her ever getting out of the room again, no wonder she felt unhappy.

"It was much pleasanter at home," thought poor Alice, "when one wasn't always growing larger and smaller, and being ordered

She's too curious—acts w/o thinking

about by mice and rabbits. I almost wish I hadn't gone down that rabbit-hole—and yet—and yet—it's rather curious, you know, this sort of life! I do wonder what *can* have happened to me! When I used to read fairy tales, I fancied that kind of thing never happened, and now here I am in the middle of one! There ought to be a book written about me, that there ought! And when I grow up, I'll write one—but I'm grown up now," she added in a sorrowful tone: "at least there's no room to grow up any more *here*."

"But then," thought Alice, "shall I *never* get any older than I am now? That'll be a comfort, one way—never to be an old woman —but then—always to have lessons to learn! Oh, I shouldn't like *that!*"

"Oh, you foolish Alice!" she answered herself. "How can you learn lessons in here? Why, there's hardly room for *you*, and no room at all for any lesson-books!"

And so she went on, taking first one side and then the other, and making quite a conversation of it altogether; but after a few minutes she heard a voice outside, and stopped to listen.

"Mary Ann! Mary Ann!" said the voice. "Fetch me my gloves this moment!" Then came a little pattering of feet on the stairs. Alice knew it was the Rabbit coming to look for her, and she trembled till she shook the house, quite forgetting that she was now about a thousand times as large as the Rabbit, and had no reason to be afraid of it.

Presently the Rabbit came up to the door, and tried to open it; but, as the door opened inwards, and Alice's elbow was pressed hard against it, that attempt proved a failure. Alice heard it say to itself "Then I'll go round and get in at the window."

"*That* you wo'n't!" thought Alice, and after waiting till she fancied she heard the Rabbit just under the window, she suddenly spread out her hand, and made a snatch in the air. She did not get hold of anything, but she heard a little shriek and a fall, and a crash of broken glass, from which she concluded that it was just possible it had fallen into a cucumber-frame,[5] or something of the sort.

5. Cucumber-frame: a low construction of wood and glass, like a small greenhouse.

Next came an angry voice—the Rabbit's—"Pat! Pat! Where are you?" And then a voice she had never heard before, "Sure then I'm here! Digging for apples, yer honour!"

"Digging for apples, indeed!" said the Rabbit angrily. "Here! Come help me out of *this*!" (Sounds of more broken glass.)

"Now tell me, Pat, what's that in the window?"

"Sure, it's an arm, yer honour!" (He pronounced it "arrum.")[6]

"An arm, you goose! Who ever saw one that size? Why, it fills the whole window!"

"Sure, it does, yer honour: but it's an arm for all that."

"Well, it's got no business there, at any rate: go and take it away!"

There was a long silence after this, and Alice could only hear whispers now and then; such as "Sure, I don't like it, yer honour, at all, at all!" "Do as I tell you, you coward!", and at last she spread out her hand again, and made another snatch in the air. This time there were *two* little shrieks, and more sounds of broken glass. "What a number of cucumber-frames there must be!" thought Alice. "I wonder what they'll do next! As for pulling me out of the window, I only wish they *could*! I'm sure I don't want to stay in here any longer!"

She waited for some time without hearing anything more: at last came a rumbling of little cart-wheels, and the sound of a good many voices all talking together: she made out the words: "Where's the other ladder?—Why, I hadn't to bring but one. Bill's got the other—Bill! Fetch it here, lad!—Here, put 'em up at this corner—No, tie 'em together first—they don't reach half high enough yet—Oh, they'll do well enough. Don't be particular—Here, Bill! Catch hold of this rope—Will the roof bear?—Mind that loose slate—Oh, it's coming down! Heads below!" (a loud crash)—"Now, who did that?—It was Bill, I fancy—Who's to go down the chimney?—Nay, *I* sha'n't! *You* do it!—*That* I wo'n't, then!—Bill's got to go down—Here, Bill! The master says you've got to go down the chimney!"

"Oh! So Bill's got to come down the chimney, has he?" said Alice to herself. "Why, they seem to put everything upon Bill! I wouldn't be in Bill's place for a good deal: this fireplace is narrow, to be sure; but I *think* I can kick a little!"

She drew her foot as far down the chimney as she could, and waited till she heard a little animal (she couldn't guess of what sort it was) scratching and scrambling about in the chimney close above

6. Dodgson does not often use dialect. The Irish dialect spoken by Pat, like the lower-class idiom used by the Gryphon later in this book and by the Frog-Footman in *Through the Looking Glass* ("wexes" for "vexes"), was a common device of nineteenth-century English humorists.

her: then, saying to herself "This is Bill", she gave one sharp kick, and waited to see what would happen next.

The first thing she heard was a general chorus of "There goes Bill!" then the Rabbit's voice alone—"Catch him, you by the hedge!" then silence, and then another confusion of voices— "Hold up his head—Brandy now—Don't choke him—How was it, old fellow? What happened to you? Tell us all about it!"

Last came a little feeble, squeaking voice ("That's Bill," thought Alice), "Well, I hardly know—No more, thank ye; I'm better now—but I'm a deal too flustered to tell you—all I know is, something comes at me like a Jack-in-the-box, and up I goes like a sky-rocket!"

"So you did, old fellow!" said the others.

"We must burn the house down!" said the Rabbit's voice. And Alice called out, as loud as she could, "If you do, I'll set Dinah at you!"

There was a dead silence instantly, and Alice thought to herself "I wonder what they *will* do next! If they had any sense, they'd take the roof off." After a minute or two they began moving about again, and Alice heard the Rabbit say "A barrowful will do, to begin with."

"A barrowful of *what?*" thought Alice. But she had not

long to doubt, for the next moment a shower of little pebbles came rattling in at the window, and some of them hit her in the face. "I'll put a stop to this," she said to herself, and shouted out "You'd better not do that again!", which produced another dead silence.

Alice noticed, with some surprise, that the pebbles were all turning into little cakes as they lay on the floor, and a bright idea came into her head. "If I eat one of these cakes," she thought, "it's sure to make *some* change in my size; and, as it ca'n't possibly make me larger, it must make me smaller, I suppose."

So she swallowed one of the cakes, and was delighted to find that she began shrinking directly. As soon as she was small enough to get through the door, she ran out of the house, and found quite a crowd of little animals and birds waiting outside. The poor little Lizard, Bill, was in the middle, being held up by two guinea-pigs, who were giving it something out of a bottle. They all made a rush at Alice the moment she appeared; but she ran off as hard as she could, and soon found herself safe in a thick wood.

"The first thing I've got to do," said Alice to herself, as she wandered about in the wood, "is to grow to my right size again; and the second thing is to find my way into that lovely garden. I think that will be the best plan."

It sounded an excellent plan, no doubt, and very neatly and simply arranged: the only difficulty was, that she had not the smallest idea how to set about it; and, while she was peering about anxiously among the trees, a little sharp bark just over her head made her look up in a great hurry.

An enormous puppy was looking down at her with large round eyes, and feebly stretching out one paw, trying to touch her. "Poor little thing!" said Alice, in a coaxing tone, and she tried hard to whistle to it; but she was terribly frightened all the time at the thought that it might be hungry, in which case it would be very likely to eat her up in spite of all her coaxing.

Hardly knowing what she did, she picked up a little bit of stick, and held it out to the puppy: whereupon the puppy jumped into the air off all its feet at once, with a yelp of delight, and rushed at the stick, and made believe to worry it: then Alice dodged behind a great thistle, to keep herself from being run over; and, the moment she appeared on the other side, the puppy made another rush at the stick, and tumbled head over heels in its hurry to get hold of it: then Alice, thinking it was very like having a game of play with a cart-horse, and expecting every moment to be trampled under its feet, ran round the thistle again: then the puppy began a series of short charges at the stick, running a very little way forwards each time and a long way back, and barking hoarsely all the while, till at

last it sat down a good way off, panting, with its tongue hanging out of its mouth, and its great eyes half shut.

This seemed to Alice a good opportunity for making her escape: so she set off at once, and ran till she was quite tired and out of breath, and till the puppy's bark sounded quite faint in the distance.

"And yet what a dear little puppy it was!" said Alice, as she leant against a buttercup to rest herself, and fanned herself with one of the leaves. "I should have liked teaching it tricks very much, if—if I'd only been the right size to do it! Oh dear! I'd nearly forgotten that I've got to grow up again! Let me see—how *is* it to be managed? I suppose I ought to eat or drink something or other; but the great question is 'What?'"

The great question certainly was "What?" Alice looked all round her at the flowers and the blades of grass, but she could not see anything that looked like the right thing to eat or drink under the circumstances. There was a large mushroom growing near her, about the same height as herself; and, when she had looked under it, and on both sides of it, and behind it, it occurred to her that she might as well look and see what was on top of it.

She stretched herself up on tiptoe, and peeped over the edge of the mushroom, and her eyes immediately met those of a large blue caterpillar, that was sitting on the top, with its arms folded, quietly smoking a long hookah, and taking not the smallest notice of her or of anything else.

Chapter V

ADVICE FROM A CATERPILLAR

The Caterpillar and Alice looked at each other for some time in silence: at last the Caterpillar took the hookah out of its mouth, and addressed her in a languid, sleepy voice.

"Who are *you*?" said the Caterpillar.

This was not an encouraging opening for a conversation. Alice replied, rather shyly, "I—I hardly know, Sir, just at present—at least I know who I *was* when I got up this morning, but I think I must have been changed several times since then."

"What do you mean by that?" said the Caterpillar, sternly. "Explain yourself!"

"I ca'n't explain *myself*, I'm afraid, Sir," said Alice, "because I'm not myself, you see."

"I don't see," said the Caterpillar.

"I'm afraid I ca'n't put it more clearly," Alice replied, very politely, "for I ca'n't understand it myself, to begin with; and being so many different sizes in a day is very confusing."

"It isn't," said the Caterpillar.

"Well, perhaps you haven't found it so yet," said Alice; "but when you have to turn into a chrysalis—you will some day, you know—and then after that into a butterfly, I should think you'll feel it a little queer, wo'n't you?"

"Not a bit," said the Caterpillar.

"Well, perhaps *your* feelings may be different," said Alice: "all I know is, it would feel very queer to *me*."

"You!" said the Caterpillar contemptuously. "Who are *you*?"

Which brought them back again to the beginning of the conversation. Alice felt a little irritated at the Caterpillar's making such *very* short remarks, and she drew herself up and said, very gravely, "I think you ought to tell me who *you* are, first."

"Why?" said the Caterpillar.

Here was another puzzling question; and, as Alice could not think of any good reason, and the Caterpillar seemed to be in a *very* unpleasant state of mind, she turned away.

"Come back!" the Caterpillar called after her. "I've something important to say!"

This sounded promising, certainly. Alice turned and came back again.

"Keep your temper," said the Caterpillar.

"Is that all?" said Alice, swallowing down her anger as well as she could.

"No," said the Caterpillar.

Alice thought she might as well wait, as she had nothing else to do, and perhaps after all it might tell her something worth hearing. For some minutes it puffed away without speaking; but at last it unfolded its arms, took the hookah out of its mouth again, and said "So you think you're changed, do you?"

"I'm afraid I am, Sir," said Alice. "I ca'n't remember things as I used—and I don't keep the same size for ten minutes together!"

"Ca'n't remember *what* things?" said the Caterpillar.

"Well, I've tried to say 'How doth the little busy bee,' but it all came different!" Alice replied in a very melancholy voice.

"Repeat 'You are old, Father William,'"[7] said the Caterpillar.

Alice folded her hands, and began:—

7. "You Are Old, Father William" is a parody of Robert Southey's "The Old Man's Comforts, and How He Gained Them," written in 1799. The last two stanzas of Southey's poem suggest the meter and form Dodgson is playing with in his parody, and the pious sentiment he is playing against:

"You are old, Father William," the
  young man cried,
"And life must be hastening away;
You are cheerful, and love to
  converse upon death:
Now tell me the reason, I pray."

"I am cheerful, young man," Father William replied;
"Let the cause thy attention engage:
In the days of my youth, I remembered my God:
And he hath not forgotten my age."

"You are old, Father William," the young man said,
  "And your hair has become very white;
And yet you incessantly stand on your head—
  Do you think, at your age, it is right?"

"In my youth," Father William replied to his son,
  "I feared it might injure the brain;
But, now that I'm perfectly sure I have none,
  Why, I do it again and again."

"You are old," said the youth, "as I mentioned before,
  And have grown most uncommonly fat;
Yet you turned a back-somersault in at the door—
  Pray, what is the reason of that?"

"In my youth," said the sage, as he shook his grey locks,
  "I kept all my limbs very supple
By the use of this ointment—one shilling the box—
  Allow me to sell you a couple?"

"You are old," said the youth, "and your jaws are too weak
  For anything tougher than suet;
Yet you finished the goose, with the bones and the beak—
  Pray, how did you manage to do it?"

"In my youth," said his father, "I took to the law,
  And argued each case with my wife;
And the muscular strength, which it gave to my jaw
  Has lasted the rest of my life."

"You are old," said the youth, "one would hardly suppose
  That your eye was as steady as ever;
Yet you balanced an eel on the end of your nose—
  What made you so awfully clever?"

"I have answered three questions, and that is enough,"
  Said his father. "Don't give yourself airs!
Do you think I can listen all day to such stuff?
  Be off, or I'll kick you down-stairs!"

"That is not said right," said the Caterpillar.

"Not *quite* right, I'm afraid," said Alice, timidly: "some of the words have got altered."

"It is wrong from beginning to end," said the Caterpillar, decidedly; and there was silence for some minutes.

The Caterpillar was the first to speak.

"What size do you want to be?" it asked.

"Oh, I'm not particular as to size," Alice hastily replied; "only one doesn't like changing so often, you know."

"I *don't* know," said the Caterpillar.

Alice said nothing: she had never been so much contradicted in all her life before, and she felt that she was losing her temper.

"Are you content now?" said the Caterpillar.

"Well, I should like to be a *little* larger, Sir, if you wouldn't mind," said Alice: "three inches is such a wretched height to be."

"It is a very good height indeed!" said the Caterpillar angrily, rearing itself upright as it spoke (it was exactly three inches high).

"But I'm not used to it!" pleaded poor Alice in a piteous tone. And she thought to herself "I wish the creatures wouldn't be so easily offended!"

"You'll get used to it in time," said the Caterpillar; and it put the hookah into its mouth, and began smoking again.

This time Alice waited patiently until it chose to speak again. In a minute or two the Caterpillar took the hookah out of its mouth, and yawned once or twice, and shook itself. Then it got down off the mushroom, and crawled away into the grass, merely remarking, as it went, "One side will make you grow taller, and the other side will make you grow shorter."

"One side of *what*? The other side of *what*?" thought Alice to herself.

"Of the mushroom," said the Caterpillar, just as if she had asked it aloud; and in another moment it was out of sight.

Alice remained looking thoughtfully at the mushroom for a minute, trying to make out which were the two sides of it; and, as it was perfectly round, she found this a very difficult question. However, at last she stretched her arms round it as far as they would go, and broke off a bit of the edge with each hand.

"And now which is which?" she said to herself, and nibbled a little of the right-hand bit to try the effect. The next moment she felt a violent blow underneath her chin: it had struck her foot!

She was a good deal frightened by this very sudden change, but she felt that there was no time to be lost, as she was shrinking rapidly: so she set to work at once to eat some of the other bit. Her chin was pressed so closely against her foot, that there was hardly room to open her mouth; but she did it at last, and managed to swallow a morsel of the left-hand bit.

*   *   *   *   *

*   *   *   *

*   *   *   *   *

"Come, my head's free at last!" said Alice in a tone of delight, which changed into alarm in another moment, when she found that her shoulders were nowhere to be found: all she could see, when she looked down, was an immense length of neck, which seemed to rise like a stalk out of a sea of green leaves that lay far below her.

"What *can* all that green stuff be?" said Alice. "And where *have* my shoulders got to? And oh, my poor hands, how is it I ca'n't see you?" She was moving them about, as she spoke, but no result seemed to follow, except a little shaking among the distant green leaves.

As there seemed to be no chance of getting her hands up to her head, she tried to get her head down to *them*, and was delighted to find that her neck would bend about easily in any direction, like a serpent. She had just succeeded in curving it down into a graceful zigzag, and was going to dive in among the leaves, which she found to be nothing but the tops of the trees under which she had been wandering, when a sharp hiss made her draw back in a hurry: a large pigeon had flown into her face, and was beating her violently with its wings.

"Serpent!" screamed the Pigeon.

"I'm *not* a serpent!" said Alice indignantly. "Let me alone!"

"Serpent, I say again!" repeated the Pigeon, but in a more sub-dued tone, and added, with a kind of sob, "I've tried every way, but nothing seems to suit them!"

"I haven't the least idea what you're talking about," said Alice.

"I've tried the roots of trees, and I've tried banks, and I've tried hedges," the Pigeon went on, without attending to her; "but those serpents! There's no pleasing them!"

Alice was more and more puzzled, but she thought there was no use in saying anything more till the Pigeon had finished.

"As if it wasn't trouble enough hatching the eggs," said the Pigeon; "but I must be on the look-out for serpents, night and day! Why, I haven't had a wink of sleep these three weeks!"

"I'm very sorry you've been annoyed," said Alice, who was begin-ning to see its meaning.

"And just as I'd taken the highest tree in the wood," continued the Pigeon, raising its voice to a shriek, "and just as I was thinking I should be free of them at last, they must needs come wriggling down from the sky! Ugh, Serpent!"

"But I'm *not* a serpent, I tell you!" said Alice. "I'm a—I'm a——"

"Well! *What* are you?" said the Pigeon. "I can see you're trying to invent something!"

"I—I'm a little girl," said Alice, rather doubtfully, as she remembered the number of changes she had gone through, that day.

"A likely story indeed!" said the Pigeon, in a tone of the deepest contempt. "I've seen a good many little girls in my time, but never *one* with such a neck as that! No, no! You're a serpent; and there's no use denying it. I suppose you'll be telling me next that you never tasted an egg!"

"I *have* tasted eggs, certainly," said Alice, who was a very truthful child; "but little girls eat eggs quite as much as serpents do, you know."

"I don't believe it," said the Pigeon; "but if they do, why, then they're a kind of serpent: that's all I can say."

This was such a new idea to Alice, that she was quite silent for a minute or two, which gave the Pigeon the opportunity of adding "You're looking for eggs, I know *that* well enough; and what does it matter to me whether you're a little girl or a serpent?"

"It matters a good deal to *me*," said Alice hastily; "but I'm not looking for eggs, as it happens; and, if I was, I shouldn't want *yours*: I don't like them raw."

"Well, be off, then!" said the Pigeon in a sulky tone, as it settled down again into its nest. Alice crouched down among the trees as well as she could, for her neck kept getting entangled among the branches, and every now and then she had to stop and untwist it. After a while she remembered that she still held the pieces of mushroom in her hands, and she set to work very carefully, nibbling first at one and then at the other, and growing sometimes taller, and sometimes shorter, until she had succeeded in bringing herself down to her usual height.

It was so long since she had been anything near the right size, that it felt quite strange at first; but she got used to it in a few minutes, and began talking to herself, as usual, "Come, there's half my plan done now! How puzzling all these changes are! I'm never sure what I'm going to be, from one minute to another! However, I've got back to my right size: the next thing is, to get into that beautiful garden—how *is* that to be done, I wonder?" As she said this, she came suddenly upon an open place, with a little house in it about four feet high. "Whoever lives there," thought Alice, "it'll never do to come upon them *this* size: why, I should frighten them out of their wits!" So she began nibbling at the right-hand bit again, and did not venture to go near the house till she had brought herself down to nine inches high.

Chapter VI

PIG AND PEPPER

For a minute or two she stood looking at the house, and wondering what to do next, when suddenly a footman in livery came running out of the wood—(she considered him to be a footman because he was in livery: otherwise, judging by his face only, she would have called him a fish)—and rapped loudly at the door with his knuckles. It was opened by another footman in livery, with a round face, and large eyes like a frog; and both footmen, Alice noticed, had powdered hair that curled all over their heads. She felt very curious to know what it was all about, and crept a little way out of the wood to listen.

The Fish-Footman began by producing from under his arm a great letter, nearly as large as himself, and this he handed over to the other, saying, in a solemn tone, "For the Duchess. An invitation from the Queen to play croquet." The Frog-Footman repeated, in the same solemn tone, only changing the order of the words a little, "From the Queen. An invitation for the Duchess to play croquet."

Then they both bowed, and their curls got entangled together.

Alice laughed so much at this, that she had to run back into the wood for fear of their hearing her; and, when she next peeped out, the Fish-Footman was gone, and the other was sitting on the ground near the door, staring stupidly up into the sky.

Alice went timidly up to the door, and knocked.

"There's no sort of use in knocking," said the Footman, "and that for two reasons. First, because I'm on the same side of the door as you are: secondly, because they're making such a noise inside, no one could possibly hear you." And certainly there *was* a most extraordinary noise going on within—a constant howling and sneezing, and every now and then a great crash, as if a dish or kettle had been broken to pieces.

"Please, then," said Alice, "how am I to get in?"

"There might be some sense in your knocking," the Footman went on, without attending to her, "if we had the door between us. For instance, if you were *inside*, you might knock, and I could let you out, you know." He was looking up into the sky all the time he was speaking, and this Alice thought decidedly uncivil. "But perhaps he ca'n't help it," she said to herself; "his eyes are so *very* nearly at the top of his head. But at any rate he might answer questions.—How am I to get in?" she repeated, aloud.

"I shall sit here," the Footman remarked, "till to-morrow——"

At this moment the door of the house opened, and a large plate came skimming out, straight at the Footman's head: it just grazed his nose, and broke to pieces against one of the trees behind him.

"——or next day, maybe," the Footman continued in the same tone, exactly as if nothing had happened.

"How am I to get in?" asked Alice again, in a louder tone.

"*Are* you to get in at all?" said the Footman. "That's the first question, you know."

It was, no doubt: only Alice did not like to be told so. "It's really dreadful," she muttered to herself, "the way all the creatures argue. It's enough to drive one crazy!"

The Footman seemed to think this a good opportunity for repeating his remark, with variations. "I shall sit here," he said, "on and off, for days and days."

"But what am *I* to do?" said Alice.

"Anything you like," said the Footman, and began whistling.

"Oh, there's no use in talking to him," said Alice desperately: "he's perfectly idiotic!" And she opened the door and went in.

The door led right into a large kitchen, which was full of smoke from one end to the other: the Duchess[8] was sitting on a three-legged stool in the middle, nursing a baby: the cook was leaning over the fire, stirring a large cauldron which seemed to be full of soup.

"There's certainly too much pepper in that soup!" Alice said to herself, as well as she could for sneezing.

There was certainly too much of it in the *air*. Even the Duchess sneezed occasionally; and as for the baby, it was sneezing and howling alternately without a moment's pause. The only two creatures in the kitchen, that did *not* sneeze, were the cook, and a large cat, which was lying on the hearth and grinning from ear to ear.

"Please would you tell me," said Alice, a little timidly, for she was not quite sure whether it was good manners for her to speak first, "why your cat grins like that?"

"It's a Cheshire-Cat,"[9] said the Duchess, "and that's why. Pig!"

8. Michael Hancher, in his excellent study of *The Tenniel Illustrations to the "Alice" Books* (see Selected Bibliography), identifies a painting attributed to the Flemish painter Quinten Massys (1465/66–1530) as the most likely source of Tenniel's drawing of the Duchess (pp. 41–48).

9. The phrase "grin like a Cheshire-Cat" is proverbial. Its origins are uncertain, but Dodgson may have read some contributions to *Notes and Queries* in 1852 that attributed the phrase to the custom of making Cheshire cheeses in the shape of grinning cats, or to the practice of a Cheshire signpainter who painted pictures of grinning cats.

She said the last word with such sudden violence that Alice quite jumped; but she saw in another moment that it was addressed to the baby, and not to her, so she took courage, and went on again:—

"I didn't know that Cheshire-Cats always grinned; in fact, I didn't know that cats *could* grin."

"They all can," said the Duchess; "and most of 'em do."

"I don't know of any that do," Alice said very politely, feeling quite pleased to have got into a conversation.

"You don't know much," said the Duchess; "and that's a fact."

Alice did not at all like the tone of this remark, and thought it would be as well to introduce some other subject of conversation. While she was trying to fix on one, the cook took the cauldron of soup off the fire, and at once set to work throwing everything within her reach at the Duchess and the baby—the fire-irons came first; then followed a shower of saucepans, plates, and dishes. The Duchess took no notice of them even when they hit her; and the baby was howling so much already, that it was quite impossible to say whether the blows hurt it or not.

"Oh, *please* mind what you're doing!" cried Alice, jumping up and down in an agony of terror. "Oh, there goes his *precious* nose!", as an unusually large saucepan flew close by it, and very nearly carried it off.

"If everybody minded their own business," the Duchess said, in a hoarse growl, "the world would go round a deal faster than it does."

"Which would *not* be an advantage," said Alice, who felt very glad to get an opportunity of showing off a little of her knowledge. "Just think what work it would make with the day and night! You see the earth takes twenty-four hours to turn round on its axis——"

"Talking of axes," said the Duchess, "chop off her head!"

Alice glanced rather anxiously at the cook, to see if she meant to take the hint; but the cook was busily stirring the soup, and seemed not to be listening, so she went on again: "Twenty-four hours, I *think*; or is it twelve? I——"

"Oh, don't bother *me*!" said the Duchess. "I never could abide figures!" And with that she began nursing her child again, singing a sort of lullaby to it as she did so, and giving it a violent shake at the end of every line:—

> "Speak roughly to your little boy,
>   And beat him when he sneezes:
> He only does it to annoy,
>   Because he knows it teases."

CHORUS
(in which the cook and the baby joined):—
"Wow! wow! wow!"

While the Duchess sang the second verse of the song, she kept tossing the baby violently up and down, and the poor little thing howled so, that Alice could hardly hear the words:—

> *"I speak severely to my boy,*
> *I beat him when he sneezes;*
> *For he can thoroughly enjoy*
> *The pepper when he pleases!"*

CHORUS
"Wow! wow! wow!"[1]

"Here! You may nurse it a bit, if you like!" the Duchess said to Alice, flinging the baby at her as she spoke. "I must go and get ready to play croquet with the Queen," and she hurried out of the room. The cook threw a frying-pan after her as she went, but it just missed her.

Alice caught the baby with some difficulty, as it was a queer-shaped little creature, and held out its arms and legs in all directions, "just like a star-fish," thought Alice. The poor little thing was snorting like a steam-engine when she caught it, and kept doubling itself up and straightening itself out again, so that altogether, for the first minute or two, it was as much as she could do to hold it.

As soon as she had made out the proper way of nursing it (which was to twist it up into a sort of knot, and then keep tight hold of its right ear and left foot, so as to prevent its undoing itself), she carried it out into the open air. "If I don't take this child away with me," thought Alice, "they're sure to kill it in a day or two. Wouldn't it be murder to leave it behind?" She said the last words out loud, and the little thing grunted in reply (it had left off sneezing by this time). "Don't grunt," said Alice; "that's not at all a proper way of expressing yourself."

The baby grunted again, and Alice looked very anxiously into its face to see what was the matter with it. There could be no doubt

1. "Speak roughly" is a parody of one stanza of a popular children's poem by David Bates, first published in 1848:

Speak gently to the little child!
   Its love be sure to gain;

Teach it in accents soft and mild—
   It may not long remain.

The poem is sometimes attributed to G. W. Langford; for the attribution to Bates, see the appendix (p. 310) to *The Lewis Carroll Handbook* (see Selected Bibliography).

that it had a *very* turn-up nose, much more like a snout than a real nose: also its eyes were getting extremely small for a baby: altogether Alice did not like the look of the thing at all. "But perhaps it was only sobbing," she thought, and looked into its eyes again, to see if there were any tears.

No, there were no tears. "If you're going to turn into a pig, my dear," said Alice, seriously, "I'll have nothing more to do with you. Mind now!" The poor little thing sobbed again (or grunted, it was impossible to say which), and they went on for some while in silence.

Alice was just beginning to think to herself, "Now, what am I to do with this creature, when I get it home?" when it grunted again, so violently, that she looked down into its face in some alarm. This time there could be *no* mistake about it: it was neither more nor less than a pig, and she felt that it would be quite absurd for her to carry it any further.

So she set the little creature down, and felt quite relieved to see it trot away quietly into the wood. "If it had grown up," she said to herself, "it would have made a dreadfully ugly child: but it makes rather a handsome pig, I think." And she began thinking over other children she knew, who might do very well as pigs, and was just saying to herself "if one only knew the right way to change them——" when she was a little startled by seeing the Cheshire-Cat sitting on a bough of a tree a few yards off.

The Cat only grinned when it saw Alice. It looked good-natured, she thought: still it had *very* long claws and a great many teeth, so she felt that it ought to be treated with respect.

"Cheshire-Puss," she began, rather timidly, as she did not at all know whether it would like the name: however, it only grinned a little wider. "Come, it's pleased so far," thought Alice, and she went on. "Would you tell me, please, which way I ought to go from here?"

"That depends a good deal on where you want to get to," said the Cat.

"I don't much care where——" said Alice.

"Then it doesn't matter which way you go," said the Cat.

"—— so long as I get *somewhere*," Alice added as an explanation.

"Oh, you're sure to do that," said the Cat, "if you only walk long enough."

Alice felt that this could not be denied, so she tried another question. "What sort of people live about here?"

"In *that* direction," the Cat said, waving its right paw round, "lives a Hatter: and in *that* direction," waving the other paw, "lives a March Hare. Visit either you like: they're both mad."[2]

"But I don't want to go among mad people," Alice remarked.

"Oh, you ca'n't help that," said the Cat: "we're all mad here. I'm mad. You're mad."

"How do you know I'm mad?" said Alice.

"You must be," said the Cat, "or you wouldn't have come here."

Alice didn't think that proved it at all: however, she went on: "And how do you know that you're mad?"

"To begin with," said the Cat, "a dog's not mad. You grant that?"

"I suppose so," said Alice.

"Well, then," the Cat went on, "you see a dog growls when it's angry, and wags its tail when it's pleased. Now *I* growl when I'm pleased, and wag my tail when I'm angry. Therefore I'm mad."

"*I* call it purring, not growling," said Alice.

---

2. "Mad as a hatter" and "mad as a March hare" are both proverbial expressions. The latter is apparently founded on the behavior of hares in their mating season; the former is a more recent phrase, although current in the mid-nineteenth century, which may have originated in the fact that the use of mercury in preparing the felt that was made into hats did produce symptoms of insanity in hatters. The Hatter also bears characteristics of one Theophilus Carter, an eccentric Oxford furniture dealer who customarily stood in the doorway of his shop wearing a top hat on the back of his head. He was also the inventor of an alarm clock bed, which at the time for which it was set tipped its occupant onto the floor. See R. L. Green's edition (p. 172) of *The Diaries of Lewis Carroll* (see Selected Bibliography).

"Call it what you like," said the Cat. "Do you play croquet with the Queen to-day?"

"I should like it very much," said Alice, "but I haven't been invited yet."

"You'll see me there," said the Cat, and vanished.

Alice was not much surprised at this, she was getting so well used to queer things happening. While she was still looking at the place where it had been, it suddenly appeared again.

"By-the-bye, what became of the baby?" said the Cat. "I'd nearly forgotten to ask."

"It turned into a pig," Alice answered very quietly, just as if the Cat had come back in a natural way.

"I thought it would," said the Cat, and vanished again.

Alice waited a little, half expecting to see it again, but it did not appear, and after a minute or two she walked on in the direction in which the March Hare was said to live. "I've seen hatters before," she said to herself: "the March Hare will be much the most interesting, and perhaps, as this is May, it wo'n't be raving mad—at least not so mad as it was in March." As she said this, she looked up, and there was the Cat again, sitting on a branch of a tree.

"Did you say 'pig', or 'fig'?" said the Cat.

"I said 'pig'," replied Alice; "and I wish you wouldn't keep appearing and vanishing so suddenly; you make one quite giddy!"

"All right," said the Cat; and this time it vanished quite slowly, beginning with the end of the tail, and ending with the grin, which remained some time after the rest of it had gone.

"Well! I've often seen a cat without a grin," thought Alice; "but a grin without a cat! It's the most curious thing I ever saw in all my life!"

She had not gone much farther before she came in sight of the house of the March Hare: she thought it must be the right house, because the chimneys were shaped like ears and the roof was thatched with fur. It was so large a house, that she did not like to go nearer till she had nibbled some more of the left-hand bit of mushroom, and raised herself to about two feet high: even then she walked up towards it rather timidly, saying to herself "Suppose it should be raving mad after all! I almost wish I'd gone to see the Hatter instead!"

Chapter VII

A MAD TEA-PARTY

There was a table set out under a tree in front of the house, and the March Hare and the Hatter were having tea at it: a Dormouse was sitting between them, fast asleep,[3] and the other two were using it as a cushion, resting their elbows on it, and talking over its head. "Very uncomfortable for the Dormouse," thought Alice; "only as it's asleep, I suppose it doesn't mind."

The table was a large one, but the three were all crowded together at one corner of it. "No room! No room!" they cried out when they saw Alice coming. "There's *plenty* of room!" said Alice indignantly, and she sat down in a large arm-chair at one end of the table.

"Have some wine," the March Hare said in an encouraging tone.

Alice looked all round the table, but there was nothing on it but tea. "I don't see any wine," she remarked.

"There isn't any," said the March Hare.

"Then it wasn't very civil of you to offer it," said Alice angrily.

3. A dormouse is a rodent that hibernates in the winter and sleeps during the day all year round.

"It wasn't very civil of you to sit down without being invited," said the March Hare.

"I didn't know it was *your* table," said Alice: "it's laid for a great many more than three."

"Your hair wants cutting," said the Hatter. He had been looking at Alice for some time with great curiosity, and this was his first speech.

"You should learn not to make personal remarks," Alice said with some severity: "it's very rude." *ironic she's telling them not to be rude, when she was doing so earlier*

The Hatter opened his eyes very wide on hearing this; but all he said was "Why is a raven like a writing-desk?"[4]

"Come, we shall have some fun now!" thought Alice. "I'm glad they've begun asking riddles—I believe I can guess that," she added aloud.

"Do you mean that you think you can find out the answer to it?" said the March Hare.

"Exactly so," said Alice.

"Then you should say what you mean," the March Hare went on.

"I do," Alice hastily replied; "at least—at least I mean what I say—that's the same thing, you know."

"Not the same thing a bit!" said the Hatter. "Why, you might just as well say that 'I see what I eat' is the same thing as 'I eat what I see'!"

"You might just as well say," added the March Hare, "that 'I like what I get' is the same thing as 'I get what I like'!" *language*

"You might just as well say," added the Dormouse, which seemed to be talking in its sleep, "that 'I breathe when I sleep' is the same thing as 'I sleep when I breathe'!"

"It *is* the same thing with you," said the Hatter, and here the conversation dropped, and the party sat silent for a minute, while Alice thought over all she could remember about ravens and writing-desks, which wasn't much.

The Hatter was the first to break the silence. "What day of the month is it?" he said, turning to Alice: he had taken his watch out of his pocket, and was looking at it uneasily, shaking it every now and then, and holding it to his ear.

Alice considered a little, and then said "The fourth."[5]

"Two days wrong!" sighed the Hatter. "I told you butter wouldn't suit the works!" he added, looking angrily at the March Hare.

4. In a later edition of *Alice's Adventures in Wonderland* Dodgson wrote that originally this riddle had no answer, and then he provided one: because it can produce a few notes, although they are very flat, and it is never put the wrong end front.
5. May fourth was Alice Liddell's birthday.

"It was the *best* butter," the March Hare meekly replied.

"Yes, but some crumbs must have got in as well," the Hatter grumbled: "you shouldn't have put it in with the bread-knife."

The March Hare took the watch and looked at it gloomily: then he dipped it into his cup of tea, and looked at it again: but he could think of nothing better to say than his first remark, "It was the *best* butter, you know."

Alice had been looking over his shoulder with some curiosity. "What a funny watch!" she remarked. "It tells the day of the month, and doesn't tell what o'clock it is!"

"Why should it?" muttered the Hatter. "Does *your* watch tell you what year it is?"

"Of course not," Alice replied very readily: "but that's because it stays the same year for such a long time together."

"Which is just the case with *mine*," said the Hatter.

Alice felt dreadfully puzzled. The Hatter's remark seemed to her to have no sort of meaning in it, and yet it was certainly English. "I don't quite understand you," she said, as politely as she could.

"The Dormouse is asleep again," said the Hatter, and he poured a little hot tea upon its nose.

The Dormouse shook its head impatiently, and said, without opening its eyes, "Of course, of course: just what I was going to remark myself."

"Have you guessed the riddle yet?" the Hatter said, turning to Alice again.

"No, I give it up," Alice replied. "What's the answer?"

"I haven't the slightest idea," said the Hatter.

"Nor I," said the March Hare.

Alice sighed wearily. "I think you might do something better with the time," she said, "than wasting it in asking riddles that have no answers."

"If you knew Time as well as I do," said the Hatter, "you wouldn't talk about wasting *it*. It's *him*."

"I don't know what you mean," said Alice.

"Of course you don't!" the Hatter said, tossing his head con-

temptuously. "I dare say you never even spoke to Time!"

"Perhaps not," Alice cautiously replied; "but I know I have to beat time when I learn music."

"Ah! That accounts for it," said the Hatter. "He wo'n't stand beating. Now, if you only kept on good terms with him, he'd do almost anything you liked with the clock. For instance, suppose it were nine o'clock in the morning, just time to begin lessons: you'd only have to whisper a hint to Time, and round goes the clock in a twinkling! Half-past one, time for dinner!"

("I only wish it was," the March Hare said to itself in a whisper.)

"That would be grand, certainly," said Alice thoughtfully; "but then—I shouldn't be hungry for it, you know."

"Not at first, perhaps," said the Hatter: "but you could keep it to half-past one as long as you liked."

"Is that the way *you* manage?" Alice asked.

The Hatter shook his head mournfully. "Not I!" he replied. "We quarreled last March—just before *he* went mad, you know——" (pointing his teaspoon at the March Hare,) "——it was at the great concert given by the Queen of Hearts, and I had to sing

> *'Twinkle, twinkle, little bat!*
> *How I wonder what you're at!'*

You know the song, perhaps?"

"I've heard something like it," said Alice.

"It goes on, you know," the Hatter continued, "in this way:—

> *'Up above the world you fly,*
> *Like a tea-tray in the sky.*
> *Twinkle, twinkle—'* "[6]

6. "Twinkle, twinkle little bat" is a parody of "The Star" by Jane Taylor, who published a popular collection, *Rhymes for the Nursery*, in 1806. The first stanza is still familiar:

> Twinkle, twinkle little star!
> How I wonder what you are.

> Up above the world so high,
> Like a diamond in the sky.

Bartholomew Price, a professor of mathematics at Oxford and once Dodgson's tutor, was nicknamed "the Bat."

Here the Dormouse shook itself, and began singing in its sleep "*Twinkle, twinkle, twinkle, twinkle——*" and went on so long that they had to pinch it to make it stop.

"Well, I'd hardly finished the first verse," said the Hatter, "when the Queen bawled out 'He's murdering the time! Off with his head!' "

"How dreadfully savage!" exclaimed Alice.

"And ever since that," the Hatter went on in a mournful tone, "he wo'n't do a thing I ask! It's always six o'clock now."

A bright idea came into Alice's head. "Is that the reason so many tea-things are put out here?" she asked.

"Yes, that's it," said the Hatter with a sigh: "it's always tea-time, and we've no time to wash the things between whiles."

"Then you keep moving round, I suppose?" said Alice.

"Exactly so," said the Hatter: "as the things get used up."

"But what happens when you come to the beginning again?" Alice ventured to ask.

"Suppose we change the subject," the March Hare interrupted, yawning. "I'm getting tired of this. I vote the young lady tells us a story."

"I'm afraid I don't know one," said Alice, rather alarmed at the proposal.

"Then the Dormouse shall!" they both cried. "Wake up, Dormouse!" And they pinched it on both sides at once.

The Dormouse slowly opened its eyes. "I wasn't asleep," it said in a hoarse, feeble voice, "I heard every word you fellows were saying."

"Tell us a story!" said the March Hare.

"Yes, please do!" pleaded Alice.

"And be quick about it," added the Hatter, "or you'll be asleep again before it's done."

"Once upon a time there were three little sisters," the Dormouse began in a great hurry; "and their names were Elsie, Lacie, and Tillie;[7] and they lived at the bottom of a well——"

"What did they live on?" said Alice, who always took a great interest in questions of eating and drinking.

"They lived on treacle,"[8] said the Dormouse, after thinking a minute or two.

---

7. Another reference to the three girls to whom Alice's adventures were first told: Lacie is an anagram of Alice; Elsie is L. C. (Lorina Charlotte); and Tillie is Edith, who was sometimes called Mathilda in her family. The Dormouse in this passage, telling his story over interruptions and falling asleep during the telling, may recall Dodgson himself. In the introductory poem to *Alice's Adventures in Wonderland*, he refers to the frequency with which his stories were interrupted by the children, and he sometimes pretended to fall asleep while he was telling them (see "Alice's Recollections of Carrollian Days," reprinted on pp. 273–78 of this edition).

8. Molasses.

"They couldn't have done that, you know," Alice gently remarked. "They'd have been ill."

"So they were," said the Dormouse; "*very* ill."

Alice tried a little to fancy to herself what such an extraordinary way of living would be like, but it puzzled her too much: so she went on: "But why did they live at the bottom of a well?"

"Take some more tea," the March Hare said to Alice, very earnestly.

"I've had nothing yet," Alice replied in an offended tone: "so I ca'n't take more."

"You mean you ca'n't take *less*," said the Hatter: "it's very easy to take *more* than nothing."

"Nobody asked *your* opinion," said Alice.

"Who's making personal remarks now?" the Hatter asked triumphantly.

Alice did not quite know what to say to this: so she helped herself to some tea and bread-and-butter, and then turned to the Dormouse, and repeated her question. "Why did they live at the bottom of a well?"

The Dormouse again took a minute or two to think about it, and then said "It was a treacle-well."

"There's no such thing!" Alice was beginning very angrily, but the Hatter and the March Hare went "Sh! Sh!" and the Dormouse sulkily remarked "If you ca'n't be civil, you'd better finish the story for yourself."

"No, please go on!" Alice said very humbly. "I wo'n't interrupt you again. I dare say there may be *one*."

"One, indeed!" said the Dormouse indignantly. However, he consented to go on. "And so these three little sisters—they were learning to draw, you know——"

"What did they draw?" said Alice, quite forgetting her promise.

"Treacle," said the Dormouse, without considering at all, this time.

"I want a clean cup," interrupted the Hatter: "let's all move one place on."

He moved on as he spoke, and the Dormouse followed him: the March Hare moved into the Dormouse's place, and Alice rather unwillingly took the place of the March Hare. The Hatter was the only one who got any advantage from the change; and Alice was a good deal worse off than before, as the March Hare had just upset the milk-jug into his plate.

Alice did not wish to offend the Dormouse again, so she began very cautiously: "But I don't understand. Where did they draw the treacle from?"

Play on words

"You can draw water out of a water-well," said the Hatter; "so I should think you could draw treacle out of a treacle-well—eh, stupid?"

language

"But they were *in* the well," Alice said to the Dormouse, not choosing to notice this last remark.

"Of course they were," said the Dormouse: "well in."

This answer so confused poor Alice, that she let the Dormouse go on for some time without interrupting it.

"They were learning to draw," the Dormouse went on, yawning and rubbing its eyes, for it was getting very sleepy; "and they drew all manner of things—everything that begins with an M——"

"Why with an M?" said Alice.

"Why not?" said the March Hare.

Alice was silent.

The Dormouse had closed its eyes by this time, and was going off into a doze; but, on being pinched by the Hatter, it woke up again with a little shriek, and went on: "——that begins with an M, such as mouse-traps, and the moon, and memory, and muchness—you know you say things are 'much of a muchness'—did you ever see such a thing as a drawing of a muchness!" *proverbial expression — much the same*

"Really, now you ask me," said Alice, very much confused, "I don't think——"

"Then you shouldn't talk," said the Hatter.

This piece of rudeness was more than Alice could bear: she got up in great disgust, and walked off: the Dormouse fell asleep instantly, and neither of the others took the least notice of her going, though she looked back once or twice, half hoping that they would call after her: the last time she saw them, they were trying to put the Dormouse into the teapot.

"At any rate I'll never go *there* again!" said Alice, as she picked her way through the wood. "It's the stupidest tea-party I ever was at in all my life!"

Just as she said this, she noticed that one of the trees had a door leading right into it. "That's very curious!" she thought. "But everything's curious to-day. I think I may as well go in at once." And in she went.

Once more she found herself in the long hall, and close to the little glass table. "Now, I'll manage better this time," she said to herself, and began by taking the little golden key, and unlocking the door that led into the garden. Then she set to work nibbling at the mushroom (she had kept a piece of it in her pocket) till she was about a foot high; then she walked down the little passage: and *then*—she found herself at last in the beautiful garden, among the bright flower-beds and the cool fountains.

Chapter VIII

THE QUEEN'S CROQUET-GROUND

A large rose-tree stood near the entrance of the garden: the roses growing on it were white, but there were three gardeners at it, busily painting them red. Alice thought this a very curious thing, and she went nearer to watch them, and, just as she came up to them, she heard one of them say "Look out now, Five! Don't go splashing paint over me like that!"

"I couldn't help it," said Five, in a sulky tone. "Seven jogged my elbow."

On which Seven looked up and said "That's right, Five! Always lay the blame on others!"

"*You'd* better not talk!" said Five. "I heard the Queen say only yesterday you deserved to be beheaded."

"What for?" said the one who had spoken first.

"That's none of *your* business, Two!" said Seven.

"Yes, it *is* his business!" said Five. "And I'll tell him—it was for bringing the cook tulip-roots instead of onions."

Seven flung down his brush, and had just begun "Well, of all the unjust things—" when his eye chanced to fall upon Alice, as she stood watching them, and he checked himself suddenly: the others looked round also, and all of them bowed low.

"Would you tell me, please," said Alice, a little timidly, "why you are painting those roses?"

Five and Seven said nothing, but looked at Two. Two began, in a low voice, "Why, the fact is, you see, Miss, this here ought to have been a *red* rose-tree, and we put a white one in by mistake; and, if the Queen was to find out, we should all have our heads cut off, you know. So you see, Miss, we're doing our best, afore she comes, to—" At this moment, Five, who had been anxiously looking across the garden, called out "The Queen! The Queen!" and the three gardeners instantly threw themselves flat upon their faces. There was a sound of many footsteps, and Alice looked round, eager to see the Queen.

First came ten soldiers carrying clubs: these were all shaped like the three gardeners, oblong and flat, with their hands and feet at the corners: next the ten courtiers: these were ornamented all over with diamonds, and walked two and two, as the soldiers did. After these came the royal children: there were ten of them, and the little dears came jumping merrily along, hand in hand, in couples: they were all ornamented with hearts. Next came the guests, mostly Kings and Queens, and among them Alice recognized the White Rabbit: it was talking in a hurried nervous manner, smiling at everything that was said, and went by without noticing her. Then followed the Knave of Hearts, carrying the King's crown on a crimson velvet cushion; and, last of all this grand procession, came THE KING AND THE QUEEN OF HEARTS.

Alice was rather doubtful whether she ought not to lie down on her face like the three gardeners, but she could not remember ever having heard of such a rule at processions; "and besides, what would be the use of a procession," thought she, "if people had all to lie down on their faces, so that they couldn't see it?" So she stood where she was, and waited.

When the procession came opposite to Alice, they all stopped and looked at her, and the Queen said, severely, "Who is this?" She said it to the Knave of Hearts, who only bowed and smiled in reply.

"Idiot!" said the Queen, tossing her head impatiently; and turning to Alice, she went on: "What's your name, child?"

"My name is Alice, so please your Majesty," said Alice very politely; but she added, to herself, "Why, they're only a pack of cards, after all. I needn't be afraid of them!"

"And who are *these*?" said the Queen, pointing to the three gardeners who were lying round the rose-tree; for, you see, as they were lying on their faces, and the pattern on their backs was the same as the rest of the pack, she could not tell whether they were gardeners, or soldiers, or courtiers, or three of her own children.

"How should *I* know?" said Alice, surprised at her own courage. "It's no business of *mine*."

The Queen turned crimson with fury, and, after glaring at her for a moment like a wild beast, began screaming "Off with her head! Off with——"

"Nonsense!" said Alice, very loudly and decidedly, and the Queen was silent.

The King laid his hand upon her arm, and timidly said "Consider, my dear: she is only a child!"

The Queen turned angrily away from him, and said to the Knave "Turn them over!"

The Knave did so, very carefully, with one foot.

"Get up!" said the Queen in a shrill, loud voice, and the three gardeners instantly jumped up, and began bowing to the King, the Queen, the royal children, and everybody else.

"Leave off that!" screamed the Queen. "You make me giddy." And then, turning to the rose-tree, she went on "What *have* you been doing here?"

"May it please your Majesty," said Two, in a very humble tone, going down on one knee as he spoke, "we were trying—"

"*I* see!" said the Queen, who had meanwhile been examining the roses. "Off with their heads!" and the procession moved on, three of the soldiers remaining behind to execute the unfortunate gardeners, who ran to Alice for protection.

"You sha'n't be beheaded!" said Alice, and she put them into a large flower-pot that stood near. The three soldiers wandered about for a minute or two, looking for them, and then quietly marched off after the others.

"Are their heads off?" shouted the Queen.

"Their heads are gone, if it please your Majesty!" the soldiers shouted in reply.

"That's right!" shouted the Queen. "Can you play croquet?"

The soldiers were silent, and looked at Alice, as the question was evidently meant for her.

"Yes!" shouted Alice.

"Come on, then!" roared the Queen, and Alice joined the procession, wondering very much what would happen next.

"It's—it's a very fine day!" said a timid voice at her side. She was walking by the White Rabbit, who was peeping anxiously into her face.

"Very," said Alice. "Where's the Duchess?"

"Hush! Hush!" said the Rabbit in a low hurried tone. He looked anxiously over his shoulder as he spoke, and then raised himself upon tiptoe, put his mouth close to her ear, and whispered "She's under sentence of execution."

"What for?" said Alice.

"Did you say 'What a pity!'?" the Rabbit said.

"No, I didn't," said Alice. "I don't think it's at all a pity. I said 'What for?'"

"She boxed the Queen's ears—" the Rabbit began. Alice gave a little scream of laughter. "Oh, hush!" the Rabbit whispered in a frightened tone. "The Queen will hear you! You see she came rather late, and the Queen said—"

"Get to your places!" shouted the Queen in a voice of thunder, and people began running about in all directions, tumbling up against each other: however, they got settled down in a minute or two, and the game began.

Alice thought she had never seen such a curious croquet-ground in her life: it was all ridges and furrows: the croquet balls were live hedgehogs, and the mallets live flamingoes, and the soldiers had to double themselves up and stand on their hands and feet, to make the arches.

The chief difficulty Alice found at first was in managing her flamingo: she succeeded in getting its body tucked away, comfortably enough, under her arm, with its legs hanging down, but generally, just as she had got its neck nicely straightened out, and was going to give the hedgehog a blow with its head, it *would* twist itself round and look up in her face, with such a puzzled expression that she could not help bursting out laughing; and, when she had got its head down, and was going to begin again, it was very provoking to find that the hedgehog had unrolled itself, and was in the act of crawling away: besides all this, there was generally a ridge or a furrow in the way wherever she wanted to send the hedgehog to, and, as the doubled-up soldiers were always getting up and walking off to other parts of the ground, Alice soon came to the conclusion that it was a very difficult game indeed.

The players all played at once, without waiting for turns, quarrel-

ing all the while, and fighting for the hedgehogs; and in a very
short time the Queen was in a furious passion, and went stamping
about, and shouting "Off with his head!" or "Off with her head!"
about once in a minute.

Alice began to feel very uneasy: to be sure, she had not as yet
had any dispute with the Queen, but she knew that it might
happen any minute, "and then," thought she, "what would become
of me? They're dreadfully fond of beheading people here: the great
wonder is, that there's any one left alive!"

She was looking about for some way of escape, and wondering
whether she could get away without being seen, when she noticed a
curious appearance in the air: it puzzled her very much at first, but
after watching it a minute or two she made it out to be a grin, and
she said to herself "It's the Cheshire-Cat: now I shall have somebody to talk to."

"How are you getting on?" said the Cat, as soon as there was
mouth enough for it to speak with.

Alice waited till the eyes appeared, and then nodded. "It's no
use speaking to it," she thought, "till its ears have come, or at least
one of them." In another minute the whole head appeared, and
then Alice put down her flamingo, and began an account of the
game, feeling very glad she had some one to listen to her. The Cat
seemed to think that there was enough of it now in sight, and no
more of it appeared.

"I don't think they play at all fairly," Alice began, in rather a
complaining tone, "and they all quarrel so dreadfully one ca'n't hear
oneself speak—and they don't seem to have any rules in particular:
at least, if there are, nobody attends to them—and you've no idea
how confusing it is all the things being alive: for instance, there's
the arch I've got to go through next walking about at the other end
of the ground—and I should have croqueted the Queen's hedgehog
just now, only it ran away when it saw mine coming!"

"How do you like the Queen?" said the Cat in a low voice.

"Not at all," said Alice: "she's so extremely—" Just then she
noticed that the Queen was close behind her, listening: so she went
on "—likely to win, that it's hardly worth while finishing the
game."

The Queen smiled and passed on.

"Who *are* you talking to?" said the King, coming up to Alice,
and looking at the Cat's head with great curiosity.

"It's a friend of mine—a Cheshire-Cat," said Alice: "allow me to
introduce it."

"I don't like the look of it at all," said the King: "however, it
may kiss my hand, if it likes."

"I'd rather not," the Cat remarked.

"Don't be impertinent," said the King, "and don't look at me like that!" He got behind Alice as he spoke.

"A cat may look at a king," said Alice. "I've read that in some book, but I don't remember where."[9]

"Well, it must be removed," said the King very decidedly; and he called to the Queen, who was passing at the moment, "My dear! I wish you would have this cat removed!"

The Queen had only one way of settling all difficulties, great or small. "Off with his head!" she said without even looking around.

"I'll fetch the executioner myself," said the King eagerly, and he hurried off.

Alice thought she might as well go back and see how the game was going on, as she heard the Queen's voice in the distance, screaming with passion. She had already heard her sentence three of the players to be executed for having missed their turns, and she did not like the look of things at all, as the game was in such confusion that she never knew whether it was her turn or not. So she went off in search of her hedgehog.

The hedgehog was engaged in a fight with another hedgehog, which seemed to Alice an excellent opportunity for croqueting one of them with the other: the only difficulty was, that her flamingo was gone across the other side of the garden, where Alice could see it trying in a helpless sort of way to fly up into a tree.

By the time she had caught the flamingo and brought it back, the fight was over, and both the hedgehogs were out of sight: "but it doesn't matter much," thought Alice, "as all the arches are gone from this side of the ground." So she tucked it away under her arm, that it might not escape again, and went back to have a little more conversation with her friend.

When she got back to the Cheshire-Cat, she was surprised to find quite a large crowd collected round it: there was a dispute going on between the executioner, the King, and the Queen, who were all talking at once, while all the rest were quite silent, and looked very uncomfortable.

The moment Alice appeared, she was appealed to by all three to settle the question, and they repeated their arguments to her, though, as they all spoke at once, she found it very hard to make out exactly what they said.

The executioner's argument was, that you couldn't cut off a head unless there was a body to cut it off from: that he had never had to do such a thing before, and he wasn't going to begin at *his* time of life.

9. "A cat may look at a king" is another proverbial expression.

The King's argument was that anything that had a head could be beheaded, and that you weren't to talk nonsense.

The Queen's argument was that, if something wasn't done about it in less than no time, she'd have everybody executed, all round. (It was this last remark that had made the whole party look so grave and anxious.)

Alice could think of nothing else to say but "It belongs to the Duchess: you'd better ask *her* about it."

"She's in prison," the Queen said to the executioner: "fetch her here." And the executioner went off like an arrow.

The Cat's head began fading away the moment he was gone, and, by the time he had come back with the Duchess, it had entirely disappeared: so the King and the executioner ran wildly up and down, looking for it, while the rest of the party went back to the game.

Chapter IX

THE MOCK TURTLE'S STORY

"You ca'n't think how glad I am to see you again, you dear old thing!" said the Duchess, as she tucked her arm affectionately into Alice's, and they walked off together.

Alice was very glad to find her in such a pleasant temper, and thought to herself that perhaps it was only the pepper that had made her so savage when they met in the kitchen.

"When *I'm* a Duchess," she said to herself (not in a very hopeful tone, though), "I wo'n't have any pepper in my kitchen *at all*. Soup does very well without—Maybe it's always pepper that makes people hot-tempered," she went on, very much pleased at having found out a new kind of rule, "and vinegar that makes them sour—and camomile that makes them bitter—and—and barley-sugar[1] and such things that make children sweet-tempered. I only wish people knew *that*: then they wouldn't be so stingy about it, you know——"

She had quite forgotten the Duchess by this time, and was a little startled when she heard her voice close to her ear. "You're thinking about something, my dear, and that makes you forget to talk. I ca'n't tell you just now what the moral of that is, but I shall remember it in a bit."

"Perhaps it hasn't one," Alice ventured to remark.

"Tut, tut, child!" said the Duchess. "Everything's got a moral, if only you can find it." And she squeezed herself up closer to Alice's side as she spoke.

Alice did not much like her keeping so close to her: first because the Duchess was *very* ugly; and secondly, because she was exactly the right height to rest her chin on Alice's shoulder, and it was an uncomfortably sharp chin. However, she did not like to be rude: so she bore it as well as she could.

"The game's going on rather better now," she said, by way of keeping up the conversation a little.

" 'Tis so," said the Duchess: "and the moral of that is—'Oh, 'tis love, 'tis love, that makes the world go round!' "

"Somebody said," Alice whispered, "that it's done by everybody minding their own business!"

"Ah well! It means much the same thing," said the Duchess, digging her sharp little chin into Alice's shoulder as she added "and

1. Camomile is a plant from which a bitter medicine, often administered as a tea, was made. Barley sugar is hard candy.

the moral of *that* is—'Take care of the sense, and the sounds will take care of themselves.' "[2]

"How fond she is of finding morals in things!" Alice thought to herself.

"I dare say you're wondering why I don't put my arm round your waist," the Duchess said, after a pause: "the reason is, that I'm doubtful about the temper of your flamingo. Shall I try the experiment?"

"He might bite," Alice cautiously replied, not feeling at all anxious to have the experiment tried.

"Very true," said the Duchess: "flamingoes and mustard both bite. And the moral of that is—'Birds of a feather flock together.' "

"Only mustard isn't a bird," Alice remarked.

"Right, as usual," said the Duchess: "what a clear way you have of putting things!"

"It's a mineral, I *think*," said Alice.

"Of course it is," said the Duchess, who seemed ready to agree to everything that Alice said: "there's a large mustard-mine near here.

2. The proverb is "Take care of the pence, and the pounds will take care of themselves." The rest of the Duchess's morals are unaltered traditional proverbs, except that she seems to have created the moral "The more there is of mine, the less there is of yours," and to be improvising her last incoherent moral.

And the moral of that is— 'The more there is of mine, the less there is of yours.' "

"Oh, I know!" exclaimed Alice, who had not attended to this last remark. "It's a vegetable. It doesn't look like one, but it is."

"I quite agree with you," said the Duchess; "and the moral of that is—'Be what you would seem to be'—or, if you'd like it put more simply—'Never imagine yourself not to be otherwise than what it might appear to others that what you were or might have been was not otherwise than what you had been would have appeared to them to be otherwise.' "

"I think I should understand that better," Alice said very politely, "if I had it written down: but I ca'n't quite follow it as you say it."

"That's nothing to what I could say if I chose," the Duchess replied, in a pleased tone.

"Pray don't trouble yourself to say it any longer than that," said Alice.

"Oh, don't talk about trouble!" said the Duchess. "I make you a present of everything I've said as yet."

"A cheap sort of present!" thought Alice. "I'm glad people don't give birthday-presents like that!" But she did not venture to say it out loud.

"Thinking again?" the Duchess asked, with another dig of her sharp little chin.

"I've a right to think," said Alice sharply, for she was beginning to feel a little worried.

"Just about as much right," said the Duchess, "as pigs have to fly; and the m——"

But here, to Alice's great surprise, the Duchess's voice died away, even in the middle of her favourite word "moral", and the arm that was linked into hers began to tremble. Alice looked up, and there stood the Queen in front of them, with her arms folded, frowning like a thunderstorm.

"A fine day, your Majesty!" the Duchess began in a low, weak voice.

"Now, I give you fair warning," shouted the Queen, stamping on the ground as she spoke; "either you or your head must be off, and that in about half no time! Take your choice!"

The Duchess took her choice, and was gone in a moment.

"Let's go on with the game," the Queen said to Alice; and Alice was too much frightened to say a word, but slowly followed her back to the croquet-ground.

The other guests had taken advantage of the Queen's absence, and were resting in the shade: however, the moment they saw her, they hurried back to the game, the Queen merely remarking that a moment's delay would cost them their lives.

All the time they were playing the Queen never left off quarreling with the other players, and shouting "Off with his head!" or "Off with her head!" Those whom she sentenced were taken into custody by the soldiers, who of course had to leave off being arches to do this, so that, by the end of half an hour or so, there were no arches left, and all the players, except the King, the Queen, and Alice, were in custody and under sentence of execution.

Then the Queen left off, quite out of breath, and said to Alice "Have you seen the Mock Turtle yet?"

"No," said Alice. "I don't even know what a Mock Turtle is."

"It's the thing Mock Turtle Soup[3] is made from," said the Queen,

"I never saw one, or heard of one," said Alice.

"Come on, then," said the Queen, "and he shall tell you his history."

As they walked off together, Alice heard the King say in a low voice, to the company, generally, "You are all pardoned." "Come, *that's* a good thing!" she said to herself, for she had felt quite unhappy at the number of executions the Queen had ordered.

They very soon came upon a Gryphon,[4] lying fast asleep in the sun. (If you don't know what a Gryphon is, look at the picture.)

3. Mock turtle soup is usually made of veal.
4. A gryphon, or griffin, is a fabulous creature, common in medieval iconography and heraldry, with the head and wings of an eagle and the body of a lion.

"Up, lazy thing!" said the Queen, "and take this young lady to see the Mock Turtle, and to hear his history. I must go back and see after some executions I have ordered;" and she walked off, leaving Alice alone with the Gryphon. Alice did not quite like the look of the creature, but on the whole she thought it would be quite as safe to stay with it as to go after that savage Queen: so she waited.

The Gryphon sat up and rubbed its eyes: then it watched the Queen till she was out of sight: then it chuckled. "What fun!" said the Gryphon, half to itself, half to Alice.

"What *is* the fun?" said Alice.

"Why, *she*," said the Gryphon. "It's all her fancy that: they never executes nobody, you know. Come on!"

"Everybody says 'come on!' here," thought Alice, as she went slowly after it: "I never was so ordered about before, in all my life, never!"

They had not gone far before they saw the Mock Turtle in the distance, sitting sad and lonely on a little ledge of rock, and, as they came nearer, Alice could hear him sighing as if his heart would break. She pitied him deeply. "What is his sorrow?" she asked the Gryphon. And the Gryphon answered, very nearly in the same words as before, "It's all his fancy, that: he hasn't got no sorrow, you know. Come on!"

So they went up to the Mock Turtle, who looked at them with large eyes full of tears, but said nothing.

"This here young lady," said the Gryphon, "she wants for to know your history, she do."

"I'll tell it her," said the Mock Turtle in a deep, hollow tone. "Sit down, both of you, and don't speak a word till I've finished."

So they sat down, and nobody spoke for some minutes. Alice thought to herself "I don't see how he can *ever* finish, if he doesn't begin." But she waited patiently.

"Once," said the Mock Turtle at last, with a deep sigh, "I was a real Turtle."

These words were followed by a very long silence, broken only by an occasional exclamation of "Hjckrrh!" from the Gryphon, and the constant heavy sobbing of the Mock Turtle. Alice was very nearly getting up and saying, "Thank you, Sir, for your interesting story," but she could not help thinking there *must* be more to come, so she sat still and said nothing.

"When we were still little," the Mock Turtle went on at last, more calmly, though still sobbing a little now and then, "we went to school in the sea. The master was an old Turtle—we used to call him Tortoise——"

"Why did you call him Tortoise,[5] if he wasn't one?" Alice asked.

"We called him Tortoise because he taught us," said the Mock Turtle angrily. "Really you are very dull!"

"You ought to be ashamed of yourself for asking such a simple question," added the Gryphon; and then they both sat silent and looked at poor Alice, who felt ready to sink into the earth. At last the Gryphon said to the Mock Turtle "Drive on, old fellow! Don't be all day about it!" and he went on in these words:—

5. Alice has in mind the conventional distinction between tortoises, a name often given to land turtles, and turtles, a name given to marine turtles. This entire passage, with its string of puns on the subjects taught in school, is Dodgson's most extensive use of puns in *Al-ice's Adventures in Wonderland*. Puns were common in mid-nineteenth-century British comic writing, especially in the theatrical pantomimes and burlesques of which Dodgson was fond.

"Yes, we went to school in the sea, though you mayn't believe it——"

"I never said I didn't!" interrupted Alice.

"You did," said the Mock Turtle.

"Hold your tongue!" added the Gryphon, before Alice could speak again. The Mock Turtle went on.

"We had the best of educations—in fact, we went to school every day——"

"*I've* been to a day-school, too," said Alice. "You needn't be so proud as all that."

"With extras?"[6] asked the Mock Turtle, a little anxiously.

"Yes," said Alice: "we learned French and music."

"And washing?" said the Mock Turtle.

"Certainly not!" said Alice indignantly.

"Ah! Then yours wasn't a really good school," said the Mock Turtle in a tone of great relief. "Now, at *ours*, they had, at the end of the bill, 'French, music, *and washing*—extra.' "

"You couldn't have wanted it much," said Alice; "living at the bottom of the sea."

"I couldn't afford to learn it," said the Mock Turtle with a sigh. "I only took the regular course."

"What was that?" inquired Alice.

"Reeling and Writhing, of course, to begin with," the Mock Turtle replied; "and then the different branches of Arithmetic— Ambition, Distraction, Uglification, and Derision."

"I never heard of 'Uglification,' " Alice ventured to say. "What is it?"

The Gryphon lifted up both its paws in surprise. "Never heard of uglifying!" it exclaimed. "You know what to beautify is, I suppose?"

"Yes," said Alice doubtfully: "it means—to—make—anything— prettier."

"Well, then," the Gryphon went on, "if you don't know what to uglify is, you *are* a simpleton."

Alice did not feel encouraged to ask any more questions about it: so she turned to the Mock Turtle, and said "What else had you to learn?"

"Well, there was Mystery," the Mock Turtle replied, counting off the subjects on his flappers—"Mystery, ancient and modern, with Seaography: then Drawling—the Drawling-master was an old

---

6. Alice interprets "extras" as subjects for whose teaching an additional charge is levied; the Mock Turtle also means services for which an extra charge is made. Alice, properly brought-up middle-class girl that she is, is indignant at the suggestion that she has been taught servile tasks, such as doing the wash.

conger-eel, that used to come once a week: *he* taught us Drawling, Stretching, and Fainting in Coils."

"What was *that* like?" said Alice.

"Well, I ca'n't show it you, myself," the Mock Turtle said: "I'm too stiff. And the Gryphon never learnt it."

"Hadn't time," said the Gryphon: "I went to the Classical master, though. He was an old crab, *he* was."

"I never went to him," the Mock Turtle said with a sigh. "He taught Laughing and Grief, they used to say."

"So he did, so he did," said the Gryphon, sighing in his turn; and both creatures hid their faces in their paws.

"And how many hours a day did you do lessons?" said Alice, in a hurry to change the subject.

"Ten hours the first day," said the Mock Turtle: "nine the next, and so on."

"What a curious plan!" exclaimed Alice.

"That's the reason they're called lessons," the Gryphon remarked: "because they lessen from day to day."

This was quite a new idea to Alice, and she thought it over a little before she made her next remark. "Then the eleventh day must have been a holiday?"

"Of course it was," said the Mock Turtle.

"And how did you manage on the twelfth?" Alice went on eagerly.

"That's enough about lessons," the Gryphon interrupted in a very decided tone. "Tell her something about the games now."

Chapter X

THE LOBSTER-QUADRILLE

The Mock Turtle sighed deeply, and drew the back of one flapper across his eyes. He looked at Alice and tried to speak, but, for a minute or two, sobs choked his voice. "Same as if he had a bone in his throat," said the Gryphon; and it set to work shaking him and punching him in the back. At last the Mock Turtle recovered his voice, and, with tears running down his cheeks, he went on again:—

"You may not have lived much under the sea—" ("I haven't," said Alice)—"and perhaps you were never even introduced to a lobster—" (Alice began to say "I once tasted——" but checked herself hastily, and said "No never") "——so you can have no idea what a delightful thing a Lobster-Quadrille is!"

"No, indeed," said Alice. "What sort of a dance is it?"

"Why," said the Gryphon, "you first form into a line along the sea-shore——"

"Two lines!" cried the Mock Turtle. "Seals, turtles, salmon, and so on: then, when you've cleared all the jelly-fish out of the way——"

"*That* generally takes some time," interrupted the Gryphon.

"—you advance twice——"

"Each with a lobster as a partner!" cried the Gryphon.

"Of course," the Mock Turtle said: "advance twice, set to partners——"

"—change lobsters, and retire in same order," continued the Gryphon.

"Then, you know," the Mock Turtle went on, "you throw the——"

"The lobsters!" shouted the Gryphon, with a bound into the air.

"—as far out to sea as you can——"

"Swim after them!" screamed the Gryphon.

"Turn a somersault in the sea!" cried the Mock Turtle, capering wildly about.

"'Change lobsters again!" yelled the Gryphon at the top of its voice.

"Back to land again, and—that's all the first figure," said the Mock Turtle, suddenly dropping his voice; and the two creatures, who had been jumping about like mad things all this time, sat down again very sadly and quietly, and looked at Alice.

"It must be a very pretty dance," said Alice timidly.

"Would you like to see a little of it?" said the Mock Turtle.

"Very much indeed," said Alice.

"Come, let's try the first figure!" said the Mock Turtle to the Gryphon. "We can do it without lobsters, you know. Which shall sing?"

"Oh, *you* sing," said the Gryphon. "I've forgotten the words."

So they began solemnly dancing round and round Alice, every now and then treading on her toes when they passed too close, and waving their fore-paws to mark the time, while the Mock Turtle sang this, very slowly and sadly:—

"Will you walk a little faster?" said a whiting to a snail,
"There's a porpoise close behind us, and he's treading on my tail.
See how eagerly the lobsters and the turtles all advance!
They are waiting on the shingle—will you come and join the
    dance?
    Will you, wo'n't you, will you, wo'n't you, will you join the
        dance?
    Will you, wo'n't you, will you, wo'n't you, wo'n't you join the
        dance?

"You can really have no notion how delightful it will be
When they take us up and throw us, with the lobsters, out to sea!"
But the snail replied "Too far, too far!", and gave a look askance—
Said he thanked the whiting kindly, but he would not join the
    dance.
    Would not, could not, would not, could not, could not join the
    dance.
    Would not, could not, would not, could not, could not join the
    dance.

"What matters it how far we go?" his scaly friend replied.
"There is another shore, you know, upon the other side.
The further off from England the nearer is to France—
Then turn not pale, beloved snail, but come and join the dance.
    Will you, wo'n't you, will you, wo'n't you, will you join the
    dance?
    Will you, wo'n't you, will you, wo'n't you, wo'n't you join the
    dance?"⁷

"Thank you, it's a very interesting dance to watch," said Alice, feeling very glad that it was over at last: "and I do so like that curious song about the whiting!"

"Oh, as to the whiting," said the Mock Turtle, "they—you've seen them, of course?"

"Yes," said Alice, "I've often seen them at dinn——" she checked herself hastily.

"I don't know where Dinn may be," said the Mock Turtle; "but, if you've seen them so often, of course you know what they're like?"

"I believe so," Alice replied thoughtfully. "They have their tails in their mouths—and they're all over crumbs."⁸

7. For the original version of this song, a parody of a minstrel song, see the passage from *Alice's Adventures Under Ground* reprinted on pp. 266–72 of this edition, and the note to an entry in Dodgson's diary for July 3, 1862, reprinted on p. 264 of this edition. The final version of the song is a parody of Mary Howitt's "The Spider and the Fly," first published in 1834. The poem begins:

"Will you walk into my parlor?"
    said the Spider to the Fly,
" 'Tis the prettiest little parlor that
    ever you did spy;
The way into my parlor is up a
    winding stair,
And I have many curious things to
    show when you are there."
"Oh no, no," said the little Fly,
    "to ask me is in vain;
For who goes up your winding stair
    can ne'er come down again."

But the fly, enticed by the spider's tributes to her green-and-purple robes and diamond-bright eyes, flies into the spider's web, is dragged into his "dismal den," and "she ne'er came out again." Like most of the poems Dodgson parodied in the Alice books, Howitt's poem ends with a strong moral:

And now, dear little children, who
    may this story read
To idle, silly, flattering words, I
    pray you ne'er give heed;
Until an evil counsellor close heart,
    and ear, and eye,
And take a lesson from the tale of
    the Spider and the Fly.

8. Whiting is a common food fish, sold with its tail tucked into its mouth or through its eyehole, and served, in Alice's experience, breaded.

"You're wrong about the crumbs," said the Mock Turtle: "crumbs would all wash off in the sea. But they *have* their tails in their mouths; and the reason is——" here the Mock Turtle yawned and shut his eyes. "Tell her about the reason and all that," he said to the Gryphon.

"The reason is," said the Gryphon, "that they *would* go with the lobsters to the dance. So they got thrown out to sea. So they had to fall a long way. So they got their tails fast in their mouths. So they couldn't get them out again. That's all."

"Thank you," said Alice, "it's very interesting. I never knew so much about a whiting before."

"I can tell you more than that, if you like," said the Gryphon. "Do you know why it's called a whiting?"

"I never thought about it," said Alice. "Why?"

"*It does the boots and shoes,*" the Gryphon replied very solemnly.

Alice was thoroughly puzzled. "Does the boots and shoes!" she repeated in a wondering tone.

"Why, what are *your* shoes done with?" said the Gryphon. "I mean, what makes them so shiny?"

Alice looked down at them, and considered a little before she gave her answer. "They're done with blacking, I believe."

"Boots and shoes under the sea," the Gryphon went on in a deep voice, "are done with whiting. Now you know."

"And what are they made of?" Alice asked in a tone of great curiosity.

"Soles and eels, of course," the Gryphon replied, rather impatiently: "any shrimp could have told you that."

"If I'd been the whiting," said Alice, whose thoughts were still running on the song, "I'd have said to the porpoise 'Keep back, please! We don't want *you* with us!'"

"They were obliged to have him with them," the Mock Turtle said. "No wise fish would go anywhere without a porpoise."

"Wouldn't it, really?" said Alice, in a tone of great surprise.

"Of course not," said the Mock Turtle. "Why, if a fish came to *me*, and told me he was going a journey, I should say 'With what porpoise?'"

"Don't you mean 'purpose'?" said Alice.

"I mean what I say," the Mock Turtle replied, in an offended tone. And the Gryphon added "Come, let's hear some of *your* adventures."

"I could tell you my adventures—beginning from this morning," said Alice a little timidly; "but it's no use going back to yesterday, because I was a different person then."

"Explain all that," said the Mock Turtle.

"No, no! The adventures first," said the Gryphon in an impatient tone: "explanations take such a dreadful time."

So Alice began telling them her adventures from the time when she first saw the White Rabbit. She was a little nervous about it, just at first, the two creatures got so close to her, one on each side, and opened their eyes and mouths so *very* wide; but she gained courage as she went on. Her listeners were perfectly quiet till she got to the part about her repeating "*You are old, Father William*," to the Caterpillar, and the words all coming different, and then the Mock Turtle drew a long breath, and said "That's very curious!"

"It's all about as curious as it can be," said the Gryphon.

"It all came different!" the Mock Turtle repeated thoughtfully. "I should like to hear her try and repeat something now. Tell her to begin." He looked at the Gryphon as if he thought it had some kind of authority over Alice.

"Stand up and repeat ' *'Tis the voice of the sluggard,*' " said the Gryphon.

"How the creatures order one about, and make one repeat lessons!" thought Alice. "I might just as well be at school at once." However, she got up, and began to repeat it, but her head was so full of the Lobster-Quadrille, that she hardly knew what she was saying; and the words came very queer indeed:—

> " *'Tis the voice of the Lobster: I heard him declare*
> '*You have baked me too brown, I must sugar my hair.*'
> *As a duck with his eyelids, so he with his nose*
> *Trims his belt and his buttons, and turns out his toes.*
> *When the sands are all dry, he is gay as a lark,*
> *And will talk in contemptuous tones of the Shark:*
> *But, when the tide rises and sharks are around,*
> *His voice has a timid and tremulous sound.*" [9]

"That's different from what *I* used to say when I was a child," said the Gryphon.

9. In the early editions of *Alice's Adventures in Wonderland* Alice's recitation ended after the first four lines. These four lines are a close parody of "The Sluggard," another poem by Isaac Watts, which, like "Against Idleness and Mischief," was published as one of his *Divine Songs for Children* in 1715:

> 'Tis the voice of the Sluggard; I
>   hear him complain,
> "You have waked me too soon, I
>   must slumber again."

> As a Door on its Hinges, so he on
>   his Bed,
> Turns his Sides and his Shoulders,
>   and his heavy Head.

When he revised the poem for a theatrical version of the Alice books prepared by Savile Clark in 1886, Dodgson added the second four lines of this part of Alice's recitation. This additional quatrain retains nothing of Watts's poem except its meter and rhyme.

"Well, *I* never heard it before," said the Mock Turtle; "but it sounds uncommon nonsense."

Alice said nothing: she had sat down with her face in her hands, wondering if anything would *ever* happen in a natural way again.

"I should like to have it explained," said the Mock Turtle.

"She ca'n't explain it," said the Gryphon hastily. "Go on with the next verse."

"But about his toes?" the Mock Turtle persisted. "How *could* he turn them out with his nose, you know?"

"It's the first position in dancing," Alice said; but she was dreadfully puzzled by the whole thing, and longed to change the subject.

"Go on with the next verse," the Gryphon repeated: "it begins '*I passed by his garden.*'"

Alice did not dare to disobey, though she felt sure it would all come wrong, and she went on in a trembling voice:—

> "*I passed by his garden, and marked, with one eye,*
> *How the Owl and the Panther were sharing a pie:*

The Panther took pie-crust, and gravy, and meat,
While the Owl had the dish as its share of the treat.
When the pie was all finished, the Owl, as a boon,
Was kindly permitted to pocket the spoon:
While the Panther received knife and fork with a growl,
And concluded the banquet by——" [1]

"What *is* the use of repeating all that stuff?" the Mock Turtle interrupted, "if you don't explain it as you go on? It's by far the most confusing thing that *I* ever heard!"

"Yes, I think you'd better leave off," said the Gryphon, and Alice was only too glad to do so.

"Shall we try another figure of the Lobster-Quadrille?" the Gryphon went on. "Or would you like the Mock Turtle to sing you another song?"

"Oh, a song, please, if the Mock Turtle would be so kind," Alice replied, so eagerly that the Gryphon said, in a rather offended tone, "Hm! No accounting for tastes! Sing her '*Turtle Soup,*' will you, old fellow?"

The Mock Turtle sighed deeply, and began, in a voice choked with sobs, to sing this:—

"Beautiful Soup, so rich and green,
Waiting in a hot tureen!
Who for such dainties would not stoop?
Soup of the evening, beautiful Soup!
Soup of the evening, beautiful Soup!
   Beau—ootiful Soo—oop!
   Beau—ootiful Soo—oop!
Soo—oop of the e—e—evening,
   Beautiful, beautiful Soup!

"Beautiful Soup! Who cares for fish,
Game, or any other dish?

1. Again, in the early editions of *Alice's Adventures in Wonderland* Alice's recitation ended after the first two lines. In this early version, the owl and an oyster shared the pie. Dodgson added two lines to this part of the poem when *The Songs from Alice's Adventures in Wonderland* were published separately in 1870, with music written by William Boyd. The lines Dodgson added in 1870 pick up some of the details of the Caucus-Race:

While the duck and the Dodo, the lizard
   and cat
Were swimming in milk round the brim of a
   hat.

Then in 1886, for Savile Clark's theatrical ver-

sion of the Alice books, Dodgson changed the oyster to the Panther, and added the concluding six lines of the poem. In his biography of his uncle (see Selected Bibliography), Stuart Collingwood prints (p. 253) yet another version of the last two lines:

But the panther obtained both the
   fork and the knife,
So, when *he* lost his temper, the owl
   lost its life.

The third stanza of Watts's "The Sluggard" does begin, "I pass'd by his garden," but there is no other reminiscence of Watt's poem in the remainder of Dodgson's parody.

> *Who would not give all else for two p*
> *ennyworth only of beautiful Soup?*
> *Pennyworth only of beautiful soup.*
> *Beau—ootiful Soo—oop!*
> *Beau—ootiful Soo—oop!*
> *Soo—oop of the e—e—evening,*
> *Beautiful, beauti—FUL SOUP!"*[2]

"Chorus again!" cried the Gryphon, and the Mock Turtle had just begun to repeat it, when a cry of "The trial's beginning!" was heard in the distance.

"Come on!" cried the Gryphon, and, taking Alice by the hand, it hurried off, without waiting for the end of the song.

"What trial is it?" Alice panted as she ran: but the Gryphon only answered "Come on!" and ran the faster, while more and more faintly came, carried on the breeze that followed them, the melancholy words:—

> *"Soo—oop of the e—e—evening,*
> *Beautiful, beautiful Soup!"*

---

2. "Beautiful Soup" is a parody of "Beautiful Star," a popular song by J. M. Sayles which Dodgson heard the Liddell children sing in August 1862, after the trip to Godstow during which he began to tell some of the adventures of Alice:

Beautiful star in heav'n so bright
Softly falls thy silv'ry light,
As thou movest from earth so far,
   Star of the evening, beautiful star,
     Beau—ti-ful star,

     Beau—ti-ful star,
   Star—of the eve—ning
     Beautiful, beautiful star.

For an early version of the Mock Turtle's song, see the passage from *Alice's Adventures Under Ground* reprinted on pp. 266–72 of this edition. Green notes in the Appendix to *The Lewis Carroll Handbook* (see Selected Bibliography) that the song had been parodied in a theatrical pantomime in 1860 (p. 311).

Chapter XI

WHO STOLE THE TARTS?

The King and Queen of Hearts were seated on their throne when they arrived, with a great crowd assembled about them—all sorts of little birds and beasts, as well as the whole pack of cards: the Knave was standing before them, in chains, with a soldier on each side to guard him; and near the King was the White Rabbit, with a trumpet in one hand, and a scroll of parchment in the other. In the very middle of the court was a table, with a large dish of tarts upon it: they looked so good, that it made Alice quite hungry to look at them—"I wish they'd get the trial done," she thought, "and hand round the refreshments!" But there seemed to be no chance of this; so she began looking at everything about her to pass away the time.

Alice had never been in a court of justice before, but she had read about them in books, and she was quite pleased to find that she knew the name of nearly everything there. "That's the judge," she said to herself, "because of his great wig."

The judge, by the way, was the King; and, as he wore his crown over the wig (look at the frontispiece if you want to see how he did it), he did not look at all comfortable, and it was certainly not becoming.

"And that's the jury-box," thought Alice; "and those twelve creatures," (she was obliged to say "creatures," you see, because some of them were animals, and some were birds,) "I suppose they are the jurors." She said this last word two or three times over to herself, being rather proud of it: for she thought, and rightly too, that very few little girls of her age knew the meaning of it at all. However, "jurymen" would have done just as well.

The twelve jurors were all writing very busily on slates. "What are they doing?" Alice whispered to the Gryphon. "They ca'n't have anything to put down yet, before the trial's begun."

"They're putting down their names," the Gryphon whispered in reply, "for fear they should forget them before the end of the trial."

"Stupid things!" Alice began in a loud indignant voice; but she stopped herself hastily, for the White Rabbit cried out "Silence in the court!", and the King put on his spectacles and looked anxiously round, to make out who was talking.

Alice could see, as well as if she were looking over their shoulders, that all the jurors were writing down "Stupid things!" on their slates, and she could even make out that one of them didn't know how to spell "stupid," and that he had to ask his neighbour to tell him. "A nice muddle their slates'll be in, before the trial's over!" thought Alice.

One of the jurors had a pencil that squeaked. This, of course, Alice could *not* stand, and she went round the court and got behind him, and very soon found an opportunity of taking it away. She did it so quickly that the poor little juror (it was Bill, the Lizard) could not make out at all what had become of it; so, after hunting all about for it, he was obliged to write with one finger for the rest of the day; and this was of very little use, as it left no mark on the slate.

"Herald, read the accusation!" said the King.

On this the White Rabbit blew three blasts on the trumpet, and then unrolled the parchment-scroll, and read as follows:—

"The Queen of Hearts, she made some tarts,
All on a summer day:
The Knave of Hearts, he stole those tarts
And took them quite away!" [3]

3. Dodgson takes over this nursery rhyme unchanged from one of its traditional versions. The traditional versions were collected in *The* *Nursery Rhymes of England* by James Orchard Halliwell (later Halliwell-Phillipps), first published in 1842.

"Consider your verdict," the King said to the jury.

"Not yet, not yet!" the Rabbit hastily interrupted. "There's a great deal to come before that!"

"'Call the first witness," said the King; and the White Rabbit blew three blasts on the trumpet, and called out "First witness!"

The first witness was the Hatter. He came in with a teacup in one hand and a piece of bread-and-butter in the other. "I beg pardon, your Majesty," he began, "for bringing these in; but I hadn't quite finished my tea when I was sent for."

"You ought to have finished," said the King. "When did you begin?"

The Hatter looked at the March Hare, who had followed him into the court, arm-in-arm with the Dormouse. "Fourteenth of March, I *think* it was," he said.

"Fifteenth," said the March Hare.

"Sixteenth," said the Dormouse.

"Write that down," the King said to the jury; and the jury eagerly wrote down all three dates on their slates, and then added them up, and reduced the answer to shillings and pence.

"Take off your hat," the King said to the Hatter.

"It isn't mine," said the Hatter.

"*Stolen!*" the King exclaimed, turning to the jury, who instantly made a memorandum of the fact.

"I keep them to sell," the Hatter added as an explanation. "I've none of my own. I'm a hatter."

Here the Queen put on her spectacles, and began staring hard at the Hatter, who turned pale and fidgeted.

"Give your evidence," said the King: "and don't be nervous, or I'll have you executed on the spot."

This did not seem to encourage the witness at all: he kept shifting from one foot to the other, looking uneasily at the Queen, and in his confusion he bit a large piece out of his teacup instead of the bread-and-butter.

Just at this moment Alice felt a very curious sensation, which puzzled her a good deal until she made out what it was: she was beginning to grow larger again, and she thought at first she would get up and leave the court; but on second thoughts she decided to remain where she was as long as there was room for her.

"I wish you wouldn't squeeze so," said the Dormouse, who was sitting next to her. "I can hardly breathe."

"I ca'n't help it," said Alice very meekly: "I'm growing."

"You've no right to grow *here*," said the Dormouse.

"Don't talk nonsense," said Alice more boldly: "you know you're growing too."

"Yes, but *I* grow at a reasonable pace," said the Dormouse: "not in that ridiculous fashion." And he got up very sulkily and crossed over to the other side of the court.

All this time the Queen had never left off staring at the Hatter, and, just as the Dormouse crossed the court, she said, to one of the officers of the court, "Bring me the list of the singers in the last concert!" on which the wretched Hatter trembled so, that he shook off both his shoes.

"Give your evidence," the King repeated angrily, "or I'll have you executed, whether you are nervous or not."

"I'm a poor man, your Majesty," the Hatter began, in a trembling voice, "and I hadn't begun my tea—not above a week or so—and what with the bread-and-butter getting so thin—and the twinkling of the tea——"

"The twinkling of *what*?" said the King.

"It *began* with the tea," the Hatter replied.

"Of course twinkling *begins* with a T!" said the King sharply. "Do you take me for a dunce? Go on!"

"I'm a poor man," the Hatter went on, "and most things twinkled after that—only the March Hare said——"

"I didn't!" the March Hare interrupted in a great hurry.

"You did!" said the Hatter.

"I deny it!" said the March Hare.

"He denies it," said the King: "leave out that part."

"Well, at any rate, the Dormouse said——" the Hatter went on, looking anxiously around to see if he would deny it too; but the Dormouse denied nothing, being fast asleep.

"After that," continued the Hatter, "I cut some more bread-and-butter——"

"But what did the Dormouse say?" one of the jury asked.

"That I ca'n't remember," said the Hatter.

"You *must* remember," remarked the King, "or I'll have you executed."

The miserable Hatter dropped his teacup and bread-and-butter, and went down on one knee. "I'm a poor man, your Majesty," he began.

"You're a *very* poor *speaker*," said the King.

Here one of the guinea-pigs cheered, and was immediately suppressed by the officers of the court. (As that is rather a hard word, I will just explain to you how it was done. They had a large canvas bag, which tied up at the mouth with strings: into this they slipped the guinea-pig, head first, and then sat upon it.)

"I'm glad I've seen that done," thought Alice. "I've so often read in the newspapers, at the end of trials, 'There was some attempt at applause, which was immediately suppressed by the officers of the court,' and I never understood what it meant till now."

"If that's all you know about it, you may stand down," continued the King.

"I ca'n't go no lower," said the Hatter: "I'm on the floor, as it is."

"Then you may *sit* down," the King replied.

Here the other guinea-pig cheered, and was suppressed.

"Come, that finishes the guinea-pigs!" thought Alice. "Now we shall get on better."

"I'd rather finish my tea," said the Hatter, with an anxious look at the Queen, who was reading the list of singers.

"You may go," said the King, and the Hatter hurriedly left the court, without even waiting to put his shoes on.

"——and just take his head off outside," the Queen added to one of the officers; but the Hatter was out of sight before the officer could get to the door.

"Call the next witness!" said the King.

The next witness was the Duchess's cook. She carried the pepper-box in her hand, and Alice guessed who it was, even before she got into the court, by the way the people near the door began sneezing all at once.

"Give your evidence," said the King.

"Sha'n't," said the cook.

The King looked anxiously at the White Rabbit, who said, in a low voice, "Your Majesty must cross-examine *this* witness."

"Well, if I must, I must," the King said with a melancholy air, and, after folding his arms and frowning at the cook till his eyes were nearly out of sight, he said, in a deep voice, "What are tarts made of?"

"Pepper, mostly," said the cook.

"Treacle," said a sleepy voice behind her.

"Collar that Dormouse!" the Queen shrieked out. "Behead that Dormouse! Turn that Dormouse out of court! Suppress him! Pinch him! Off with his whiskers!'"

For some minutes the whole court was in confusion, getting the Dormouse turned out, and, by the time they had settled down again, the cook had disappeared.

"Never mind!" said the King, with an air of great relief. "Call the next witness." And, he added, in an undertone to the Queen, "Really, my dear, *you* must cross-examine the next witness. It quite makes my forehead ache!"

Alice watched the White Rabbit as he fumbled over the list, feeling very curious to see what the next witness would be like, "—for they haven't got much evidence *yet*," she said to herself. Imagine her surprise, when the White Rabbit read out, at the top of his shrill little voice, the name "Alice!"

Chapter XII

ALICE'S EVIDENCE

"Here!" cried Alice, quite forgetting in the flurry of the moment how large she had grown in the last few minutes, and she jumped up in such a hurry that she tipped over the jury-box with the edge of her skirt, upsetting all the jurymen on to the heads of the crowd below, and there they lay sprawling about, reminding her very much of a globe of gold-fish she had accidentally upset the week before.

"Oh, I *beg* your pardon!" she exclaimed in a tone of great dismay, and began picking them up again as quickly as she could, for the accident of the gold-fish kept running in her head, and she had a vague sort of idea that they must be collected at once and put back into the jury-box, or they would die.

"The trial cannot proceed," said the King, in a very grave voice, "until all the jurymen are back in their proper places—*all*," he repeated with great emphasis, looking hard at Alice as he said so.

Alice looked at the jury-box, and saw that, in her haste, she had put the Lizard in head downwards, and the poor little thing was waving its tail about in a melancholy way, being quite unable to move. She soon got it out again, and put it right; "not that it signifies much," she said to herself; "I should think it would be *quite* as much use in the trial one way up as the other."

As soon as the jury had a little recovered from the shock of being upset, and their slates and pencils had been found and handed back to them, they set to work very diligently to write out a history of the accident, all except the Lizard, who seemed too much overcome to do anything but sit with its mouth open, gazing up into the roof of the court.

"What do you know about this business?" the King said to Alice.

"Nothing," said Alice.

"Nothing *whatever*?" persisted the King.

"Nothing whatever," said Alice.

"That's very important," the King said, turning to the jury. They were just beginning to write this down on their slates, when the White Rabbit interrupted: "*Un*important, your Majesty means, of course," he said, in a very respectful tone, but frowning and making faces at him as he spoke.

"*Un*important, of course, I meant," the King hastily said, and went on to himself in an undertone, "important—unimportant—unimportant—important——" as if he were trying which word sounded best.

Some of the jury wrote it down "important," and some "unimportant." Alice could see this, as she was near enough to look over their slates; "but it doesn't matter a bit," she thought to herself.

At this moment the King, who had been for some time busily writing in his note-book, called out "Silence!", and read out from his book, "Rule Forty-two. *All persons more than a mile high to leave the court.*"

Everybody looked at Alice.

"*I'm* not a mile high," said Alice.

"You are," said the King.

"Nearly two miles high," added the Queen.

"Well, I sha'n't go, at any rate," said Alice; "besides, that's not a regular rule: you invented it just now."

"It's the oldest rule in the book," said the King.

"Then it ought to be Number One," said Alice.

The King turned pale, and shut his note-book hastily. "Consider your verdict," he said to the jury, in a low trembling voice.

"There's more evidence to come yet, please your Majesty," said the White Rabbit, jumping up in a great hurry: "this paper has just been picked up."

"What's in it?" said the Queen.

"I haven't opened it yet," said the White Rabbit; "but it seems to be a letter, written by the prisoner to—to somebody."

"It must have been that," said the King, "unless it was written to nobody, which isn't usual, you know."

"Who is it directed to?" said one of the jurymen.

"It isn't directed at all," said the White Rabbit: "in fact, there's nothing written on the *outside*." He unfolded the paper as he spoke, and added "It isn't a letter, after all: it's a set of verses."

"Are they in the prisoner's handwriting?" asked another of the jurymen.

"No, they're not," said the White Rabbit, "and that's the queerest thing about it." (The jury all looked puzzled.)

"He must have imitated somebody else's hand," said the King. (The jury all brightened up again.)

"Please, your Majesty," said the Knave, "I didn't write it, and they ca'n't prove that I did: there's no name signed at the end."

"If you didn't sign it," said the King, "that only makes the matter worse. You *must* have meant some mischief, or else you'd have signed your name like an honest man."

There was a general clapping of hands at this: it was the first really clever thing the King had said that day.

"That *proves* his guilt, of course," said the Queen, "so, off with——"

"It doesn't prove anything of the sort!" said Alice. "Why, you don't even know what they're about!"

"Read them," said the King.

The White Rabbit put on his spectacles. "Where shall I begin, please your Majesty?" he asked.

"Begin at the beginning," the King said, very gravely, "and go on till you come to the end: then stop."

There was dead silence in the court, whilst the White Rabbit read out these verses:—

> "*They told me you had been to her,*
> *And mentioned me to him:*
> *She gave me a good character,*
> *But said I could not swim.*

He sent them word I had not gone
   (We know it to be true):
If she should push the matter on,
   What would become of you?

I gave her one, they gave him two,
   You gave us three or more;
They all returned from him to you,
   Though they were mine before.

If I or she should chance to be
   Involved in this affair,
He trusts to you to set them free,
   Exactly as we were.

My notion was that you had been
   (Before she had this fit)
An obstacle that came between
   Him, and ourselves, and it.

Don't let him know she liked them best,
   For this must ever be
A secret, kept from all the rest,
   Between yourself and me."[4]

"That's the most important piece of evidence we've heard yet," said the King, rubbing his hands; "so now let the jury——"

"If any one of them can explain it," said Alice, (she had grown so large in the last few minutes that she wasn't a bit afraid of interrupting him,) "I'll give him sixpence. *I* don't believe there's an atom of meaning in it."

The jury all wrote down, on their slates, "*She* doesn't believe there's an atom of meaning in it," but none of them attempted to explain the paper.

"If there's no meaning in it," said the King, "that saves a world of trouble, you know, as we needn't try to find any. And yet I don't know," he went on, spreading out the verses on his knee, and looking at them with one eye; "I seem to see some meaning in them, after all. '—*said I could not swim*—' you ca'n't swim, can you?" he added, turning to the Knave.

The Knave shook his head sadly. "Do I look like it?" he said. (Which he certainly did *not*, being made entirely of cardboard.)

"All right, so far," said the King; and he went on muttering over the verses to himself: " '*We know it to be true*'—that's the jury, of

4. For an early version of this poem, see pp. 253–54 of this edition. The early version begins as a parody of "Alice Gray," an early nineteenth-century popular ballad by William Mee. The relationship between this later version and "Alice Gray" is slight.

course—'*If she should push the matter on*'—that must be the Queen—'*What would become of you?*'—What, indeed!—'*I gave her one, they gave him two*'—why, that must be what he did with the tarts, you know——"

"But it goes on '*they all returned from him to you,*'" said Alice.

"Why, there they are!" said the King triumphantly, pointing to the tarts on the table. "Nothing can be clearer than *that*. Then again—'*before she had this fit*'—you never had fits, my dear, I think?" he said to the Queen.

"Never!" said the Queen, furiously, throwing an inkstand at the Lizard as she spoke. (The unfortunate little Bill had left off writing on his slate with one finger, as he found it made no mark; but he now hastily began again, using the ink, that was trickling down his face, as long as it lasted.)

"Then the words don't *fit* you," said the King looking round the court with a smile. There was a dead silence.

"It's a pun!" the King added in an angry tone, and everybody laughed. "Let the jury consider their verdict," the King said, for about the twentieth time that day.

"No, no!" said the Queen. "Sentence first—verdict afterwards."

"Stuff and nonsense!" said Alice loudly. "The idea of having the sentence first!"

"Hold your tongue!" said the Queen, turning purple.

"I wo'n't!" said Alice.

"Off with her head!" the Queen shouted at the top of her voice. Nobody moved.

"Who cares for *you*?" said Alice (she had grown to her full size by this time). "You're nothing but a pack of cards!"

At this the whole pack rose up into the air, and came flying down upon her; she gave a little scream, half of fright and half of anger, and tried to beat them off, and found herself lying on the

bank, with her head in the lap of her sister, who was gently brushing away some dead leaves that had fluttered down from the trees upon her face.

"Wake up, Alice dear!" said her sister. "Why, what a long sleep you've had!"

"Oh, I've had such a curious dream!" said Alice. And she told her sister, as well as she could remember them, all these strange Adventures of hers that you have just been reading about; and, when she had finished, her sister kissed her, and said "It *was* a curious dream, dear, certainly; but now run in to your tea: it's getting late." So Alice got up and ran off, thinking while she ran, as well she might, what a wonderful dream it had been.

But her sister sat still just as she left her, leaning her head on her hand, watching the setting sun, and thinking of little Alice and all her wonderful Adventures, till she too began dreaming after a fashion, and this was her dream:—

First, she dreamed about little Alice herself: once again the tiny hands were clasped upon her knee, and the bright eager eyes were looking up into hers—she could hear the very tones of her voice, and see that queer little toss of her head to keep back the wandering hair that *would* always get into her eyes—and still as she listened, or seemed to listen, the whole place around her became alive with the strange creatures of her little sister's dream.

The long grass rustled at her feet as the White Rabbit hurried by—the frightened Mouse splashed his way through the neighbouring pool—she could hear the rattle of the teacups as the March Hare and his friends shared their never-ending meal, and the shrill voice of the Queen ordering off her unfortunate guests to execution—once more the pig-baby was sneezing on the Duchess's knee, while plates and dishes crashed around it—once more the shriek of the Gryphon, the squeaking of the Lizard's slate-pencil, and the choking of the suppressed guinea-pigs, filled the air, mixed up with the distant sob of the miserable Mock Turtle.

So she sat on, with closed eyes, and half believed herself in Wonderland, though she knew she had but to open them again, and all would change to dull reality—the grass would be only rustling in the wind, and the pool rippling to the waving of the reeds—the rattling teacups would change to tinkling sheep-bells, and the Queen's shrill cries to the voice of the shepherd-boy—and the sneeze of the baby, the shriek of the Gryphon, and all the other queer noises, would change (she knew) to the confused clamour of the busy farm-yard—while the lowing of the cattle in the distance would take the place of the Mock Turtle's heavy sobs.

Lastly, she pictured to herself how this same little sister of hers would, in the after-time, be herself a grown woman; and how she would keep, through all her riper years, the simple and loving heart of her childhood; and how she would gather about her other little children, and make *their* eyes bright and eager with many a strange tale, perhaps even with the dream of Wonderland of long ago; and how she would feel with all their simple sorrows, and find a pleasure in all their simple joys, remembering her own child-life, and the happy summer days.

Why have last chunk?
- Reflection of Lewis Carroll (tried to hold on to his childhood)
- better ending for adults

sister's dream is all scary things - nightmarish

The Text of

Through the
Looking-Glass
and what Alice found there

Through the Looking-Glass
and what Alice found there

setting up Alice w/ diff. personality
(than seen in A in W) -dreamy, clarovoyant

Child of the pure unclouded brow
  And dreaming eyes of wonder!
Though time be fleet, and I and thou
  Are half a life asunder,
Thy loving smile will surely hail
The love-gift of a fairy-tale.

I have not seen thy sunny face,
  Nor heard thy silver laughter:
No thought of me shall find a place
  In thy young life's hereafter—
Enough that now thou wilt not fail
To listen to my fairy-tale.

A tale begun in other days,
  When summer suns were glowing—
A simple chime, that served to time
  The rhythm of our rowing—
Whose echoes live in memory yet,
Though envious years would say "forget."

Come, hearken then, ere voice of dread,
  With bitter tidings laden,
Shall summon to unwelcome bed
  A melancholy maiden!
We are but older children, dear,
Who fret to find our bedtime near.

somewhat dark
setting/tone

Without, the frost, the blinding snow,
  The storm-wind's moody madness—
Within, the firelight's ruddy glow,
  And childhood's nest of gladness.
The magic words shall hold thee fast:
Thou shalt not heed the raving blast.

And, though the shadow of a sigh
  May tremble through the story,
For "happy summer days" gone by,
  And vanish'd summer glory—
It shall not touch, with breath of bale,
The pleasance of our fairy-tale.[1]

nostalgia - good days
have past

1. Alice Liddell's middle name was Pleasance. *Through the Looking-Glass* was published in December 1871; its title page bears the date 1872. Alice Liddell was sixteen and a half years old at the end of 1871. In *Through the Looking-Glass* Alice is seven and a half years old, six months older than she is in the first Alice book. The first book is set in May; *Through the Looking-Glass* ("Without, the frost, the blinding snow") is set in November.

RED

WHITE

White Pawn (Alice) to play, and win in eleven moves.

As the chess-problem, given on the previous page, has puzzled some of my readers, it may be well to explain that it is correctly worked out, so far as the *moves* are concerned. The *alternation* of Red and White is perhaps not so strictly observed as it might be, and the "castling" of the three Queens is merely a way of saying that they entered the palace; but the "check" of the White King at move 6, the capture of the Red Knight at move 7, and the final "checkmate" of the Red King, will be found, by any one who will take the trouble to set the pieces and play the moves as directed, to be strictly in accordance with the laws of the game.[2]

The new words, in the poem "Jabberwocky," have given rise to some differences of opinion as to their pronunciation: so it may be well to give instructions on *that* point also. Pronounce "slithy" as if it were the two words "sly, the": make the "g" *hard* in "gyre" and "gimble": and pronounce "rath" to rhyme with "bath."

For this sixty-first thousand, fresh electrotypes have been taken from the wood-blocks (which, never having been used for printing from, are in as good condition as when first cut in 1871), and the whole book has been set up afresh with new type. If the artistic qualities of this re-issue fall short, in any particular, of those possessed by the original issue, it will not be for want of painstaking on the part of author, publisher, or printer.[3]

I take this opportunity of announcing that the Nursery "Alice," hitherto priced at four shillings, net, is now to be had on the same terms as the ordinary shilling picture-books—although I feel sure that it is, in every quality (except the *text* itself, on which I am not qualified to pronounce), greatly superior to them. Four shillings was a perfectly reasonable price to charge, considering the very heavy initial outlay I had incurred: still, as the Public have practically said "We will *not* give more than a shilling for a picture-book, however artistically got-up," I am content to reckon my outlay on the book as so much dead loss, and, rather than let the little ones, for whom it was written, go without it, I am selling it at a price which is, to me, much the same thing as *giving* it away.

Christmas, 1896

2. See the passage reprinted from A. L. Taylor's *The White Knight* on pp. 373–80 of this edition for an explanation of the chess game—really the chess lesson—which is played in the book. See also Martin Gardner's explanation (pp. 170–72) in *The Annotated Alice* (see Selected Bibliography).

3. Dodgson, who was himself painstaking about the appearance of his books, had agreed to recall 2,000 copies of the first issue of *Alice's Adventures in Wonderland* because Tenniel was dissatisfied with the appearance of the plates. Dodgson was also, as the last paragraph of this preface suggests, acutely interested in the sales and profits of his books. The authors of the 1970 edition of *The Lewis Carroll Handbook* (see Selected Bibliography) estimate that 110,000 copies of *Alice's Adventures in Wonderland* were issued before Dodgson's death in 1898 (p. 30). In addition, 61,000 copies of *Through the Looking-Glass* had been issued by 1896, and 10,000 copies of *The Nursery Alice*, a simplified version of the first Alice book, were distributed in 1890. (An edition printed in 1889, also of 10,000 copies, was rejected by Dodgson because the colors of the illustrations were too bright; some of the sheets were bound into copies sold in the United States, and the rest were made into a People's Edition published in 1891.)

Chapter I

LOOKING-GLASS HOUSE

One thing was certain, that the *white* kitten had had nothing to do with it—it was the black kitten's fault entirely. For the white kitten had been having its face washed by the old cat for the last quarter of an hour (and bearing it pretty well, considering): so you see that it *couldn't* have had any hand in the mischief.

The way Dinah[4] washed her children's faces was this: first she held the poor thing down by its ear with one paw, and then with the other paw she rubbed its face all over, the wrong way, beginning at the nose: and just now, as I said, she was hard at work on the white kitten, which was lying quite still and trying to purr—no doubt feeling that it was all meant for its good.

But the black kitten had been finished with earlier in the afternoon, and so, while Alice was sitting curled up in a corner of the great armchair, half talking to herself and half asleep, the kitten had been having a grand game of romps with the ball of worsted Alice had been trying to wind up, and had been rolling it up and down till it had all come undone again; and there it was, spread over the hearth-rug, all knots and tangles, with the kitten running after its own tail in the middle.

"Oh, you wicked wicked little thing!" cried Alice, catching up the kitten, and giving it a little kiss to make it understand that it was in disgrace. "Really, Dinah ought to have taught you better

4. Dinah, the Liddells' cat, is also named in *Alice's Adventures in Wonderland.*

manners! You *ought*, Dinah, you know you ought!" she added, looking reproachfully at the old cat, and speaking in as cross a voice as she could manage—and then she scrambled back into the arm-chair, taking the kitten and the worsted with her, and began winding up the ball again. But she didn't get on very fast, as she was talking all the time, sometimes to the kitten, and sometimes to herself. Kitty sat very demurely on her knee, pretending to watch the progress of the winding, and now and then putting out one paw and gently touching the ball, as if it would be glad to help if it might.

"Do you know what to-morrow is, Kitty?" Alice began. "You'd have guessed if you'd been up in the window with me—only Dinah was making you tidy, so you couldn't. I was watching the boys getting in sticks for the bonfire[5]—and it wants plenty of sticks, Kitty! Only it got so cold, and it snowed so, they had to leave off. Never mind, Kitty, we'll go and see the bonfire to-morrow." Here Alice wound two or three turns of the worsted round the kitten's neck, just to see how it would look: this led to a scramble, in which the ball rolled down upon the floor, and yards and yards of it got unwound again.

"Do you know, I was so angry, Kitty," Alice went on, as soon as they were comfortably settled again, "when I saw all the mischief you had been doing, I was very nearly opening the window, and putting you out into the snow! And you'd have deserved it, you little mischievous darling! What have you got to say for yourself? Now don't interrupt me!" she went on, holding up one finger. "I'm going to tell you all your faults. Number one: you squeaked twice while Dinah was washing your face this morning. Now you ca'n't deny it, Kitty: I heard you! What's that you say?" (pretending that the kitten was speaking). "Her paw went into your eye? Well, that's *your* fault, for keeping your eyes open—if you'd shut them tight up, it wouldn't have happened. Now don't make any more excuses, but listen! Number two: you pulled Snowdrop away by the tail just as I had put down the saucer of milk before her! What, you were thirsty, were you? How do you know she wasn't thirsty too? Now for number three: you unwound every bit of the worsted while I wasn't looking!

"That's three faults, Kitty, and you've not been punished for any of them yet. You know I'm saving up all your punishments for Wednesday week[6]—Suppose they had saved up all *my* punish-

---

5. If "tomorrow" is Guy Fawkes Day, on which the frustration of a seventeenth-century attempt to blow up the house of Parliament is commemorated by the building of bonfires, then the date of the story is November 4. Alice Liddell's birthday was May 4; later (p. 153) she tells the White Queen that she is exactly seven and a half years old.
6. A week from Wednesday.

ments?" she went on, talking more to herself than the kitten. "What *would* they do at the end of a year? I should be sent to prison, I suppose, when the day came. Or—let me see—suppose each punishment was to be going without a dinner: then, when the miserable day came, I should have to go without fifty dinners at once! Well, I shouldn't mind *that* much! I'd far rather go without them than eat them!

"Do you hear the snow against the window-panes, Kitty? How nice and soft it sounds! Just as if someone was kissing the window all over outside. I wonder if the snow *loves* the trees and fields, that it kisses them so gently? And then it covers them up snug, you know, with a white quilt; and perhaps it says 'Go to sleep, darlings, till the summer comes again.' And when they wake up in the summer, Kitty, they dress themselves all in green, and dance about—whenever the wind blows—oh, that's very pretty!" cried Alice, dropping the ball of worsted to clap her hands. "And I do so *wish* it was true! I'm sure the woods look sleepy in the autumn, when the leaves are getting brown.

"Kitty, can you play chess? Now, don't smile, my dear. I'm asking it seriously. Because, when we were playing just now, you watched just as if you understood it: and when I said 'Check!' you purred! Well, it *was* a nice check, Kitty, and really I might have won, if it hadn't been for that nasty Knight, that came wriggling down among my pieces. Kitty dear, let's pretend——" And here I wish I could tell you half the things Alice used to say, beginning with her favourite phrase "Let's pretend." She had had quite a long argument with her sister only the day before—all because Alice had begun with "Let's pretend we're kings and queens;" and her sister, who liked being very exact, had argued that they couldn't, because there were only two of them, and Alice had been reduced at last to say "Well, *you* can be one of them, then, and *I'll* be all the rest." And once she had really frightened her old nurse by shouting suddenly in her ear, "Nurse! Do let's pretend that I'm a hungry hyæna, and you're a bone!"

But this is taking us away from Alice's speech to the kitten. "Let's pretend that you're the Red Queen, Kitty! Do you know, I think if you sat up and folded your arms, you'd look exactly like her. Now do try, there's a dear!" And Alice got the Red Queen off the table, and set it up before the kitten as a model for it to imitate: however, the thing didn't succeed, principally, Alice said, because the kitten wouldn't fold its arms properly. So, to punish it, she held it up to the Looking-glass, that it might see how sulky it was, "—and if you're not good directly," she added, "I'll put you through into Looking-glass House. How would you like *that*?

"Now, if you'll only attend, Kitty, and not talk so much, I'll tell you all my ideas about Looking-glass House. First, there's the room you can see through the glass—that's just the same as our drawing-room, only the things go the other way. I can see all of it when I get upon a chair—all but the bit just behind the fireplace. Oh! I do so wish I could see *that* bit! I want so much to know whether they've a fire in the winter: you never *can* tell, you know, unless our fire smokes, and then smoke comes up in that room too—but that may be only pretence, just to make it look as if they had a fire. Well then, the books are something like our books, only the words go the wrong way: I know *that*, because I've held up one of our books to the glass, and then they hold up one in the other room.

"How would you like to live in Looking-glass House, Kitty? I wonder if they'd give you milk in there? Perhaps Looking-glass milk

isn't good to drink—but oh, Kitty! now we come to the passage.
You can just see a little *peep* of the passage in Looking-glass
House, if you leave the door of our drawing-room wide open: and
it's very like our passage as far as you can see, only you know it
may be quite different on beyond. Oh, Kitty, how nice it would be
if we could only get through into Looking-glass House! I'm sure it's
got, oh! such beautiful things in it! Let's pretend there's a way of
getting through into it, somehow, Kitty. Let's pretend the glass has
got all soft like gauze, so that we can get through. Why, it's turning into a sort of mist now, I declare! It'll be easy enough to get
through——" She was up on the chimney-piece while she said this,
though she hardly knew how she had got there. And certainly the
glass *was* beginning to melt away, just like a bright silvery mist.

In another moment Alice was through the glass, and had jumped lightly down into the Looking-glass room. The very first thing she did was to look whether there was a fire in the fireplace, and she was quite pleased to find that there was a real one, blazing away as brightly as the one she had left behind. "So I shall be as warm here as I was in the old room," thought Alice: "warmer, in fact, because there'll be no one here to scold me away from the fire. Oh, what fun it'll be, when they see me through the glass in here, and ca'n't get at me!"

Then she began looking about, and noticed that what could be seen from the old room was quite common and uninteresting, but that all the rest was as different as possible. For instance, the pictures on the wall next the fire seemed to be all alive, and the very clock on the chimney-piece (you know you can only see the back of it in the Looking-glass) had got the face of a little old man, and grinned at her.

"They don't keep this room so tidy as the other," Alice thought to herself, as she noticed several of the chessmen down in the hearth among the cinders; but in another moment, with a little "Oh!" of surprise, she was down on her hands and knees watching them. The chessmen were walking about, two and two!

"Here are the Red King and the Red Queen," Alice said (in a whisper, for fear of frightening them), "and there are the White King and the White Queen sitting on the edge of the shovel—and here are two Castles walking arm in arm—I don't think they can hear me," she went on, as she put her head closer down, "and I'm nearly sure they ca'n't see me. I feel somehow as if I was getting invisible——"

Here something began squeaking on the table behind Alice, and made her turn her head just in time to see one of the White Pawns roll over and begin kicking: she watched it with great curiosity to see what would happen next.

"It is the voice of my child!" the White Queen cried out, as she rushed past the King, so violently that she knocked him over among the cinders. "My precious Lily! My imperial kitten!" and she began scrambling wildly up the side of the fender.[7]

7. Fender: see n. 5 on p. 14.

"Imperial fiddlestick!" said the King, rubbing his nose, which had been hurt by the fall. He had a right to be a *little* annoyed with the Queen, for he was covered with ashes from head to foot.

Alice was very anxious to be of use, and, as the poor little Lily was nearly screaming herself into a fit, she hastily picked up the Queen and set her on the table by the side of her noisy little daughter.

The Queen gasped, and sat down: the rapid journey through the air had quite taken away her breath, and for a minute or two she could do nothing but hug the little Lily in silence. As soon as she had recovered her breath a little, she called out to the White King, who was sitting sulkily among the ashes, "Mind the volcano!"

"What volcano?" said the King, looking up anxiously into the fire, as if he thought that was the most likely place to find one.

"Blew—me—up," panted the Queen, who was still a little out of breath. "Mind you come up—the regular way—don't get blown up!"

Alice watched the White King as he slowly struggled up from bar to bar, till at last she said "Why, you'll be hours and hours getting to the table, at that rate. I'd far better help you, hadn't I?" But the King took no notice of the question: it was quite clear that he could neither hear her nor see her.

So Alice picked him up very gently, and lifted him across more

slowly than she had lifted the Queen, that she mightn't take his breath away; but, before she put him on the table, she thought she might as well dust him a little, he was so covered with ashes.

She said afterwards that she had never seen in all her life such a face as the King made, when he found himself held in the air by an invisible hand, and being dusted: he was far too much astonished to cry out, but his eyes and his mouth went on getting larger and larger, and rounder and rounder, till her hand shook so with laughter that she nearly let him drop upon the floor.

"Oh! *please* don't make such faces, my dear!" she cried out, quite forgetting that the King couldn't hear her. "You make me laugh so that I can hardly hold you! And don't keep your mouth so wide open! All the ashes will get into it—there, now I think you're tidy enough!" she added, as she smoothed his hair, and set him upon the table near the Queen.

The King immediately fell flat on his back, and lay perfectly still; and Alice was a little alarmed at what she had done, and went round the room to see if she could find any water to throw over him. However, she could find nothing but a bottle of ink, and when she got back with it she found he had recovered, and he and the Queen were talking together in a frightened whisper—so low, that Alice could hardly hear what they said.

The King was saying "I assure you, my dear, I turned cold to the very ends of my whiskers!"

To which the Queen replied "You haven't got any whiskers."

"The horror of that moment," the King went on, "I shall never, *never* forget!"

"You will, though," the Queen said, "if you don't make a memorandum of it."

Alice looked on with great interest as the King took an enormous memorandum-book out of his pocket, and began writing. A sudden thought struck her, and she took hold of the end of the pencil, which came some way over his shoulder, and began writing for him.

The poor King looked puzzled and unhappy, and struggled with the pencil for some time without saying anything; but Alice was too strong for him, and at last he panted out "My dear! I really *must* get a thinner pencil. I ca'n't manage this one a bit: it writes all manner of things that I don't intend——"

"What manner of things?" said the Queen, looking over the book (in which Alice had put '*The White Knight is sliding down the poker. He balances very badly*'). "That's not a memorandum of *your* feelings!"

There was a book lying near Alice on the table, and while she sat watching the White King (for she was still a little anxious about him, and had the ink all ready to throw over him, in case he fainted again), she turned over the leaves, to find some part that she could read, "—for it's all in some language I don't know," she said to herself.

It was like this.

JABBERWOCKY

'Twas brillig, and the slithy toves
Did gyre and gimble in the wabe:
All mimsy were the borogoves,
And the mome raths outgrabe.

She puzzled over this for some time, but at last a bright thought struck her. "Why, it's a Looking-glass book, of course! And, if I hold it up to a glass, the words will all go the right way again."

This was the poem that Alice read

JABBERWOCKY

'Twas brillig, and the slithy toves
Did gyre and gimble in the wabe:
All mimsy were the borogoves,
And the mome raths outgrabe.

"Beware the Jabberwock, my son!
     The jaws that bite, the claws that catch!
Beware the Jubjub bird, and shun
          The frumious Bandersnatch!"

He took his vorpal sword in hand:
     Long time the manxome foe he sought—
So rested he by the Tumtum tree,
          And stood awhile in thought.

And, as in uffish thought he stood,
     The Jabberwock, with eyes of flame,
Came whiffling through the tulgey wood,
          And burbled as it came!

One, two! One, two! And through and through
     The vorpal blade went snicker-snack!
He left it dead, and with its head
          He went galumphing back.

"And, hast thou slain the Jabberwock?
     Come to my arms, my beamish boy!
O frabjous day! Callooh! Callay!"
          He chortled in his joy.

'Twas brillig, and the slithy toves
     Did gyre and gimble in the wabe:
All mimsy were the borogoves,
          And the mome raths outgrabe.[8]

"It seems very pretty," she said when she had finished it, "but it's *rather* hard to understand!" (You see she didn't like to confess, even to herself, that she couldn't make it out at all.) "Somehow it seems to fill my head with ideas—only I don't exactly know what they are! However, *somebody* killed *something*: that's clear, at any rate——"

8. Dodgson wrote the first stanza of "Jabberwocky," then titled "Stanza of Anglo-Saxon Poetry," and tricked out in a fake Old English script, for the manuscript miscellany he put together between 1855 and 1862 under the title *Mischmasch* (see Selected Bibliography for Florence Milner's edition). Later in *Through the Looking-Glass*, Humpty Dumpty explicates part of "Jabberwocky" (pp. 164–66 of this edition), and Carroll further explicates the poem in his preface to *The Hunting of the Snark* (see pp. 219–20 of this edition). See also Elizabeth Sewell's essay, "The Balance of Brillig" (pp. 380–88 of this edition), Eric Partridge's "The Nonsense Words of Edward Lear and Lewis Carroll" in *Here, There, and Everywhere* (see Selected Bibliography), and Martin Gardner's *The Annotated Alice* (see Selected Bibliography) for further glosses on the vocabulary of "Jabberwocky."

Roger Lancelyn Green suggests in the *Times Literary Supplement* (March 1, 1957, p. 126) that the story of "Jabberwocky" is a condensation of the plot of "The Shepherd of the Giant Mountains," a poem by Menella Bute Smedley. The comma after "And" in the first line of the penultimate stanza was included in the corrections Dodgson made when he prepared an 1897 edition of the Alice books, but this correction was not included in the 1897 edition. See Stanley Goodman, "Lewis Carroll's Final Corrections to 'Alice,'" *Times Literary Supplement*, 2 May 1958, 248.

"But oh!" thought Alice, suddenly jumping up, "if I don't make haste, I shall have to go back through the Looking-glass, before I've seen what the rest of the house is like! Let's have a look at the garden first!" She was out of the room in a moment, and ran down stairs—or, at least, it wasn't exactly running, but a new invention for getting down stairs quickly and easily, as Alice said to herself. She just kept the tips of her fingers on the hand-rail, and floated gently down without even touching the stairs with her feet: then she floated on through the hall, and would have gone straight out at the door in the same way, if she hadn't caught hold of the door-post. She was getting a little giddy with so much floating in the air, and was rather glad to find herself walking again in the natural way.

Chapter II

THE GARDEN OF LIVE FLOWERS

"I should see the garden far better," said Alice to herself, "if I could get to the top of that hill: and here's a path that leads straight to it—at least, no, it doesn't do *that*——" (after going a few yards along the path, and turning several sharp corners), "but I suppose it will at last. But how curiously it twists! It's more like a corkscrew than a path! Well *this* turn goes to the hill, I suppose—no, it doesn't! This goes straight back to the house! Well then, I'll try it the other way."

And so she did: wandering up and down, and trying turn after turn, but always coming back to the house, do what she would. Indeed, once, when she turned a corner rather more quickly than usual, she ran against it before she could stop herself.

"It's no use talking about it," Alice said, looking up at the house and pretending it was arguing with her. "I'm *not* going in again yet. I know I should have to get through the Looking-glass again—back into the old room—and there'd be an end of all my adventures!"

So, resolutely turning her back upon the house, she set out once more down the path, determined to keep straight on till she got to the hill. For a few minutes all went on well, and she was just saying "I really *shall* do it this time——" when the path gave a sudden twist and shook itself (as she described it afterwards), and the next moment she found herself actually walking in at the door.

"Oh, it's too bad!" she cried. "I never saw such a house for getting in the way! Never!"

However, there was the hill full in sight, so there was nothing to be done but start again. This time she came upon a large flower-bed,[9] with a border of daisies, and a willow-tree growing in the middle.

"O Tiger-lily!" said Alice, addressing herself to one that was waving gracefully about in the wind, "I *wish* you could talk!"

"We *can* talk," said the Tiger-lily, "when there's anybody worth talking to."

9. The flowers, and their announcement of the coming of the Red Queen, are taken from a stanza in Tennyson's *Maud* (1855) in which the lover waits for his lady in a garden:

> There has fallen a splendid tear
> From the passion-flower at the gate.
> She is coming, my dove, my dear;
> She is coming, my life, my fate;
> The red rose cries, "She is near,"

And the white rose weeps, "She is late;"
The larkspur listens, "I hear;"
And the lily whispers, "I wait."

Dodgson changed the passion-flower to a tiger-lily when he learned that because of its markings the passion-flower was associated with the passion of Christ.

Alice was so astonished that she couldn't speak for a minute: it quite seemed to take her breath away. At length, as the Tiger-lily only went on waving about, she spoke again, in a timid voice—almost in a whisper. "And can *all* the flowers talk?"

"As well as *you* can," said the Tiger-lily. "And a great deal louder."

"It isn't manners for us to begin, you know," said the Rose, "and I really was wondering when you'd speak! Said I to myself, 'Her face has got *some* sense in it, though it's not a clever one!' Still, you're the right colour, and that goes a long way."

"I don't care about the colour," the Tiger-lily remarked. "If only her petals curled up a little more, she'd be all right."

Alice didn't like being criticized, so she began asking questions. "Aren't you sometimes frightened at being planted out here, with nobody to take care of you?"

"There's the tree in the middle," said the Rose. "What else is it good for?"

"But what could it do, if any danger came?" Alice asked.

"It could bark," said the Rose.

"It says 'Bough-wough!' " cried a Daisy. "That's why its branches are called boughs!"[1]

"Didn't you know *that*?" cried another Daisy. And here they all began shouting together, till the air seemed quite full of little shrill voices. "Silence, every one of you!" cried the Tiger-lily, waving itself passionately from side to side, and trembling with excitement. "They know I ca'n't get at them!" it panted, bending its quivering head towards Alice, "or they wouldn't dare to do it!"

"Never mind!" Alice said in a soothing tone, and, stooping down to the daisies, who were just beginning again, she whispered "If you don't hold your tongues, I'll pick you!"

There was silence in a moment, and several of the pink daisies turned white.

"That's right!" said the Tiger-lily. "The daisies are worst of all. When one speaks, they all begin together, and it's enough to make one wither to hear the way they go on!"

"How is it you can all talk so nicely?" Alice said, hoping to get it into a better temper by a compliment. "I've been in many gardens before, but none of the flowers could talk."

"Put your hand down, and feel the ground," said the Tiger-lily. "Then you'll know why."

Alice did so. "It's very hard," she said; "but I don't see what that has to do with it."

"In most gardens," the Tiger-lily said, "they make the beds too soft—so that the flowers are always asleep."

This sounded a very good reason, and Alice was quite pleased to know it. "I never thought of that before!" she said.

"It's *my* opinion that you never think *at all*," the Rose said, in a rather severe tone.

"I never saw anybody that looked stupider," a Violet said, so suddenly, that Alice quite jumped; for it hadn't spoken before.

"Hold *your* tongue!" cried the Tiger-lily. "As if *you* ever saw anybody! You keep your head under the leaves, and snore away

---

1. This is the first of several passages in the book that play with the question of whether words are entirely arbitrary signs or whether, as the Daisy here suggests, the name of a thing is somehow intrinsically connected with its nature. If Dodgson fulfilled his intention, recorded in his diary (see p. 250 of this edition), of reading Horne Tooke's *The Diversions of Purley* (1786; 1805), he would have found there etymologies as fanciful as that advanced by the Daisy: for example, that because the *bark* of a tree and the *bark* of a dog are used for defense, both words derive from *bar*, meaning to defend against. The phrase "bow-wow theory" was also current in nineteenth-century philological study, referring to the idea that human speech developed from animal sounds.

there, till you know no more what's going on in the world, than if you were a bud!"

"Are there any more people in the garden besides me?" Alice said, not choosing to notice the Rose's last remark.

"There's one other flower in the garden that can move about like you," said the Rose. "I wonder how you do it———" ("You're always wondering," said the Tiger-lily), "but she's more bushy than you are."

"Is she like me?" Alice asked eagerly, for the thought crossed her mind, "There's another little girl in the garden, somewhere!"

"Well, she has the same awkward shape as you," the Rose said: "but she's redder—and her petals are shorter, I think."

"They're done up close, like a dahlia," said the Tiger-lily: "not tumbled about, like yours."

"But that's not *your* fault," the Rose added kindly. "You're beginning to fade, you know—and then one ca'n't help one's petals getting a little untidy."

Alice didn't like this idea at all: so, to change the subject, she asked "Does she ever come out here?"

"I daresay you'll see her soon," said the Rose. "She's one of the kind that has nine spikes, you know." *crown*

"Where does she wear them?" Alice asked with some curiosity.

"Why, all round her head, of course," the Rose replied. "I was wondering *you* hadn't got some too. I thought it was the regular rule."

"She's coming!" cried the Larkspur. "I hear her footstep, thump, thump, along the gravel-walk!"

Alice looked round eagerly and found that it was the Red Queen. "She's grown a good deal!" was her first remark. She had *size* indeed: when Alice first found her in the ashes, she had been only three inches high—and here she was, half a head taller than Alice herself!

"It's the fresh air that does it," said the Rose: "wonderfully fine air it is, out here."

"I think I'll go and meet her," said Alice, for, though the flowers were interesting enough, she felt that it would be far grander to have a talk with a real Queen.

"You ca'n't possibly do that," said the Rose: "I should advise you to walk the other way."

This sounded nonsense to Alice, so she said nothing, but set off at once towards the Red Queen. To her surprise she lost sight of her in a moment, and found herself walking in at the front-door again.

A little provoked, she drew back, and, after looking everywhere for the Queen (whom she spied out at last, a long way off), she

124 · *Through the Looking-Glass*

thought she would try the plan, this time, of walking in the opposite direction.

It succeeded beautifully. She had not been walking a minute before she found herself face to face with the Red Queen, and full in sight of the hill she had been so long aiming at.

drives story "Where do you come from?" said the Red Queen. "And where are you going? Look up, speak nicely, and don't twiddle your fingers all the time."

Alice attended to all these directions, and explained, as well as she could, that she had lost her way.

language "I don't know what you mean by *your* way," said the Queen: "all the ways about here belong to *me*—but why did you come out here at all?" she added in a kinder tone. "Curtsey while you're thinking what to say. It saves time."

Alice wondered a little at this, but she was too much in awe of the Queen to disbelieve it. "I'll try it when I go home," she thought to herself, "the next time I'm a little late for dinner."

"It's time for you to answer now," the Queen said, looking at her watch: "open your mouth a *little* wider when you speak, and always say 'your Majesty.' "

"I only wanted to see what the garden was like, your Majesty——"

"That's right," said the Queen, patting her on the head, which Alice didn't like at all: "though, when you say 'garden'—*I've* seen gardens, compared with which this would be a wilderness."

Alice didn't dare to argue the point, but went on: "—and I thought I'd try and find my way to the top of that hill——"

"When you say 'hill'," the Queen interrupted, "*I* could show you hills, in comparison with which you'd call that a valley."

"No, I shouldn't," said Alice, surprised into contradicting her at last: "a hill *ca'n't* be a valley, you know. That would be nonsense——"

The Red Queen shook her head. "You may call it 'nonsense' if you like," she said, "but *I've* heard nonsense, compared with which that would be as sensible as a dictionary!"

Alice curtseyed again, as she was afraid from the Queen's tone that she was a *little* offended: and they walked on in silence till they got to the top of the little hill.

For some minutes Alice stood without speaking, looking out in all directions over the country—and a most curious country it was. There were a number of tiny little brooks running straight across it from side to side, and the ground between was divided up into squares by a number of little green hedges, that reached from brook to brook.

"I declare it's marked out just like a large chess-board!" Alice said at last. "There ought to be some men moving about somewhere—and so there are!" she added in a tone of delight, and her heart began to beat quick with excitement as she went on. "It's a great huge game of chess that's being played—all over the world—if this *is* the world at all, you know. Oh, what fun it is! How I *wish* I was one of them! I wouldn't mind being a Pawn, if only I might join—though of course I should *like* to be a Queen, best."

She glanced rather shyly at the real Queen as she said this, but her companion only smiled pleasantly, and said "That's easily managed. You can be the White Queen's Pawn, if you like, as Lily's too young to play, and you're in the Second Square to begin with: when you get to the Eighth Square you'll be a Queen——" Just at this moment, somehow or other, they began to run.

Alice never could quite make out, in thinking it over afterwards, how it was that they began: all she remembers is, that they were running hand in hand, and the Queen went so fast that it was all she could do to keep up with her: and still the Queen kept crying "Faster! Faster!", but Alice felt she *could not* go faster, though she had no breath left to say so.

The most curious part of the thing was, that the trees and the other things round them never changed their places at all: however fast they went, they never seemed to pass anything. "I wonder if all the things move along with us?" thought poor puzzled Alice. And the Queen seemed to guess her thoughts, for she cried "Faster! Don't try to talk!"

Not that Alice had any idea of doing *that*. She felt as if she would never be able to talk again, she was getting so much out of breath: and still the Queen cried "Faster! Faster!", and dragged her along. "Are we nearly there?" Alice managed to pant out at last.

"Nearly there!" the Queen repeated. "Why, we passed it ten minutes ago! Faster!" And they ran on for a time in silence, with the wind whistling in Alice's ears, and almost blowing her hair off her head, she fancied.

"Now! Now!" cried the Queen. "Faster! Faster!" And they went so fast that at last they seemed to skim through the air, hardly touching the ground with their feet, till suddenly, just as Alice was getting quite exhausted, they stopped, and she found herself sitting on the ground, breathless and giddy.

The Queen propped her up against a tree, and said kindly, "You may rest a little, now."

Alice looked round her in great surprise. "Why, I do believe we've been under this tree the whole time! Everything's just as it was!"

"Of course it is," said the Queen. "What would you have it?"

"Well, in *our* country," said Alice, still panting a little, "you'd generally get to somewhere else—if you ran very fast for a long time as we've been doing."

"A slow sort of country!" said the Queen. "Now, *here, you see,* it takes all the running *you* can do, to keep in the same place. If you want to get somewhere else, you must run at least twice as fast as that!"

"I'd rather not try, please!" said Alice. "I'm quite content to stay here—only I *am* so hot and thirsty!"

"I know what *you'd* like!" the Queen said good-naturedly, taking a little box out of her pocket. "Have a biscuit?"

Alice thought it would not be civil to say "No," though it wasn't at all what she wanted. So she took it, and ate it as well as she could: and it was *very* dry: and she thought she had never been so nearly choked in all her life.

"While you're refreshing yourself," said the Queen, "I'll just take the measurements." And she took a ribbon out of her pocket, marked in inches, and began measuring the ground, and sticking little pegs in here and there.[2]

"At the end of two yards," she said, putting in a peg to mark the distance, "I shall give you your directions—have another biscuit?"

"No, thank you," said Alice: "one's *quite* enough!"

"Thirst quenched, I hope?" said the Queen. *how does a dry biscuit quench [your] thirst?*

Alice did not know what to say to this, but luckily the Queen

2. See the diagram with which Dodgson prefaced the book. See also the passage from A. L. Taylor's *The White Knight* (see Selected Bibliography) on pp. 373–80 of this edition for an explanation of the Red Queen's disappearance. Alice will move straight ahead; the Red Queen is marking off distances within the square adjacent to Alice, and when she reaches the last peg, she moves into another square. Until she becomes a queen, Alice will never see or converse with a piece or character who is not in or adjacent to the square she is occupying.

did not wait for an answer, but went on. "At the end of *three* yards I shall repeat them—for fear of your forgetting them. At the end of *four*, I shall say good-bye. And at the end of *five*, I shall go!"

She had got all the pegs put in by this time, and Alice looked on with great interest as she returned to the tree, and then began slowly walking down the row.

At the two-yard peg she faced round, and said "A pawn goes two squares in its first move, you know. So you'll go *very* quickly through the Third Square—by railway, I should think—and you'll find yourself in the Fourth Square in no time. Well, *that* square belongs to Tweedledum and Tweedledee—the Fifth is mostly water—the Sixth belongs to Humpty Dumpty—But you make no remark?"

"I—I didn't know I had to make one—just then," Alice faltered out.

"You *should* have said," the Queen went on in a tone of grave reproof, " 'It's extremely kind of you to tell me all this'—however, we'll suppose it said—the Seventh Square is all forest—however, one of the Knights will show you the way—and in the Eighth Square we shall be Queens together, and it's all feasting and fun!" Alice got up and curtseyed, and sat down again.

At the next peg the Queen turned again, and this time she said "Speak in French when you ca'n't think of the English for a thing—turn out your toes as you walk—and remember who you are!" She did not wait for Alice to curtsey, this time, but walked on quickly to the next peg, where she turned for a moment to say "Good-bye," and then hurried on to the last.

How it happened, Alice never knew, but exactly as she came to the last peg, she was gone. Whether she vanished into the air, or whether she ran quickly into the wood ("and she *can* run very fast!" thought Alice), there was no way of guessing, but she was gone, and Alice began to remember that she was a Pawn, and that it would soon be time for her to move.

Chapter III

LOOKING-GLASS INSECTS

Of course the first thing to do was to make a grand survey of the country she was going to travel through. "It's something very like learning geography," thought Alice, as she stood on tiptoe in hopes of being able to see a little further. "Principal rivers—there *are* none. Principal mountains—I'm on the only one, but I don't think it's got any name. Principal towns—why, what *are* those creatures, making honey down there? They ca'n't be bees—nobody ever saw bees a mile off, you know——" and for some time she stood silent, watching one of them that was bustling about among the flowers, poking its proboscis into them, "just as if it was a regular bee," thought Alice.

However, this was anything but a regular bee: in fact, it was an elephant—as Alice soon found out, though the idea quite took her breath away at first. "And what enormous flowers they must be!" was her next idea. "Something like cottages with the roofs taken off, and stalks put to them—and what quantities of honey they must make! I think I'll go down and—no, I wo'n't go *just* yet," she went on, checking herself just as she was beginning to run down the hill, and trying to find some excuse for turning shy so suddenly. "It'll never do to go down among them without a good long branch to brush them away—and what fun it'll be when they ask me how I liked my walk. I shall say 'Oh, I liked it well enough——' (here came the favourite little toss of the head), 'only it *was* so dusty and hot, and the elephants *did* tease so!'"

"I think I'll go down the other way," she said after a pause; "and perhaps I may visit the elephants later on. Besides, I *do* so want to get into the Third Square!"

So, with this excuse, she ran down the hill, and jumped over the first of the six little brooks.

*   *   *   *   *

*   *   *   *

*   *   *   *   *

"Tickets, please!" said the Guard, putting his head in at the window. In a moment everybody was holding out a ticket: they were about the same size as the people, and quite seemed to fill the carriage.

"Now then! Show your ticket, child!" the Guard went on, looking angrily at Alice. And a great many voices all said together ("like the chorus of a song," thought Alice) "Don't keep him waiting, child! Why, his time is worth a thousand pounds a minute!"

"I'm afraid I haven't got one," Alice said in a frightened tone: "there wasn't a ticket-office where I came from." And again the chorus of voices went on. "There wasn't room for one where she came from. The land there is worth a thousand pounds an inch!"

"Don't make excuses," said the Guard: "you should have bought one from the engine-driver." And once more the chorus of voices went on with "The man that drives the engine. Why, the smoke alone is worth a thousand pounds a puff!"

Alice thought to herself "Then there's no use in speaking." The voices didn't join in, *this* time, as she hadn't spoken, but, to her great surprise, they all *thought* in chorus (I hope you understand what *thinking in chorus* means—for I must confess that *I* don't), "Better say nothing at all. Language is worth a thousand pounds a word!"

"I shall dream about a thousand pounds to-night, I know I shall!" thought Alice.

All this time the Guard was looking at her, first through a telescope, then through a microscope, and then through an opera-glass. At last he said "You're traveling the wrong way," and shut up the window, and went away.

"So young a child," said the gentleman sitting opposite to her, (he was dressed in white paper,)[3] "ought to know which way she's going, even if she doesn't know her own name!"

3. There is nothing in the text to make it appropriate that in Tenniel's drawing the man dressed in paper unmistakably resembles Benjamin Disraeli, unless it is his advice to take a return ticket every time the train stops: Disraeli had briefly been prime minister in 1868, was replaced in that year by Gladstone, and did not return to office until 1874.

A Goat, that was sitting next to the gentleman in white, shut his eyes and said in a loud voice, "She ought to know her way to the ticket-office, even if she doesn't know her alphabet!"

There was a Beetle sitting next the Goat (it was a very queer carriage-full of passengers altogether), and, as the rule seemed to be that they should all speak in turn, *he* went on with "She'll have to go back from here as luggage!"

Alice couldn't see who was sitting beyond the Beetle, but a hoarse voice spoke next. "Change engines——" it said, and there it choked and was obliged to leave off.

"It sounds like a horse," Alice thought to herself. And an extremely small voice, close to her ear, said "You might make a joke on that—something about 'horse' and 'hoarse,' you know."

Then a very gentle voice in the distance said, "She must be labeled 'Lass, with care,'[4] you know——"

And after that other voices went on ("What a number of people there are in the carriage!" thought Alice), saying "She must go by post, as she's got a head[5] on her——" "She must be sent as a message by the telegraph——" "She must draw the train herself the rest of the way——," and so on.

But the gentleman dressed in white paper leaned forwards and whispered in her ear, "Never mind what they all say, my dear, but take a return-ticket every time the train stops."

"Indeed I sha'n't!" Alice said rather impatiently. "I don't belong to this railway journey at all—I was in a wood just now—and I wish I could get back there!'"

"You might make a joke on *that*," said the little voice close to her ear: "something about 'you *would* if you could,' you know." language

"Don't tease so," said Alice, looking about in vain to see where the voice came from. "If you're so anxious to have a joke made, why don't you make one yourself?"

The little voice sighed deeply. It was *very* unhappy, evidently, and Alice would have said something pitying to comfort it, "if it would only sigh like other people!" she thought. But this was such a wonderfully small sigh, that she wouldn't have heard it all, if it hadn't come *quite* close to her ear. The consequence of this was that it tickled her ear very much, and quite took off her thoughts from the unhappiness of the poor little creature.

"I know you are a friend," the little voice went on: "a dear friend, and an old friend. And you wo'n't hurt me, though I *am* an insect."

"What kind of insect?" Alice inquired, a little anxiously. What she really wanted to know was, whether it could sting or not, but she thought this wouldn't be quite a civil question to ask.

4. I.e., "Glass, with care."
5. Mid-nineteenth-century postage stamps bore a portrait of the head of Queen Victoria.

"What, then you don't—" the little voice began, when it was drowned by a shrill scream from the engine, and everybody jumped up in alarm, Alice among the rest.

The Horse, who had put his head out of the window, quietly drew it in and said "It's only a brook we have to jump over." Everybody seemed satisfied with this, though Alice felt a little nervous at the idea of trains jumping at all. "However, it'll take us into the Fourth Square, that's some comfort!" she said to herself. In another moment she felt the carriage rise straight up into the air, and in her fright she caught at the thing nearest to her hand, which happened to be the Goat's beard.

*   *   *   *   *

*   *   *   *

*   *   *   *   *

But the beard seemed to melt away as she touched it, and she found herself sitting quietly under a tree—while the Gnat (for that was the insect she had been talking to) was balancing itself on a twig just over her head, and fanning her with its wings.

It certainly was a *very* large Gnat: "about the size of a chicken," Alice thought. Still, she couldn't feel nervous with it, after they had been talking together so long.

"—then you don't like *all* insects?" the Gnat went on, as quietly as if nothing had happened.

"I like them when they can talk," Alice said. "None of them ever talk, where *I* come from."

"What sort of insects do you rejoice in, where *you* come from?" the Gnat inquired.

"I don't *rejoice* in insects at all," Alice explained, "because I'm rather afraid of them—at least the large kinds. But I can tell you the names of some of them."

"Of course they answer to their names?" the Gnat remarked carelessly.

"I never knew them do it."

"What's the use of their having names," the Gnat said, "if they wo'n't answer to them?"

"No use to *them*," said Alice; "but it's useful to the people that name them, I suppose. If not, why do things have names at all?"[6]

"I ca'n't say," the Gnat replied. "Further on, in the wood down there, they've got no names—however, go on with your list of insects: you're wasting time."

6. Alice here plays with another theory of language, later to be developed by Humpty Dumpty: that names are arbitrary designations imposed on things for the convenience of humans.

"Well, there's the Horse-fly," Alice began, counting off the names on her fingers.

"All right," said the Gnat. "Half way up that bush, you'll see a Rocking-horse-fly, if you look. It's made entirely of wood, and gets about by swinging itself from branch to branch."

"What does it live on?" Alice asked, with great curiosity.

"Sap and sawdust," said the Gnat. "Go on with the list."

Alice looked at the Rocking-horse-fly with great interest, and made up her mind that it must have been just repainted, it looked so bright and sticky; and then she went on.

"And there's the Dragon-fly."

"Look on the branch above your head," said the Gnat, "and there you'll find a Snap-dragon-fly. Its body is made of plum-pudding, its wings of holly-leaves, and its head is a raisin burning in brandy."

"And what does it live on?" Alice asked, as before.

"Frumenty[7] and mince-pie," the Gnat replied; "and it makes its nest in a Christmas-box."

"And then there's the Butterfly," Alice went on, after she had taken a good look at the insect with its head on fire, and had thought to herself, "I wonder if that's the reason insects are so fond of flying into candles—because they want to turn into Snap-dragon-flies!"

"Crawling at your feet," said the Gnat (Alice drew her feet back in some alarm), "you may observe a Bread-and-butter-fly. Its wings are thin slices of bread-and-butter, its body is a crust, and its head is a lump of sugar."

"And what does *it* live on?"

"Weak tea with cream in it."

A new difficulty came into Alice's head. "Supposing it couldn't find any?" she suggested.

"Then it would die, of course."

"But that must happen very often," Alice remarked thoughtfully.

"It always happens," said the Gnat.

After this, Alice was silent for a minute or two, pondering. The Gnat amused itself meanwhile by humming round and round her head: at last it settled again and remarked "I suppose you don't want to lose your name?"

"No, indeed," Alice said, a little anxiously.

"And yet I don't know," the Gnat went on in a careless tone: "only think how convenient it would be if you could manage to go

7. Frumenty is a dessert made of boiled wheat flavored with sugar, spice, or raisins.

home without it! For instance, if the governess wanted to call you to your lessons, she would call out 'Come here——,' and there she would have to leave off, because there wouldn't be any name for her to call, and of course you wouldn't have to go, you know."

"That would never do, I'm sure," said Alice: "the governess would never think of excusing me lessons for that. If she couldn't remember my name, she'd call me 'Miss,' as the servants do."

"Well, if she said 'Miss,' and didn't say anything more," the Gnat remarked, "of course you'd miss your lessons. That's a joke. I wish *you* had made it." *language*

"Why do you wish *I* had made it?" Alice asked. "It's a very bad one."

But the Gnat only sighed deeply, while two large tears came rolling down its cheeks.

"You shouldn't make jokes," Alice said, "if it makes you so unhappy."

Then came another of those melancholy little sighs, and this time the poor Gnat really seemed to have sighed itself away, for, when Alice looked up, there was nothing whatever to be seen on the twig, and, as she was getting quite chilly with sitting still so long, she got up and walked on.

She very soon came to an open field, with a wood on the other side of it: it looked much darker than the last wood, and Alice felt a *little* timid about going into it. However, on second thoughts, she made up her mind to go on: "for I certainly won't go *back*," she thought to herself, and this was the only way to the Eighth Square.

"This must be the wood," she said thoughtfully to herself, "where things have no names. I wonder what'll become of *my* name when I go in? I shouldn't like to lose it at all—because they'd have to give me another, and it would be almost certain to be an ugly one. But then the fun would be, trying to find the creature that had got my old name! That's just like the advertisements, you know, when people lose dogs——'*answers to the name of* "Dash": *had on a brass collar*'—just fancy calling everything you met 'Alice,' till one of them answered! Only they wouldn't answer at all, if they were wise."

She was rambling on in this way when she reached the wood: it looked very cool and shady. "Well, at any rate it's a great comfort," she said as she stepped under the trees, "after being so hot, to get into the—into the—into *what*?" she went on, rather surprised at not being able to think of the word. "I mean to get under the—under the—under *this*, you know!" putting her hand on the trunk of the tree. "What *does* it call itself, I wonder? I do believe

language

it's got no name—why, to be sure it hasn't!"

She stood silent for a minute, thinking: then she suddenly began again. "Then it really *has* happened, after all! And now, who am I? I *will* remember, if I can! I'm determined to do it!" But being determined didn't help her much, and all she could say, after a great deal of puzzling, was "L, I *know* it begins with L!"[8]

Just then a Fawn came wandering by: it looked at Alice with its large gentle eyes, but didn't seem at all frightened. "Here then! Here then!" Alice said, as she held out her hand and tried to stroke it; but it only started back a little, and then stood looking at her again.

"What do you call yourself?" the Fawn said at last. Such a soft sweet voice it had!

"I wish I knew!" thought poor Alice. She answered, rather sadly, "Nothing, just now."

"Think again," it said: "that wo'n't do."

Alice thought, but nothing came of it. "Please, would you tell me what *you* call yourself?" she said timidly. "I think that might help a little."

8. Liddell begins with L.

"I'll tell you, if you'll come a little further on," the Fawn said. "I ca'n't remember *here*."

So they walked on together through the wood, Alice with her arms clasped lovingly round the soft neck of the Fawn, till they came out into another open field, and here the Fawn gave a sudden bound into the air, and shook itself free from Alice's arm. "I'm a Fawn!" it cried out in a voice of delight. "And, dear me! you're a human child!" A sudden look of alarm came into its beautiful brown eyes, and in another moment it had darted away at full speed.

language

Alice stood looking after it, almost ready to cry with vexation at having lost her dear little fellow-traveler so suddenly. "However, I know my name now," she said: "that's *some* comfort. Alice—Alice—I wo'n't forget it again. And now, which of these finger-posts ought I to follow, I wonder?"

It was not a very difficult question to answer, as there was only one road through the wood, and the two finger-posts both pointed along it. "I'll settle it," Alice said to herself, "when the road divides and they point different ways."

But this did not seem likely to happen. She went on and on, a long way, but, wherever the road divided, there were sure to be two finger-posts pointing the same way, one marked "TO TWEEDLEDUM'S HOUSE," and the other "TO THE HOUSE OF TWEEDLEDEE."

"I do believe," said Alice at last, "that they live in the *same* house! I wonder I never thought of that before—But I ca'n't stay there long. I'll just call and say 'How d'ye do?' and ask them the way out of the wood. If I could only get to the Eighth Square before it gets dark!" So she wandered on, talking to herself as she went, till, on turning a sharp corner, she came upon two fat little men, so suddenly that she could not help starting back, but in another moment she recovered herself, feeling sure that they must be

Chapter IV

TWEEDLEDUM AND TWEEDLEDEE

They were standing under a tree, each with an arm round the other's neck, and Alice knew which was which in a moment, because one of them had 'DUM' embroidered on his collar, and the other 'DEE.' "I suppose they've each got 'TWEEDLE' round at the back of the collar," she said to herself.

They stood so still that she quite forgot they were alive, and she was just going round to see if the word 'TWEEDLE' was written at the back of each collar, when she was startled by a voice coming from the one marked 'DUM.'

"If you think we're wax-works," he said, "you ought to pay, you know. Wax-works weren't made to be looked at for nothing. Nohow!"

"Contrariwise," added the one marked 'DEE,' "if you think we're alive, you ought to speak."

"I'm sure I'm very sorry," was all Alice could say; for the words of the old song kept ringing through her head like the ticking of a clock, and she could hardly help saying them out loud:—

> *"Tweedledum and Tweedledee*
> *Agreed to have a battle;*
> *For Tweedledum said Tweedledee*
> *Had spoiled his nice new rattle.*

> *Just then flew down a monstrous crow,*
>   *As black as a tar-barrel;*
> *Which frightened both the heroes so,*
>   *They quite forgot their quarrel.*"[9]

"I know what you're thinking about," said Tweedledum; "but it isn't so, nohow."

"Contrariwise," continued Tweedledee, "if it was so, it might be; and if it were so, it would be; but as it isn't, it ain't. That's logic."

"I was thinking," Alice said politely, "which is the best way out of this wood: it's getting so dark. Would you tell me, please?"

But the fat little men only looked at each other and grinned.

They looked so exactly like a couple of great schoolboys, that Alice couldn't help pointing her finger at Tweedledum, and saying "First Boy!"

"Nohow!" Tweedledum cried out briskly, and shut his mouth up again with a snap.

"Next Boy!" said Alice, passing on to Tweedledee, though she felt quite certain he would only shout out "Contrariwise!" and so he did.

"You've begun wrong!" cried Tweedledum. "The first thing in a visit is to say 'How d'ye do?' and shake hands!" And here the two brothers gave each other a hug, and then they held out the two hands that were free, to shake hands with her.

Alice did not like shaking hands with either of them first, for fear of hurting the other one's feelings; so, as the best way out of the difficulty, she took hold of both hands at once: the next moment they were dancing round in a ring. This seemed quite natural (she remembered afterwards), and she was not even surprised to hear music playing: it seemed to come from the tree under which they were dancing, and it was done (as well as she could make it out) by the branches rubbing one across the other, like fiddles and fiddle-sticks.

"But it certainly *was* funny," (Alice said afterwards, when she was telling her sister the history of all this,) "to find myself singing *'Here we go round the mulberry bush.'* I don't know when I began it, but somehow I felt as if I'd been singing it a long long time!"

The other two dancers were fat, and very soon out of breath. "Four times round is enough for one dance," Tweedledum panted

9. Dodgson takes over this nursery rhyme unaltered from one of its traditional versions. The rhyme was collected in James Orchard Halliwell's *The Nursery Rhymes of England* (first edition, 1842). .

out, and they left off dancing as suddenly as they had begun: the music stopped at the same moment.

Then they let go of Alice's hands, and stood looking at her for a minute: there was a rather awkward pause, as Alice didn't know how to begin a conversation with people she had just been dancing with. "It would never do to say 'How d'ye do?' *now*," she said to herself: "we seem to have got beyond that, somehow!"

"I hope you're not much tired?" she said at last.

"Nohow. And thank you *very* much for asking," said Tweedledum.

"So *much* obliged!" added Tweedledee. "You like poetry?"

"Ye-es, pretty well—*some* poetry," Alice said doubtfully. "Would you tell me which road leads out of the wood?"

"What shall I repeat to her?" said Tweedledee, looking round at Tweedledum with great solemn eyes, and not noticing Alice's question.

" '*The Walrus and the Carpenter*' is the longest," Tweedledum replied, giving his brother an affectionate hug.

Tweedledee began instantly:

> "*The sun was shining——*"

Here Alice ventured to interrupt him. "If it's *very* long," she said, as politely as she could, "would you please tell me first which road——"

Tweedledee smiled gently, and began again:

> "*The sun was shining on the sea,*
>   *Shining with all his might:*
> *He did his very best to make*
>   *The billows smooth and bright—*
> *And this was odd, because it was*
>   *The middle of the night.*
>
> *The moon was shining sulkily,*
>   *Because she thought the sun*
> *Had got no business to be there*
>   *After the day was done—*
> *'It's very rude of him,' she said,*
>   *'To come and spoil the fun!'*
>
> *The sea was wet as wet could be,*
>   *The sands were dry as dry.*
> *You could not see a cloud, because*
>   *No cloud was in the sky:*
> *No birds were flying overhead—*
>   *There were no birds to fly.*

The Walrus and the Carpenter
    Were walking close at hand:
They wept like anything to see
    Such quantities of sand:
'If this were only cleared away,'
    They said, 'it would be grand!'

'If seven maids with seven mops
    Swept it for half a year,
Do you suppose,' the Walrus said,
    'That they could get it clear?'
'I doubt it,' said the Carpenter,
    And shed a bitter tear.

'O Oysters, come and walk with us!'
    The Walrus did beseech.
'A pleasant walk, a pleasant talk,
    Along the briny beach:
We cannot do with more than four,
    To give a hand to each.'

The eldest Oyster looked at him,
    But never a word he said:
The eldest Oyster winked his eye,
    And shook his heavy head—
Meaning to say he did not choose
    To leave the oyster-bed.

But four young Oysters hurried up,
   All eager for the treat:
Their coats were brushed, their faces washed,
   Their shoes were clean and neat—
And this was odd, because, you know,
   They hadn't any feet.

Four other Oysters followed them,
   And yet another four;
And thick and fast they came at last,
   And more, and more, and more—
All hopping through the frothy waves,
   And scrambling to the shore.

The Walrus and the Carpenter
   Walked on a mile or so,
And then they rested on a rock
   Conveniently low:
And all the little Oysters stood
   And waited in a row.

'The time has come,' the Walrus said,
   'To talk of many things:
Of shoes—and ships—and sealing wax—
   Of cabbages—and kings—
And why the sea is boiling hot—
   And whether pigs have wings.'

'But wait a bit,' the Oysters cried,
    'Before we have our chat;
For some of us are out of breath,
    And all of us are fat!'
'No hurry!' said the Carpenter.
    They thanked him much for that.

'A loaf of bread,' the Walrus said,
    'Is what we chiefly need:
Pepper and vinegar besides
    Are very good indeed—
Now, if you're ready, Oysters dear,
    We can begin to feed.'

'But not on us!' the Oysters cried,
    Turning a little blue.
'After such kindness, that would be
    A dismal thing to do!'
'The night is fine,' the Walrus said.
    'Do you admire the view?

'It was so kind of you to come!
    And you are very nice!'
The Carpenter said nothing but
    'Cut us another slice.
I wish you were not quite so deaf—
    I've had to ask you twice!'

'It seems a shame,' the Walrus said,
    'To play them such a trick,
After we've brought them out so far,
    And made them trot so quick!'
The Carpenter said nothing but
    'The butter's spread too thick!'

> '*I weep for you,*' *the Walrus said:*
> '*I deeply sympathize.*'
> *With sobs and tears he sorted out*
> *Those of the largest size,*
> *Holding his pocket-handkerchief*
> *Before his streaming eyes.*
>
> '*O Oysters,*' *said the Carpenter,*
> '*You've had a pleasant run!*
> *Shall we be trotting home again?*'
> *But answer came there none—*
> *And this was scarcely odd, because*
> *They'd eaten every one.*"[1]

"I like the Walrus best," said Alice: "because he was a *little* sorry for the poor oysters."

"He ate more than the Carpenter, though," said Tweedledee. "You see he held his handkerchief in front, so that the Carpenter couldn't count how many he took: contrariwise."

"That was mean!" Alice said indignantly. "Then I like the Carpenter best—if he didn't eat so many as the Walrus."

"But he ate as many as he could get," said Tweedledum.

This was a puzzler. After a pause, Alice began, "Well! They were *both* very unpleasant characters——" Here she checked herself in some alarm, at hearing something that sounded to her like the puffing of a large steam-engine in the wood near them, though she feared it was more likely to be a wild beast. "Are there any lions or tigers about here?" she asked timidly.

"It's only the Red King snoring," said Tweedledee.

"Come and look at him!" the brothers cried, and they each took one of Alice's hands, and led her up to where the King was sleeping.

"Isn't he a *lovely* sight?" said Tweedledum.

Alice couldn't say honestly that he was. He had a tall red night-cap on, with a tassel, and he was lying crumpled up into a sort of untidy heap, and snoring loud—"fit to snore his head off!" as Tweedledum remarked.

"I'm afraid he'll catch cold with lying on the damp grass," said Alice, who was a very thoughtful little girl.

1. "The Walrus and the Carpenter" is written in the meter of Thomas Hood's "The Dream of Eugene Aram" (1832), a poem about a schoolteacher who is discovered to be a murderer. For Savile Clark's theatrical version of the Alice books, Dodgson added a final stanza:

> The Carpenter he ceased to sob;
>   The Walrus ceased to weep;
> They'd finished all the oysters;

> And they laid them down to sleep—
> And of their craft and cruelty
>   The punishment to reap.

This verse was followed by a scene in which the ghosts of three oysters enter and stamp on the chests of the sleeping Walrus and Carpenter. The scene is reprinted on pp. 446–47 of R. L. Green's edition of *The Diaries of Lewis Carroll* (see Selected Bibliography).

"He's dreaming now," said Tweedledee: "and what do you think he's dreaming about?"

Alice said "Nobody can guess that."

"Why, about *you!*" Tweedledee exclaimed, clapping his hands triumphantly. "And if he left off dreaming about you, where do you suppose you'd be?"

"Where I am now, of course," said Alice.

"Not you!" Tweedledee retorted contemptuously. "You'd be nowhere. Why, you're only a sort of thing in his dream!"

"'If that there King was to wake," added Tweedledum, "you'd go out—bang!—just like a candle!"

"I shouldn't!" Alice exclaimed indignantly. "Besides, if *I'm* only a sort of thing in his dream, what are *you,* I should like to know?"

"Ditto," said Tweedledum.

"Ditto, ditto!" cried Tweedledee.

He shouted this so loud that Alice couldn't help saying "Hush! You'll be waking him, I'm afraid, if you make so much noise."

"Well, it's no use *your* talking about waking him," said Tweedledum, "when you're only one of the things in his dream. You know very well you're not real."

"I *am* real!" said Alice, and began to cry.

"You wo'n't make yourself a bit realler by crying," Tweedledee remarked: "there's nothing to cry about."

"If I wasn't real," Alice said—half laughing through her tears, it all seemed so ridiculous—"I shouldn't be able to cry."

"I hope you don't suppose those are *real* tears?" Tweedledum interrupted in a tone of great contempt.

"I know they're talking nonsense," Alice thought to herself: "and it's foolish to cry about it." So she brushed away her tears, and went on, as cheerfully as she could, "At any rate I'd better be getting out of the wood, for really it's coming on very dark. Do you think it's going to rain?"

Tweedledum spread a large umbrella over himself and his brother, and looked up into it. "No, I don't think it is," he said: "at least—not under *here*. Nohow."

"But it may rain *outside*?"

"It may—if it chooses," said Tweedledee: "we've no objection. Contrariwise."

"Selfish things!" thought Alice, and she was just going to say "Good-night" and leave them, when Tweedledum sprang out from under the umbrella, and seized her by the wrist.

"Do you see *that*?" he said, in a voice choking with passion, and his eyes grew large and yellow all in a moment, as he pointed with a trembling finger at a small white thing lying under the tree.

"It's only a rattle," Alice said, after a careful examination of the little white thing. "Not a rattle-*snake*, you know," she added hastily, thinking that he was frightened: "only an old rattle—quite old and broken."

"I knew it was!" cried Tweedledum, beginning to stamp about wildly and tear his hair. "It's spoilt, of course!" Here he looked at Tweedledee, who immediately sat down on the ground, and tried to hide himself under the umbrella.

Alice laid her hand upon his arm, and said, in a soothing tone, "You needn't be so angry about an old rattle."

"But it *isn't* old!" Tweedledum cried, in a greater fury than ever. "It's *new*, I tell you——I bought it yesterday—my nice NEW RATTLE!" and his voice rose to a perfect scream.

All this time Tweedledee was trying his best to fold up the umbrella, with himself in it: which was such an extraordinary thing to do, that it quite took off Alice's attention from the angry brother. But he couldn't quite succeed, and it ended in his rolling over, bundled up in the umbrella, with only his head out: and there he lay, opening and shutting his mouth and his large eyes— "looking more like a fish than anything else," Alice thought.

"Of course you agree to have a battle?" Tweedledum said in a calmer tone.

"I suppose so," the other sulkily replied, as he crawled out of the umbrella: "only *she* must help us to dress up, you know."

So the two brothers went off hand-in-hand into the wood, and returned in a minute with their arms full of things—such as bolsters, blankets, hearth-rugs, table-cloths, dish-covers, and coal-scuttles. "I hope you're a good hand at pinning and tying strings?" Tweedledum remarked. "Every one of these things has got to go on, somehow or other."

Alice said afterwards she had never seen such a fuss made about anything in all her life—the way those two bustled about—and the quantity of things they put on—and the trouble they gave her in tying strings and fastening buttons—"Really they'll be more like bundles of old clothes than anything else, by the time they're ready!" she said to herself, as she arranged a bolster round the neck of Tweedledee, "to keep his head from being cut off," as he said.

"You know," he added very gravely, "it's one of the most serious things that can possibly happen to one in a battle—to get one's head cut off."

Alice laughed loud: but she managed to turn it into a cough, for fear of hurting his feelings.

"Do I look very pale?" said Tweedledum, coming up to have his helmet tied on. (He *called* it a helmet, though it certainly looked much more like a saucepan.)

"Well—yes—a *little*," Alice replied gently.

"I'm very brave, generally," he went on in a low voice: "only to-day I happen to have a headache."

"And *I've* got a toothache!" said Tweedledee, who had over-heard the remark. "I'm far worse than you!"

"Then you'd better not fight to-day," said Alice, thinking it a good opportunity to make peace.

"We *must* have a bit of a fight, but I don't care about going on long," said Tweedledum. "What's the time now?"

Tweedledee looked at his watch, and said "Half-past four."

"Let's fight till six, and then have dinner," said Tweedledum.

"Very well," the other said, rather sadly: "and *she* can watch us—only you'd better not come *very* close," he added: "I generally hit every thing I can see—when I get really excited."

"And *I* hit every thing within reach," cried Tweedledum, "whether I can see it or not!"

Alice laughed. "You must hit the *trees* pretty often, I should think," she said.

Tweedledum looked round him with a satisfied smile. "I don't suppose," he said, "there'll be a tree left standing, for ever so far round, by the time we've finished!"

"And all about a rattle!" said Alice, still hoping to make them a *little* ashamed of fighting for such a trifle.

"I shouldn't have minded it so much," said Tweedledum, "if it hadn't been a new one."

"I wish the monstrous crow would come!" thought Alice.

"There's only one sword, you know," Tweedledum said to his brother: "but *you* can have the umbrella—it's quite as sharp. Only we must begin quick. It's getting as dark as it can."

"And darker," said Tweedledee.

It was getting dark so suddenly that Alice thought there must be a thunderstorm coming on. "What a thick black cloud that is!" she said. "And how fast it comes! Why, I do believe it's got wings!"

"It's the crow!" Tweedledum cried out in a shrill voice of alarm; and the two brothers took to their heels and were out of sight in a moment.

Alice ran a little way into the wood, and stopped under a large tree. "It can never get at me *here*," she thought: "it's far too large to squeeze itself in among the trees. But I wish it wouldn't flap its wings so—it makes quite a hurricane in the wood—here's somebody's shawl being blown away!"

Chapter V

WOOL AND WATER

She caught the shawl as she spoke, and looked about for the owner: in another moment the White Queen came running wildly through the wood, with both arms stretched out wide, as if she were flying, and Alice very civilly went to meet her with the shawl.

"I'm very glad I happened to be in the way," Alice said, as she helped her to put on her shawl again.

The White Queen only looked at her in a helpless frightened sort of way, and kept repeating something in a whisper to herself that sounded like "Bread-and-butter, bread-and-butter," and Alice felt that if there was to be any conversation at all, she must manage it herself. So she began rather timidly: "Am I addressing the White Queen?"

"Well, yes, if you call that a-dressing," the Queen said. "It isn't *my* notion of the thing, at all."

Alice thought it would never do to have an argument at the very beginning of their conversation, so she smiled and said "If your Majesty will only tell me the right way to begin, I'll do it as well as I can."

"But I don't want it done at all!" groaned the poor Queen. "I've been a-dressing myself for the last two hours."

It would have been all the better, as it seemed to Alice, if she had got some one else to dress her, she was so dreadfully untidy. "Every single thing's crooked," Alice thought to herself, "and she's all over pins!—May I put your shawl straight for you?" she added aloud.

"I don't know what's the matter with it!" the Queen said, in a melancholy voice. "It's out of temper, I think. I've pinned it here, and I've pinned it there, but there's no pleasing it!"

"It *ca'n't* go straight, you know, if you pin it all on one side," Alice said as she gently put it right for her; "and dear me, what a state your hair is in!"

"The brush has got entangled in it!" the Queen said with a sigh. "And I lost the comb yesterday."

Alice carefully released the brush, and did her best to get the hair into order. "Come, you look rather better now!" she said, after altering most of the pins. "But really you should have a lady's maid!"

"I'm sure I'll take *you* with pleasure!" the Queen said. "Two pence a week, and jam every other day."

Alice couldn't help laughing, as she said "I don't want you to hire *me*—and I don't care for jam."

"It's very good jam," said the Queen.

"Well, I don't want any *to-day*, at any rate."

"You couldn't have it if you *did* want it," the Queen said. "The rule is, jam to-morrow and jam yesterday—but never jam *to-day*."

"It *must* come sometimes to 'jam to-day,' " Alice objected.

"No, it ca'n't," said the Queen. "It's jam every *other* day: to-day isn't any *other* day, you know."

"I don't understand you," said Alice. "Its dreadfully confusing!"

"That's the effect of living backwards," the Queen said kindly: "it always makes one a little giddy at first—"

"Living backwards!" Alice repeated in great astonishment. "I never heard of such a thing!"

"—but there's one great advantage in it, that one's memory works both ways."

"I'm sure *mine* only works one way," Alice remarked. "I ca'n't remember things before they happen."

"It's a poor sort of memory that only works backwards," the Queen remarked.

"What sort of things do *you* remember best?" Alice ventured to ask.

"Oh, things that happened the week after next," the Queen replied in a careless tone. "For instance, now," she went on, sticking a large piece of plaster[2] on her finger as she spoke, "there's the King's Messenger. He's in prison now, being punished: and the trial doesn't even begin till next Wednesday: and of course the crime comes last of all."

"Suppose he never commits the crime?" said Alice.

"That would be all the better, wouldn't it?" the Queen said, as she bound the plaster round her finger with a bit of ribbon.

Alice felt there was no denying *that*. "Of course it would be all the better," she said: "but it wouldn't be all the better his being punished."

"You're wrong *there*, at any rate," said the Queen. "Were *you* ever punished?"

"Only for faults," said Alice.

"And you were all the better for it, I know!" the Queen said triumphantly.

"Yes, but then I *had* done the things I was punished for," said Alice: "that makes all the difference."

"But if you *hadn't* done them," the Queen said, "that would have been better still; better, and better, and better!" Her voice went higher with each "better," till it got quite to a squeak at last.

Alice was just beginning to say "There's a mistake somewhere———," when the Queen began screaming, so loud that she

2. An adhesive bandage.

had to leave the sentence unfinished. "Oh, oh, oh!" shouted the Queen, shaking her hand about as if she wanted to shake it off. "My finger's bleeding! Oh, oh, oh, oh!"

Her screams were so exactly like the whistle of a steam-engine, that Alice had to hold both her hands over her ears.

"What *is* the matter?" she said, as soon as there was a chance of making herself heard. "Have you pricked your finger?"

"I haven't pricked it *yet*," the Queen said, "but I soon shall—oh, oh, oh!"

"When do you expect to do it?" Alice said, feeling very much inclined to laugh.

"When I fasten my shawl again," the poor Queen groaned out: "the brooch will come undone directly. Oh, oh!" As she said the words the brooch flew open, and the Queen clutched wildly at it, and tried to clasp it again.

"Take care!" cried Alice. "You're holding it all crooked!" And she caught at the brooch; but it was too late: the pin had slipped, and the Queen had pricked her finger.

"That accounts for the bleeding, you see," she said to Alice with a smile. "Now you understand the way things happen here."

"But why don't you scream *now*?" Alice asked, holding her hands ready to put over her ears again.

"Why, I've done all the screaming already," said the Queen. "What would be the good of having it all over again?"

By this time it was getting light. "The crow must have flown away, I think," said Alice: "I'm so glad it's gone. I thought it was the night coming on."

"I wish *I* could manage to be glad!" the Queen said. "Only I never can remember the rule. You must be very happy, living in this wood, and being glad whenever you like!"

"Only it is so *very* lonely here!" Alice said in a melancholy voice; and, at the thought of her loneliness, two large tears came rolling down her cheeks.

"Oh, don't go on like that!" cried the poor Queen, wringing her hands in despair. "Consider what a great girl you are. Consider what a long way you've come to-day. Consider what o'clock it is. Consider anything, only don't cry!"

Alice could not help laughing at this, even in the midst of her tears. "Can *you* keep from crying by considering things?" she asked.[3]

---

3. In the preface to *Pillow-Problems*, the second part of *Curiosa Mathematica*, published in 1893 under Dodgson's own name, he recommends the working-out in one's head of mathematical problems as a way to keep skeptical, blasphemous, and unholy thoughts at bay during wakeful night-time hours.

"That's the way it's done," the Queen said with great decision: "nobody can do two things at once, you know. Let's consider your age to begin with——how old are you?"

"I'm seven and a half, exactly."

"You needn't say 'exactly,' " the Queen remarked. "I can believe it without that. Now I'll give *you* something to believe. I'm just one hundred and one, five months and a day."

"I ca'n't believe *that*!" said Alice.

"Ca'n't you?" the Queen said in a pitying tone. "Try again: draw a long breath, and shut your eyes."

Alice laughed. "There's no use trying," she said: "one *ca'n't* believe impossible things."

"I daresay you haven't had much practice," said the Queen. "When I was your age, I always did it for half-an-hour a day. Why, sometimes I've believed as many as six impossible things before breakfast. There goes the shawl again!"

The brooch had come undone as she spoke, and a sudden gust of wind blew the Queen's shawl across a little brook. The Queen spread out her arms again, and went flying after it, and this time she succeeded in catching it for herself. "I've got it!" she cried in a triumphant tone. "Now you shall see me pin it on again, all by myself!"

"Then I hope your finger is better now?" Alice said very politely, as she crossed the little brook after the Queen.

*   *   *   *   *

*   *   *   *   *

*   *   *   *   *

"Oh, much better!" cried the Queen, her voice rising into a squeak as she went on. "Much be-etter! Be-etter! Be-e-e-etter! Be-e-ehh!" The last word ended in a long bleat, so like a sheep that Alice quite started.

She looked at the Queen, who seemed to have suddenly wrapped herself up in wool. Alice rubbed her eyes, and looked again. She couldn't make out what had happened at all. Was she in a shop? And was that really—was it really a *sheep* that was sitting on the other side of the counter? Rub as she would, she could make nothing more of it: she was in a little dark shop, leaning with her elbows on the counter, and opposite to her was an old Sheep, sitting in an arm-chair, knitting, and every now and then leaving off to look at her through a great pair of spectacles.[4]

4. One of the central features of the theatrical pantomimes Dodgson frequently attended was a series of transformation scenes in which one setting was ingeniously transformed into another. This transformation, like others in *Through the Looking-Glass*, owes something to pantomime. Tenniel's illustration of the Shop itself is modeled on a shop in Oxford.

"What is it you want to buy?" the Sheep said at last, looking up for a moment from her knitting.

"I don't *quite* know yet," Alice said very gently. "I should like to look all round me first, if I might."

"You may look in front of you, and on both sides, if you like," said the Sheep; "but you ca'n't look *all* round you—unless you've got eyes at the back of your head."

But these, as it happened, Alice had *not* got: so she contented herself with turning round, looking at the shelves as she came to them.

The shop seemed to be full of all manner of curious things—but the oddest part of it all was that, whenever she looked hard at any shelf, to make out exactly what it had on it, that particular shelf was always quite empty, though the others round it were crowded as full as they could hold.

"Things flow about so here!" she said at last in a plaintive tone, after she had spent a minute or so in vainly pursuing a large bright thing that looked sometimes like a doll and sometimes·like a work-box, and was always in the shelf next above the one she was looking at. "And this one is the most provoking of all—but I'll tell you what——" she added, as a sudden thought struck her. "I'll follow it up to the very top shelf of all. It'll puzzle it to go through the ceiling, I expect!"

But even this plan failed: the 'thing' went through the ceiling as quietly as possible, as if it were quite used to it.

"Are you a child or a teetotum?"[5] the Sheep said, as she took up another pair of needles. "You'll make me giddy soon, if you go on turning round like that." She was now working with fourteen pairs at once, and Alice couldn't help looking at her in great astonishment.

"How *can* she knit with so many?" the puzzled child thought to herself. "She gets more and more like a porcupine every minute!"

"Can you row?" the Sheep asked, handing her a pair of knitting-needles as she spoke.

"Yes, a little—but not on land—and not with needles——" Alice was beginning to say, when suddenly the needles turned into oars in her hands, and she found they were in a little boat, gliding along between banks: so there was nothing for it but to do her best.

"Feather!" cried the Sheep, as she took up another pair of needles.

This didn't sound like a remark that needed any answer: so Alice said nothing, but pulled away. There was something very queer about the water, she thought, as every now and then the oars got fast in it, and would hardly come out again.

"Feather! Feather!" the Sheep cried again, taking more needles. "You'll be catching a crab directly."[6]

"A dear little crab!" thought Alice. "I should like that."

"Didn't you hear me say 'Feather'?" the Sheep cried angrily, taking up quite a bunch of needles.

"Indeed I did," said Alice: "you've said it very often—and very loud. Please, where *are* the crabs?"

"In the water, of course!" said the Sheep, sticking some of the needles into her hair, as her hands were full. "Feather, I say!"

"*Why* do you say 'Feather' so often?" Alice asked at last, rather vexed. "I'm not a bird!"

"You are," said the Sheep: "you're a little goose."

5. A small top with several flat surfaces bearing numbers. It is used to play games—to direct players the number of spaces they may move on a board, for example.
6. To feather is to turn an oar-blade horizontally on the return stroke. If the blade touches the water on the return stroke, the rower has caught a crab. Because the rower's body is moving forward on the return stroke, to catch a crab may drive the oar handle into her chest or chin and even, as happens to Alice, unseat her.

This offended Alice a little, so there was no more conversation for a minute or two, while the boat glided gently on, sometimes among beds of weeds (which made the oars stick fast in the water, worse than ever), and sometimes under trees, but always with the same tall river-banks frowning over their heads.

"Oh, please! There are some scented rushes!" Alice cried in a sudden transport of delight. "There really are—and *such* beauties!"

"You needn't say 'please' to *me* about 'em," the Sheep said, without looking up from her knitting: "I didn't put 'em there, and I'm not going to take 'em away."

"No, but I meant—please, may we wait and pick some?" Alice pleaded. "If you don't mind stopping the boat for a minute."

"How am *I* to stop it?" said the Sheep. "If you leave off rowing, it'll stop of itself."

So the boat was left to drift down the stream as it would, till it glided gently in among the waving rushes. And then the little sleeves were carefully rolled up, and the little arms were plunged in elbow-deep, to get hold of the rushes a good long way down before breaking them off—and for a while Alice forgot all about the Sheep and the knitting, as she bent over the side of the boat, with just the ends of her tangled hair dipping into the water—while with bright eager eyes she caught at one bunch after another of the darling scented rushes.

"I only hope the boat wo'n't tipple over!" she said to herself. "Oh, *what* a lovely one! Only I couldn't quite reach it." And it certainly *did* seem a little provoking ("almost as if it happened on purpose," she thought) that, though she managed to pick plenty of beautiful rushes as the boat glided by, there was always a more lovely one that she couldn't reach.

"The prettiest are always further!" she said at last, with a sigh at the obstinacy of the rushes in growing so far off, as, with flushed cheeks and dripping hair and hands, she scrambled back into her place, and began to arrange her new-found treasures.

What mattered it to her just then that the rushes had begun to fade, and to lose all their scent and beauty, from the very moment that she picked them? Even real scented rushes, you know, last only a very little while—and these, being dream-rushes, melted away almost like snow, as they lay in heaps at her feet—but Alice hardly noticed this, there were so many other curious things to think about.

They hadn't gone much farther before the blade of one of the oars got fast in the water and *wouldn't* come out again (so Alice explained it afterwards), and the consequence was that the handle of it caught her under the chin, and, in spite of a series of little shrieks of "Oh, oh, oh!" from poor Alice, it swept her straight off

the seat, and down among the heap of rushes.

However, she wasn't a bit hurt, and was soon up again: the Sheep went on with her knitting all the while, just as if nothing had happened. "That was a nice crab you caught!" she remarked, as Alice got back into her place, very much relieved to find herself still in the boat.

"Was it? I didn't see it," said Alice, peeping cautiously over the side of the boat into the dark water. "I wish it hadn't let go—I should so like a little crab to take home with me!" But the Sheep only laughed scornfully, and went on with her knitting.

"Are there many crabs here?" said Alice.

"Crabs, and all sorts of things," said the Sheep: "plenty of choice, only make up your mind. Now, what *do* you want to buy?"

"To buy!" Alice echoed in a tone that was half astonished and half frightened—for the oars, and the boat, and the river, had vanished all in a moment, and she was back again in the little dark shop.

"I should like to buy an egg, please," she said timidly. "How do you sell them?"

"Fivepence farthing for one—twopence for two," the Sheep replied.

"Then two are cheaper than one?" Alice said in a surprised tone, taking out her purse.

"Only you *must* eat them both, if you buy two," said the Sheep.

"Then I'll have *one*, please," said Alice, as she put the money down on the counter. For she thought to herself, "They mightn't be at all nice, you know."[7]

The Sheep took the money, and put it away in a box: then she said "I never put things into people's hands—that would never do—you must get it for yourself." And so saying, she went off to the other end of the shop, and set the egg upright on a shelf.

"I wonder *why* it wouldn't do?" thought Alice, as she groped her way among the tables and chairs, for the shop was very dark towards the end. "The egg seems to get further away the more I walk towards it. Let me see, is this a chair? Why, it's got branches, I declare! How very odd to find trees growing here! And actually here's a little brook! Well, this is the very queerest shop I ever saw!"

*　　　*　　　*　　　*　　　*

*　　　*　　　*　　　*

*　　　*　　　*　　　*　　　*

So she went on, wondering more and more at every step, as everything turned into a tree the moment she came up to it, and she quite expected the egg to do the same.

7. In his edition of Dodgson's diaries (see Selected Bibliography), R. L. Green quotes one of Dodgson's contemporaries at Oxford as saying that "a Christ Church undergraduate knew that if he ordered one boiled egg he was served with two, but one was invariably bad" (p. 176).

Chapter VI

HUMPTY DUMPTY

However, the egg only got larger and larger, and more and more human: when she had come within a few yards of it, she saw that it had eyes and a nose and a mouth; and, when she had come close to it, she saw clearly that it was HUMPTY DUMPTY himself. "It ca'n't be anybody else!" she said to herself. "I'm as certain of it, as if his name were written all over his face!"

It might have been written a hundred times, easily, on that enormous face. Humpty Dumpty was sitting, with his legs crossed like a Turk, on the top of a high wall—such a narrow one that Alice quite wondered how he could keep his balance—and, as his eyes were steadily fixed in the opposite direction, and he didn't take the least notice of her, she thought he must be a stuffed figure after all.

"And how exactly like an egg he is!" she said aloud, standing with her hands ready to catch him, for she was every moment expecting him to fall.

"It's *very* provoking," Humpty Dumpty said after a long silence, looking away from Alice as he spoke, "to be called an egg—*very!*"

"I said you *looked* like an egg, Sir," Alice gently explained. "And some eggs are very pretty, you know," she added, hoping to turn her remark into a sort of compliment.

"Some people," said Humpty Dumpty, looking away from her as usual, "have no more sense than a baby!"

Alice didn't know what to say to this: it wasn't at all like conversation, she thought, as he never said anything to *her*; in fact, his last remark was evidently addressed to a tree—so she stood and softly repeated to herself:—

> *"Humpty Dumpty sat on a wall:*
> *Humpty Dumpty had a great fall.*
> *All the King's horses and all the King's men*
> *Couldn't put Humpty Dumpty in his place again."*[8]

"That last line is much too long for the poetry," she added, almost out loud, forgetting that Humpty Dumpty would hear her.

8. This nursery rhyme, which again Dodgson takes over in one of its traditional forms, is very old and common in several languages. It is, as Iona and Peter Opie point out in *The Oxford Dictionary of Nursery Rhymes* (Oxford, 1951: pp. 213–16), a riddle, which may explain why Humpty Dumpty does not know or will not admit that he is an egg, and begins his conversation with Alice with a riddling contest.

The usual last line is: "Couldn't put Humpty together again." Alice's misremembering of the line not only gives it two additional syllables, as she notices, but also charitably protects Humpty from a graphic description of his fate.

"Don't stand chattering to yourself like that," Humpty Dumpty said, looking at her for the first time, "but tell me your name and your business."

"My *name* is Alice, but——"

"It's a stupid name enough!" Humpty Dumpty interrupted impatiently. "What does it mean?"

"*Must* a name mean something?" Alice asked doubtfully.

"Of course it must," Humpty Dumpty said with a short laugh: "*my* name means the shape I am[9]—and a good handsome shape it is, too. With a name like yours, you might be any shape, almost."

"Why do you sit out here all alone?" said Alice, not wishing to begin an argument.

"Why, because there's nobody with me!" cried Humpty Dumpty. "Did you think I didn't know the answer to *that*? Ask another."

"Don't you think you'd be safer down on the ground?" Alice went on, not with any idea of making another riddle, but simply in her good-natured anxiety for the queer creature. "That wall is so *very* narrow!"

"What tremendously easy riddles you ask!" Humpty Dumpty growled out. "Of course I don't think so! Why, if ever I *did* fall off—which there's no chance of—but if I did——" Here he pursed up his lips, and looked so solemn and grand that Alice could hardly help laughing. "If I *did* fall," he went on, "*the King has promised me*—ah, you may turn pale, if you like! You didn't think I was going to say that, did you? *The King has promised me—with his very own mouth*—to—to——"

"To send all his horses and all his men," Alice interrupted, rather unwisely.

"Now I declare that's too bad!" Humpty Dumpty cried, breaking into a sudden passion. "You've been listening at doors—and behind trees—and down chimneys—or you couldn't have known it!"

"I haven't indeed!" Alice said very gently. "It's in a book."

"Ah, well! They may write such things in a *book*," Humpty Dumpty said in a calmer tone. "That's what you call a History of England, that is. Now, take a good look at me! I'm one that has spoken to a King, *I* am: mayhap you'll never see such another: and, to show you I'm not proud, you may shake hands with me!" And he grinned almost from ear to ear, as he leant forwards (and as

9. Humpty Dumpty here advances the theory that names have something to do with the nature of the thing they name. Later, in his re-

marks about "glory," he picks up the other theory Dodgson plays with in this book, that words are wholly arbitrary signs.

nearly as possible fell off the wall in doing so) and offered Alice his hand. She watched him a little anxiously as she took it. "If he smiled much more the ends of his mouth might meet behind," she thought: "And then I don't know *what* would happen to his head! I'm afraid it would come off!"

"Yes, all his horses and all his men," Humpty Dumpty went on. "They'd pick me up again in a minute, *they* would! However, this conversation is going on a little too fast: let's go back to the last remark but one."

"I'm afraid I ca'n't quite remember it," Alice said, very politely.

"In that case we start afresh," said Humpty Dumpty, "and it's my turn to choose a subject——" ("He talks about it just as if it was a game!" thought Alice.) "So here's a question for you. How old did you say you were?"

Alice made a short calculation, and said "Seven years and six months."

"Wrong!" Humpty Dumpty exclaimed triumphantly. "You never said a word like it!"

"I thought you meant 'How old *are* you?'" Alice explained.

"If I'd meant that, I'd have said it," said Humpty Dumpty.

Alice didn't want to begin another argument, so she said nothing.

"Seven years and six months!" Humpty Dumpty repeated thoughtfully. "An uncomfortable sort of age. Now if you'd asked *my* advice, I'd have said 'Leave off at seven'——but it's too late now."

"I never ask advice about growing," Alice said indignantly.

"Too proud?" the other enquired.

Alice felt even more indignant at this suggestion. "I mean," she said, "that one ca'n't help growing older."

"*One* ca'n't, perhaps," said Humpty Dumpty; "but *two* can. With proper assistance, you might have left off at seven."

"What a beautiful belt you've got on!" Alice suddenly remarked. (They had had quite enough of the subject of age, she thought: and, if they really were to take turns in choosing subjects, it was *her* turn now.) "At least," she corrected herself on second thoughts, "a beautiful cravat, I should have said—no, a belt, I mean—I beg your pardon!" she added in dismay, for Humpty Dumpty looked thoroughly offended, and she began to wish she hadn't chosen that subject. "If only I knew," she thought to herself, "which was neck and which was waist!"

Evidently Humpty Dumpty was very angry, though he said nothing for a minute or two. When he *did* speak again, it was in a deep growl.

"It is a—*most*—*provoking*—thing," he said at last, "when a person doesn't know a cravat from a belt!"

"I know it's very ignorant of me," Alice said, in so humble a tone that Humpty Dumpty relented.

"It's a cravat, child, and a beautiful one, as you say. It's a present from the White King and Queen. There now!"

"It is really?" said Alice, quite pleased to find that she *had* chosen a good subject, after all.

"They gave it me," Humpty Dumpty continued thoughtfully, as he crossed one knee over the other and clasped his hands round it, "they gave it me—for an un-birthday present."

"I beg your pardon?" Alice said with a puzzled air.

"I'm not offended," said Humpty Dumpty.

"I mean, what *is* an un-birthday present?"

"A present given when it isn't your birthday, of course."

Alice considered a little. "I like birthday presents best," she said at last.

"You don't know what you're talking about!" cried Humpty Dumpty. "How many days are there in a year?"

"Three hundred and sixty-five," said Alice.

"And how many birthdays have you?"

"One."

"And if you take one from three hundred and sixty-five what remains?"

"Three hundred and sixty-four, of course."

Humpty Dumpty looked doubtful. "I'd rather see that done on paper," he said.

Alice couldn't help smiling as she took out her memorandum-book, and worked the sum for him:

$$365$$
$$\underline{1}$$
$$\underline{364}$$

Humpty Dumpty took the book, and looked at it carefully. "That *seems* to be done right——" he began.

"You're holding it upside down!" Alice interrupted.

"To be sure I was!" Humpty Dumpty said gaily, as she turned it round for him. "I thought it looked a little queer. As I was saying, that *seems* to be done right—though I haven't time to look it over thoroughly just now—and that shows that there are three hundred and sixty-four days when you might get un-birthday presents——"

"Certainly," said Alice.

"And only *one* for birthday presents, you know. There's glory for you!"

"I don't know what you mean by 'glory,'" Alice said.

Humpty Dumpty smiled contemptuously. "Of course you don't—till I tell you. I meant 'there's a nice knock-down argument for you!'"

"But 'glory' doesn't mean 'a nice knock-down argument,'" Alice objected.

"When I use a word," Humpty Dumpty said, in rather a scornful tone, "it means just what I choose it to mean—neither more nor less." "I'm king of language"

"The question is," said Alice, "whether you *can* make words mean so many different things."

"The question is," said Humpty Dumpty, "which is to be master——that's all."

Alice was too much puzzled to say anything; so after a minute Humpty Dumpty began again. "They've a temper, some of them—particularly verbs: they're the proudest—adjectives you can do anything with, but not verbs—however, *I* can manage the whole lot of them! Impenetrability! That's what *I* say!"

"Would you tell me, please," said Alice, "what that means?"

"Now you talk like a reasonable child," said Humpty Dumpty, looking very much pleased. "I meant by 'impenetrability' that we've had enough of that subject, and it would be just as well if you'd mention what you mean to do next, as I suppose you don't mean to stop here all the rest of your life."

"That's a great deal to make one word mean," Alice said in a thoughtful tone.

"When I make a word do a lot of work like that," said Humpty Dumpty, "I always pay it extra."

"Oh!" said Alice. She was too much puzzled to make any other remark.

"Ah, you should see 'em come round me of a Saturday night," Humpty Dumpty went on, wagging his head gravely from side to side, "for to get their wages, you know."

(Alice didn't venture to ask what he paid them with; and so you see I ca'n't tell *you*.)

"You seem very clever at explaining words, Sir," said Alice. "Would you kindly tell me the meaning of the poem called 'Jabberwocky'?"

"Let's hear it," said Humpty Dumpty. "I can explain all the poems that ever were invented—and a good many that haven't been invented just yet."

This sounded very hopeful, so Alice repeated the first verse:—

> " '*Twas brillig, and the slithy toves*
> *Did gyre and gimble in the wabe:*
> *All mimsy were the borogoves,*
> *And the mome raths outgrabe.*"

"That's enough to begin with," Humpty Dumpty interrupted: "there are plenty of hard words there. '*Brillig*' means four o'clock in the afternoon—the time when you begin *broiling* things for dinner."

"That'll do very well," said Alice: "and '*slithy*'?"

"Well, '*slithy*' means 'lithe and slimy.' 'Lithe' is the same as 'active.' You see it's like a pormanteau[1]—there are two meanings packed up into one word."

"I see it now," Alice remarked thoughtfully: "and what are '*toves*'?"

"Well '*toves*' are something like badgers—they're something like lizards—and they're something like corkscrews."

"They must be very curious-looking creatures."

"They are that," said Humpty Dumpty; "also they make their nests under sun-dials—also they live on cheese."

1. A portmanteau is a traveling bag that opens, like a book, into two equal compartments. For a further discussion by Dodgson of the portmanteau words of "Jabberwocky," see the preface to *The Hunting of the Snark*, on pp. 219–20 of this edition.

"And what's to '*gyre*' and to '*gimble*'?"

"To '*gyre*' is to go round and round like a gyroscope. To '*gimble*' is to make holes like a gimblet."

"And '*the wabe*' is the grass-plot round a sun-dial, I suppose?" said Alice, surprised at her own ingenuity.

"Of course it is. It's called '*wabe*', you know, because it goes a long way before it, and a long way behind it——"

"And a long way beyond it on each side," Alice added.

"Exactly so. Well then, '*mimsy*' is 'flimsy and miserable' (there's another portmanteau for you). And a '*borogove*' is a thin shabby-looking bird with its feathers sticking out all round—something like a live mop."

"And then '*mome raths*'?" said Alice. "I'm afraid I'm giving you a great deal of trouble."

"Well, a '*rath*' is a sort of green pig: but '*mome*' I'm not certain about. I think it's short for 'from home'—meaning that they'd lost their way, you know."

"And what does '*outgrabe*' mean?"

"Well, '*outgribing*' is something between bellowing and whistling, with a kind of sneeze in the middle: however, you'll hear it done, maybe—down in the wood yonder—and, when you've once heard it, you'll be *quite* content. Who's been repeating all that hard stuff to you?"

"I read it in a book," said Alice. "But I *had* some poetry repeated to me much easier than that, by—Tweedledee, I think it was."

"As to poetry, you know," said Humpty Dumpty, stretching out one of his great hands, "I can repeat poetry as well as other folk, if it comes to that——"

"Oh, it needn't come to that!" Alice hastily said, hoping to keep him from beginning.

"The piece I'm going to repeat," he went on without noticing her remark, "was written entirely for your amusement."

Alice felt that in that case she really *ought* to listen to it; so she sat down, and said "Thank you" rather sadly,

> "*In winter, when the fields are white,*
> *I sing this song for your delight——*

only I don't sing it," he added, as an explanation.

"I see you don't," said Alice.

"If you can *see* whether I'm singing or not, you've sharper eyes than most," Humpty Dumpty remarked severely. Alice was silent.

> "*In spring, when woods are getting green,*
> *I'll try and tell you what I mean:*"

"Thank you very much," said Alice.

> "*In summer, when the days are long,*
> *Perhaps you'll understand the song:*
>
> *In autumn, when the leaves are brown,*
> *Take pen and ink, and write it down.*"

"I will, if I can remember it so long," said Alice.

"You needn't go on making remarks like that," Humpty Dumpty said: "they're not sensible, and they put me out."

> "*I sent a message to the fish:*
> *I told them 'This is what I wish.'*

The little fishes of the sea,
They sent an answer back to me.

The little fishes' answer was
'We cannot do it, Sir, because——' "

"I'm afraid I don't quite understand," said Alice.
"It gets easier further on," Humpty Dumpty replied.

"I sent to them again to say
'It will be better to obey.'

The fishes answered, with a grin,
'Why, what a temper you are in!'

I told them once, I told them twice:
They would not listen to advice.

I took a kettle large and new,
Fit for the deed I had to do.

My heart went hop, my heart went thump:
I filled the kettle at the pump.

Then some one came to me and said
'The little fishes are in bed.'

I said to him, I said it plain,
'Then you must wake them up again.'

I said it very loud and clear:
I went and shouted in his ear."

Humpty Dumpty raised his voice almost to a scream as he repeated this verse, and Alice thought, with a shudder, "I wouldn't have been the messenger for *anything!*"

> *"But he was very stiff and proud:*
> *He said, 'You needn't shout so loud!'*
>
> *And he was very proud and stiff:*
> *He said 'I'd go and wake them, if——'*
>
> *I took a corkscrew from the shelf:*
> *I went to wake them up myself.*
>
> *And when I found the door was locked,*
> *I pulled and pushed and kicked and knocked.*
>
> *And when I found the door was shut,*
> *I tried to turn the handle, but——"*

There was a long pause.

"Is that all?" Alice timidly asked.

"That's all," said Humpty Dumpty. "Good-bye."

This was rather sudden, Alice thought: but, after such a *very* strong hint that she ought to be going, she felt that it would hardly be civil to stay. So she got up, and held out her hand. "Good-bye, till we meet again!" she said as cheerfully as she could.

"I shouldn't know you again if we *did* meet," Humpty Dumpty replied in a discontented tone, giving her one of his fingers to shake: "you're so exactly like other people."

"The *face* is what one goes by, generally," Alice remarked in a thoughtful tone.

"That's just what I complain of," said Humpty Dumpty. "Your face is the same as everybody has—the two eyes, so——" (marking their places in the air with his thumb) "nose in the middle, mouth under. It's always the same. Now if you had the two eyes on the same side of the nose, for instance—or the mouth at the top—that would be *some* help."

"It wouldn't look nice," Alice objected. But Humpty Dumpty only shut his eyes, and said "Wait till you've tried."

Alice waited a minute to see if he would speak again, but, as he never opened his eyes or took any further notice of her, she said "Good-bye!" once more, and, getting no answer to this, she quietly walked away: but she couldn't help saying to herself, as she went, "Of all the unsatisfactory——" (she repeated this aloud, as it was a great comfort to have such a long word to say) "of all the unsatisfactory people I *ever* met——" She never finished the sentence, for at this moment a heavy crash shook the forest from end to end.

H-D fell

Chapter VII

THE LION AND THE UNICORN

The next moment soldiers came running through the wood, at first in twos and threes, then ten or twenty together, and at last in such crowds that they seemed to fill the whole forest. Alice got behind a tree, for fear of being run over, and watched them go by.

She thought that in all her life she had never seen soldiers so uncertain on their feet: they were always tripping over something or other, and whenever one went down, several more always fell over him, so that the ground was soon covered with little heaps of men.

Then came the horses. Having four feet, these managed rather

better than the foot-soldiers; but even *they* stumbled now and then; and it seemed to be a regular rule that, whenever a horse stumbled, the rider fell off instantly. The confusion got worse every moment, and Alice was very glad to get out of the wood into an open place, where she found the White King seated on the ground, busily writing in his memorandum-book.

"I've sent them all!" the King cried in a tone of delight, on seeing Alice. "Did you happen to meet any soldiers, my dear, as you came through the wood?"

"Yes, I did," said Alice: "several thousand, I should think."

"Four thousand two hundred and seven, that's the exact number," the King said, referring to his book. "I couldn't send all the horses, you know, because two of them are wanted in the game.[2] And I haven't sent the two Messengers, either. They're both gone to the town. Just look along the road, and tell me if you can see either of them."

"I see nobody on the road," said Alice.

"I only wish I had such eyes," the King remarked in a fretful tone. "To be able to see Nobody! And at that distance too! Why, it's as much as I can do to see real people, by this light!"

All this was lost on Alice, who was still looking intently along the road, shading her eyes with one hand. "I see somebody now!" she exclaimed at last. "But he's coming very slowly—and what curious attitudes he goes into!" (For the Messenger kept skipping up and down, and wriggling like an eel, as he came along, with his great hands spread out like fans on each side.)

"Not at all," said the King. "He's an Anglo-Saxon Messenger—and those are Anglo-Saxon attitudes.[3] He only does them when he's happy. His name is Haigha." (He pronounced it so as to rhyme with 'mayor.')

"I love my love with an H," Alice couldn't help beginning, "because he is Happy. I hate him with an H, because he is Hideous. I fed him with—with—with Ham-sandwiches and Hay. His name is Haigha, and he lives——"

"He lives on the Hill," the King remarked simply, without the least idea that he was joining in the game, while Alice was still hesitating for the name of a town beginning with H. "The other Mes-

---

2. The White King holds back two horses (knights) for the chess game.

3. Harry Morgan Ayres, in *Carroll's Alice* (see Selected Bibliography), reproduces (pp. 70–71) some illustrations from a tenth-century Old English manuscript in which figures strike attitudes similar to those described in this passage. The burlesque of the seemingly rude and awkward line and composition of medieval tapestry and woodcuts was a common practice of mid-nineteenth-century comic draftsmen: Richard Doyle, for example, published a popular series in *Punch* in the 1850s in which he parodied the style of the Bayeux tapestry to depict the customs of nineteenth-century England.

senger's called Hatta. I must have *two*, you know—to come and go. One to come, and one to go."[4]

"I beg your pardon?" said Alice.

"It isn't respectable to beg," said the King.

"I only meant that I didn't understand," said Alice. "Why one to come and one to go?"

"Don't I tell you?" the King repeated impatiently. "I must have *two*—to fetch and carry. One to fetch, and one to carry."

At this moment the Messenger arrived: he was far too much out of breath to say a word, and could only wave his hands about, and make the most fearful faces at the poor King.

"This young lady loves you with an H," the King said, introducing Alice in the hope of turning off the Messenger's attention from himself—but it was of no use—the Anglo-Saxon attitudes only got more extraordinary every moment, while the great eyes rolled wildly from side to side.

"You alarm me!" said the King. "I feel faint—Give me a ham sandwich!"

4. In *Carroll's Alice*, Ayres also suggests (pp. 66–72) that the name of Haigha is derived from that of Daniel Henry Haigh, a nineteenth-century student of Anglo-Saxon language and literature; and that the name of Hatta may derive from a misconception by an early nineteenth-century author of a history of the Anglo-Saxons that the word *hatte* ("is called") in an early manuscript is a surname. *Hatte, Hatta,* and *Hatter*—Hatta turns out to be the Mad Hatter—is a conjunction of words and sounds that Dodgson may very well have exploited in a book so interested in words.

The White King's interruption in a sense saves Alice. She is playing a parlor game in which each player must complete a set of statements with words beginning with the same letter. If she fails to think of a town whose name begins with an H, she will fall out of the game.

On which the Messenger, to Alice's great amusement, opened a bag that hung round his neck, and handed a sandwich to the King, who devoured it greedily.

"Another sandwich!" said the King.

"There's nothing but hay left now," the Messenger said, peeping into the bag.

"Hay, then," the King murmured in a faint whisper.

Alice was glad to see that it revived him a good deal. "There's nothing like eating hay when you're faint," he remarked to her, as he munched away.

"I should think throwing cold water over you would be better," Alice suggested: "—or some sal-volatile."[5]

"I didn't say there was nothing *better*," the King replied. "I said there was nothing *like* it." Which Alice did not venture to deny.

"Who did you pass on the road?" the King went on, holding out his hand to the Messenger for some hay.

"Nobody," said the Messenger.

"Quite right," said the King: "this young lady saw him too. So of course Nobody walks slower than you."

"I do my best," the Messenger said in a sullen tone. "I'm sure nobody walks much faster than I do!"

"He ca'n't do that," said the King, "or else he'd have been here first. However, now you've got your breath, you may tell us what's happened in the town."

"I'll whisper it," said the Messenger, putting his hands to his mouth in the shape of a trumpet and stooping so as to get close to the King's ear. Alice was sorry for this, as she wanted to hear the news too. However, instead of whispering, he simply shouted, at the top of his voice, "They're at it again!"

"Do you call *that* a whisper?" cried the poor King, jumping up and shaking himself. "If you do such a thing again, I'll have you buttered! It went through and through my head like an earthquake!"

"It would have to be a very tiny earthquake!" thought Alice. "Who are at it again?" she ventured to ask.

"Why, the Lion and the Unicorn, of course," said the King.

"Fighting for the crown?"

"Yes, to be sure," said the King: "and the best of the joke is, that it's *my* crown all the while! Let's run and see them." And they trotted off, Alice repeating to herself, as she ran, the words of the old song:—

> *"The Lion and the Unicorn were fighting for the crown:*
> *The Lion beat the Unicorn all round the town.*

5. An ammonia solution used as smelling salts.

> *Some gave them white bread, some gave them brown:*
> *Some gave them plum-cake and drummed them out of town."*[6]

"Does——the one——that wins——get the crown?" she asked, as well as she could, for the run was putting her quite out of breath.

"Dear me, no!" said the King. "What an idea!"

"Would you——be good enough——" Alice panted out, after running a little further, "to stop a minute—just to get—one's breath again?"

"I'm *good* enough," the King said, "only I'm not *strong* enough. You see, a minute goes by so fearfully quick. You might as well try to stop a Bandersnatch!"

Alice had no more breath for talking; so they trotted on in silence, till they came into sight of a great crowd, in the middle of which the Lion and Unicorn were fighting. They were in such a cloud of dust, that at first Alice could not make out which was which; but she soon managed to distinguish the Unicorn by his horn.

They placed themselves close to where Hatta, the other Messenger, was standing watching the fight, with a cup of tea in one hand and a piece of bread-and-butter in the other.

"He's only just out of prison,[7] and he hadn't finished his tea when he was sent in," Haigha whispered to Alice: "and they only give them oyster-shells in there—so you see he's very hungry and thirsty. How are you, dear child?" he went on, putting his arm affectionately round Hatta's neck.

Hatta looked round and nodded, and went on with his bread-and-butter.

"Were you happy in prison, dear child?" said Haigha.

Hatta looked round once more, and this time a tear or two trickled down his cheek; but not a word would he say.

"Speak, ca'n't you!" Haigha cried impatiently. But Hatta only munched away, and drank some more tea.

"Speak, wo'n't you!" cried the King. "How are they getting on with the fight?"

---

6. Again, Dodgson takes over a traditional version of this nursery rhyme. The contest between the lion and the unicorn is traditional too, and in the rhyme, which was current in England in the eighteenth century, the contest may specifically refer to the placing of the unicorn from the Scottish coat of arms on the British coat of arms after the union of Scotland and England. Tenniel's unicorn looks a good deal like Disraeli, and his lion somewhat like William Ewart Gladstone, Disraeli's great parliamentary rival who succeeded him as prime minister in 1868. At the time he illustrated the Alice books, Tenniel was best known for his political cartoons in *Punch*. In his book on Tenniel's illustrations (see Selected Bibliography), Michael Hancher remarks many similarities between Tenniel's work in *Punch* and his illustrations of the Alice books.

7. Although the White Queen does not name Hatta in an earlier reference (p. 151) to one of the King's messengers, Tenniel has already pictured him as the Mad Hatter, who left the King of Hearts' court hurriedly at the end of *Alice's Adventures in Wonderland*, just before the Queen of Hearts ordered his execution.

Hatta made a desperate effort, and swallowed a large piece of bread-and-butter. "They're getting on very well," he said in a choking voice: "each of them has been down about eighty-seven times."

"Then I suppose they'll soon bring the white bread and the brown?" Alice ventured to remark.

"It's waiting for 'em now," said Hatta; "this is a bit of it as I'm eating."

There was a pause in the fight just then, and the Lion and the Unicorn sat down, panting, while the King called out "Ten minutes allowed for refreshments!" Haigha and Hatta set to work at once, carrying round trays of white and brown bread. Alice took a piece to taste, but it was *very* dry.

"I don't think they'll fight any more to-day," the King said to Hatta: "go and order the drums to begin." And Hatta went bounding away like a grasshopper

For a minute or two Alice stood silent, watching him. Suddenly she brightened up. "Look, look!" she cried, pointing eagerly. "There's the White Queen running across the country! She came flying out of the wood over yonder——How fast those Queens *can* run!"

"There's some enemy after her, no doubt," the King said, without even looking round. "That wood's full of them."

"But aren't you going to run and help her?" Alice asked, very much surprised at his taking it so quietly.

"No use, no use!" said the King. "She runs so fearfully quick. You might as well try to catch a Bandersnatch! But I'll make a memorandum about her, if you like——She's a dear good creature," he repeated softly to himself, as he opened his memorandum-book. "Do you spell 'creature' with a double 'e'?"

At this moment the Unicorn sauntered by them, with his hands in his pockets. "I had the best of it this time?" he said to the King, just glancing at him as he passed.

"A little—a little," the King replied, rather nervously. "You shouldn't have run him through with your horn, you know."

"It didn't hurt him," the Unicorn said carelessly, and he was going on, when his eye happened to fall upon Alice: he turned round instantly, and stood for some time looking at her with an air of the deepest disgust.

"What—is—this?" he said at last.

"This is a child!" Haigha replied eagerly, coming in front of Alice to introduce her, and spreading out both his hands towards her in an Anglo-Saxon attitude. "We only found it to-day. It's as large as life, and twice as natural!"

"I always thought they were fabulous monsters!" said the Unicorn. "Is it alive?"

"It can talk," said Haigha solemnly.

The Unicorn looked dreamily at Alice, and said "Talk, child."

Alice could not help her lips curling up into a smile as she began: "Do you know, I always thought Unicorns were fabulous monsters, too? I never saw one alive before!"

"Well, now that we *have* seen each other," said the Unicorn, "if you'll believe in me, I'll believe in you. Is that a bargain?"

"Yes, if you like," said Alice.

"Come, fetch out the plum-cake, old man!" the Unicorn went on, turning from her to the King. "None of your brown bread for me!"

"Certainly—certainly!" the King muttered, and beckoned to Haigha. "Open the bag!" he whispered. "Quick! Not that one— that's full of hay!"

Haigha took a large cake out of the bag, and gave it to Alice to hold, while he got out a dish and carving-knife. How they all came out of it Alice couldn't guess. It was just like a conjuring-trick, she thought.

The Lion had joined them while this was going on: he looked very tired and sleepy, and his eyes were half shut. "What's this!" he said, blinking lazily at Alice, and speaking in a deep hollow tone that sounded like the tolling of a great bell.

"Ah, what *is* it, now?" the Unicorn cried eagerly. "You'll never guess! *I* couldn't."

The Lion looked at Alice wearily. "Are you animal—or vegetable—or mineral?" he said, yawning at every other word.

"It's a fabulous monster!" the Unicorn cried out, before Alice could reply.

"Then hand round the plum-cake, Monster," the Lion said, lying down and putting his chin on his paws. "And sit down, both of you," (to the King and the Unicorn): "fair play with the cake, you know!"

The King was evidently very uncomfortable at having to sit down between the two great creatures; but there was no other place for him.

"What a fight we might have for the crown, *now*!" the Unicorn said, looking slyly up at the crown, which the poor King was nearly shaking off his head, he trembled so much.

"I should win easy," said the Lion.

"I'm not so sure of that," said the Unicorn.

"Why, I beat you all round the town, you chicken!" the Lion replied angrily, half getting up as he spoke.

Here the King interrupted, to prevent the quarrel going on: he was very nervous, and his voice quite quivered. "All round the town?" he said. "That's a good long way. Did you go by the old bridge, or the market-place? You get the best view by the old bridge."

"I'm sure I don't know," the Lion growled out as he lay down again. "There was too much dust to see anything. What a time the Monster is, cutting up that cake!"

Alice had seated herself on the bank of a little brook, with the great dish on her knees, and was sawing away diligently with the knife. "It's very provoking!" she said, in reply to the Lion (she was getting quite used to being called 'the Monster'). "I've cut several slices already, but they always join on again!"

"You don't know how to manage Looking-glass cakes," the Unicorn remarked. "Hand it round first, and cut it afterwards."

This sounded nonsense, but Alice very obediently got up, and carried the dish round, and the cake divided itself into three pieces as she did so. "*Now* cut it up," said the Lion, as she returned to her place with the empty dish.

"I say, this isn't fair!" cried the Unicorn, as Alice sat with the knife in her hand, very much puzzled how to begin. "The Monster has given the Lion twice as much as me!"

"She's kept none for herself, anyhow," said the Lion. "Do you like plum-cake, Monster?"

But before Alice could answer him, the drums began.

Where the noise came from, she couldn't make out: the air seemed full of it, and it rang through and through her head till she felt quite deafened. She started to her feet and sprang across the little brook in her terror, and had just time to see the Lion and the

         *   *   *   *   *

              *   *   *   *

         *   *   *   *   *

Unicorn rise to their feet, with angry looks at being interrupted in their feast, before she dropped to her knees, and put her hands over her ears, vainly trying to shut out the dreadful uproar.

"If *that* doesn't 'drum them out of town,' " she thought to herself, "nothing ever will!"

Chapter VIII

"IT'S MY OWN INVENTION"

After a while the noise seemed gradually to die away, till all was dead silence, and Alice lifted up her head in some alarm. There was no one to be seen, and her first thought was that she must have been dreaming about the Lion and the Unicorn and those queer Anglo-Saxon Messengers. However, there was the great dish still lying at her feet, on which she had tried to cut the plum-cake, 'So I wasn't dreaming, after all," she said to herself, "unless—unless we're all part of the same dream. Only I do hope it's *my* dream, and not the Red King's! I don't like belonging to another person's dream," she went on in a rather complaining tone: "I've a great mind to go and wake him, and see what happens!"

At this moment her thoughts were interrupted by a loud shouting of "Ahoy! Ahoy! Check!" and a Knight, dressed in crimson armour, came galloping down upon her, brandishing a great club. Just as he reached her, the horse stopped suddenly: "You're my prisoner!" the Knight cried, as he tumbled off his horse.

Startled as she was, Alice was more frightened for him than for herself at the moment, and watched him with some anxiety as he mounted again. As soon as he was comfortably in the saddle, he began once more "You're my——" but here another voice broke in "Ahoy! Ahoy! Check!" and Alice looked round in some surprise for the new enemy.

This time it was a White Knight. He drew up at Alice's side, and tumbled off his horse just as the Red Knight had done: then he got on again, and the two Knights sat and looked at each other for some time without speaking. Alice looked from one to the other in some bewilderment.

"She's *my* prisoner, you know!" the Red Knight said at last.

"Yes, but then *I* came and rescued her!" the White Knight replied.

"Well, we must fight for her, then," said the Red Knight, as he took up his helmet (which hung from the saddle, and was something the shape of a horse's head) and put it on.

"You will observe the Rules of Battle, of course?" the White Knight remarked, putting on his helmet too.

"I always do," said the Red Knight, and they began banging away at each other with such fury that Alice got behind a tree to be out of the way of the blows.

"I wonder, now, what the Rules of Battle are," she said to herself, as she watched the fight, timidly peeping out from her hiding-place. "One Rule seems to be, that if one Knight hits the other, he knocks him off his horse; and, if he misses, he tumbles off himself—and another Rule seems to be that they hold their clubs with their arms, as if they were Punch and Judy[8]——What a noise they make when they tumble! Just like a whole set of fire-irons falling into the fender! And how quiet the horses are! They let them get on and off them just as if they were tables!"

Another Rule of Battle, that Alice had not noticed, seemed to be that they always fell on their heads; and the battle ended with their both falling off in this way, side by side. When they got up again, they shook hands, and then the Red Knight mounted and galloped off.

"It was a glorious victory, wasn't it?" said the White Knight, as he came up panting.

8. The hand puppets in a Punch and Judy show necessarily hold their clubs (there is a good deal of beating in the Punch and Judy story) pressed between their bodies and their crossed arms, as in Tenniel's illustration.

"I don't know," Alice said doubtfully. "I don't want to be anybody's prisoner. I want to be a Queen."

"So you will, when you've crossed the next brook," said the White Knight. "I'll see you safe to the end of the wood—and then I must go back, you know. That's the end of my move."

"Thank you very much," said Alice. "May I help you off with your helmet?" It was evidently more than he could manage by himself: however, she managed to shake him out of it at last.

"Now one can breathe more easily," said the Knight, putting back his shaggy hair with both hands, and turning his gentle face and large mild eyes to Alice. She thought she had never seen such a strange-looking soldier in all her life.

He was dressed in tin armour, which seemed to fit him very badly, and he had a queer-shaped little deal box[9] fastened across his shoulders, upside-down, and with the lid hanging open. Alice looked at it with great curiosity.

"I see you're admiring my little box," the Knight said in a friendly tone. "It's my own invention[1]—to keep clothes and sandwiches in. You see I carry it upside-down, so that the rain ca'n't get in."

"But the things can get *out*," Alice gently remarked. "Do you know the lid's open?"

"I didn't know it," the Knight said, a shade of vexation passing over his face. "Then all the things must have fallen out! And the box is no use without them." He unfastened it as he spoke, and was just going to throw it into the bushes, when a sudden thought seemed to strike him, and he hung it carefully on a tree. "Can you guess why I did that?" he said to Alice.

Alice shook her head.

"In hopes some bees may make a nest in it—then I should get the honey."

"But you've got a bee-hive—or something like one—fastened to the saddle," said Alice.

"Yes, it's a very good bee-hive," the Knight said in a discontented tone, "one of the best kind. But not a single bee has come near it yet. And the other thing is a mouse-trap. I suppose the mice keep the bees out—or the bees keep the mice out, I don't know which."

9. A deal box is made of pine.
1. Many commentators have found Dodgson in the White Knight. Dodgson too was an inventory of such devices as a map of London cut in sections so that it could be carried as a book in a pocket, and the Nyctograph, an invention designed to assist writing in the dark. The association between Dodgson and the White Knight is both strengthened and made poignant by the White Knight's departure from Alice, who really leaves him to become a queen.

"I was wondering what the mouse-trap was for," said Alice. "It isn't very likely there would be any mice on the horse's back."

"Not very likely, perhaps," said the Knight; "but, if they *do* come, I don't choose to have them running all about."

"You see," he went on after a pause, "it's as well to be provided for *everything*. That's the reason the horse has all those anklets round his feet."

"But what are they for?" Alice asked in a tone of great curiosity.

"To guard against the bites of sharks," the Knight replied. "It's an invention of my own. And now help me on. I'll go with you to the end of the wood—What's that dish for?"

"It's meant for plum-cake," said Alice.

"We'd better take it with us," the Knight said. "It'll come in handy if we find any plum-cake. Help me to get it into this bag."

This took a long time to manage, though Alice held the bag open very carefully, because the Knight was so *very* awkward in putting in the dish: the first two or three times that he tried he fell in himself instead. "It's rather a tight fit, you see," he said, as they got it in at last; "there are so many candlesticks in the bag." And he hung it to the saddle, which was already loaded with bunches of carrots, and fire-irons, and many other things.

"I hope you've got your hair well fastened on?" he continued, as they set off.

"Only in the usual way," Alice said, smiling.

"That's hardly enough," he said, anxiously. "You see the wind is so *very* strong here. It's as strong as soup."

"Have you invented a plan for keeping the hair from being blown off?" Alice enquired.

"Not yet," said the Knight. "But I've got a plan for keeping it from *falling* off."

"I should like to hear it, very much."

"First you take an upright stick," said the Knight. "Then you make your hair creep up it, like a fruit-tree. Now the reason hair falls off is because it hangs *down*—things never fall *upwards*, you know. It's a plan of my own invention. You may try it if you like."

It didn't sound a comfortable plan, Alice thought, and for a few minutes she walked on in silence, puzzling over the idea, and every now and then stopping to help the poor Knight, who certainly was *not* a good rider.

Whenever the horse stopped (which it did very often), he fell off in front; and, whenever it went on again (which it generally did rather suddenly), he fell off behind. Otherwise he kept on pretty well, except that he had a habit of now and then falling off side-

ways; and, as he generally did this on the side on which Alice was walking, she soon found that it was the best plan not to walk *quite* close to the horse.

"I'm afraid you've not had much practice in riding," she ventured to say, as she was helping him up from his fifth tumble.

The Knight looked very much surprised, and a little offended at the remark. "What makes you say that?" he asked, as he scrambled back into the saddle, keeping hold of Alice's hair with one hand, to save himself from falling over on the other side.

"Because people don't fall off quite so often, when they've had much practice."

"I've had plenty of practice," the Knight said very gravely: "plenty of practice!"

Alice could think of nothing better to say than "Indeed?" but she said it as heartily as she could. They went on a little way in silence after this, the Knight with his eyes shut, muttering to himself, and Alice watching anxiously for the next tumble.

"The great art of riding," the Knight suddenly began in a loud voice, waving his right arm as he spoke, "is to keep——" Here the sentence ended as suddenly as it had begun, as the Knight fell heavily on the top of his head exactly in the path where Alice was walking. She was quite frightened this time, and said in an anxious tone, as she picked him up, "I hope no bones are broken?"

"None to speak of," the Knight said, as if he didn't mind breaking two or three of them. "The great art of riding, as I was saying is—to keep your balance properly. Like this, you know————"

He let go the bridle, and stretched out both his arms to show Alice what he meant, and this time he fell flat on his back, right under the horse's feet.

"Plenty of practice!" he went on repeating, all the time that Alice was getting him on his feet again. "Plenty of practice!"

"It's too ridiculous!" cried Alice, losing all her patience this time. "You ought to have a wooden horse on wheels, that you ought!"

"Does that kind go smoothly?" the Knight asked in a tone of great interest, clasping his arms round the horse's neck as he spoke, just in time to save himself from tumbling off again.

"Much more smoothly than a live horse," Alice said, with a little scream of laughter, in spite of all she could do to prevent it.

"I'll get one," the Knight said thoughtfully to himself. "One or two—several."

There was a short silence after this, and then the Knight went on again. "I'm a great hand at inventing things. Now, I daresay you noticed, the last time you picked me up, that I was looking rather thoughtful?"

"You *were* a little grave," said Alice.

"Well, just then I was inventing a new way of getting over a gate—would you like to hear it?"

"Very much indeed," Alice said politely.

"I'll tell you how I came to think of it," said the Knight. "You see, I said to myself 'The only difficulty is with the feet: the *head* is high enough already.' Now, first I put my head on the top of the gate—then the head's high enough—then I stand on my head—then the feet are high enough, you see—then I'm over, you see."

"Yes, I suppose you'd be over when that was done," Alice said thoughtfully: "but don't you think it would be rather hard?"

"I haven't tried it yet," the Knight said, gravely; "so I ca'n't tell for certain—but I'm afraid it *would* be a little hard."

He looked so vexed at the idea, that Alice changed the subject hastily. "What a curious helmet you've got!" she said cheerfully. "Is that your invention too?"

The Knight looked down proudly at his helmet, which hung from the saddle. "Yes," he said; "but I've invented a better one

than that—like a sugar-loaf.[2] When I used to wear it, if I fell off
the horse, it always touched the ground directly. So I had a *very*
little way to fall, you see—But there *was* the danger of falling *into*
it, to be sure. That happened to me once—and the worst of it was,
before I could get out again, the other White Knight came and put
it on. He thought it was his own helmet."

The Knight looked so solemn about it that Alice did not dare to
laugh. "I'm afraid you must have hurt him," she said in a trembling voice, "being on the top of his head."

"I had to kick him, of course," the Knight said, very seriously.
"And then he took the helmet off again—but it took hours and
hours to get me out. I was as fast as—as lightning, you know."

"But that's a different kind of fastness," Alice objected.

The Knight shook his head. "It was all kinds of fastness with
me, I can assure you!" he said. He raised his hands in some excitement as he said this, and instantly rolled out of the saddle, and fell
headlong into a deep ditch.

Alice ran to the side of the ditch to look for him. She was rather
startled by the fall, as for some time he had kept on very well, and
she was afraid that he really *was* hurt this time. However, though
she could see nothing but the soles of his feet, she was much
relieved to hear that he was talking on in his usual tone. "All kinds
of fastness," he repeated: "but it was careless of him to put
another man's helmet on—with the man in it, too."

"How *can* you go on talking so quietly, head downwards?" Alice

2. A sugar-loaf is usually cone-shaped. Hats called "sugar-loaf hats" were common in the sixteenth
and seventeeh centuries.

asked, as she dragged him out by the feet, and laid him in a heap on the bank.

The Knight looked surprised at the question. "What does it matter where my body happens to be?" he said. "My mind goes on working all the same. In fact, the more head-downwards I am, the more I keep inventing new things."

"Now the cleverest thing of the sort that I ever did," he went on after a pause, "was inventing a new pudding during the meat-course."

"In time to have it cooked for the next course?" said Alice. "Well, that *was* quick work, certainly!"

"Well, not the *next* course," the Knight said in slow thoughtful tone: "no, certainly not the next *course*."

"Then it would have to be the next day. I suppose you wouldn't have two pudding-courses in one dinner?"

"Well, not the *next* day," the Knight repeated as before: "not the next *day*. In fact," he went on, holding his head down, and his voice getting lower and lower, "I don't believe that pudding ever *was* cooked! In fact, I don't believe that pudding ever *will* be cooked! And yet it was a very clever pudding to invent."

"What did you mean it to be made of?" Alice asked, hoping to cheer him up, for the poor Knight seemed quite low-spirited about it.

"It began with blotting-paper," the Knight answered with a groan.

"That wouldn't be very nice, I'm afraid——"

"Not very nice *alone*," he interrupted, quite eagerly: "but you've no idea what a difference it makes, mixing it with other things—such as gunpowder and sealing-wax. And here I must leave you." They had just come to the end of the wood.

Alice could only look puzzled: she was thinking of the pudding.

"You are sad," the Knight said in an anxious tone: "let me sing you a song to comfort you."

"Is it very long?" Alice asked, for she had heard a good deal of poetry that day.

"It's long," said the Knight, "but it's very, *very* beautiful. Everybody that hears me sing it—either it brings the *tears* into their eyes, or else——"

"Or else what?" said Alice, for the Knight had made a sudden pause.

"Or else it doesn't, you know. The name of the song is called '*Haddocks' Eyes*.'"

"Oh, that's the name of the song, is it?" Alice said, trying to feel interested.

"No, you don't understand," the Knight said, looking a little vexed. "That's what the name *is called*. The name really *is* 'The Aged Aged Man.' "

"Then I ought to have said 'That's what the *song* is called'?" Alice corrected herself.

"No, you oughtn't: that's quite another thing! The *song* is called '*Ways and Means*': but that's only what it's *called*, you know!"

"Well, what *is* the song, then?" said Alice, who was by this time completely bewildered.

"I was coming to that," the Knight said. "The song really *is* '*A-sitting On A Gate*': and the tune's my own invention."

So saying, he stopped his horse and let the reins fall on its neck: then, slowly beating time with one hand, and with a faint smile lighting up his gentle foolish face, as if he enjoyed the music of his song, he began.

Of all the strange things that Alice saw in her journey Through The Looking-Glass, this was the one that she always remembered most clearly. Years afterwards she could bring the whole scene back again, as if it had been only yesterday—the mild blue eyes and kindly smile of the Knight—the setting sun gleaming through his hair, and shining on his armour in a blaze of light that quite dazzled her—the horse quietly moving about, with the reins hanging loose on his neck, cropping the grass at her feet—and the black shadows of the forest behind—all this she took in like a picture, as, with one hand shading her eyes, she leant against a tree, watching the strange pair, and listening, in a half-dream, to the melancholy music of the song.

"But the tune *isn't* his own invention," she said to herself: "it's '*I give thee all, I can no more*.' "[3] She stood and listened very attentively, but no tears came into her eyes.

> "*I'll tell thee everything I can:*
>   *There's little to relate.*
> *I saw an aged aged man,*
>   *A-sitting on a gate.*
> '*Who are you, aged man?*' *I said.*
>   '*And how is it you live?*'
> *And his answer trickled through my head,*
>   *Like water through a sieve.*

---

3. "I give thee all—I can no more" is the first line of a song entitled "My Heart and Lute," by Thomas Moore. The White Knight's song retains, until the last lines of the poem, the meter and rhyme scheme of Moore's song. But Dodgson's poem itself is a burlesque of Wordsworth's "Resolution and Independence," in which an inexplicably saddened speaker is heartened by a colloquy with an aged but resolute leech-gatherer. See pp. 255–56 of this edition for an earlier version of this parody.

He said 'I look for butterflies
   That sleep among the wheat:
I make them into mutton-pies,
   And sell them in the street.
I sell them unto men,' he said,
   'Who sail on stormy seas;
And that's the way I get my bread—
   A trifle, if you please.'

But I was thinking of a plan
   To dye one's whiskers green,
And always use so large a fan
   That they could not be seen.
So, having no reply to give
   To what the old man said,
I cried 'Come, tell me how you live!'
   And thumped him on the head.

His accents mild took up the tale:
   He said 'I go my ways,
And when I find a mountain-rill,
   I set it in a blaze;
And thence they make a stuff they call
   Rowland's Macassar-Oil—[4]
Yet twopence-halfpenny is all
   They give me for my toil.'

But I was thinking of a way
   To feed oneself on batter,
And so go on from day to day
   Getting a little fatter.
I shook him well from side to side,
   Until his face was blue:
'Come, tell me how you live,' I cried,
   'And what it is you do!'

He said 'I hunt for haddocks' eyes
   Among the heather bright,
And work them into waistcoat-buttons
   In the silent night.
And these I do not sell for gold
   Or coin of silvery shine,
But for a copper halfpenny,
   And that will purchase nine.

'I sometimes dig for buttered rolls,
   Or set limed twigs for crabs:[5]

4. Rowland's Macassar-Oil was a widely advertised hair dressing.

5. Lime twigs are branches covered with bird lime, used to catch birds.

I sometimes search for grassy knolls
    For wheels of Hansom-cabs.[6]
And that's the way' (he gave a wink)
    'By which I get my wealth—
And very gladly will I drink
    Your Honour's noble health.'

I heard him then, for I had just
    Completed my design
To keep the Menai bridge[7] from rust
    By boiling it in wine.
I thanked him much for telling me
    The way he got his wealth,
But chiefly for his wish that he
    Might drink my noble health.

And now, if e'er by chance I put
    My fingers into glue,
Or madly squeeze a right-hand foot
    Into a left-hand shoe,
Or if I drop upon my toe
    A very heavy weight,
I weep, for it reminds me so
Of that old man I used to know—

6. A hansom-cab is a two-wheeled carriage; it became very common as a hired conveyance, especially in London, in the latter half of the nineteenth century.
7. The Menai Bridge is a suspension bridge in Wales.

> *Whose look was mild, whose speech was slow,*
> *Whose hair was whiter than the snow,*
> *Whose face was very like a crow,*
> *With eyes, like cinders, all aglow,*
> *Who seemed distracted with his woe,*
> *Who rocked his body to and fro,*
> *And muttered mumblingly and low,*
> *As if his mouth were full of dough,*
> *Who snorted like a buffalo——*
> *That summer evening long ago,*
>   *A-sitting on a gate."*

As the Knight sang the last words of the ballad, he gathered up the reins, and turned his horse's head along the road by which they had come. "You've only a few yards to go," he said, "down the hill and over that little brook, and then you'll be a Queen——But you'll stay and see me off first?" he added as Alice turned with an eager look in the direction to which he pointed. "I sha'n't be long. You'll wait and wave your handkerchief when I get to that turn in the road? I think it'll encourage me, you see."

"Of course I'll wait," said Alice: "and thank you very much for coming so far—and for the song—I liked it very much."

"I hope so," the Knight said doubtfully: "but you didn't cry so much as I thought you would."

So they shook hands, and then the Knight rode slowly away into the forest. "It wo'n't take long to see him *off,* I expect," Alice said to herself, as she stood watching him. "There he goes! Right on his head as usual! However, he gets on again pretty easily—that comes of having so many things hung round the horse——" So she went on talking to herself, as she watched the horse walking leisurely along the road, and the Knight tumbling off, first on one side and then on the other. After the fourth or fifth tumble he reached the turn, and then she waved her handkerchief to him, and waited till he was out of sight.

"I hope it encouraged him," she said, as she turned to run down the hill: "and now for the last brook, and to be a Queen! How grand it sounds!" A very few steps brought her to the edge of the brook[8] "The Eighth Square at last!" she cried as she bounded

*   *   *   *   *
   *   *   *   *
*   *   *   *   *

8. Dodgson wrote an episode about Alice and "The Wasp in a Wig" and placed it at this point in Alice's journey. He deleted the episode after the book had been set in galley proofs. See pp. 210–14 of this edition.

across, and threw herself down to rest on a lawn as soft as moss, with little flowerbeds dotted about it here and there. "Oh, how glad I am to get here! And what *is* this on my head?" she exclaimed in a tone of dismay, as she put her hands up to something very heavy, that fitted tight round her head.

"But how *can* it have got there without my knowing it?" she said to herself, as she lifted it off, and set it on her lap to make out what it could possibly be.

It was a golden crown.

Chapter IX

QUEEN ALICE

"Well, this *is* grand!" said Alice. "I never expected I should be a Queen so soon—and I'll tell you what it is, your Majesty," she went on, in a severe tone (she was always rather fond of scolding herself), "it'll never do for you to be lolling about on the grass like that! Queens have to be dignified, you know!"

So she got up and walked about—rather stiffly just at first, as she was afraid that the crown might come off: but she comforted herself with the thought that there was nobody to see her, "and if I really am a Queen," she said as she sat down again, "I shall be able to manage it quite well in time."

Everything was happening so oddly that she didn't feel a bit surprised at finding the Red Queen and the White Queen sitting close to her, one on each side: she would have liked very much to ask them how they came there, but she feared it would not be quite civil. However, there would be no harm, she thought, in asking if the game was over. "Please, would you tell me——" she began, looking timidly at the Red Queen.

"Speak when you're spoken to!" the Queen sharply interrupted her.

"But if everybody obeyed that rule," said Alice, who was always ready for a little argument, "and if you only spoke when you were spoken to, and the other person always waited for *you* to begin, you see nobody would ever say anything, so that——"

"Ridiculous!" cried the Queen. "Why, don't you see, child——" here she broke off with a frown, and, after thinking for a minute, suddenly changed the subject of the conversation. "What do you mean by 'If you really are a Queen'? What right have you to call yourself so? You ca'n't be a Queen, you know, till you've passed the proper examination. And the sooner we begin it, the better."

"I only said 'if'!" poor Alice pleaded in a piteous tone.

The two Queens looked at each other, and the Red Queen remarked, with a little shudder, "She *says* she only said 'if'——"

"But she said a great deal more than that!" the White Queen moaned, wringing her hands. "Oh, ever so much more than that!"

"So you did, you know," the Red Queen said to Alice. "Always speak the truth—think before you speak—and write it down afterwards."

"I'm sure I didn't mean——" Alice was beginning, but the Red Queen interrupted her impatiently.

"That's just what I complain of! You *should* have meant! What do you suppose is the use of a child without any meaning? Even a joke should have some meaning—and a child's more important than a joke, I hope. You couldn't deny that, even if you tried with both hands."

"I don't deny things with my *hands*," Alice objected.

"Nobody said you did," said the Red Queen. "I said you couldn't if you tried."

"She's in that state of mind," said the White Queen, "that she wants to deny *something*—only she doesn't know what to deny!"

"A nasty, vicious temper," the Red Queen remarked; and then there was an uncomfortable silence for a minute or two.

The Red Queen broke the silence by saying, to the White Queen, "I invite you to Alice's dinner-party this afternoon."

The White Queen smiled feebly, and said "And I invite *you*."

"I didn't know I was to have a party at all," said Alice; "but, if there *is* to be one, I think *I* ought to invite the guests."

"We gave you the opportunity of doing it," the Red Queen remarked: "but I daresay you've not had many lessons in manners yet?"

"Manners are not taught in lessons," said Alice. "Lessons teach you to do sums, and things of that sort."

"Can you do Addition?" the White Queen asked. "What's one and one and one and one and one and one and one and one and one and one?"

"I don't know," said Alice. "I lost count."

"She ca'n't do Addition," the Red Queen interrupted. "Can you do Subtraction? Take nine from eight."

"Nine from eight I ca'n't, you know," Alice replied very readily: "but——"

"She ca'n't do Subtraction," said the White Queen. "Can you do Division? Divide a loaf by a knife—what's the answer to *that*?"

"I suppose——" Alice was beginning, but the Red Queen answered for her. "Bread-and-butter, of course. Try another Subtraction sum. Take a bone from a dog: what remains?"

Alice considered. "The bone wouldn't remain, of course, if I took it—and the dog wouldn't remain: it would come to bite me—and I'm sure *I* shouldn't remain!"

"Then you think nothing would remain?" said the Red Queen.

"I think that's the answer."

"Wrong, as usual," said the Red Queen: "the dog's temper would remain."

"But I don't see how——"

"Why, look here!" the Red Queen cried. "The dog would lose its temper, wouldn't it?"

"Perhaps it would," Alice replied cautiously.

"Then if the dog went away, its temper would remain!" the Queen exclaimed triumphantly.

Alice said, as gravely as she could, "They might go different ways." But she couldn't help thinking to herself "What dreadful nonsense we *are* talking!"

"She ca'n't do sums a *bit*!" the Queens said together, with great emphasis.

"Can *you* do sums?" Alice said, turning suddenly on the White Queen, for she didn't like being found fault with so much.

The Queen gasped and shut her eyes. "I can do Addition," she said, "if you give me time—but I ca'n't do Subtraction under *any* circumstances!"

"Of course you know your ABC?" said the Red Queen.

"To be sure I do," said Alice.

"So do I," the White Queen whispered: "we'll often say it over together, dear. And I'll tell you a secret—I can read words of one letter! Isn't *that* grand? However, don't be discouraged. You'll come to it in time."

Here the Red Queen began again. "Can you answer useful questions?" she said. "How is bread made?"

"I know *that*!" Alice cried eagerly. "You take some flour——"

"Where do you pick the flower?" the White Queen asked: "In a garden or in the hedges?"

"Well, it isn't *picked* at all," Alice explained: "it's *ground*——"

"How many acres of ground?" said the White Queen. "You mustn't leave out so many things."

"Fan her head!" the Red Queen anxiously interrupted. "She'll be feverish after so much thinking." So they set to work and fanned her with bunches of leaves, till she had to beg them to leave off, it blew her hair about so.

"She's all right again now," said the Red Queen. "Do you know Languages? What's the French for fiddle-de-dee?"

"Fiddle-de-dee's not English," Alice replied gravely.

"Who ever said it was?" said the Red Queen.

Alice thought she saw a way out of the difficulty, this time. "If you'll tell me what language 'fiddle-de-dee' is, I'll tell you the French for it!" she exclaimed triumphantly.

But the Red Queen drew herself up rather stiffly, and said "Queens never make bargains."

"I wish Queens never asked questions," Alice thought to herself.

"Don't let us quarrel," the White Queen said in an anxious tone. "What is the cause of lightning?"

"The cause of lightning," Alice said very decidedly, for she felt quite certain about this, "is the thunder—no, no!" she hastily corrected herself. "I meant the other way."

"It's too late to correct it," said the Red Queen: "when you've once said a thing, that fixes it, and you must take the consequences."

"Which reminds me——" the White Queen said, looking down and nervously clasping and unclasping her hands, "we had *such* a thunderstorm last Tuesday—I mean one of the last set of Tuesdays, you know."

Alice was puzzled. "In *our* country," she remarked, "there's only one day at a time."

The Red Queen said "That's a poor thin way of doing things. Now *here*, we mostly have days and nights two or three at a time, and sometimes in the winter we take as many as five nights together—for warmth, you know."

"Are five nights warmer than one night, then?" Alice ventured to ask.

"Five times as warm, of course."

"But they should be five times as *cold*, by the same rule——"

"Just so!" cried the Red Queen. "Five times as warm, *and* five times as cold—just as I'm five times as rich as you are, *and* five times as clever!"

Alice sighed and gave it up. "It's exactly like the riddle with no answer!" she thought.

"Humpty Dumpty saw it too," the White Queen went on in a low voice, more as if she were talking to herself. "He came to the door with a corkscrew in his hand——"

"What did he want?" said the Red Queen.

"He said he *would* come in," the White Queen went on, "because he was looking for a hippopotamus. Now, as it happened, there wasn't such a thing in the house, that morning."

"Is there generally?" Alice asked in an astonished tone.

"Well, only on Thursdays," said the Queen.

"I know what he came for," said Alice: "he wanted to punish the fish, because——"[9]

Here the White Queen began again. "It was *such* a thunderstorm, you ca'n't think!" ("She *never* could, you know," said the Red Queen.) "And part of the roof came off, and ever so much thunder got in—and it went rolling round the room in great lumps—and knocking over the tables and things—till I was so frightened, I couldn't remember my own name!"

Alice thought to herself "I never should *try* to remember my name in the middle of an accident! Where would be the use of it?" but she did not say this aloud, for fear of hurting the poor Queen's feelings.

"Your Majesty must excuse her," the Red Queen said to Alice, taking one of the White Queen's hands in her own, and gently stroking it: "she means well, but she ca'n't help saying foolish things, as a general rule."

The White Queen looked timidly at Alice, who felt she *ought* to say something kind, but really couldn't think of anything at the moment.

"She never was really well brought up," the Red Queen went on: "but it's amazing how good-tempered she is! Pat her on the head, and see how pleased she'll be!" But this was more than Alice had courage to do.

"A little kindness—and putting her hair in papers[1]—would do wonders with her——"

The White Queen gave a deep sigh, and laid her head on Alice's shoulder. "I *am* so sleepy!" she moaned.

"She's tired, poor thing!" said the Red Queen. "Smoothe[2] her hair—lend her your nightcap—and sing her a soothing lullaby."

"I haven't got a nightcap with me," said Alice, as she tried to

9. See Humpty Dumpty's song on pp. 166–68 of this edition.
1. Curlers.
2. "Smoothe" for "Smooth" is the second (and last) of the corrections by Dodgson intended for an 1897 edition of the two Alice books that were not included in the edition. See Stanley Goodman, "Lewis Carroll's Final Corrections to 'Alice,' " *Times Literary Supplement*, May 2, 1958, p. 248.

obey the first direction: "and I don't know any soothing lullabies."

"I must do it myself, then," said the Red Queen, and she began:—

> "*Hush-a-by lady, in Alice's lap!*
> *Till the feast's ready, we've time for a nap.*
> *When the feast's over, we'll go to the ball—*
> *Red Queen, and White Queen, and Alice, and all!*[3]

"And now you know the words," she added, as she put her head down on Alice's other shoulder, "just sing it through to *me*. I'm getting sleepy, too." In another moment both Queens were fast asleep, and snoring loud.

"What *am* I to do?" exclaimed Alice, looking about in great perplexity, as first one round head, and then the other, rolled down from her shoulder, and lay like a heavy lump in her lap. "I don't think it *ever* happened before, that any one had to take care of two Queens asleep at once! No, not in all the History of England—it couldn't, you know, because there never was more than one Queen at a time. Do wake up, you heavy things!" she went on in an impatient tone; but there was no answer but a gentle snoring.

The snoring got more distinct every minute, and sounded more like a tune: at last she could even make out words, and she listened so eagerly that, when the two great heads suddenly vanished from her lap, she hardly missed them.

---

3. This song is the only parody of a nursery rhyme in the Alice books. The rhyme, "Hush-a-by baby" or "Rock-a-by baby," was well known by the eighteenth century.

She was standing before an arched doorway, over which were the words "QUEEN ALICE" in large letters, and on each side of the arch there was a bell-handle; one was marked "Visitors' Bell," and the other "Servants' Bell."[4]

"I'll wait till the song's over," thought Alice, "and then I'll ring the—the—*which* bell must I ring?" she went on, very much puzzled by the names. "I'm not a visitor, and I'm not a servant. There *ought* to be one marked 'Queen,' you know——"

Just then the door opened a little way, and a creature with a long beak put its head out for a moment and said "No admittance till the week after next!" and shut the door again with a bang.

Alice knocked and rang in vain for a long time; but at last a very old Frog, who was sitting under a tree, got up and hobbled slowly

4. A. L. Taylor in *The White Knight* (see Selected Bibliography) speculates that Alice has come full circle to a point where several sets of opposites meet: front door ("Visitors' Bell") and back door ("Servants' Bell"), the two ends of the chess board, beginning and end (pp. 106–7). This scene is the last of the transformation scenes in the book, except for the final dissolving scene.

towards her: he was dressed in bright yellow, and had enormous boots on.

"What is it, now?" the Frog said in a deep hoarse whisper.

Alice turned round, ready to find fault with anybody. "Where's the servant whose business it is to answer the door?" she began angrily.

"Which door?" said the Frog.

Alice almost stamped with irritation at the slow drawl in which he spoke. "*This* door, of course!"

The Frog looked at the door with his large dull eyes for a minute: then he went nearer and rubbed it with his thumb, as if he were trying whether the paint would come off: then he looked at Alice.

"To answer the door?" he said. "What's it been asking of?" He was so hoarse that Alice could scarcely hear him.

"I don't know what you mean," she said.

"I speaks English, doesn't I?" the Frog went on. "Or are you deaf? What did it ask you?"

"Nothing!" Alice said impatiently. "I've been knocking at it!"

"Shouldn't do that—shouldn't do that——" the Frog muttered. "Wexes it, you know." Then he went up and gave the door a kick with one of his great feet. "You let *it* alone," he panted out, as he hobbled back to his tree, "and it'll let *you* alone, you know."

At this moment the door was flung open, and a shrill voice was heard singing:—

"To the Looking-Glass world it was Alice that said
'I've a sceptre in hand, I've a crown on my head.
Let the Looking-Glass creatures, whatever they be,
Come and dine with the Red Queen, the White Queen, and me!' "

And hundreds of voices joined in the chorus:—

"Then fill up the glasses as quick as you can,
And sprinkle the table with buttons and bran:
Put cats in the coffee, and mice in the tea—
And welcome Queen Alice with thirty-times-three!"

Then followed a confused noise of cheering, and Alice thought to herself "Thirty times three makes ninety. I wonder if any one's counting?" In a minute there was silence again, and the same shrill voice sang another verse:—

" 'O Looking-Glass creatures,' quoth Alice, 'draw near!
'Tis an honour to see me, a favour to hear:
'Tis a privilege high to have dinner and tea
Along with the Red Queen, the White Queen, and me!' "

Then came the chorus again:—

> *"Then fill up the glasses with treacle and ink,*
> *Or anything else that is pleasant to drink:*
> *Mix sand with the cider, and wool with the wine—*
> *And welcome Queen Alice with ninety-times-nine!"*[5]

"Ninety times nine!" Alice repeated in despair. "Oh, that'll never be done! I'd better go in at once———" and in she went, and there was a dead silence the moment she appeared.

Alice glanced nervously along the table, as she walked up the large hall, and noticed that there were about fifty guests, of all kinds: some were animals, some birds, and there were even a few flowers among them. "I'm glad they've come without waiting to be asked," she thought: "I should never have known who were the right people to invite!"

There were three chairs at the head of the table: the Red and White Queens had already taken two of them, but the middle one was empty. Alice sat down in it, rather uncomfortable at the silence, and longing for some one to speak.

At last the Red Queen began. "You've missed the soup and fish," she said. "Put on the joint!" And the waiters set a leg of mutton before Alice, who looked at it rather anxiously, as she had never had to carve a joint before.

"You look a little shy: let me introduce you to that leg of mutton," said the Red Queen. "Alice———Mutton: Mutton—Alice." The leg of mutton got up in the dish and made a little bow to Alice; and Alice returned the bow, not knowing whether to be frightened or amused.

"May I give you a slice?" she said, taking up the knife and fork, and looking from one Queen to the other.

"Certainly not," the Red Queen said, very decidedly: "it isn't etiquette to cut[6] any one you've been introduced to. Remove the joint!" And the waiters carried it off, and brought a large plum-pudding in its place.

"I wo'n't be introduced to the pudding, please," Alice said rather hastily, "or we shall get no dinner at all. May I give you some?"

But the Red Queen looked sulky, and growled "Pudding———Alice: Alice———Pudding. Remove the pudding!", and the waiters took it away so quickly that Alice couldn't return its bow.

However, she didn't see why the Red Queen should be the only one to give orders; so, as an experiment, she called out "Waiter!

---

5. The song that greets Alice is a parody of "Bonny Dundee," by Sir Walter Scott, first published in 1830. Scott's poem begins, "To the Lords of Convention 'twas Claver'se who spoke"; and its chorus begins with the line "Come fill my cup, come fill my can."

6. To "cut" someone is to fail to acknowledge his or her greeting.

Bring back the pudding!" and there it was again in a moment, like
a conjuring-trick. It was so large that she couldn't help feeling a
little shy with it, as she had been with the mutton; however, she
conquered her shyness by a great effort, and cut a slice and handed
it to the Red Queen.

"What impertinence!" said the Pudding. "I wonder how you'd
like it, if I were to cut a slice out of *you*, you creature!"

It spoke in a thick, suety sort of voice, and Alice hadn't a word
to say in reply: she could only sit and look at it and gasp.

"Make a remark," said the Red Queen: "it's ridiculous to leave
all the conversation to the pudding!"

"Do you know, I've had such a quantity of poetry repeated to
me to-day," Alice began, a little frightened at finding that, the
moment she opened her lips, there was dead silence, and all eyes
were fixed upon her; "and it's a very curious thing, I think—every
poem was about fishes in some way. Do you know why they're so
fond of fishes, all about here?"

She spoke to the Red Queen, whose answer was a little wide of
the mark. "As to fishes," she said, very slowly and solemnly, putting her mouth close to Alice's ear, "her White Majesty knows a
lovely riddle—all in poetry—all about fishes. Shall she repeat it?"

"Her Red Majesty's very kind to mention it," the White Queen
murmured into Alice's other ear, in a voice like the cooing of a
pigeon. "It would be *such* a treat! May I?"

"Please do," Alice said very politely.

The White Queen laughed with delight, and stroked Alice's cheek. Then she began:

> " 'First, the fish must be caught.'
> *That is easy: a baby, I think, could have caught it.*
> *'Next, the fish must be bought.'*
> *That is easy: a penny, I think, could have bought it.*
>
> *'Now cook me the fish!'*
> *That is easy, and will not take more than a minute.*
> *'Let it lie in a dish!'*
> *That is easy, because it already is in it.*
>
> *'Bring it here! Let me sup!'*
> *It is easy to set such a dish on the table.*
> *'Take the dish-cover up!'*
> *Ah, that is so hard that I fear I'm unable!*
>
> *For it holds it like glue—*
> *Holds the lid to the dish, while it lies in the middle:*
> *Which is easiest to do,*
> *Un-dish-cover the fish, or dishcover the riddle?"*[7]

"Take a minute to think about it, and then guess," said the Red Queen. "Meanwhile, we'll drink your health—Queen Alice's health!" she screamed at the top of her voice, and all the guests began drinking it directly, and very queerly they managed it: some of them put their glasses upon their heads like extinguishers, and drank all that trickled down their faces—others upset the decanters, and drank the wine as it ran off the edges of the table—and three of them (who looked like kangaroos) scrambled into the dish of roast mutton, and began eagerly lapping up the gravy, "just like pigs in a trough!" thought Alice.

"You ought to return thanks in a neat speech," the Red Queen said, frowning at Alice as she spoke.

"We must support you, you know," the White Queen whispered, as Alice got up to do it, very obediently, but a little frightened.

"Thank you very much," she whispered in reply, "but I can do quite well without."

"That wouldn't be at all the thing," the Red Queen said very decidedly: so Alice tried to submit to it with good grace.

("And they *did* push so!" she said afterwards, when she was telling her sister the history of her feast. "You would have thought they wanted to squeeze me flat!")

In fact it was rather difficult for her to keep in her place while

---

7. Dodgson apparently did not provide an answer to this riddle, as he later did to the Mad Hatter's riddle in *Alice's Adventures in Won-derland*. Martin Gardner in *The Annotated Alice* (see Selected Bibliography) suggests that the answer is: an oyster (p. 333).

she made her speech: the two Queens pushed her so, one on each side, that they nearly lifted her up into the air. "I rise to return thanks——" Alice began: and she really *did* rise as she spoke, several inches; but she got hold of the edge of the table, and managed to pull herself down again.

"Take care of yourself!" screamed the White Queen, seizing Alice's hair with both her hands. "Something's going to happen!"

And then (as Alice afterwards described it) all sorts of things happened in a moment. The candles all grew up to the ceiling, looking something like a bed of rushes with fireworks at the top. As to the bottles, they each took a pair of plates, which they hastily fitted on as wings, and so, with forks for legs, went fluttering about in all directions: "and very like birds they look," Alice thought to herself, as well as she could in the dreadful confusion that was beginning.

At this moment she heard a hoarse laugh at her side, and turned to see what was the matter with the White Queen; but, instead of the Queen, there was the leg of mutton sitting in the chair. "Here I am!" cried a voice from the soup-tureen, and Alice turned again, just in time to see the Queen's broad good-natured face grinning at her for a moment over the edge of the tureen, before she disappeared into the soup.

There was not a moment to be lost. Already several of the guests were lying down in the dishes, and the soup ladle was walking up the table towards Alice's chair, and beckoning to her impatiently to get out of its way.

"I ca'n't stand this any longer!" she cried, as she jumped up and seized the tablecloth with both hands: one good pull, and plates, dishes, guests, and candles came crashing down together in a heap on the floor.

"And as for *you*," she went on, turning fiercely upon the Red Queen, whom she considered as the cause of all the mischief—but the Queen was no longer at her side—she had suddenly dwindled down to the size of a little doll, and was now on the table, merrily running round and round after her own shawl, which was trailing behind her.

At any other time, Alice would have felt surprised at this, but she was far too much excited to be surprised at anything *now*. "As for *you*," she repeated, catching hold of the little creature in the very act of jumping over a bottle which had just lighted upon the table, "I'll shake you into a kitten, that I will!"

Chapter X

SHAKING

She took her off the table as she spoke, and shook her backwards and forwards with all her might.

The Red Queen made no resistance whatever: only her face grew very small, and her eyes got large and green: and still, as Alice went on shaking her, she kept on growing shorter—and fatter—and softer—and rounder—and——

Chapter XI

WAKING

—it really *was* a kitten, after all.

Chapter XII

WHICH DREAMED IT?

"Your Red Majesty shouldn't purr so loud," Alice said, rubbing her eyes, and addressing the kitten, respectfully, yet with some severity. "You woke me out of oh! such a nice dream! And you've been along with me, Kitty—all through the Looking-Glass world. Did you know it, dear?"

It is a very inconvenient habit of kittens (Alice had once made the remark) that, whatever you say to them, they *always* purr. "If they would only purr for 'yes,' and mew for 'no,' or any rule of that sort," she had said, "so that one could keep up a conversation! But how *can* you talk with a person if they *always* say the same thing?"

On this occasion the kitten only purred: and it was impossible to guess whether it meant "yes" or "no."

So Alice hunted among the chessmen on the table till she had found the Red Queen: then she went down on her knees on the hearth-rug, and put the kitten and the Queen to look at each other. "Now, Kitty!" she cried, clapping her hands triumphantly. "Confess that was what you turned into!"

("But it wouldn't look at it," she said, when she was explaining the thing afterwards to her sister: "it turned away its head, and pretended not to see it: but it looked a *little* ashamed of itself, so I think it *must* have been the Red Queen.")

"Sit up a little more stiffly, dear!" Alice cried with a merry laugh. "And curtsey while you're thinking what to—what to purr. It saves time, remember!" And she caught it up and gave it one little kiss, "just in honour of its having been a Red Queen."

"Snowdrop, my pet!" she went on, looking over her shoulder at the White Kitten, which was still patiently undergoing its toilet, "when *will* Dinah have finished with your White Majesty, I wonder? That must be the reason you were so untidy in my dream.——Dinah! Do you know that you're scrubbing a White Queen? Really, it's most disrespectful of you!

"And what did *Dinah* turn to, I wonder?" she prattled on, as she settled comfortably down, with one elbow on the rug, and her chin in her hand, to watch the kittens. "Tell me, Dinah, did you turn to Humpty Dumpty? I *think* you did—however, you'd better not mention it to your friends just yet, for I'm not sure.

"By the way, Kitty, if only you'd been really with me in my dream, there was one thing you *would* have enjoyed——I had such a quantity of poetry said to me, all about fishes! To-morrow morning you shall have a real treat. All the time you're eating your breakfast, I'll repeat 'The Walrus and the Carpenter' to you; and then you can make believe it's oysters, dear!

"Now, Kitty, let's consider who it was that dreamed it all. This is a serious question, my dear, and you should *not* go on licking your paw like that—as if Dinah hadn't washed you this morning! You see, Kitty, it *must* have been either me or the Red King. He was part of my dream, of course—but then I was part of his dream, too! *Was* it the Red King, Kitty? You were his wife, my dear, so you ought to know——Oh, Kitty, *do* help to settle it! I'm sure your paw can wait!" But the provoking kitten only began on the other paw, and pretended it hadn't heard the question.

Which do *you* think it was?

A boat, beneath a sunny sky
Lingering onward dreamily
In an evening of July—

Children three that nestle near,
Eager eye and willing ear,
Pleased a simple tale to hear—

Long has paled that sunny sky:
Echoes fade and memories die:
Autumn frosts have slain July.

Still she haunts me, phantomwise.
Alice moving under skies
Never seen by waking eyes.

Children yet, the tale to hear,
Eager eye and willing ear,
Lovingly shall nestle near.

In a Wonderland they lie,
Dreaming as the days go by,
Dreaming as the summers die:

Ever drifting down the stream—
Lingering in the golden gleam—
Life, what is it but a dream?[8]

8. The initial letters of each line in this poem, when read downward, spell Alice Pleasance Liddell.

The Wasp in a Wig

The episode of the wasp in a wig was intended to occur between the White Knight's departure from Alice and her entrance into the eighth square at the end of chapter 8. In his biography of his uncle, Stuart Dodgson Collingwood quotes John Tenniel as objecting that "a *wasp* in a *wig* is altogether beyond the appliances of art." Collingwood reproduces another letter in which Tenniel judged the episode to be uninteresting and suggested, "If you want to shorten the book, I can't help thinking—with all submission— that *there* is your opportunity" (146). Even though Alice's kindness to the rude and threatening Wasp furnishes a satisfying transition between the gentle interlude with the White Knight and the nightmare of the coronation dinner, Carroll apparently did want to shorten his book. He therefore simply brought Alice to the boundary of the brook and had her jump across immediately, rather than turn back to hear the wasp's story.

It has been known since the publication of Collingwood's book in 1898 that the episode had been eliminated from the final version of *Through the Looking-Glass*. But the content of the episode was not known until the galley sheets were offered at auction in 1974. The episode was published in 1977 by the Lewis Carroll Society of North America and Macmillan in *The Wasp in a Wig* (New York and London: Macmillan, 1977). The text used here is that of the 1977 publication.

The Wasp in a Wig†

. . . and she was just going to spring over, when she heard a deep sigh, which seemed to come from the wood behind her.

"There's somebody *very* unhappy there," she thought, looking anxiously back to see what was the matter. Something like a very old man (only that his face was more like a wasp) was sitting on the ground, leaning against a tree, all huddled up together, and shivering as if he were very cold.

"I don't *think* I can be of any use to him," was Alice's first thought, as she turned to spring over the brook:——"but I'll just ask him what's the matter," she added, checking herself on the very edge. "If I once jump over, everything will change, and then I can't help him."

So she went back to the Wasp——rather unwillingly, for she was *very* anxious to be a Queen.

"Oh, my old bones, my old bones!" he was grumbling on as Alice came up to him.

"It's rheumatism, I should think," Alice said to herself, and she stooped over him, and said very kindly, "I hope you're not in much pain?"

The Wasp only shook his shoulders, and turned his head away. "Ah, deary me!" he said to himself.

"Can I do anything for you?" Alice went on. "Aren't you rather cold here?"

"How you go on!" the Wasp said in a peevish tone. "Worrity, worrity![1] There never was such a child!"

Alice felt rather offended at this answer, and was very nearly walking on and leaving him, but she thought to herself "Perhaps it's only pain that makes him so cross." So she tried once more.

"Won't you let me help you round to the other side? You'll be out of the cold wind there."

The Wasp took her arm, and let her help him round the tree, but when he got settled down again he only said, as before, "Worrity, worrity! Can't you leave a body alone?"

† Reprinted with the permission of A P Watt Limited on behalf of the Lewis Carroll Society of North America and the Executors of the C. L. Dodgson Estate, and of Macmillan, London and Basingstoke.
1. Worrity: worry. Here and in several other words and phrases, the Wasp uses words common in lower-class dialect.

"Would you like me to read you a bit of this?" Alice went on, as she picked up a newspaper which had been lying at his feet.

"You may read it if you've a mind to," the Wasp said, rather sulkily. "Nobody's hindering you, that I know of."

So Alice sat down by him, and spread out the paper on her knees, and began. "*Latest News. The Exploring Party have made another tour in the Pantry, and have found five new lumps of white sugar, large and in fine condition. In coming back——*"

"Any brown sugar?" the Wasp interrupted.

Alice hastily ran her eye down the paper and said "No. It says nothing about brown."

"No brown sugar!" grumbled the Wasp. "A nice exploring party!"

"*In coming back,*" Alice went on reading, "*they found a lake of treacle. The banks of the lake were blue and white, and looked like china. While tasting the treacle, they had a sad accident: two of their party were engulphed——*"[2]

"Were *what?*" the Wasp asked in a very cross voice.

"En-gulph-ed," Alice repeated, dividing the word into syllables.

"There's no such word in the language!" said the Wasp.

"It's in this newspaper, though," Alice said a little timidly.

"Let it stop there!" said the Wasp, fretfully turning away his head.

Alice put down the newspaper. "I'm afraid you're not well," she said in a soothing tone. "Can't I do anything for you?"

"It's all along of[3] the wig," the Wasp said in a much gentler voice.

"Along of the wig?" Alice repeated, quite pleased to find that he was recovering his temper.

"You'd be cross too, if you'd a wig like mine," the Wasp went on. "They jokes at one. And they worrits one. And then I gets cross. And I gets cold. And I gets under a tree. And I gets a yellow handkerchief. And I ties up my face——as at the present."

Alice looked pityingly at him. "Tying up the face is very good for the toothache," she said.

"And it's good for the conceit," added the Wasp.

Alice didn't catch the word exactly. "Is that a kind of toothache?" she asked.

The Wasp considered a little. "Well, no," he said: "it's when you hold up your head——so——without bending your neck."

"Oh, you mean stiff-neck," said Alice.

The Wasp said "That's a new-fangled name. They called it conceit in my time."

"Conceit isn't a disease at all," Alice remarked.

---

2. An archaic spelling of "engulfed." The Wasp of course does not see the spelling; he only hears Alice's pronunciation of the word.

3. All along of: because of, another phrase from lower-class dialect.

"It is, though," said the Wasp: "wait till you have it, and then you'll know. And when you catches it, just try tying a yellow handkerchief round your face. It'll cure you in no time!"

He untied the handkerchief as he spoke, and Alice looked at his wig in great surprise. It was bright yellow like the handkerchief, and all tangled and tumbled about like a heap of sea-weed. "You would make your wig much neater," she said, "if only you had a comb."

"What, you're a Bee, are you?" the Wasp said, looking at her with more interest. "And you've got a comb. Much honey?"

"It isn't that kind," Alice hastily explained. "It's to comb hair with—your wig's so *very* rough, you know."

"I'll tell you how I came to wear it," the Wasp said. "When I was young, you know, my ringlets used to wave——"

A curious idea came into Alice's head. Almost every one she had met had repeated poetry to her, and she thought she would try if the Wasp couldn't d it too. "Would you mind saying it in rhyme?" she asked very politely.

"It ain't what I'm used to," said the Wasp: "however I'll try; wait a bit." He was silent for a few moments, and then began again—

> *"When I was young, my ringlets waved*
> *And curled and crinkled on my head:*
> *And then they said 'You should be shaved,*
> *And wear a yellow wig instead.'*
>
> *But when I followed their advice,*
> *And they had noticed the effect,*
> *They said I did not look so nice*
> *As they had ventured to expect.*
>
> *They said it did not fit, and so*
> *It made me look extremely plain:*
> *But what was I to do, you know?*
> *My ringlets would not grow again.*
>
> *So now that I am old and gray,*
> *And all my hair is nearly gone,*
> *They take my wig from me and say*
> *'How can you put such rubbish on?'*
>
> *And still, whenever I appear,*
> *They hoot at me and call me 'Pig!'*
> *And that is why they do it, dear,*
> *Because I wear a yellow wig."*[4]

"I'm very sorry for you," Alice said heartily: "and I think if your wig fitted a little better, they wouldn't tease you quite so much."

---

4. The Wasp's poem does not seem to be a parody.

"*Your* wig fits very well," the Wasp murmured, looking at her with an expression of admiration: "it's the shape of your head as does it. Your jaws ain't well shaped, though——I should think you couldn't bite well?"

Alice began with a little scream of laughter, which she turned into a cough as well as she could. At last she managed to say gravely, "I can bite anything I want."

"Not with a mouth as small as that," the Wasp persisted. "If you was a-fighting, now——could you get hold of the other one by the back of the neck?"

"I'm afraid not," said Alice.

"Well, that's because your jaws are too short," the Wasp went on: "but the top of your head is nice and round." He took off his own wig as he spoke, and stretched out one claw towards Alice, as if he wished to do the same for her, but she kept out of reach, and would not take the hint. So he went on with his criticisms.

"Then your eyes——they're too much in front, no doubt. One would have done as well as two, if you *must* have them so close——"

Alice did not like having so many personal remarks made on her, and as the Wasp had quite recovered his spirits, and was getting very talkative, she thought she might safely leave him. "I think I must be going on now," she said. "Good-bye."

"Good-bye, and thank-ye," said the Wasp, and Alice tripped down the hill again, quite pleased that she had gone back and given a few minutes to making the poor old creature comfortable.

The Text of

The Hunting
of the Snark

An Agony, in Eight Fits

An Easter Greeting

My dear child,

Please to fancy, if you can, that you are reading a real letter, from a real friend whom you have seen, and whose voice you can seem to yourself to hear, wishing you, as I do now with all my heart, a happy Easter.

Do you know that delicious dreamy feeling, when one first wakes on a summer morning, with the twitter of birds in the air, and the fresh breeze coming in at the open window——when, lying lazily with eyes half shut, one sees as in a dream green boughs waving, or waters rippling in a golden light? It is a pleasure very near to sadness, bringing tears to one's eyes like a beautiful picture or poem. And is not that a Mother's gentle hand that undraws your curtains, and a Mother's sweet voice that summons you to rise? To rise and forget, in the bright sunlight, the ugly dreams that frightened you so when all was dark——to rise and enjoy another happy day, first kneeling to thank that unseen Friend who sends you the beautiful sun?

Are these strange words from a writer of such tales as "Alice"? And is this a strange letter to find in a book of nonsense? It may be so. Some perhaps may blame me for thus mixing together things grave and gay; others may smile and think it odd that any one should speak of solemn things at all, except in Church and on a Sunday: but I think——nay, I am sure——that some children will read this gently and lovingly, and in the spirit in which I have written it.

For I do not believe God means us thus to divide life into two halves—to wear a grave face on Sunday, and to think it out-of-place to even so much as mention Him on a week-day. Do you think He cares to see only kneeling figures and to hear only tones of prayer——and that He does not also love to see the lambs leaping in the sunlight, and to hear the merry voices of the children, as they roll among the hay? Surely their innocent laughter is as sweet in His ears as the grandest anthem that ever rolled up from the "dim religious light" of some solemn cathedral?

And if I have written anything to add to those stores of innocent and healthy amusement that are laid up in books for the children I love so well, it is surely something I may hope to look back upon without shame and sorrow (as how much of life must then be recalled!) when *my* turn comes to walk through the valley of shadows.

† Dodgson wrote this greeting in the spring of 1876, intending that it be inserted in copies of *The Hunting of the Snark*, which was published in March of that year. The greeting was also sold separately in 1876, and in 1880 Dodgson authorized another separate printing. The version printed above is a final version, slightly revised in its punctuation and a few other minor points, which was published around 1885.

This Easter sun will rise on you, dear child, "feeling your life in every limb," and eager to rush out into the fresh morning air——and many an Easter-day will come and go, before it finds you feeble and grey-headed, creeping wearily out to bask once more in the sunlight—but it is good, even now, to think sometimes of that great morning when "the Sun of righteousness" shall "arise with healing in his wings."

Surely your gladness need not be the less for the thought that you will one day see a brighter dawn than this——when lovelier sights will meet your eyes than any waving trees or rippling waters——when angel-hands shall undraw your curtains, and sweeter tones than ever loving Mother breathed shall wake you to a new and glorious day—and when all the sadness, and the sin, that darkened life on this little earth, shall be forgotten like the dreams of a night that is past!

Your affectionate Friend,
LEWIS CARROLL.

Inscribed to a Dear Child:

IN MEMORY OF GOLDEN SUMMER HOURS

AND WHISPERS OF A SUMMER SEA[1]

Girt with a boyish garb for boyish task,
 Eager she wields her spade: yet loves as well
Rest on a friendly knee, intent to ask
 The tale he loves to tell.

Rude spirits of the seething outer strife,
 Unmeet to read her pure and simple spright,
Deem, if you list, such hours a waste of life,
 Empty of all delight!

Chat on, sweet Maid, and rescue from annoy
 Hearts that by wiser talk are unbeguiled,
Ah, happy he who owns that tenderest joy,
 The heart-love of a child!

Away, fond thoughts, and vex my soul no more!
 Work claims my wakeful nights, my busy days—
Albeit bright memories of that sunlit shore
 Yet haunt my dreaming gaze!

1. The first letters of each line spell, and the first syllables of each stanza sound, the name of Gertrude Chataway, a young girl Dodgson had met during a vacation by the sea in September 1875. He had already begun to write *The Hunting of the Snark* by this date. The last line of the poem, he wrote in his diary (November 6, 1875), came into his head July 18, 1874 (see also his statement in "*Alice* on the Stage," on pp. 280–82 of this edition); he wrote the first stanza of the poem on July 22, 1874; and he wrote a good deal of the poem in the fall and winter of 1873–76, completing it in the spring of 1876. The poem was published in March 1876.

Preface

If—and the thing is wildly possible—the charge of writing non-sense were ever brought against the author of this brief but instructive poem, it would be based, I feel convinced, on the line

"Then the bowsprit[2] got mixed with the rudder sometimes."

In view of this painful possibility, I will not (as I might) appeal indignantly to my other writings as a proof that I am incapable of such a deed: I will not (as I might) point to the strong moral purpose of this poem itself, to the arithmetical principles so cautiously inculcated in it, or to its noble teachings in Natural History—I will take the more prosaic course of simply explaining how it happened.

The Bellman, who was almost morbidly sensitive about appearances, used to have the bowsprit unshipped once or twice a week to be revarnished, and it more than once happened, when the time came for replacing it, that no one on board could remember which end of the ship it belonged to. They knew it was not of the slightest use to appeal to the Bellman about it—he would only refer to his Naval Code, and read out in pathetic tones Admiralty Instructions which none of them had ever been able to understand—so it generally ended in its being fastened on, anyhow, across the rudder. The helmsman* used to stand by with tears in his eyes: *he* knew it was all wrong, but alas! Rule 42 of the Code, "*No one shall speak to the Man at the Helm*," had been completed by the Bellman himself with the words "*and the Man at the Helm shall speak to no one.*" So remonstrance was impossible, and no steering could be done till the next varnishing day. During these bewildering intervals the ship usually sailed backwards.

As this poem is to some extent connected with the lay of the Jabberwock, let me take this opportunity of answering a question that has often been asked me, how to pronounce "slithy toves." The "i" in "slithy" is long, as in "writhe"; and "toves" is pronounced so as to rhyme with "groves." Again, the first "o" in "borogroves" is pronounced like the "o" in "borrow." I have heard people try to give it the sound of the "o" in "worry." Such is Human Perversity.

This also seems a fitting occasion to notice the other hard words in that poem. Humpty-Dumpty's theory, of two meanings packed into one word like a portmanteau, seems to me the right explanation for all.

---

2. A boom or spar projecting forward from the bow of a ship.
* This office was usually undertaken by the Boots, who found in it a refuge from the Baker's constant complaints about the insufficient blacking of his three pairs of boots [*Dodgson's note*].

For instance, take the two words "fuming" and "furious." Make up your mind that you will say both words, but leave it unsettled which you will say first. Now open your mouth and speak. If your thoughts incline ever so little towards "fuming," you will say "fuming-furious;" if they turn, by even a hair's breadth, towards "furious," you will say "furious-fuming;" but if you have the rarest of gifts, a perfectly balanced mind, you will say "frumious."

Supposing that, when Pistol uttered the well-known words—

> "Under which King, Bezonian? Speak or die!"

Justice Shallow[3] had felt certain that it was either William or Richard, but had not been able to settle which, so that he could not possibly say either name before the other, can it be doubted that, rather than die, he would have gasped out "Rilchiam!"

Fit the First.

THE LANDING.

"Just the place for a Snark!" the Bellman[4] cried,
  As he landed his crew with care;
Supporting each man on the top of the tide
  By a finger entwined in his hair.

"Just the place for a Snark! I have said it twice:
  That alone should encourage the crew.
Just the place for a Snark! I have said it thrice:
  What I tell you three times is true."

The crew was complete: it included a Boots—
  A maker of Bonnets and Hoods—
A Barrister, brought to arrange their disputes—
  And a Broker, to value their goods.

A Billiard-marker, whose skill was immense,
  Might perhaps have won more than his share—
But a Banker, engaged at enormous expense,
  Had the whole of their cash in his care.

There was also a Beaver, that paced on the deck,
  Or would sit making lace in the bow:
And had often (the Bellman said) saved them from wreck,
  Though none of the sailors knew how.

3. Pistol and Shallow conduct this conversation in act 5, scene 3, of the second part of Shakespeare's *King Henry IV*.
4. A bellman is a town crier. Among the other occupations named in the first fit, a boots is a servant in a hotel who, among other menial tasks, cleans and shines boots; a barrister is a lawyer who is admitted to plead before a court; and a billiard-marker is the score-keeper of a billiards game. The broker, who values goods, may be a pawnbroker.

There was one who was famed for the number of things
    He forgot when he entered the ship:
His umbrella, his watch, all his jewels and rings,
    And the clothes he had bought for the trip.

He had forty-two boxes, all carefully packed,
    With his name painted clearly on each:
But, since he omitted to mention the fact,
    They were all left behind on the beach.

The loss of his clothes hardly mattered, because
    He had seven coats on when he came,
With three pair of boots—but the worst of it was,
    He had wholly forgotten his name.

He would answer to "Hi!" or to any loud cry,
    Such as "Fry me!" or "Fritter my wig!"
To "What-you-may-call-um!" or "What-was-his name!"
    But especially "Thing-um-a-jig!"

While, for those who preferred a more forcible word,
    He had different names from these:
His intimate friends called him "Candle-ends,"
    And his enemies "Toasted-cheese."

"His form is ungainly—his intellect small—"
    (So the Bellman would often remark)
"But his courage is perfect! And that, after all,
    Is the thing that one needs with a Snark."

He would joke with hyænas, returning their stare
    With an impudent wag of the head:
And he once went a walk, paw-in-paw, with a bear,
    "Just to keep up its spirits," he said.

He came as a Baker: but owned, when too late—
    And it drove the poor Bellman half-mad—
He could only bake Bride-cake[5]—for which, I may state,
    No materials were to be had.

The last of the crew needs especial remark,
    Though he looked an incredible dunce:
He had just one idea—but, that one being "Snark,"
    The good Bellman engaged him at once.

He came as a Butcher: but gravely declared,
    When the ship had been sailing a week,
He could only kill Beavers. The Bellman looked scared,
    And was almost too frightened to speak:

But at length he explained, in a tremulous tone,
    There was only one Beaver on board;
And that was a tame one he had of his own,
    Whose death would be deeply deplored.

5. Wedding cake.

The Beaver, who happened to hear the remark,
    Protested, with tears in its eyes,
That not even the rapture of hunting the Snark
    Could atone for that dismal surprise!

It strongly advised that the Butcher should be
    Conveyed in a separate ship:
But the Bellman declared that would never agree
    With the plans he had made for the trip:

Navigation was always a difficult art,
    Though with only one ship and one bell:
And he feared he must really decline, for his part,
    Undertaking another as well.

The Beaver's best course was, no doubt, to procure
    A second-hand dagger-proof coat—
So the Baker advised it—and next, to insure
    Its life in some Office of note:

This the Banker suggested, and offered for hire[6]
    (On moderate terms), or for sale,
Two excellent Policies, one Against Fire
    And one Against Damage From Hail.

Yet still, ever after that sorrowful day,
    Whenever the Butcher was by,
The Beaver kept looking the opposite way,
    And appeared unaccountably shy.

Fit the Second.

THE BELLMAN'S SPEECH.

The Bellman himself they all praised to the skies—
    Such a carriage, such ease and such grace!
Such solemnity, too! One could see he was wise,
    The moment one looked in his face!

He had bought a large map representing the sea,[7]
    Without the least vestige of land:
And the crew were much pleased when they found it to be
    A map they could all understand.

"What's the good of Mercator's[8] North Poles and Equators,
    Tropics, Zones, and Meridian Lines?"
So the Bellman would cry: and the crew would reply
    "They are merely conventional signs!

---

6. Rent.
7. In Henry Holiday's illustration, the map is an entirely blank rectangle marked on its margins by the directions of the compass and such phrases as "Torrid Zone," "Equator," and "South Pole."
8. Gerhardus Mercator was the sixteenth-century cartographer who devised a means of depicting the round earth on a flat map.

"Other maps are such shapes, with their islands and capes!
    But we've got our brave Captain to thank"
(So the crew would protest) "that he's bought *us* the best—
    A perfect and absolute blank!"

This was charming, no doubt: but they shortly found out
    That the Captain they trusted so well
Had only one notion for crossing the ocean,
    And that was to tingle his bell.

He was thoughtful and grave—but the orders he gave
    Were enough to bewilder a crew.
When he cried "Steer to starboard, but keep her head larboard!"
    What on earth was the helmsman to do?

Then the bowsprit got mixed with the rudder sometimes:
    A thing, as the Bellman remarked,
That frequently happens in tropical climes,
    When a vessel is, so to speak, "snarked."

But the principal failing occured in the sailing,
    And the Bellman, perplexed and distressed,
Said he *had* hoped, at least, when the wind blew due East,
    That the ship would *not* travel due West!

But the danger was past—they had landed at last,
    With their boxes, portmanteaus, and bags:
Yet at first sight the crew were not pleased with the view,
    Which consisted of chasms and crags.

The Bellman perceived that their spirits were low,
    And repeated in musical tone
Some jokes he had kept for a season of woe—
    But the crew would do nothing but groan.

He served out some grog with a liberal hand,
    And bade them sit down on the beach:
And they could not but own that their Captain looked grand,
    As he stood and delivered his speech.

"Friends, Romans, and countrymen, lend me your ears!"[9]
    (They were all of them fond of quotations:
So they drank to his health, and they gave him three cheers,
    While he served out additional rations).

"We have sailed many months, we have sailed many weeks,
    (Four weeks to the month you may mark),
But never as yet ('tis your Captain who speaks)
    Have we caught the least glimpse of a Snark!

"We have sailed many weeks, we have sailed many days,
    (Seven days to the week I allow),

9. The Bellman misquotes the first line of Mark Antony's oration in Shakespeare's *Julius Caesar*:
the speech begins, "Friends, Romans, countrymen."

But a Snark, on the which we might lovingly gaze,
    We have never beheld till now!

"Come, listen, my men, while I tell you again
    The five unmistakable marks
By which you may know, wheresoever you go,
    The warranted genuine Snarks.

"Let us take them in order. The first is the taste,
    Which is meagre and hollow, but crisp:
Like a coat that is rather too tight in the waist,
    With a flavour of Will-o-the-Wisp.

"Its habit of getting up late you'll agree
    That it carries too far, when I say
That it frequently breakfasts at five-o'clock tea,
    And dines on the following day.

"The third is its slowness in taking a jest.
    Should you happen to venture on one,
It will sigh like a thing that is deeply distressed:
    And it always looks grave at a pun.

"The fourth is its fondness for bathing-machines,[1]
    Which it constantly carries about,
And believes that they add to the beauty of scenes—
    A sentiment open to doubt.

"The fifth is ambition. It next will be right
    To describe each particular batch:
Distinguishing those that have feathers, and bite,
    From those that have whiskers, and scratch.

"For, although common Snarks do no manner of harm,
    Yet, I feel it my duty to say,
Some are Boojums—" The Bellman broke off in alarm,
    For the Baker had fainted away.

Fit the Third.

THE BAKER'S TALE.

They roused him with muffins—they roused him with ice—
    They roused him with mustard and cress—
They roused him with jam and judicious advice—
    They set him conundrums to guess.

When at length he sat up and was able to speak,
    His sad story he offered to tell;
And the Bellman cried "Silence! Not even a shriek!"
    And excitedly tingled his bell.

1. Bathing-machines: see note 8, p. 17.

There was silence supreme! Not a shriek, not a scream,
    Scarcely even a howl or a groan,
As the man they called "Ho!" told his story of woe
    In an antediluvian tone.[2]

"My father and mother were honest, though poor—"
    "Skip all that!" cried the Bellman in haste.
"If it once becomes dark, there's no chance of a Snark—
    We have hardly a minute to waste!"

"I skip forty years," said the Baker, in tears,
    "And proceed without further remark
To the day when you took me aboard of your ship
    To help you in hunting the Snark.

"A dear uncle of mine (after whom I was named)
    Remarked, when I bade him farewell—"
"Oh, skip your dear uncle!" the Bellman exclaimed,
    And he angrily tingled his bell.

"He remarked to me then," said the mildest of men,
    " 'If your Snark be a Snark, that is right:
Fetch it home by all means—you may serve it with greens,
    And it's handy for striking a light.

" 'You may seek it with thimbles—and seek it with care;
    You may hunt it with forks and hope;
You may threaten its life with a railway-share;
    You may charm it with smiles and soap—' "

("That's exactly the method," the Bellman bold
    In a hasty parenthesis cried,
"That's exactly the way I have always been told
    That the capture of Snarks should be tried!")

" 'But oh, beamish[3] nephew, beware of the day,
    If your Snark be a Boojum! For then
You will softly and suddenly vanish away,
    And never be met with again!'

"It is this, it is this that oppresses my soul,
    When I think of my uncle's last words:
And my heart is like nothing so much as a bowl
    Brimming over with quivering curds!

"It is this, it is this—" "We have had that before!"
    The Bellman indignantly said.
And the Baker replied "Let me say it once more.
    It is this, it is this that I dread!

"I engage with the Snark—every night after dark—
    In a dreamy delirious fight:

2. Dodgson's willfully inaccurate use of "antediluvian"—which means "before the Deluge"—predicts the Baker's catastrophic fate.

3. Like *uffish*, *galumphing*, *Jubjub*, *outgrate*, and some other words and names in the poem, this word is borrowed from "Jabberwocky."

I serve it with greens in those shadowy scenes,
  And I use it for striking a light:

"But if ever I meet with a Boojum, that day,
  In a moment (of this I am sure),
I shall softly and suddenly vanish away—
  And the notion I cannot endure!"

Fit the Fourth.

THE HUNTING.

The Bellman looked uffish, and wrinkled his brow.
  "If only you'd spoken before!
It's excessively awkward to mention it now,
  With the Snark, so to speak, at the door!

"We should all of us grieve, as you well may believe,
  If you never were met with again—
But surely, my man, when the voyage began,
  You might have suggested it then?

"It's excessively awkward to mention it now—
  As I think I've already remarked."
And the man they called "Hi!" replied, with a sigh,
  "I informed you the day we embarked.

"You may charge me with murder—or want of sense—
  (We are all of us weak at times):
But the slightest approach to a false pretence
  Was never among my crimes!

"I said it in Hebrew—I said it in Dutch—
  I said it in German and Greek:
But I wholly forgot (and it vexes me much)
  That English is what you speak!"

" 'Tis a pitiful tale," said the Bellman, whose face
  Had grown longer at every word:
"But, now that you've stated the whole of your case,
  More debate would be simply absurd.

"The rest of my speech" (he exclaimed to his men)
  "You shall hear when I've leisure to speak it.
But the Snark is at hand, let me tell you again!
  'Tis your glorious duty to seek it!

"To seek it with thimbles, to seek it with care;
  To pursue it with forks and hope;
To threaten its life with a railway-share;
  To charm it with smiles and soap!

"For the Snark's a peculiar creature, that won't
    Be caught in a commonplace way.
Do all that you know, and try all that you don't:
    Not a chance must be wasted to-day!

"For England expects[4]—I forbear to proceed:
    'Tis a maxim tremendous, but trite:
And you'd best be unpacking the things that you need
    To rig yourselves out for the fight."

Then the Banker endorsed a blank cheque (which he crossed),
    And changed his loose silver for notes.[5]
The Baker with care combed his whiskers and hair,
    And shook the dust out of his coats.

The Boots and the Broker were sharpening a spade—
    Each working the grindstone in turn:
But the Beaver went on making lace, and displayed
    No interest in the concern:

Though the Barrister tried to appeal to its pride,
    And vainly proceeded to cite
A number of cases, in which making laces
    Had been proved an infringement of right.

The maker of Bonnets ferociously planned
    A novel arrangement of bows:
While the Billiard-marker with quivering hand
    Was chalking the tip of his nose.

But the Butcher turned nervous, and dressed himself fine,
    With yellow kid gloves and a ruff—
Said he felt it exactly like going to dine,
    Which the Bellman declared was all "stuff."[6]

"Introduce me, now there's a good fellow," he said,
    "If we happen to meet it together!"
And the Bellman, sagaciously nodding his head,
    Said "That must depend on the weather."

The Beaver went simply galumphing about,
    At seeing the Butcher so shy:
And even the Baker, though stupid and stout,
    Made an effort to wink with one eye.

"Be a man!" cried the Bellman in wrath, as he heard
    The Butcher beginning to sob.

4. The trite maxim is Lord Nelson's admonition to the men of his fleet before the battle of Trafalgar in 1805: "England expects every man to do his duty."
5. To cross a check is to draw lines across it, indicating that it is not negotiable but must be deposited in the account of the person to whom it is made out. "Notes" are banknotes.
6. "Stuff" was a slang expression used to describe meaningless or pointless words and gestures.

"Should we meet with a Jubjub, that desperate bird,
  We shall need all our strength for the job!"

Fit the Fifth.

THE BEAVER'S LESSON.

They sought it with thimbles, they sought it with care;
  They pursued it with forks and hope;
They threatened its life with a railway-share;
  They charmed it with smiles and soap.

Then the Butcher contrived an ingenious plan
  For making a separate sally;
And had fixed on a spot unfrequented by man,
  A dismal and desolate valley.

But the very same plan to the Beaver occurred:
  It had chosen the very same place:
Yet neither betrayed, by a sign or a word,
  The disgust that appeared in his face.

Each thought he was thinking of nothing but "Snark"
  And the glorious work of the day;
And each tried to pretend that he did not remark
  That the other was going that way.

But the valley grew narrow and narrower still,
  And the evening got darker and colder,
Till (merely from nervousness, not from good will)
  They marched along shoulder to shoulder.

Then a scream, shrill and high, rent the shuddering sky,
  And they knew that some danger was near:
The Beaver turned pale to the tip of its tail,
  And even the Butcher felt queer.

He thought of his childhood, left far behind—
  That blissful and innocent state—
The sound so exactly recalled to his mind
  A pencil that squeaks on a slate!

" 'Tis the voice of the Jubjub!" he suddenly cried.
  (This man, that they used to call "Dunce.")
"As the Bellman would tell you," he added with pride,
  "I have uttered that sentiment once.

" 'Tis the note of the Jubjub! Keep count, I entreat;
  You will find I have told it you twice.
'Tis the song of the Jubjub! The proof is complete.
  If only I've stated it thrice."

The Beaver had counted with scrupulous care,
　　Attending to every word:
But it fairly lost heart, and outgrabe in despair,
　　When the third repetition occurred.

It felt that, in spite of all possible pains,
　　It had somehow contrived to lose count,
And the only thing now was to rack its poor brains
　　By reckoning up the amount.

"Two added to one—if that could but be done,"
　　It said, "with one's fingers and thumbs!"
Recollecting with tears how, in earlier years,
　　It had taken no pains with its sums.

"The thing can be done," said the Butcher, "I think.
　　The thing must be done, I am sure.
The thing shall be done! Bring me paper and ink,
　　The best there is time to procure."

The Beaver brought paper, portfolio, pens,
　　And ink in unfailing supplies:
While strange creepy creatures came out of their dens,
　　And watched them with wondering eyes.

So engrossed was the Butcher, he heeded them not,
　　As he wrote with a pen in each hand,
And explained all the while in a popular style
　　Which the Beaver could well understand.

"Taking Three as the subject to reason about—
　　A convenient number to state—
We add Seven, and Ten, and then multiply out
　　By One Thousand diminished by Eight.

"The result we proceed to divide, as you see,
　　By Nine Hundred and Ninety and Two:
Then subtract Seventeen, and the answer must be
　　Exactly and perfectly true.

"The method employed I would gladly explain,
　　While I have it so clear in my head,
If I had but the time and you had but the brain—
　　But much yet remains to be said.

"In one moment I've seen what has hitherto been
　　Enveloped in absolute mystery,
And without extra charge I will give you at large
　　A Lesson in Natural History."

In his genial way he proceeded to say
　　(Forgetting all laws of propriety,
And that giving instruction, without introduction,
　　Would have caused quite a thrill in Society),

"As to temper the Jubjub's a desperate bird,
  Since it lives in perpetual passion: .
Its taste in costume is entirely absurd—
  It is ages ahead of the fashion:

"But it knows any friend it has met once before:
  It never will look at a bribe:
And in charity-meetings it stands at the door,
  And collects—though it does not subscribe.[7]

"Its flavour when cooked is more exquisite far
  Than mutton, or oysters, or eggs:
(Some think it keeps best in an ivory jar,
  And some, in mahogany kegs:)

"You boil it in sawdust: you salt it in glue:
  You condense it with locusts and tape:
Still keeping one principal object in view—
  To preserve its symmetrical shape."

The Butcher would gladly have talked till next day,
  But he felt that the Lesson must end,
And he wept with delight in attempting to say
  He considered the Beaver his friend.

While the Beaver confessed, with affectionate looks
  More eloquent even than tears,
It had learned in ten minutes far more than all books
  Would have taught it in seventy years.

They returned hand-in-hand, and the Bellman, unmanned
  (For a moment) with noble emotion,
Said "This amply repays all the wearisome days
  We have spent on the billowy ocean!"

Such friends, as the Beaver and Butcher became,
  Have seldom if ever been known;
In winter or summer, 'twas always the same—
  You could never meet either alone.

And when quarrels arose—as one frequently finds
  Quarrels will, spite of every endeavour—
The song of the Jubjub recurred to their minds,
  And cemented their friendship for ever!

Fit the Sixth.

THE BARRISTER'S DREAM.

They sought it with thimbles, they sought it with care;
  They pursued it with forks and hope;

---

7. To subscribe to a charity is to contribute money.

They threatened its life with a railway-share;
    They charmed it with smiles and soap.

But the Barrister, weary of proving in vain
    That the Beaver's lace-making was wrong,
Fell asleep, and in dreams saw the creature quite plain
    That his fancy had dwelt on so long.

He dreamed that he stood in a shadowy Court,
    Where the Snark, with a glass in its eye,
Dressed in gown, bands, and wig,[8] was defending a pig
    On the charge of deserting its sty.

The Witnesses proved, without error or flaw,
    That the sty was deserted when found:
And the Judge kept explaining the state of the law
    In a soft under-current of sound.

The indictment had never been clearly expressed,
    And it seemed that the Snark had begun,
And had spoken three hours, before any one guessed
    What the pig was supposed to have done.

The Jury had each formed a different view
    (Long before the indictment was read),
And they all spoke at once, so that none of them knew
    One word that the others had said.

"You must know—" said the Judge: but the Snark exclaimed
    "Fudge!
    That statute is obsolete quite!
Let me tell you, my friends, the whole question depends
    On an ancient manorial right.

"In the matter of Treason the pig would appear
    To have aided, but scarcely abetted:
While the charge of Insolvency fails, it is clear,
    If you grant the plea 'never indebted.'[9]

"The fact of Desertion I will not dispute:
    But its guilt, as I trust, is removed
(So far as relates to the costs of this suit)
    By the Alibi which has been proved.

"My poor client's fate now depends on your votes."
    Here the speaker sat down in his place,
And directed the Judge to refer to his notes
    And briefly to sum up the case.

But the Judge said he never had summed up before;
    So the Snark undertook it instead,

---

8. Wig, gown, and bands (a pair of cloth strips hanging from the neck of the gown) are worn by barristers when they plead before a judge.

9. "Never indebted" is a proper plea in an action for debt: it is not a proper plea in an insolvency or bankruptcy action.

And summed it so well that it came to far more
  Than the Witnesses ever had said!

When the verdict was called for, the Jury declined,
  As the word was so puzzling to spell;
But they ventured to hope that the Snark wouldn't mind
  Undertaking that duty as well.

So the Snark found the verdict, although, as it owned,
  It was spent with the toils of the day:
When it said the word "GUILTY!" the Jury all groaned,
  And some of them fainted away.

Then the Snark pronounced sentence, the Judge being quite
  Too nervous to utter a word:
When it rose to its feet, there was silence like night,
  And the fall of a pin might be heard.

"Transportation for life"[1] was the sentence it gave,
  "And *then* to be fined forty pound."
The Jury all cheered, though the Judge said he feared
  That the phrase was not legally sound.

But their wild exultation was suddenly checked
  When the jailer informed them, with tears,
Such a sentence would have not the slightest effect,
  As the pig had been dead for some years.

The Judge left the Court, looking deeply disgusted:
  But the Snark, though a little aghast,
As the lawyer to whom the defence was intrusted,
  Went bellowing on to the last.

Thus the Barrister dreamed, while the bellowing seemed
  To grow every moment more clear:
Till he woke to the knell of a furious bell,
  Which the Bellman rang close at his ear.

Fit the Seventh.

THE BANKER'S FATE.

They sought it with thimbles, they sought it with care;
  They pursued it with forks and hope;

1. During the eighteenth century and part of the nineteenth, persons convicted of crimes in England were frequently transported, that is, sent to one of the British colonies to work out their sentences as convict laborers. Commonly, sentences of transportation in the nineteenth century sent convicts to Australia or New Zealand. This is one of several references in the poem (another is the Baker's inability to recall his name) that persuaded some contemporary reviewers that it was a satire on the trial in the early 1870s of an Australian butcher who claimed to be Sir Roger Tichborne, a wealthy Englishman who had been presumed lost at sea. The Tichborne impostor was found guilty of perjury.

They threatened its life with a railway-share;
　They charmed it with smiles and soap.

And the Banker, inspired with a courage so new
　It was matter for general remark,
Rushed madly ahead and was lost to their view
　In his zeal to discover the Snark.

But while he was seeking with thimbles and care,
　A Bandersnatch swiftly drew nigh
And grabbed at the Banker, who shrieked in despair,
　For he knew it was useless to fly.

He offered large discount—he offered a cheque
　(Drawn "to bearer") for seven-pounds-ten:
But the Bandersnatch merely extended its neck
　And grabbed at the Banker again.

Without rest or pause—while those frumious jaws
　Went savagely snapping around—
He skipped and he hopped, and he floundered and flopped
　Till fainting he fell to the ground.

The Bandersnatch fled as the others appeared
　Led on by that fear-stricken yell:
And the Bellman remarked "It is just as I feared!"
　And solemnly tolled on his bell.

He was black in the face, and they scarcely could trace
　The least likeness to what he had been:
While so great was his fright that his waistcoat turned white—
　A wonderful thing to be seen!

To the horror of all who were present that day,
　He uprose in full evening dress,
And with senseless grimaces endeavoured to say
　What his tongue could no longer express.

Down he sank in a chair—ran his hands through his hair—
　And chanted in mimsiest tones
Words whose utter inanity proved his insanity,
　While he rattled a couple of bones.[2]

"Leave him here Ho his fate—it is getting so late!"
　The Bellman exclaimed in a fright.
"We have lost half the day. Any further delay,
　And we sha'n't catch a Snark before night!"

2. One of the performers in a conventional minstrel show—Mr. Bones—rattled a pair of bones to punctuate nonsensical exchanges with other performers. Minstrel shows were enormously popular in England from the 1840s until near the end of the century. For a parody by Dodgson of a song from a minstrel show, see note 4, p. 264 of this edition.

Fit the Eighth.

THE VANISHING.

They sought it with thimbles, they sought it with care;
  They pursued it with forks and hope;
They threatened its life with a railway-share;
  They charmed it with smiles and soap.

They shuddered to think that the chase might fail,
  And the Beaver, excited at last,
Went bounding along on the tip of its tail,
  For the daylight was nearly past.

"There is Thingumbob shouting!" the Bellman said.
  "He is shouting like mad, only hark!
He is waving his hands, he is wagging his head,
  He has certainly found a Snark!"

They gazed in delight, while the Butcher exclaimed
  "He was always a desperate wag!"
They beheld him—their Baker—their hero unnamed—
  On the top of a neighbouring crag,

Erect and sublime, for one moment of time.
  In the next, that wild figure they saw
(As if stung by a spasm) plunge into a chasm,
  While they waited and listened in awe.

"It's a Snark!" was the sound that first came to their ears,
  And seemed almost too good to be true.
Then followed a torrent of laughter and cheers:
  Then the ominous words "It's a Boo—"

Then, silence. Some fancied they heard in the air
  A weary and wandering sigh
That sounded like "—jum!" but the others declare
  It was only a breeze that went by.

They hunted till darkness came on, but they found
  Not a button, or feather, or mark,
By which they could tell that they stood on the ground
  Where the Baker had met with the Snark.

In the midst of the word he was trying to say,
  In the midst of his laughter and glee,
He had softly and suddenly vanished away—
  For the Snark *was* a Boojum, you see.

THE END.

Backgrounds

Early Life

DEREK HUDSON

[Parents and Childhood]†

* * *

The family background explains much in Lewis Carroll's character—his sense of religion and tradition, of loyalty and service; a certain pride in social standing; an innate conservatism that struggled with his own originality of mind. It is necessary now to detach from the rich confusion of this parade of gifted relatives, the substantial figure of his father Charles Dodgson, who was born at Hamilton, Lanarkshire, in 1800.

A photograph of the father of Lewis Carroll, which appears in Collingwood's Life of his son,[1] shows a solid and rather gloomy-looking divine, though one whose obvious authority and piety admit the lurking possibility of a sense of humour. We are assured that he had "the rare power of telling anecdotes effectively", although Collingwood adds that "his reverence for sacred things was so great that he was never known to relate a story which included a jest upon words from the Bible" (the same might be said, word for word, of Lewis Carroll as he developed).

In fact, there is no doubt that Lewis Carroll's father had a remarkably vivid, profuse and indeed ruthless sense of fantastic fun. He demonstrates it generously in an unpublished letter, written to his son Charles at the age of eight, which is among the Dodgson Family Papers:

> . . . I will not forget your commission. As soon as I get to Leeds I shall scream out in the middle of the street, Ironmongers—Iron-mongers—Six hundred men will rush out of their shops in a moment—fly, fly, in all directions—ring the bells, call the constables—set the town on fire. I *will* have a file & a screwdriver, & a ring, & if they are not brought directly, in forty seconds I will leave nothing but one small cat alive in the whole town of Leeds, & I shall only leave that, because I am afraid I shall not have time to kill it.

† From *Lewis Carroll: An Illustrated Biography* (New York: Clarkson Potter; London: Constable, 1977) 35–37, 46–50. Copyright (c) by Derek Hudson. This extract and those be-ginning on pp. 257, 261, and 302 of this edition are reprinted by permission of Clarkson N. Potter, Inc. and Constable and Company. 1. See Selected Bibliography [*Editor*].

Then what a bawling & a tearing of hair there will be! Pigs & babies, camels & butterflies, rolling in the gutter together—old women rushing up the chimneys & cows after them—ducks hiding themselves in coffee cups, & fat geese trying to squeeze themselves into pencil cases—at last the Mayor of Leeds will be found in a soup plate covered up with custard & stuck full of almonds to make him look like a sponge cake that he may escape the dreadful destruction of the Town. . . .

And so he goes on, until he concludes:

At last they bring the things which I ordered & then I spare the Town & send off in fifty waggons & under the protection of 10,000 soldiers, a file & a screwdriver and a ring as a present to Charles Lutwidge Dodgson from his affec^nt. Papa.[2]

Surely no boy of eight could ever have received more direct encouragement to devote himself to the writing of nonsense than this? The Rev. Charles Dodgson was heavy-handed; his son refined the process to a sensitive art. But the element of ruthlessness in this letter reappears in the work of Lewis Carroll.

The father would not now be remembered if it were not for his son, but he had in abundant measure the qualities necessary to the success of a nineteenth-century clergyman, and they brought him in due course to the Archdeaconry of Richmond and to a Canonry at Ripon Cathedral. He was a distinguished classical scholar who took a "double first" at Christ Church, Oxford, published a translation of Tertullian and a number of books on theological and religious subjects, and, besides all this, had a special interest in mathematical studies.[3] His generosity to the poor was proverbial in the character of his famous son—though more, perhaps, that belongs to the formal presentation of C. L. Dodgson, the Oxford don, than to the artist who wrote as Lewis Carroll.

* * * it is beyond dispute that Lewis Carroll modelled his outward character largely on his authoritarian father. This would make it all the more likely that, as a grown man, he would turn back again and again to his memories of the love of an affectionate mother, who died on the day before his nineteenth birthday. It seems clear that students of heredity must look to his mother for much of the gentleness, the graceful simplicity, and perhaps, too, the whimsical poetry, without which the "Alice" books could never have been written. In his "Easter Greeting", written long afterwards, he remembered "a Mother's gentle hand that undraws your curtains and a Mother's

2. The entire letter is published in Morton Cohen's edition of *The Letters of Lewis Carroll* 1: 4. See Selected Bibliography [*Editor*].
3. An archdeacon ranks just below the bishop of the diocese; a canon serves on the ecclesiastical staff of a cathedral. A "double-first" is the winning of first-class honors in examinations in two subjects. Tertullian was a theologian of the early Roman church [*Editor*].

sweet voice that summons you to rise". Collingwood quotes an estimate of Mrs Dodgson as

> one of the sweetest and gentlest women that ever lived, whom to know
> was to love. The earnestness of her simple faith and love shone forth in
> all she did and said; she seemed to live always in the conscious presence
> of God. It has been said by her children that they never in all their lives
> remember to have heard an impatient or harsh word from her lips. (8)

This picture might appear almost too idealistic to be quite convincing. But a perusal of some of Mrs Dodgson's letters—written in a sensitive, swiftly running hand—show that she was essentially a practical angel, who lived effectively on this earth: a very busy person who often wrote "in a tearing hurry" or "at a gallop", and whose family, husband, house, garden and servants filled her life.

* * *

As a boy Lewis Carroll devoted himself wholeheartedly to the entertainment of his brothers and sisters; and because the sisters were in the majority he naturally acquired from an early age those special skills in amusing little girls which he practised so willingly for the rest of his life. The minute box of carpenter's tools, measuring 2 inches by 1½ inches and inscribed on the lid "Tool box E.L.D. from C.L.D.", which he made for his sister Elizabeth at Croft, shows that he was remarkably deft with his fingers. He was a successful conjurer, and, according to Collingwood, he made, with the assistance of the village carpenter and members of his family, a troupe of marionettes and a theatre for them to perform in—thus early establishing his life-long passion for the stage. Apparently he also owned, as a boy, a contemporary German puppet-theatre.

* * *

It may not be out of place to insert here some remarks made many years later by a Christ Church friend of Lewis Carroll:

> My own view has always been that Dodgson was a great dramatic genius,
> who had found his opening as "Dramatist of Childhood": this was his
> work in life, and was consciously, or, perhaps more often, subconsciously,
> present to him in seeking the friendship of children: it was a "dramatic"
> as well as a "personal" friendship that he sought.[4]

Lewis Carroll never did, in fact, complete a play for the professional stage, and in later life produced only a few prologues, etc., for amateurs, although * * * he once seriously considered writing a play

---

4. Quoted in S. H. Williams and Falconer Madan, A *Handbook of the Literature of the Rev. C. I. Dodgson (Lewis Carroll)* (Oxford, 1931) xx. The friend's name is not given [*Editor*].

and got so far as sketching an outline for it. There is no doubt, however, that the dialogues which contribute so much to the success of the "Alice" books are informed with a keen dramatic sense; and he cast his *Euclid and his Modern Rivals*[5] effectively into dramatic shape. It is important therefore to understand that his early enthusiasm for the drama was an essential element in his crowded childhood.

But, soon after his arrival at Croft[6] he also began to write poems and stories, and to set aside a special little book for humorous sketches, in which he was already taking great pleasure. Throughout his life he continued to draw with remarkable zest and perseverance, never attaining to a professional facility, but showing more than ordinary talent. His drawings were naïve, but enjoyed the advantages of sincerity and simplicity; the best of them are masterpieces of the amateur, and have their own validity as expressions of character. Thus we can trace the progress of his artistic talent from the lively, grotesque, uninhibited drawings of his first youth—which often have a wild brilliance; through the imaginative but still primitive designs for the first draft of *Alice's Adventures in Wonderland*; until it peters out in conventional sketches of little girls at the seaside, painstaking but weak.

At Croft he was soon illustrating the manuscript magazines which he edited, and largely composed, for the amusement of his family (his interest in illustration, persisting throughout his life, helps to explain the usually happy results that he obtained from artist-collaborators in his later books). The first of the family magazines was *Useful and Instructive Poetry*, composed for "W.L.D." and "L.F.D.", his younger brother and sister, Wilfred (aged seven) and Louisa (aged five). The editor tells us that it was written "about the year 1845" and "lasted about half a year". Many of the verses poke fun at copybook maxims. Thus, "Rules and Regulations":

> Learn well your grammar,
> And never stammer,[7]
> Write well and neatly,
> And sing most sweetly,
> Be enterprising,
> Love early rising,
> Go walk of six miles,
> Have ready quick smiles,
> With lightsome laughter,

5. *Euclid and His Modern Rivals*, published in 1879, was intended to demonstrate that for pedagogical purposes a revised version of Euclid was preferable to any of the geometries that proposed to replace it [*Editor*].
6. The rectory to which the family moved in 1843 [*Editor*].

7. These allusions were something more than convenient rhymes. Several of the children stammered, among them Lewis Carroll, who suffered from a hesitation of speech throughout his life. But four of the children did not stammer at all. Wilfred was one of those who escaped the affliction.

Soft flowing after.
Drink tea, not coffee;
Never eat toffy.
Eat bread with butter.
Once more, don't stutter.
Don't waste your money.
Abstain from honey.
Shut doors behind you,
(Don't slam them mind you.)
Drink beer, not porter.[8]
Don't enter the water
Till to swim you are able.
Sit close to the table.
Take care of a candle.
Shut a door by the handle,
Don't push with your shoulder
Until you are older.
Lose not a button.
Refuse cold mutton.
Starve your canaries.
Believe in fairies. . . .

The first poem in the magazine, which the editor declares was suggested by a piece in Praed's *Etonian*,[9] takes up the theme of belief in fairies in a manner intimate and personal. It is called "My Fairy":

I have a fairy by my side
    Which says I must not sleep.
When once in pain I loudly cried
    It said "You must not weep".

If, full of mirth, I smile and grin,
    It says "You must not laugh";
When once I wished to drink some gin
    It said "You must not quaff".

When once a meal I wished to taste
    It said "You must not bite";
When to the wars I went in haste
    It said "You must not fight."

"What may I do?" at length I cried,
    Tired of the painful task.
The fairy quietly replied,
  ˙ And said "You must not ask."

Moral: "You mustn't".

8. Porter is a weak, sweet beer [*Editor*].
9. Winthrop Mackworth Praed was a writer of light verse whose school magazine, *The Eton-* *ian*, was republished in several London editions in the 1820s [*Editor*].

This tiresome fairy, conjured up by Lewis Carroll at the age of thirteen, seems to have kept in touch with him during most of his life, and to have been particularly assiduous in its attentions after he had passed forty. Was this the fairy who gave him his insomnia and his stoicism, who set such strict bounds to his natural humour, who put him on to a sparse diet, and who ultimately told him "You must not ask" as the answer to several large questions? There is no end to the almost uncanny anticipations that we find in this remarkable childhood. The same magazine contains "A Tale of a Tail", with a drawing of a very long dog's tail which seems to anticipate the Mouse's tail in "Alice", and a poem about someone who insisted on standing on a wall but eventually fell off it—strongly suggestive of Humpty Dumpty. The pages are as full of "Morals" as the conversation of the Ugly Duchess. There is also a significant emphasis throughout on dreams and visions, and a hint—at thirteen!—of what G. M. Young has called "the new, unpietistic handling of childhood". It is not quite enough to say of Lewis Carroll that the child was father of the man. In his case the child and the man were curiously, indeed uniquely, blended.

* * *

ANNE CLARK

[School]†

* * * One major advantage of his improved financial status was that Mr Dodgson could now invest money in his children's future.[1] For his daughters he considered that insurances provided the best securities, but for his sons he felt that an investment in their education would reap the greatest dividends in later life. He was determined to obtain the very best education possible for his eldest son. So it was that Charles Dodgson, at the age of twelve, left home on 1 August 1844, equipped by his devoted family with a superfluity of clothes and comforts, and became a boarder at Richmond School, some ten miles away.

* * *

† From *Lewis Carroll: A Biography* (New York: Schocken; London: J. M. Dent, 1979) 36–43. Copyright (c) 1979 by Anne Clark. This extract and that on p. 305 of this edition are reprinted by permission of Schocken Books, published by Pantheon Books, a division of Random House, Inc., and by permission of the author and J. M. Dent & Sons, Ltd.
1. In 1843 Mr. Dodgson was appointed to the parish of Croft, which provided a substantial income of over £1,000 a year along with a house and garden [*Editor*].

The old schoolhouse was replaced in 1850 and ultimately demolished, but Richmond School as Charles knew it was a one-storey building erected in 1677 and situated in a corner of the churchyard. Originally it had consisted of a single room forty-five feet long and twenty feet wide, but in 1815 a second had been added. Heating was by a large open fire. The headmaster had a rostrum at one end, and the boys sat on benches round the walls in enclosures that looked like pews. Charles, like all the other pupils, had a sloping bookboard with a shelf beneath where he could keep text books, writing materials and so forth.

Despite his shyness, Charles settled down quickly at the school. As a newcomer he was expected to undergo various initiation ceremonies in the churchyard where the children used to play, and these he described to his eldest sisters Fanny and Memy in a letter written only five days after the start of term:

> The boys have played two tricks upon me which were these—they first proposed to play at 'King of the Cobblers' and asked if I would be king, to which I agreed. Then they made me sit down and sat (on the ground) in a circle round me, and they told me to say 'Go to work' which I said, and they immediately began kicking me and knocking me on all sides. The next game they proposed was 'Peter, the red lion', and they made a mark on a tombstone (for we were playing in the churchyard) and one of the boys walked with his eyes shut, holding out his finger to touch, trying to touch the mark; then a little boy came forward to lead the rest and led a good many very near the mark; at last it was my turn; they told me to shut my eyes well, and the next minute I had my finger in the mouth of one of the boys, who had stood (I believe) before the tombstone with his mouth open.[2]

Once he had proved his mettle, the teasing stopped. * * * His parents, who drove over from Croft on 10 August 1844 to find out at first hand how he was getting on at the school, were well satisfied with the way in which he adapted himself to his first experience of life outside the family circle.

* * *

Charles quickly proved his scholastic ability, achieving an outstanding rating in mathematics. At the end of the first term the headmaster wrote of him, 'He has past [sic] an excellent examination just now in mathematics, exhibiting at times an illustration of that love of precise argument, which seems to him natural. He is not however *classed* because the subjects in which he and the two others were tried, do not allow of a strict comparison with the other Mathematical Pupils.' Classical studies came less easily to him, but he

2. The entire letter, dated August 5, 1844, is printed in Cohen's edition of the *Letters* 1: 5–6 [*Editor*].

showed considerable promise despite grammatical errors and difficulties with Latin metrical form, for schoolboys of his era had not only to achieve proficiency in prose composition, but to write Latin verse, modelling themselves on the great classical poets, and observing scrupulously the complicated rules of syllabic quantity. He was, in the words of his headmaster [James Tate II], 'marvellously ingenious in replacing the ordinary inflexions of nouns and verbs, as detailed in our grammars, by more exact analogies, or convenient forms of his own devising', and when he read aloud from Virgil or Ovid, failed to observe the correct scansion.

James Tate II showed an almost uncanny ability to analyse Charles Dodgson's true potential. After only a single term he wrote to Mr and Mrs Dodgson:

> I do not hesitate to express my opinion that he possesses, along with other and natural endowments, a very uncommon share of genius. Gentle and cheerful in his intercourse with others, playful and ready in conversation, he is capable of acquirements and knowledge far beyond his years, while his reason is so clear and so jealous of error, that he will not rest satisfied without a most exact solution of whatever appears to him obscure. . . . You must not entrust your son with a full knowledge of his superiority over other boys. Let him discover this as he proceeds. The love of excellence is far beyond the love of excelling; and if he should once be bewitched into a mere ambition to surpass others I need not urge that the very quality of his knowledge would be materially injured, and that his character would receive a stain of a more serious description still.[3]

* * *

Westminster, his father's own old school, would have seemed an obvious choice for Charles to progress to, for Christ Church drew a high percentage of its men from this source. It had fallen into a sharp decline in the first half of the nineteenth century, however, and on careful consideration Mr Dodgson decided that this was not the place for Charles. * * * Rugby, on the other hand, under the headmastership of the famous Dr Thomas Arnold, and encouraged by the new London to Birmingham Railway, which made it more readily accessible, had risen to the foremost ranks of public schools. When Arnold had accepted the headmastership in 1828, most public schools found their numbers dwindling because parents were increasingly reluctant to submit their sons to the brutality of school life. Yet his methods had met with widespread approbation, and despite fees which stood at more than fifty guineas a term, Mr Dodgson resolved to send his eldest son there.[4] Charles Dodgson's

---

3. Quoted in Collingwood (see Selected Bibliography) 25.
4. Arnold added mathematics and modern history and languages to the curriculum, and trusted some of the governance of the school to exceptionally upright senior boys. Fifty guineas was over fifty-two pounds; at mid-century a working-man earned about a pound a week [*Editor*].

name was accordingly entered in the school register on 27 January 1846. He was exactly fourteen years old.

* * *

From every point of view life at Rugby was a personal disaster for young Dodgson. He could not accept the transition from the intimate family atmosphere of Richmond School, where work had been a pleasure and the kind old schoolmaster a well-loved friend, to the vast impersonality of Rugby. * * * He did not object to the work, though this was rigorous: the boys worked from 7 a.m. until 10 p.m. six days a week, and only marginally less on Sundays, when normal studies were replaced by Biblical ones. But the endless imposition of lines for trifling offences took all the pleasure out of learning and wasted hours which could have been better spent. Even worse was the bullying to which younger pupils were subjected. Though Tait modified the powers of the Praeposters, or sixth formers, who had dominated the school even in Arnold's day, and severely curbed their right to inflict punishments, he could not eliminate bullying altogether.[5] As a scholarly boy who was poor at games, Charles was an obvious target for abuse. Worse still, his distressing stammer caused him acute embarrassment. Yet he could have borne all the humiliation and misery had he been safe from interference at night. Though the practice of sleeping four or five to a bed, which had so shocked Dr Arnold, had been abolished, there were no separate sleeping quarters. Like all the younger boys in the dormitories, Charles was often stripped of his bedclothes, and spent many cold, wretched nights longing for the warm family atmosphere at Croft Rectory and counting the days till the school holidays.

* * *

Predictably, Dodgson's academic record was outstanding, and he rarely returned home for the holidays without prizes. His proud mother, meticulous as ever, kept a record of the books he won. It was against the rules for any scholar to win more than one prize per term, and though in his form of more than fifty boys he was often placed first in more than one subject, his prizes averaged out at one per half year from December 1846 onwards. Usually the choice of books, which rested with the scholar himself, was biographical, historical and religious. Even at the age of fourteen he was consciously building up for himself a library which would be of lasting value, and in choosing books either as prizes or from his own money he relied heavily on his father's opinion. Of his total of eleven prize

5. Archibald Campbell Tait went on to a distinguished career in the Church of England, becoming archbishop of Canturbury in 1868.

The sixth form is the highest class in a British school, equivalent to the senior class [*Editor*].

books from Rugby, at least three were for Classics, including Latin composition, which effectively dispels any suggestion that he was weak in these subjects. It would be fairer to say that he was better at Mathematics than Classics, and that as his life progressed, his greater inclination to the former led him to devote himself to Mathematics at the expense of his work in Latin and Greek. As time went on, Divinity also emerged as a subject in which he excelled, and in his last term at the school, the headmaster wrote to his father, 'his examination for the Divinity prize was one of the most creditable exhibitions I have ever seen.'

* * *

STUART DODGSON COLLINGWOOD

[Oxford]†

* * *

On May 23, 1850, he matriculated at Christ Church, the venerable college which had numbered his father's among other illustrious names. A letter from Dr. Jelf, one of the canons of Christ Church, to Archdeacon Dodgson, written when the former heard that his old friend's son was coming up to "the House," contains the following words: "I am sure I express the common feeling of all who remember you at Christ Church when I say that we shall rejoice to see a son of yours worthy to tread in your footsteps."

Lewis Carroll came into residence on January 24, 1851. From that day to the hour of his death—a period of forty-seven years—he belonged to "the House," never leaving it for any length of time, becoming almost a part of it. * * *

Only a few days after term began, Mrs. Dodgson died suddenly at Croft. The shock was a terrible one to the whole family, and especially to her devoted husband. * * *

Lewis Carroll was summoned home to attend the funeral—a sad interlude amidst the novel experiences of a first term of College. * * *

Early rising then was strictly enforced, as the following extract from one of his letters will show:—

> I am not so anxious as usual to begin my personal history, as the first thing I have to record is a very sad incident, namely, my missing morning chapel; before, however, you condemn me, you must hear how accidental

† From *The Life and Letters of Lewis Carroll (Rev. C. L. Dodgson)* (London: T. Fisher Unwin, 1898) 46–52, 57–60.

it was. For some days now I have been in the habit of, I will not say getting up, but of being called at a quarter past six, and generally managing to be down soon after seven. In the present instance I had been up the night before till about half-past twelve, and consequently when I was called I fell asleep again, and was thunderstruck to find on waking that it was ten minutes past eight. I have had no imposition, nor heard anything about it. It is rather vexatious to have happened so soon, as I had intended never to be late.[1]

* * *

On November 1st [1851] he won a Boulter scholarship, and at the end of the following year obtained First Class Honours in Mathematics and a Second in Classical Moderations. On Christmas Eve he was made a Student on Dr. Pusey's nomination, for at that time the Dean and Canons nominated to Studentships by turn.[2] The only conditions on which these old Studentships were held were that the Student should remain unmarried, and should proceed to Holy Orders. No statute precisely defined what work was expected of them, that question being largely left to their own discretion. * * *

In the early part of 1854 Mr. Dodgson was reading hard for "Greats." For the last three weeks before the examination he worked thirteen hours a day, spending the whole night before the *viva voce*[3] over his books. But philosophy and history were not very congenial subjects to him, and when the list was published his name was only in the third class.

He spent the Long Vacation at Whitby, reading Mathematics with Professor Price.[4] His work bore good fruit, for in October he obtained First Class Honours in the Final Mathematical School. "I am getting quite tired of being congratulated on various subjects," he writes; "there seems to be no end of it. If I had shot the Dean I could hardly have had more said about it."

In another letter dated December 13th, [1854], he says:

Enclosed you will find a list which I expect you to rejoice over considerably; it will take me more than a day to believe it, I expect—I feel at present very like a child with a new toy, but I daresay I shall be tired of it soon, and wish to be Pope of Rome next. . . . I have just been to Mr. Price to see how I did in the papers, and the result will I hope be

---

1. The letter is to his sister Mary, dated March 6, 1851. A complete text, somewhat different in its punctuation, is published in Cohen's edition of *Letters* 1: 12–15 [*Editor*].
2. Dodgson won the Boulter scholarship less than a year after he entered Oxford. He was awarded the Studentship at the end of 1852, after two years at Oxford. Edward Bouverie Pusey was canon of Christ Church, regius professor of Hebrew, and one of the founders of the Oxford Movement, an attempt to emphasize the spiritual character of the Church of England and its historical relationships with the early Christian church of Rome [*Editor*].
3. "Greats" was a name for the final examination at Oxford in classical letters and culture. *Viva voce* is an oral examination [*Editor*].
4. Bartholomew Price was a tutor and mathematical lecturer at Oxford, and perhaps the "Bat" of "Twinkle, twinkle little bat." The Long Vacation was the period in August and September between the close of one academic year the beginning of the next [*Editor*].

gratifying to you. The following were the sums total for each in the first Class, as nearly as I can remember:

Dodgson	...	...	...	279
Bosanquet	...	...	...	261
Cookson	...	...	...	254
Fowler	...	...	...	225
Ranken	...	...	...	213

He also said he never remembered so good a set of men in. All this is very satisfactory. I must also add (this is a very boastful letter) that I ought to get the senior scholarship next term. . . . One thing more I will add, to crown all, and that is, I find I am the next First Class Mathematical Student to Faussett (with the exception of Kitchin who had given up Mathematics), so that I stand next (as Bosanquet is going to leave) for the Lectureship.[5]

* * *

* * * On February 15th [1855] he was made Sub-Librarian. "This will add £35 to my income," he writes, "not much towards independence." For he was most anxious to have a sufficient income to make him his own master, that he might enter on the literary and artistic career of which he was already dreaming. On May 14th he wrote in his Diary: "The Dean and Canons have been pleased to give me one of the Bostock scholarships, said to be worth £20 a year—this very nearly raises my income this year to independence. Courage!"

His college work, during 1855, was chiefly taking private pupils, but he had, in addition, about three and a half hours a day of lecturing during the last term of the year. He did not, however, work as one of the regular staff of lecturers until the next year. From that date his work rapidly increased, and he soon had to devote regularly as much as seven hours a day to delivering lectures, to say nothing of the time required for preparing them.

* * *

5. This letter is also to his sister Mary. See Cohen, *Letters* 1: 29–30 [*Editor*].

LEWIS CARROLL

From the Letters [1855]†

To his sister Henrietta and brother Edwin

My dear Henrietta,
My dear Edwin,
I am very much obliged by your nice little birthday gift—it was much better than a cane would have been—I have got it on my watch chain, but the Dean has not yet remarked it.

My one pupil had begun his work with me, and I will give you a description how the lecture is conducted. It is the most important point, you know, that the tutor should be *dignified*, and at a distance from the pupil, and that the pupil should be as much as possible *degraded*—otherwise you know, they are not humble enough. So I sit at the further end of the room; outside the door (*which is shut*) sits the scout;¹ outside the outer door (*also shut*) sits the sub-scout; halfway down stairs sits the sub-sub-scout; and down in the yard sits the *pupil*.

The questions are shouted from one to the other, and the answers come back in the same way—it is rather confusing till you are well used to it. The lecture goes on, something like this.

> *Tutor.* "What is twice three?"
> *Scout.* "What's a rice tree?"
> *Sub-Scout.* "When is ice free?"
> *Sub-sub-Scout.* "What's a nice fee?"
> *Pupil* (timidly). "Half a guinea!"
> *Sub-sub-Scout.* "Can't forge any!"
> *Sub-Scout.* "Ho for Jinny!"
> *Scout.* "Don't be a ninny!"
> *Tutor* (looks offended, but tries another question). "Divide a hundred by twelve!"
> *Scout.* "Provide wonderful bells!"
> *Sub-Scout.* "Go ride under it yourself."
> *Sub-sub-Scout.* "Deride the dunder-headed elf!"
> *Pupil* (surprised). "Who do you mean?"
> *Sub-sub-Scout.* "Doings between!"
> *Sub-Scout.* "Blue is the screen!"
> *Scout.* "Soup-tureen!"

† From *The Letters of Lewis Carroll*, ed. Morton Cohen (New York: Oxford, 1979) 1: 31. Reprinted by permission of Oxford University Press and Macmillan, London and Basingstoke.
1. A scout is a servant [*Editor*].

And so the lecture proceeds.
 Such is Life—from

Your most affectionate brother,
Charles L. Dodgson

From the Diaries [1855–56]†

Mar: 13. (Tu). [1855].I have been trying to form some practicable scheme for reading history, and have decided on beginning with Smythe's[1] *Lectures*, of which I read the first this evening. When these scholarships are over I shall be more at leisure for general reading. I hope to carry out some such scheme as this:—

Classics. Review methodically all the books I have read, and perhaps add a new one—Aeschylus?

Divinity. Keep up Gospels and Acts in Greek, and go on to Epistles.

History. As guided by Smythe.

Languages. Read something French—begin Italian—(I think German had better be postponed).

Poetry. Read whole poets, or at least whole poems—I think in this order: Shakespeare, Milton, Byron, Coleridge, Wordsworth(?).

Mathematics. Go regularly on from the points I have fairly reached—this needs a scheme to itself.

Novels. Scott's over again to begin with (?).

Miscellaneous Studies. I should like to go on with *Etymology* and read White—and all Trench's books—and Horne Tooke—2nd *Logic*, finish Mill and dip into Dugald Stewart.[2]

Divinity reading for Ordination. This should take precedence of all other, I must consult my Father on the subject.

† From *The Diaries of Lewis Carroll*, ed. Roger Lancelyn Green (New York: Oxford, 1954) 1: 43–44, 55, 71, 76–77. This extract and those on the following pages are reprinted by permission of AP Watt Limited on behalf of the executors of the C. L. Dodgson Estate and Richard Gordon Lancelyn Green. I have added, within brackets, the year of each entry. Unless otherwise noted, all other bracketed additions are Mr. Green's. I have indicated omissions within an entry for a single date by asterisks. I have not indicated when I have omitted material between entries. The dates of the entries make it clear that these extracts are not usually continuous [*Editor*].

1. Green suggests that this reference is to William Smyth's *Lectures on Modern History* (1840) [*Editor*].

2. "White": perhaps the reference is to Walter Whiter, whose *Etymologican Universale, or Universal Etymological Dictionary* was published in 1822–25. Richard Chenevix Trench published the first edition of *The Study of Words* in 1851, and his lectures on *English, Past and Present* in 1855. The first volume of John Horne Tooke's Ἔπεα πτεροεντα, *Or, The Diversions of Purley*, was published in 1786, and the second volume in 1805; Charles Richardson published an exposition of Horne Tooke's work, *On the Study of Language*, in 1854. John Stuart Mill's *A System of Logic* was published in 1843; and an edition of the writings of Dugald Stewart—an early 19th century Scottish philosopher who wrote on topics in logic and epistemology—was being published in 1854–58 [*Editor*].

Other Subjects. Scripture History—Church Architecture—Anglo-Saxon—Gothic.

July 5. (Th). [1855]. I went to the Boys' School in the morning to hear my Father teach, as I want to begin trying myself soon. Some of the boys were much more intelligent than I expected.

July 8. (Sun). [1855]. I took the 1st and 2nd class of the Boys' School in the morning—we did part of the life of St. John, one of the "lessons" on Scripture lives. I liked my first attempt in teaching very much.

July 10. (Tu). [1855]. I have an idea for a new drama for the Marionette Theatre—*Alfred the Great,* but have not yet begun to write it. His adventures in disguise in the neatherd's hut, and in the Danish Camp, will furnish two very effective scenes.

Yesterday I heard from Menella Smedley, returning 'The Three Voices' which she borrowed to show Frank Smedley: she says that he wishes to be instrumental in publishing it and others—I do not think I have yet written anything worthy of real publication (in which I do not include *The Whitby Gazette* or *The Oxonian Advertiser*), but I do not despair of doing so some day.[3]

Jan: 7. (M). [1856]. * * * Finished *Alton Locke.*[4] It tells the tale well of the privations and miseries of the poor, but I wish he would propose some more definite remedy, and especially that he would tell us what he wishes to substitute for the iniquitous 'sweating' system in tailoring and other trades.

If the book were but a little more definite, it might stir up many fellow-workers in the same good field of social improvement. Oh that God, in His good providence, may make me hereafter such a

3. Menella Bute Smedley, Dodgson's first cousin once removed, wrote for magazines and published several volumes of heroic poetry and poems for children. Roger Lancelyn Green suggests (*Times Literary Supplement,* March 1, 1957: 136) that one of her poems founded on a German legend, "The Shepherd of the Giant Mountains," furnished some of the details for "Jabberwocky." Frank Smedley, Menella Smedley's cousin, was a novelist and essayist who was associated with Edmund Yates in the publication of the *Comic Times* and *The Train* (see below), in which Dodgson was to publish some of his early writing. *The Oxonian Advertiser* and the *Whitby Gazette* were local newspapers in which Dodgson published several comic poems and a prose sketch in 1854.

"The Three Voices," a parody of a poem by Tennyson, was included in *Mischmasch,* a scrapbook of his writing Dodgson constructed at Oxford; the poem was later (1856) published in *The Train.* Dodgson's contributions to the *Oxonian Advertiser* have not been definitively identified; see *The Lewis Carroll Handbook* (see Selected Bibliography), 6–7. Dodgson contributed a poem, "The Lady of the Ladle," and a prose sketch, "Wilhelm Von Schmitz," to the *Whitby Gazette;* both are reprinted, along with "The Three Voices," in the Nonesuch and Modern Library collections of his writings (see Selected Bibliography) [*Editor*].
4. A novel by Charles Kingsley, published in 1850, about the miseries and exploitations of the tailoring trade [*Editor*].

worker! But, alas, what are the means? Each has his own nostrum to propound, and in the Babel of voices nothing is done. I would thankfully spend and be spent so long as I were sure of really effecting something by the sacrifice, and not merely lying down under the wheels of some irrestible Juggernaut.

    * * * How few seem to care for the only subjects of real interest in life.—What am I, to say so? Am *I* a deep philosopher, or a great genius? I think neither. What talents I have, I desire to devote to His service, and may He purify me, and take away my pride and selfishness. Oh that *I* might hear 'Well done, good and faithful servant'!

Feb: 8. (F). [1856]. The school class[5] noisy and inattentive—the novelty of the thing is wearing off, and I find them rather unmanageable. Was a good deal tired with the six hours consecutive lecturing.

    Heard from Mr. Yates[6]—he is going to use the verses on 'Solitude', and the 'Carpette Knyghte'. He wishes me to alter the signature 'B.B.' and proposed that I should adopt some 'Nom de plume': accordingly I sent 'Dares'. At the same time I suggested a picture to illustrate the verse—if Bennett will deign to draw it—a group of children at play * * *

Feb: 10. (Sun). [1856]. Heard again from Mr. Yates—he wants me to choose another name, as Dares is too much like a newspaper signature. With reference to the picture he says he has already handed the verses over for illustration, and that the idea he gave the artist was, a man lying stretched under a large tree on a hill, a brook meandering in the distance, and a general sense of solitude and stillness pervading the picture.

Feb: 11. (M). [1856]. Wrote to Mr. Yates sending him a choice of names: 1. *Edgar Cuthwellis* (made by transposition out of 'Charles Lutwidge'). 2. *Edgar U. C. Westhill* (ditto). 3. *Louis Carroll*, (derived from Lutwidge = Ludovic = Louis, and Charles [Carolus]). 4. *Lewis Carroll.* (ditto)

---

5. In January of this year Dodgson had accepted a part-time appointment teaching in a boys' school in Oxford. He gave up the appointment in February [*Editor*].

6. Edmund Yates, a popular novelist and an enterprising journalist, was the editor of the *Comic Times*, which survived for sixteen weekly numbers in 1855, and its successor, *The Train*, a monthly magazine that lasted a little over a year. "B. B." was the signature Dodgson

had used for his two contributions to the *Whitby Gazette*. Charles Henry Bennett was a comic draftsman who wrote and illustrated children's books, drew for comic periodicals, and ended his career as one of the principal artists of *Punch*. "Ye Carpette Knyghte" appeared in *The Train* in March, 1856; it is reprinted in both the Nonesuch and Modern Library collections of Dodgson's writings [*Editor*].

LEWIS CARROLL

Early Poems

She's All My Fancy Painted Him†

A POEM

This affecting fragment was found in MS. among the papers of
the well-known author of "Was it You or I?" a tragedy, and the two
popular novels, "Sister and Son", and "The Niece's Legacy, or the
Grateful Grandfather".

> She's all my fancy painted him
> (I make no idle boast);
> If he or you had lost a limb,
> Which would have suffered most?
>
> He said that you had been to her,
> And seen me here before:
> But, in another character,
> She was the same of yore.
>
> There was not one that spoke to us,
> Of all that thronged the street:
> So he sadly got into a 'bus,
> And pattered with his feet.
>
> They sent him word I had not gone
> (We know it to be true);
> If she should push the matter on,
> What would become of you?
>
> They gave her one, they gave me two,
> They gave us three or more;
> They all returned from him to you,
> Though they were mine before.
>
> If I or she should chance to be
> Involved in this affair,
> He trusts to you to set them free,
> Exactly as we were.
>
> It seemed to me that you had been
> (Before she had this fit)

---

† First printed in a home-made scrapbook of
Carroll's writings, *Mischmasch*, in 1855, and
then in the *Comic Times* later in the same year.
Reprinted in Florence Milner's edition of *The
Rectory Umbrella and Mischmasch*, and in
both the Nonesuch and Modern Library collections of Dodgson's writing (see Selected Bibliography). The poem begins as a parody of
"Alice Gray," a popular ballad by William Mee
published about 1815. It is also an early version
of the White Rabbit's evidence in *Alice's Adventures in Wonderland* (see pp. 94–95 of this
edition) [*Editor*].

An obstacle, that came between
    Him, and ourselves, and it.

Don't let him know she liked them best,
    For this must ever be
A secret, kept from all the rest,
    Between yourself and me.

Solitude†

I love the stillness of the wood:
    I love the music of the rill:
I love to couch in pensive mood
    Upon some silent hill.

Scarce heard, beneath yon arching trees,
    The silver-crested ripples pass;
And, like a mimic brook, the breeze
    Whispers among the grass.

Here from the world I win release,
    Nor scorn of men, nor footstep rude,
Break in to mar the holy peace
    Of this great solitude.

Here may the silent tears I weep
    Lull the vexed spirit into rest,
As infants sob themselves to sleep
    Upon a mother's breast.

But when the bitter hour is gone,
    And the keen throbbing pangs are still,
Oh, sweetest then to couch alone
    Upon some silent hill!

To live in joys that once have been,
    To put the cold world out of sight,
And deck life's drear and barren scene
    With hues of rainbow-light.

For what to man the gift of breath,
    If sorrow be his lot below;
If all the day that ends in death
    Be dark with clouds of woe?

Shall the poor transport of an hour
    Repay long years of sore distress—
The fragrance of a lonely flower
    Make glad the wilderness?

† First published in *The Train* in March 1856. Reprinted by Dodgson in *Phantasmagoria* (1869) and *Three Sunsets* (1898), collections he made of his verse: in the latter, Dodgson added the date of the poem's composition.

Ye golden hours of Life's young spring,
    Of innocence, of love and truth!
Bright, beyond all imagining,
    Thou fairy-dream of youth!

I'd give all wealth that years have piled,
    The slow result of Life's decay,
To be once more a little child
    For one bright summer-day.

March 16, 1853

Upon the Lonely Moor†

I met an aged, aged man
    Upon the lonely moor:
I knew I was a gentleman,
    And he was but a boor.
So I stopped and roughly questioned him,
    "Come, tell me how you live!"
But his words impressed my ear no more
    Than if it were a sieve.

He said, "I look for soap-bubbles,
    That lie among the wheat,
And bake them into mutton-pies,
    And sell them in the street.
I sell them unto men," he said,
"Who sail on stormy seas;
And that's the way I get my bread—
    A trifle, if you please."

But I was thinking of a way
    To multiply by ten,
And always, in the answer, get
    The question back again.
I did not hear a word he said,
    But kicked that old man calm,
And said, "Come, tell me how you live!"
    And pinched him in the arm.

His accents mild took up the tale:
    He said, "I go my ways,
And when I find a mountain-rill,
    I set it in a blaze.
And thence they make a stuff they call
    Rowland's Macassar Oil;[1]

† Published, without a signature, in *The Train* in October 1856. The poem is a parody of Wordsworth's "Resolution and Independence," and an early version of the White Knight's song in *Through the Looking-Glass* (see pp. 187–90 of this edition).
1. A hairdressing.

But fourpence-halfpenny is all
　　They give me for my toil."

But I was thinking of a plan
　　To paint one's gaiters green,
So much the colour of the grass
　　That they could ne'er be seen.
I gave his ear a sudden box,
　　And questioned him again,
And tweaked his grey and reverend locks,
　　And put him into pain.

He said, "I hunt for haddocks' eyes
　　Among the heather bright,
And work them into waistcoat-buttons
　　In the silent night.
And these I do not sell for gold,
　　Or coin of silver-mine,
But for a copper-halfpenny,
　　And that will purchase nine.

"I sometimes dig for buttered rolls,
　　Or set limed twigs[2] for crabs;
I sometimes search the flowery knolls
　　For wheels of hansom cabs.
And that's the way" (he gave a wink)
　　"I get my living here,
And very gladly will I drink
　　Your Honour's health in beer."

I heard him then, for I had just
　　Completed my design
To keep the Menai bridge[3] from rust
　　By boiling it in wine.
I duly thanked him, ere I went,
　　For all his stories queer,
But chiefly for his kind intent
　　To drink my health in beer.

And now if e'er by chance I put
　　My fingers into glue,
Or madly squeeze a right-hand foot
　　Into a left-hand shoe;
Or if a statement I aver
　　Of which I am not sure,
I think of that strange wanderer
　　Upon the lonely moor.

---

2. Setting limed twigs is a practice of bird-catchers.　　3. An iron suspension bridge in Wales.

DEREK HUDSON

[Ordination]†

✼   ✼   ✼

"An unimaginative person", said Ruskin, "can neither be reverent nor kind." It is a perceptive remark, and may properly be applied to C. L. Dodgson, in whom there was much kindness, not always revealed on surface acquaintance, and deep inherent reverence. This being the case, it was natural that he should have been greatly exercised in his mind when the time came for him to decide whether he should take Holy Orders, a necessary step if he was to continue in his Christ Church Studentship, which he had no wish to abandon. Many years later (September 10th, 1885) he wrote an important letter to his cousin and godson William Wilcox, who was then himself contemplating the priesthood, which will be read with interest:

> . . . I will tell you a few facts about myself, which may be useful to you. When I was about 19, the Studentships at Ch. Ch. were in the gift of the Dean & Chapter—each Canon having a turn: & Dr Pusey, having a turn, sent for me, & told me he would like to nominate me, but had made a rule to nominate *only* those who were going to take Holy Orders. I told him that was my intention, & he nominated me. That was a sort of "condition", no doubt: but I am quite sure, if I had told him, when the time came to be ordained, that I had changed my mind, he would not have considered it as in any way a breach of contract.
>
> When I reached the age for taking Deacon's Orders, I found myself established as the Mathematical Lecturer, & with no sort of inclination to give it up & take parochial work: & I had grave doubts whether it would not be my duty *not* to take Orders. I took advice on this point (Bp Wilberforce was one that I applied to), & came to the conclusion that, so far from educational work (even Mathematics) being unfit occupation for a clergyman, it was distinctly a *good* thing that many of our educators should be men in Holy Orders.
>
> And a further doubt occurred—I could not feel that I should ever wish to take *Priest's* Orders—And I asked Dr Liddon whether he thought I shd be justified in taking Deacon's Orders as a sort of experiment, which would enable me to try how the occupation of a clergyman suited me, & *then* decide whether I would take full Orders. He said "most certainly"— & that a Deacon is in a totally different position from a Priest: & much more free to regard himself as *practically* a layman. So I took Deacon's Orders in that spirit. And now, for several reasons, I have given up all idea of taking full Orders, & regard myself (tho' occasionally doing small

† From *Lewis Carroll*, 103–6.

clerical acts, such as helping at the Holy Communion) as practically a layman.[1]

This was Dodgson's view of his commitments as he looked back, when he was past fifty, on his career as a clergyman. In summarising the story, he did not touch on many considerations that had been important to him at the time.

It was, no doubt, the general intention in his family, from very early days, that he would marry and settle down as a parish priest in one of the Christ Church livings,[2] as his father had done. Canon Dodgson diligently proposed to him a system of personal saving and insurance which had this in prospect, but Dodgson eventually came to the decision "that it will be best not to effect any insurance at present, but simply to save as much as I reasonably can from year to year. If at any future period I contemplate marriage (of which I see no present likelihood), it will be quite time enough to begin paying the premium then." (Diary, July 31st, 1857.)

That he was still a bachelor when the time came for him to take a decision about his ordination must obviously have been an influencing factor, for the idea of relinquishing an agreeable existence at Christ Church to settle down as a solitary country curate or parson cannot have had many attractions. Moreover, there were other important considerations. Dodgson was already an ardent theatregoer: yet Bishop Wilberforce—to whose pronouncements as Bishop of Oxford Dodgson was obliged to give ear—had expressed the opinion that the "resolution to attend theatres or operas was an absolute disqualification for Holy Orders", so far as the parochial clery was concerned. And, perhaps most conclusive of all, there was the disability of his stammer.

In view of all these obstacles, it is not surprising that Dodgson should have abandoned any half-formed idea of attempting parochial work. That he felt himself generally unfitted for the day-to-day encounters of a parish can be gathered from a remark which he made in his diary after an argument with his brother Wilfred on college duties and the need for submission to discipline (in which Dodgson apparently believed more strongly than Wilfred): "This also suggests to me grave doubts as to the work of the ministry which I am looking forward to—if I find it so hard to prove a plain duty to one individual, and that one unpractised in argument, how can I ever be ready to

1. The entire letter is published in Cohen, *Letters* 1: 602–3. Samuel Wilberforce was bishop of Oxford. H. P. Liddon was Dodgson's colleague at Christ Church, and later canon of St. Paul's. He was also Dodgson's companion on a journey to Russia in 1867, Dodgson's only significant travel outside England. Hudson quotes Liddon as writing, "I have never been inside a theatre since I took Orders in 1852, and I do not intend to go into one, please God, while I live" (140) [*Editor*].

2. In the nineteenth-century Church of England, individuals and institutions such as Christ Church controlled appointments to parishes and other ecclesiastical preferments [*Editor*].

face the countless sophisms and ingenious arguments against religion
which a clergyman must meet with!" (Diary, February 2nd, 1857.)

* * *

There is no evidence that Dodgson was disturbed in his faith, or
that his hesitations over ordination derived from anything but his
own sense of diffidence and unworthiness. In the end he decided to
take Deacon's Orders—as he put it, "as a sort of experiment"—and
after studying at Cuddesdon was ordained by the Bishop of Oxford
on December 22nd, 1861. The diary shows that, after he had been
ordained Deacon, Dean Liddell maintained that he was obliged to
take Priest's Orders, but on further reflection the Dean did not press
the point.

That he sufficiently conquered his stammer to undertake even a
small part in the services of the Church is a great proof of Dodgson's
courage. There are records in the Croft baptismal register of his
conducting baptisms on August 2nd, 1863, and on September 11th,
1864—his entry as "Officiating Minister" on that occasion followed
immediately after an entry in his father's hand, a comparison of the
two writings suggesting how closely he identified himself with his
father. His diary shows that he first conducted a funeral on October
5th, 1862. He was able to preach occasional sermons, and did so
with increasing success in his later years, though he always had to
speak slowly. But the stammer—much though he worked at it, by
reciting scenes from Shakespeare—remained a constant problem.
The diary of Sunday, August 31st, 1862, records that he read the
service that afternoon in the church at Putney, where his uncle lived:
"I got through it all with great success, till I came to read out the
first verse of the hymn before the sermon, where the two words
'strife, strengthened', coming together were too much for me. . . ."
And thirty year later his friend Vere Bayne noted (December 10th,
1891) that "Dodgson read the Lesson in Morn^g Chapel, but got into
difficulties toward the end". It was indeed the curse of his life.

* * *

The Alice Books

DEREK HUDSON

[Child Friends]†

* * * His delight in the companionship of children—particularly of little girls—was to sustain and encourage him until his death. It had all begun, of course, when he played with his brothers and sisters and their friends at Daresbury and Croft; but we see the process continuing in the first surviving diary of his early manhood. On August 21st, at Tynemouth, he met the "three nice little children" of a Mrs Crawshay, and wrote: "I took a great fancy to Florence, the eldest, a child of very sweet manners—she has a very striking, though not a pretty face, and may possibly turn out a beautiful brunette." At about the same time he made the acquaintance at Whitburn of Frederika Liddell, a niece of Dr Liddell, the new Dean of Christ Church—"one of the most lovely children I ever saw, gentle and innocent looking, not an inanimate doll-beauty". He sketched her on the sea-shore, and she soon became "one of the nicest children I have ever seen, as well as the prettiest: dear, sweet, pretty little Frederika!" But Frederika had a younger sister who also caught his eye: "The youngest Liddell, Gertrude, is even prettier than my little favourite, Freddie: indeed she has quite the most lovely face I ever saw in a child" (September 21st, 1855).[1]

Collingwood's remark [365] that "his first child-friend, so far as I know, was Miss Alice Liddell" is therefore misleading. Dodgson had made friends with a number of children before he ever met Alice, including two of her cousins. It is not surprising that, as an artist, he should have been attracted primarily to good-looking children— and the Liddell family, as a whole, seems to have been exceptionally well-favoured. Soon after Dean Liddell had installed himself at Christ Church, Dodgson was on friendly terms with his two eldest children, Harry, aged eight or nine, and Lorina, aged six or seven. The diary of March 6th, 1856, records: "Made friends with little Harry Liddell (whom I first spoke to down at the boats last week): he is certainly the handsomest boy I ever saw." It seems that he did

---

† From *Lewis Carroll*, 87–89.
1. These quotations are from Green's edition of the *Diaries* (see Selected Bibliography) 1: 60–

65. Hudson identifies subsequent quotations from the *Diaries* by date [*Editor*].

not meet the second daughter, Alice, who was nearing her fourth birthday, until April 25th of that year, when he went over to the Deanery with his friend Southey to try to take a photograph of the Cathedral from the garden. "The three little girls"—the third was Edith, about two years old—"were in the garden most of the time, and we became excellent friends: we tried to group them in the foreground of the picture, but they were not patient sitters." Although the photographs of the Cathedral proved failures, and although the diary gives no further details, there must have been some special quality about this first meeting with Alice Liddell that impressed Dodgson, for he added to his diary entry a comment which he reserved for outstanding occasions: "I mark this day with a white stone".

Thereafter Dodgson was frequently at the Deanery. In June he photographed the young Liddells, and, with his cousin Frank, took Harry and Ina (as Lorina was generally known) on a successful river excursion. But his early photographic attempts often ended in failure, especially when he tried to take pictures in bad light. He soon discovered that Mrs Liddell, the mother of these desirably "photogenic" children, was as formidable as she was handsome; and before long she had apparently decided that Dodgson's photography was becoming a nuisance. After twice attempting to take photographs of Harry and Ina in November, Dodgson wrote in his diary (November 14th, 1856):

> I found Mrs Liddell had said they were not to be taken till all can be taken in a group. This may be meant as a hint that I have intruded on the premises long enough: I am quite of the same opinion myself; and, partly for this reason, partly because I cannot afford to waste any more time on portraits at such a bad season of the year, I have resolved not to go again for the present, nor at all without invitation, except just to pack up the things and bring them back.

It was a passing cloud: a hypersensitive young man's readiness to seize offence. Within a few days he was dining at the Deanery and attending a musical party there. Yet it appears probable that Mrs Liddell did not take particularly kindly to Dodgson, for when he offered to teach Henry Liddell his sums, she "seemed to think it would take up too much of my time" [Dec. 12, 1856]. (He succeeded eventually in his determination, though the lessons did not last long.)

In 1856 Dr Liddell's health compelled him to winter in Madeira. His wife accompanied him. It is noteworthy, perhaps, that—the very day after they left in December—Dodgson went over to the Deanery and stayed to "nursery" dinner.

Despite the temperamental difficulties of association with Mrs

Liddell, Dodgson soon established himself as a close friend of her children—he gave "little Alice" a present for her fifth birthday—and he obviously gained the confidence of their governess, Miss Prickett. Even this had its drawbacks in Victorian Oxford, however, for on May 17th, 1857, he commented: "I find to my great surprise that my notice of them (the children) is construed by some men into attentions to the governess, Miss Prickett." After a serious discussion with a colleague about this unexpected problem, he decided that, "though for my own part I should give little importance to the existence of so groundless a rumour, it would be inconsiderate to the governess to give any further occasion for remarks of the sort. For this reason I shall avoid taking any public notice of the children in future, unless any occasion should arise when such an interpretation is impossible".

Miss Prickett—"Pricks" to the children—was not, according to Alice's son, Caryl Hargreaves, "the highly educated governess of the present day"; in due course she became Mrs Foster and died the proprietress of the Mitre Hotel.[2] The idea that Dodgson might have been attracted to her is delightfully absurd. Indeed, the very suggestion shows that Dodgson's contemporaries simply could not contemplate the possibility that a young man in his twenties might have a disinterested love of children for their own sake.

* * *

LEWIS CARROLL

From the Diaries [1856–63]†

June 5. (Th.) [1856]. From 4.30 to 7 Frank[1] and I made a boating excursion with Harry and Ina [Lorina]: the latter, much to my surprise, having got permission from the Dean to come. We went down to the island, and made a kind of picnic there, taking biscuits with us, and buying ginger beer and lemonade there. Harry as before rowed stroke most of the way, and fortunately, considering the wild spirits of the children, we got home without accidents, having attracted by our remarkable crew a good deal of attention from almost everyone we met. Mark this day, annalist, not only with a white stone, but as altogether 'Dies mirabilis'.

2. Caryl and Alice Hargreaves, "Alice's Recollections of Carrollian Days," *Cornhill,* n.s. 73 (1932): 1–12.

† *The Diaries of Lewis Carroll,* ed. Roger Lancelyn Green, 1: 86, 178, 181–86, 188, 208.
1. Frank Dodgson, his cousin [*Editor*].

June 17. *(Tu)*. [1862]. Expedition to Nuneham. Duckworth[2] (of Trinity) and Ina, Alice and Edith came with us. We set out about 12.30 and got to Nuneham about 2; dined there, then walked in the park and set off for home about 4.30. About a mile above Nuneham heavy rain came on, and after bearing it a short time I settled that we had better leave the boat and walk: three miles of this drenched us all pretty well. I went on first with the children * * * and took them to the only house I knew in Sandford, Mrs. Broughton's, where Ranken lodges. I left them with her to get their clothes dried, and went off to find a vehicle, but none was to be had there, so on the others arriving, Duckworth and I walked on to Iffley, whence we sent them a fly. We all had tea in my rooms about 8.30, after which I took the children home, and we adjourned to Bayne's rooms for music and singing.

July 3. *(Th)*. [1862]. * * * Atkinson[3] and I went to lunch at the Deanery, after which we were to have gone down the river with the children, but as it rained, we remained to hear some music and singing instead—the three sang 'Sally come up' with great spirit.[4] Then croquet at which Duckworth joined us, and he and Atkinson afterwards dined with me. I mark this day with a white stone.

July 4. *(F)*. [1862]. Atkinson brought over to my rooms some friends of his, a Mrs. and Miss Peters, of whom I took photographs, and who afterwards looked over my album and stayed to lunch. They then went off to the Museum, and Duckworth and I made an expedition *up* the river to Godstow with the three Liddells: we had tea on the bank there, and did not reach Christ Church again till quarter past eight, when we took them on to my rooms to see my collection of micro-photographs, and restored them to the Deanery just before nine. [Mr. Green notes: On the opposite page Dodgson added on Feb. 10, 1863,]: On which occasion I told them the fairy-tale of *Alice's Adventures Underground*, which I undertook to write out for

---

2. Robinson Duckworth was in 1862 a fellow of Trinity; later he became chaplain in ordinary to the queen and canon of Westminster. He was present on the expedition on July 4 during which many of Alice's adventures were told, and he appears as the Duck in *Alice's Adventures in Wonderland* and its predecessor, *Alice's Adventures Under Ground*. This episode of June 17 is undoubtedly the origin of the caucus-race chapters in both books (see pp. 21–26, 266–69 of this edition) [*Editor*].

3. F. H. Atkinson was a clergyman who was spending a holiday in Oxford [*Editor*].
4. Green (181) prints the words of a minstrel song by T. Ramsey and E. W. Mackney, whose chorus is:

> Sally come up! Sally go down!
> Sally come twist your heel around!
> De old man he's gone to town—
> Oh, Sally come down de middle!
> [*Editor*]

Alice, and which is now finished (as to the text) though the pictures are not yet nearly done.

July 5. (Sat). [1862]. Left with Atkinson for London at 9.2, meeting at the station the Liddells who went up by the same train. [Mr. Green notes: On Sept. 13, 1864 (the day on which he finished the pictures), Dodgson noted concerning *Alice's Adventures Underground* 'headings written out (on my way to London) July 5, 1862'.]

Aug: 1. (F). [1862]. As the Dean's children are still here, * * * I went over to see if they could come on the river today or tomorrow, and remained a short time, for me to write the names in the books for crests etc. which I have given to Alice and Edith, and to hear them play their trio and sing 'Beautiful Star'.[5]

Aug: 6. (W). [1862]. Left the papers at the Delegates' room: we have 250 plucked out of 600. In the afternoon Harcourt[6] and I took the three Liddells up to Godstow, where we had tea; we tried the game of 'the Ural Mountains' on the way, but it did not prove very successful, and I had to go on with my interminable fairy-tale of *Alice's Adventures*. We got back soon after eight, and had supper in my rooms, the children coming over for a short while. A very enjoyable expedition—the last, I should think, to which Ina is likely to be allowed to come—her fourteenth time.[7]

Nov: 13. (Th). [1862]. Walked with Liddon. On returning to Christ Church I found Ina, Alice and Edith in the quadrangle, and had a little talk with them—a rare event of late. Began writing the fairy-tale for Alice, which I told them July 4, going to Godstow—I hope to finish it by Christmas.

Dec: 19. (Sat). [1863]. * * * At five went over to the Deanery, where I stayed till eight, making a sort of dinner at their tea. The nominal object of my going was to play croquet, but it never came to that, music, talk, etc. occupying the whole of a very pleasant evening. The Dean was away: Mrs. Liddell was with us part of the time. It is nearly six months (June 25th) since I have seen anything of them, to speak of. I mark this day with a white stone.

5. "Beautiful Star" was parodied in both *Alice's Adventures Under Ground* and *Alice's Adventures in Wonderland* as "Beautiful Soup." See note 2 on pp. 84–85 of this edition [*Editor*].

6. Augustus George Vernon Harcourt was a reader and tutor in chemistry and a colleague of Dodgson's in Christ Church. "Plucked"; failed [*Editor*].

7. Lorina, whom Mr. Hudson guesses (88) to have been six or seven years old when Dodgson met her in 1856, would have been twelve or thirteen years old in August of 1862 [*Editor*].

Dec: 31. *(Th)*. [1863]. Here, at the close of another year, how much of neglect, carelessness, and sin have I to remember! I had hoped, during the year, to have made a beginning in parochial work, to have thrown off habits of evil, to have advanced in my work at Christ Church. How little, next to nothing, has been done of all this! Now I have a fresh year before me: once more let me set myself to do something worthy of life 'before I go hence, and be no more seen'.

LEWIS CARROLL

From *Alice's Adventures Under Ground*†

[*The Mouse's Tale*]

They were indeed a curious looking party that assembled on the bank—the birds with draggled feathers, the animals with their fur clinging close to them—all dripping wet, cross, and uncomfortable. The first question of course was, how to get dry: they had a consultation about this, and Alice hardly felt at all surprised at finding herself talking familiarly with the birds, as if she had known them all her life. Indeed, she had quite a long argument with the Lory,[1] who at last turned sulky, and would only say "I am older than you, and must know best," and this Alice would not admit without knowing how old the Lory was, and as the Lory positively refused to tell its age, there was nothing more to be said.

At last the mouse, who seemed to have some authority among them, called out "sit down, all of you, and attend to me! I'll soon make you dry enough!" They all sat down at once, shivering, in a large ring, Alice in the middle, with her eyes anxiously fixed on the mouse, for she felt sure she would catch a bad cold if she did not get dry very soon.

"Ahem!" said the mouse, with a self-important air, "are you all ready? This is the driest thing I know. Silence all round, if you please!

"William the Conqueror, whose cause was favoured by the pope, was soon submitted to by the English, who wanted leaders, and had been of late much accustomed to usurpation and conquest. Edwin and Morcar, the earls of Mercia and Northumbria—"

"Ugh!" said the Lory with a shiver.

---

† *Alice Adventures Under Ground, Being a Facsimile of the Original Ms. Book Afterwards Developed Into "Alice's Adventures in Wonderland,"* New York, 1932, 24–30, 76–90.

1. One of the nicknames of Lorina Liddell, who was the oldest of the Liddell daughters [*Editor*].

"I beg your pardon?" said the mouse, frowning, but very politely, "did you speak?"

"Not I!" said the Lory hastily.

"I thought you did," said the mouse, "I proceed. Edwin and Morcar, the earls of Mercia and Northumbria, declared for him; and even Stigand, the patriotic archbishop of Canterbury, found it advisable to go with Edgar Atheling to meet William and offer him the crown. William's conduct was at first moderate[2]—, how are you getting on now, dear?" said the mouse, turning to Alice as it spoke.

"As wet as ever," said poor Alice, "it doesn't seem to dry me at all."

"In that case," said the Dodo[3] solemnly, rising to his feet, "I move that the meeting adjourn, for the immediate adoption of more energetic remedies—"

"Speak English!" said the Duck, "I don't know the meaning of half those long words, and what's more, I don't believe you do either!" And the Duck quacked a comfortable laugh to itself. Some of the other birds tittered audibly.

"I only meant to say," said the Dodo in a rather offended tone, "that I know of a house near here, where we could get the young lady and the rest of the party dried, and then we could listen comfortably to the story which I think you were good enough to promise to tell us," bowing gravely to the mouse.

The mouse made no objection to this, and the whole party moved along the river bank, (for the pool had by this time begun to flow out of the hall, and the edge of it was fringed with rushes and forget-me-nots,) in a slow procession, the Dodo leading the way. After a time the Dodo became impatient, and, leaving the Duck to bring up the rest of the party, moved on at a quicker pace with Alice, the Lory, and the Eaglet,[4] and soon brought them to a little cottage, and there they sat snugly by the fire, wrapped up in blankets, until the rest of the party had arrived, and they were all dry again.

Then they all sat down again in a large ring on the bank, and begged the mouse to begin his story.

"Mine is a long and a sad tale!" said the mouse, turning to Alice, and sighing.

"It *is* a long tail, certainly," said Alice, looking down with wonder at the mouse's tail, which was coiled nearly all round the party, "but why do you call it sad?" and she went on puzzling about this as the mouse went on speaking, so that her idea of the tale was something like this:

---

2. R. L. Green (*Diaries* 1: 2) has identified this passage as a quotation from Haviland Chepmell's *Short Course of History*, published in 1862 [*Editor*].
3. Dodgson: the Duck is Duckworth [*Editor*].
4. Edith Liddell [*Editor*].

We lived beneath the mat
Warm and snug and fat
But one woe, & that
Was the cat!
To our joys
a clog, In
our eyes a
fog, On our
hearts a log
Was the dog!
When the
cat's away,
Then
the mice
will
play,
But, alas!
one day, (So they say)
Came the dog and
cat, Hunting
for a
rat,
Crushed
the mice
all flat,
Each
one
as
he
sat
Underneath the mat,
Warm & snug & fat. Think of that!

"You are not attending!" said the mouse to Alice severely, "what are you thinking of?"

"I beg your pardon," said Alice very humbly, "you had got to the fifth bend, I think?"

"I had *not*!" cried the mouse, sharply and very angrily.

"A knot!" said Alice, always ready to make herself useful, and looking anxiously about her, "oh, do let me help to undo it!"

"I shall do nothing of the sort!" said the mouse, getting up and walking away from the party, "you insult me by talking such nonsense!"

"I didn't mean it!" pleaded poor Alice, "but you're easily offended, you know."

The mouse only growled in reply.

"Please come back and finish your story!" Alice called after it, and the others all joined in chorus "yes, please do!' but the mouse only shook its ears, and walked quickly away, and was soon out of sight.

"What a pity it wouldn't stay!" sighed the Lory, and an old Crab took the opportunity of saying to its daughter "Ah, my dear! let this be a lesson to you never to lose *your* temper!" "Hold your tongue, Ma!" said the young Crab, a little snappishly, "you're enough to try the patience of an oyster!"

"I wish I had our Dinah here, I know I do!" said Alice aloud, addressing no one in particular, "*she'd* soon fetch it back!"

"And who is Dinah, if I might venture to ask the question?" said the Lory.

Alice replied eagerly, for she was always ready to talk about her pet, "Dinah's our cat. And she's such a capital one for catching mice, you ca'n't think! And oh! I wish you could see her after the birds! Why, she'll eat a little bird as soon as look at it!"

This answer caused a remarkable sensation among the party; some of the birds hurried off at once; one old magpie began wrapping itself up very carefully, remarking "I really must be getting home: the night air does not suit my throat," and a canary called out in a trembling voice to its children "come away from her, my dears, she's no fit company for you!" On various pretexts, they all moved off, and Alice was soon left alone.

*   *   *

[*The Lobster Quadrille*]

"You may not have lived much under the sea—" ("I haven't," said Alice,) "and perhaps you were never introduced to a lobster—" (Alice began to say "I once tasted—" but hastily checked herself, and said "no, never," instead;) "so you can have no idea what a delightful thing a Lobster Quadrille is!"

"No, indeed," said Alice, "what sort of a thing is it?"

"Why," said the Gryphon, "you form into a line along the sea shore—"

"Two lines!" cried the Mock Turtle, "seals, turtles, salmon, and so on—advance twice—"

"Each with a lobster as partner!" cried the Gryphon.

"Of course," the Mock Turtle said, "advance twice, set to partners—"

"Change lobsters, and retire in same order—" interrupted the Gryphon.

"Then, you know," continued the Mock Turtle, "you throw the—"

"The lobsters!" shouted the Gryphon, with a bound into the air.

"As far out to sea as you can—"

"Swim after them!" screamed the Gryphon.

"Turn a somersault in the sea!" cried the Mock Turtle, capering wildly about.

"Change lobsters again!" yelled the Gryphon at the top of its voice, "and then—"

"That's all," said the Mock Turtle, suddenly dropping its voice, and the two creatures, who had been jumping about like mad things all this time, sat down again very sadly and quietly, and looked at Alice.

"It must be a very pretty dance," said Alice timidly.

"Would you like to see a little of it?" said the Mock Turtle.

"Very much indeed," said Alice.

"Come, let's try the first figure!" said the Mock Turtle to the Gryphon, "we can do it without lobsters, you know. Which shall sing?"

"Oh! *you* sing!" said the Gryphon, "I've forgotten the words."

So they began solemnly dancing round and round Alice, every now and then treading on her toes when they came too close, and waving their fore-paws to mark the time, while the Mock Turtle sang slowly and sadly, these words:

> "Beneath the waters of the sea
> Are lobsters thick as thick can be—
> They love to dance with you and me,
> My own, my gentle Salmon!"

The Gryphon joined in singing the chorus, which was:

> "Salmon come up! Salmon go down!
> Salmon come twist your tail around!
> Of all the fishes of the sea
> There's none so good as Salmon!"

"Thank you," said Alice, feeling very glad that the figure was over.

"Shall we try the second figure?" said the Gryphon, "or would you prefer a song?"

"Oh, a song, please!" Alice replied, so eagerly, that the Gryphon said, in a rather offended tone, "hm! no accounting for tastes! Sing her 'Mock Turtle Soup', will you, old fellow!"

The Mock Turtle sighed deeply, and began, in a voice sometimes choked with sobs, to sing this:

"Beautiful Soup, so rich and green,
Waiting in a hot tureen!
Who for such dainties would not stoop?
Soup of the evening, beautiful Soup!
Soup of the evening, beautiful Soup!
   Beau—ootiful Soo—oop!
   Beau—ootiful Soo—oop!
Soo—op of the e—e—evening,
   Beautiful beautiful Soup!"[5]

"Chorus again!" cried the Gryphon, and the Mock Turtle had just begun to repeat it, then a cry of "the trial's beginning!" was heard in the distance.

"Come on!" cried the Gryphon, and, taking Alice by the hand, he hurried off, without waiting for the end of the song.

"What trial is it?" panted Alice as she ran, but the Gryphon only answered "come on!" and ran the faster, and more and more faintly came, borne on the breeze that followed them, the melancholy words

   "Soo—oop of the e—e—evening,
   Beautiful beautiful Soup!"

The King and Queen were seated on their throne when they arrived, with a great crowd assembled around them: the Knave was in custody: and before the King stood the white rabbit, with a trumpet in one hand, and a scroll of parchment in the other.

"Herald! read the accusation!" said the King.

On this the white rabbit blew three blasts on the trumpet, and then unrolled the parchment scroll, and read as follows:

   "The Queen of Hearts she made some tarts
     All on a summer day:
   The Knave of Hearts he stole those tarts,
     And took them quite away!"[6]

"Now for the evidence," said the King, "and then the sentence."

"No!" said the Queen, "first the sentence and then the evidence!"

"Nonsense!" cried Alice, so loudly that everybody jumped, "the idea of having the sentence first!"

"Hold your tongue!" said the Queen.

"I won't" said Alice, "you're nothing but a pack of cards! Who cares for you?"

At this the whole pack rose up into the air, and came flying down upon her: she gave a little scream of fright, and tried to beat them

---

5. For the minstrel song of which the first version of the Lobster Quadrille is a parody, see note 4 on p. 264 of this edition. For the stanza of "Beautiful Star" that is parodied in "Beau-tiful Soup," see note 2 on p. 85 of this edition [*Editor*].

6. Dodgson uses a traditional version of this nursery rhyme [*Editor*].

off, and found herself lying on the bank, with her head in the lap of her sister, who was gently brushing away some leaves that had fluttered down from the trees on to her face.

"Wake up! Alice dear!" said her sister, "what a nice long sleep you've had!"

"Oh, I've had such a curious dream!" said Alice, and she told her sister all her Adventures Under Ground, as you have read them, and when she had finished, her sister kissed her and said "it *was* a curious dream, dear, certainly! But now run in to your tea: it's getting late."

So Alice ran off, thinking while she ran (as well she might) what a wonderful dream it had been.

But her sister sat there some while longer, watching the setting sun, and thinking of little Alice and her Adventures, till she too began dreaming after a fashion, and this was her dream.

She saw an ancient city, and a quiet river winding near it along the plain, and up the stream went slowly gliding a boat with a merry party of children on board—she could hear their voices and laughter like music over the water—and among them was another little Alice, who sat listening with bright eager eyes to a tale that was being told, and she listened for the words of the tale, and lo! it was the dream of her own little sister. So the boat wound slowly along, beneath the bright summer-day, with its merry crew and its music of voices and laughter, till it passed round one of the many turnings of the stream, and she saw it no more.

Then she thought, (in a dream within the dream, as it were,) how this same little Alice would, in the after-time, be herself a grown woman: and how she would keep, through her riper years, the simple and loving heart of her childhood: and how she would gather around her other little children, and make *their* eyes bright and eager with many a wonderful tale, perhaps even with these very adventures of the little Alice of long-ago: and how she would feel with all their simple sorrows, and find a pleasure in all their simple joys, remembering her own child-life, and the happy summer days.

THE END

ALICE AND CARYL HARGREAVES

Alice's Recollections of Carrollian Days†

Soon after we went to live in the old grey stone-built Deanery, there were two additions to the family in the shape of two tiny tabby kittens. One called Villikens, was given to my eldest brother Harry, but died at an early age of some poison. The other, Dinah, which was given to Ina, became my special pet, and lived to be immortalised in the *Alice*.[1] Every day these kittens were bathed by us in imitation of our own upbringing. Dinah I was devoted to, but there were some other animals of which we were terrified. When my father went to Christ Church, he had some carved lions (wooden representations of the Liddell crest) placed on top of each of the corner posts in the banisters going upstairs and along the gallery. When we went to bed we had to go along this gallery, and we always ran as hard as we could along it, because we *knew* that the lions got down from their pedestals and ran after us. And then the swans on the river when we went out with Mr. Dodgson! But, even then, we were always much too happy little girls to be really frightened. We had some canaries, but there was never a white rabbit in the family. That was a pure invention of Mr. Dodgson's.

We were all very fond of games, and our favourite card games were Pope Joan, and Beggar my Neighbour, followed later by Whist. About the time when the *Alice* was told, we used to spend a good many happy hours in the Deanery garden trying to play croquet. Chess came later. The deanery is a fair-sized house, one side of which looks out into Tom Quad, while the other looks on to a garden which is also overlooked by the Christ Church Library. It was very modern for those days in that it had a big bath, but with the un-modern limitation that only cold water was laid on! So the young ladies had a cold bath every morning! It was in this house, built by Cardinal Wolsey, but adapted to the comforts of the day, that we spent the happy years of childhood.

*   *   *

But my great joy was to go out riding with my father. As soon as we had a pony, he used to take one of us out with him every morning. The first pony we ever had was one given to my eldest brother Harry, called Tommy. Harry was away at school most of the time, and in any case did not care much about riding, so we always kept his pony

---

† From "Alice's Recollections of Carrollian Days. As Told to Her Son, Caryl Hargreaves," *Cornhill*, n.s. (1932): 1–12. Reprinted by permission of John Murray (Publishers), Ltd.

1. The kittens owed their names to the contemporary song, "Villikens and his Dinah" [*Editor*].

exercised for him. I began to ride soon after we went to Oxford. We were taught up and down a path running at an angle to the Broad Walk (the triangular piece of grass between the two paths being called the Dean's Ham) by Bultitude.[2] With my father we used to ride on Port Meadow, or to go to Abingdon through Radley, and there were the most lovely rides through Wytham Woods. * * * When Tommy got too old, my father bought a bigger pony for us. One Boxing Day this pony crossed its legs, and came down with me on the Abingdon road. My father had to leave me by the side of the road while he went off to get help. While he was gone, some strangers, out for an excursion, passed, and were kind enough to send me back to Oxford in their wagonette, lying on a feather bed, borrowed from a near-by farm. The bottom of the wagonette was not quite long enough when the door was shut, and this caused me great pain, so perhaps I was not as grateful as I should have been, for, when I got home and Bultitude was carrying me indoors, I said to him, "*You* won't let them hurt me any more, will you?" at which, as he told my mother afterwards, he "nearly let Miss Alice drop." As it was, I was on my back for six weeks with a broken thigh. During all these weeks Mr. Dodgson never came to see me. If he had, perhaps the world might have known some more of Alice's Adventures. As it is, I think many of my earlier adventures must be irretrievably lost to posterity, because Mr. Dodgson told us many, many stories before the famous trip up the river to Godstow. No doubt he added some of the earlier adventures to make up the difference between *Alice in Wonderland* and *Alice's Adventures Underground*, which latter was nearly all told on that one afternoon. Much of *Through the Looking Glass* is made up of them too, particularly the ones to do with chessmen, which are dated by the period when we were excitedly learning chess. But even then, I am afraid that many must have perished for ever in his waste-paper basket, for he used to illustrate the meaning of his stories on any piece of paper that he had handy.

The stories that he illustrated in this way owed their existence to the fact that Mr. Dodgson was one of the first amateur photographers, and took many photographs of us. He did not draw when telling stories on the river expeditions. When the time of year made picnics impossible, we used to go to his rooms in the Old Library, leaving the Deanery by the back door, escorted by our nurse. When we got there, we used to sit on the big sofa on each side of him, while he told us stories, illlustrating them by pencil or ink drawings as he went along. When we were thoroughly happy and amused at his stories, he used to pose us, and expose the plates before the right mood had passed. He seemed to have an endless store of these

---

2. The Liddells' coachman [*Editor*].

fantastical tales, which he made up as he told them, drawing busily on a large sheet of paper all the time. They were not always entirely new. Sometimes they were new versions of old stories: sometimes they started on the old basis, but grew into new tales owing to the frequent interruptions which opened up fresh and undreamed-of possibilities. In this way the stories, slowly enunciated in his quiet voice with its curious stutter, were perfected. Occasionally he pretended to fall asleep, to our great dismay. Sometimes he said "That is all till next time," only to resume on being told that it was already next time. Being photographed was therefore a joy to us and not a penance as it is to most children. We looked forward to the happy hours in the mathematical tutor's rooms.

But much more exciting than being photographed was being allowed to go into the dark room, and watch him develop the large glass plates. What could be more thrilling than to see the negative gradually take shape, as he gently rocked it to and fro in the acid bath? Besides, the dark room was so mysterious, and we felt that any adventure might happen there! There were all the joys of preparation, anticipation, and realisation, besides the feeling that we were assisting at some secret rite usually reserved for grown-ups! Then there was the additional excitement, after the plates were developed, of seeing what we looked like in a photograph. Looking at the photographs now, it is evident that Mr. Dodgson was far in advance of his time in the art of photography and of posing his subjects.

We never went to tea with him, nor did he come to tea with us. In any case, five-o'clock tea had not become an established practice in those days. He used sometimes to come to the Deanery on the afternoons when we had a half-holiday. At the time when we first went to Oxford, my parents, having had luncheon at one o'clock, did not have another meal until dinner, which they took at 6.30 p.m. * * * In those days, instead of five-o'clock tea, coffee and tea were served after dinner in the drawing-room. It was not until we were nearly grown up that afternoon tea was started, and then only as a treat. When the weather was too bad to go out, we used to say, "Now then, it's a rainy day, let's have some tea." On the other hand, when we went on the river for the afternoon with Mr. Dodgson, which happened at most four or five times every summer term, he always brought out with him a large basket full of cakes, and a kettle, which we used to boil under a haycock, if we could find one. On rarer occasions we went out for the whole day with him, and then we took a larger basket with luncheon—cold chicken and salad and all sorts of good things. One of our favourite whole-day excursions was to row down to Nuneham and picnic in the woods there, in one of the huts specially provided by Mr. Harcourt for picnickers. On landing at Nuneham, our first duty was to choose the hut, and then to borrow plates, glasses, knives and forks from the cottages by the riverside. To us the hut might have been a Fairy King's palace, and the picnic a banquet in our honour. Sometimes we were told stories after luncheon that transported us into Fairyland. Sometimes we spent the afternoon wandering in the more material fairyland of the Nuneham woods until it was time to row back to Oxford in the long summer evening. On these occasions we did not get home until about seven o'clock.

The party usually consisted of five—one of Mr. Dodgson's men friends as well as himself and us three. His brother occasionally took an oar in the merry party, but our most usual fifth was Mr. Duckworth, who sang well. On our way back we generally sang songs popular at the time, such as,

"Star of the evening, beautiful star,"

and

"Twinkle, twinkle, little star,"

and

"Will you walk into my parlour, said the spider to the fly," all of which are parodied in the *Alice*.

* * *

In the usual way, after we had chosen our boat with great care, we three children were stowed away in the stern, and Mr. Dodgson took the stroke oar. A pair of sculls was always laid in the boat for us little girls to handle when being taught to row by our indulgent host. He succeeded in teaching us in the course of these excursions, and it proved an unending joy to us. When we had learned enough to manage the oars, we were allowed to take our turn at them, while the two men watched and instructed us. * * * I can remember what hard work it was rowing upstream from Nuneham, but this was nothing if we thought we were learning and getting on. It was a proud day when we could "feather our oars" properly. The verse at the beginning of the *Alice* describes our rowing. We thought it nearly as much fun as the stories. Sometimes (a treat of great importance in the eyes of the fortunate one) one of us was allowed to take the tiller ropes: and, if the course was a little devious, little blame was accorded to the small but inexperienced coxswain.

Nearly all of *Alice's Adventures Underground* was told on that blazing summer afternoon with the heat haze shimmering over the meadows where the party landed to shelter for awhile in the shadow cast by the haycocks near Godstow. I think the stories he told us that afternoon must have been better than usual, because I have such a distinct recollection of the expedition, and also, on the next day I started to pester him to write down the story for me, which I had never done before. It was due to my "going on" and importunity that, after saying he would think about it, he eventually gave the-hesitating promise which started him writing it down at all. This he referred to in a letter written in 1883 in which he writes of me as the "one without whose infant patronage I might possibly never have written at all." What a nuisance I must have made of myself! Still, I am glad I did it now; and so was Mr. Dodgson afterwards. It does not do to think what pleasure would have been missed if his little bright-eyed favourite had not bothered him to put pen to paper. The result was that for several years, when he went away on vacation, he took the little black book about with him, writing the manuscript in his own peculiar script, and drawing the illustrations. Finally the book was finished and given to me. But in the meantime, friends who had seen and heard bits of it while he was at work on it, were so thrilled that they persuaded him to publish it. I have been told, though I doubt its being true, that at first he thought that it should be published at the publisher's expense, but that the London publishers were reluctant to do so, and he therefore decided to publish it at his own expense. In any case, after Macmillans had agreed to publish it, there arose the question of the illustrations. At first he tried to do them himself, on the lines of those in the manuscript book, but he came to the conclusion that he could not do them well enough, as they had to be drawn on wood, and he did not know how. He eventually approached Mr. (later Sir John) Tenniel. Fortunately, as I think most people will agree, the latter accepted. As a rule Tenniel used Mr. Dodgson's drawings as the basis for his own illustrations and they held frequent consultations about them. One point, which was not settled for a long time and until after many trials and consultations, was whether Alice in Wonderland should have her hair cut straight across her forehead as Alice Liddell had always worn it, or not. Finally it was decided that Alice in Wonderland should have no facial resemblance to her prototype.

Unfortunately my mother tore up all the letters that Mr. Dodgson wrote to me when I was a small girl. I cannot remember what any of them were like, but it is an awful thought to contemplate what may have perished in the Deanery waste-paper basket. Mr. Dodgson always wore black clergyman's clothes in Oxford, but, when he took us out on the river, he used to wear white flannel trousers. He also replaced his black top-hat by a hard white straw hat on these occasions, but of course retained his black boots, because in those days white tennis shoes had never been heard of. He always carried himself upright, almost more than upright, as if he had swallowed a poker.

On the occasion of the marriage of King Edward and Queen Alexandra, the whole of Oxford was illuminated, and Mr. Dodgson and his brother took me out to see the illuminations. The crowd in the streets was very great, and I clung tightly on to the hand of the strong man on either side of me. The colleges were all lit up, and the High Street was a mass of illuminations of all sorts and kinds. One in particular took my fancy, in which the words "May they be happy" appeared in large letters of fire. My enthusiasm prompted Mr. Dodgson to draw a caricature of it next day for me, in which underneath those words appeared two hands holding very formidable birches[3] with the words "Certainly not." Even if the joke was not very good, the drawing pleased me enormously, and I wish I had it still! Little did we dream then that this shy but almost brilliant logic tutor, with a bent for telling fairy stories to little girls, and for taking photographs of elderly dons, would before so many years be known all over the civilised world, and that his fairy stories would be translated into almost every European language, into Chinese and Japanese, and some of them even into Arabic! But perhaps only a brilliant logician could have written *Alice in Wonderland!*

LEWIS CARROLL

From the Diaries [1863–65]†

May 9. (Sat.) [1863]. Heard from Mrs. MacDonald[1] about *Alice's Adventures Underground*, which I had lent them to read, and which they wish me to publish.

Jan: 25. (M). [1864]. Called at the "Board of Health" and saw Mr. Tom Taylor.[2] He gave me a note of introduction to Mr. Tenniel (to whom he had before applied, for me, about pictures for *Alice's Adventures*). I called at Mr. Tenniel's, whom I found at home; he was very friendly, and seemed to think favourably of undertaking the pictures, but must see the book before deciding. * * *

April 5. (Tu). [1864]. Heard from Tenniel that he consents to draw the pictures for *Alice's Adventures Underground.* * * *

---

3. Flexible wooden switches used to punish children [*Editor*].

† *The Diaries of Lewis Carroll*, ed. Roger Lancelyn Green, 1: 196, 210, 212, 215, 222, 230–31, 234–35, 236.

1. Mrs. MacDonald was the wife of George MacDonald, who had served as a minister of the Congregational Church but was at this time earning his living in London by lecturing, preaching, and writing poem and novels. He had already published one of his best-known fantastic romances, *Phantases* (1858); he was later to publish collections of fairy-stories and his most famous children's books, *At the Back of the North Wind* and *The Princess and the Goblin* (both 1871). His children, Mary and Greville, were among Dodgson's first child-friends [*Editor*].

2. In addition to serving as secretary to the Board of Health, Tom Taylor was a prolific and successful playwright, and a frequent contributor to *Punch*, whose editor he became in 1874.

John (later Sir John) Tenniel had been drawing for *Punch* since 1850. In 1864 he was drawing its principal weekly political cartoon and was soon to become its principal cartoonist. Tenniel had made an early success in the 1840s with his illustrations to an edition of *Aesop's Fables*, but he did not often illustrate books [*Editor*].

May 2. (*M*). [1864]. Sent Tenniel the first slip set up for *Alice's Adventures*—from the beginning of Chap: III. * * *

Sept. 13. (*Tu*). [1864]. At Croft. Finished drawing the pictures in the MS. copy of *Alice's Adventures*. [In his text of the diaries, Mr. Green inserts here this additional entry by Dodgson: "MS. finally sent to Alice, Nov: 26, (*Sat.*) 1864."]

May 11. (*Th*). [1865]. Met Alice and Miss Prickett in the quadrangle: Alice seems changed a good deal, and hardly for the better—probably going through the usual awkward stage of transition.[3]

May 26. (*F*). [1865]. Received from Macmillan a copy (blank all but the first sheet) of *Alice's Adventures in Wonderland* bound in red cloth as a specimen.

July 20. (*Th*). [1865]. Called on Macmillan, and showed him Tenniel's letter about the fairy-tale—he is entirely dissatisfied with the printing of the pictures, and I suppose we shall have to do it again.

Aug. 2. (*W*). [1865]. Finally decided on the re-print of *Alice*, and that the first 2000 shall be sold as waste paper. Wrote about it to Macmillan, Combe and Tenniel. That total cost will be:

	[£]
Drawing pictures	138
Cutting	142
Printing (by Clay)	240
Binding and advertising (say)	80
	600

i.e. 6/-a copy on the 2000. If I make £500 by sale, this will be a loss of £100, and the loss on the first 2000 will probably be £100, leaving me £200 out of pocket. But if a second 2000 could be sold it would cost £300, and bring in £500, thus squaring accounts and any further sale would be a gain, but that I can hardly hope for.

Nov: 8. (*W*). [1865]. My work has now reached a climax: lectures from nine to two, and five to six, and a good deal of looking over papers, etc. besides.

3. Alice Liddell, who was ten years old in the summer of the expedition to Godstow (1862), had turned thirteen in May of 1865 [*Editor*].

Nov: 9. (Th). [1865]. Received from Macmillan a copy of the new
impression of *Alice*—very *far* superior to the old, and in fact a perfect
piece of artistic printing.

LEWIS CARROLL

From *Alice* on the Stage†

*   *   *

Many a day we rowed together on that quiet stream—the three
little maidens and I—and many a fairy tale had been extemporised
for their benefit—whether it were at times when the narrator was "i'
the vein," and fancies unsought came crowding thick upon him, or
at times when the jaded Muse was goaded into action, and plodded
meekly on, more because she had to say something than that she
had something to say—yet none of these many tales got written down:
they lived and died, like summer midges, each in its own golden
afternoon until there came a day when, as it chanced, one of my
little listeners petitioned that the tale might be written out for her.
That was many a year ago, but I distinctly remember, now as I write,
how, in a desperate attempt to strike out some new line of fairy-lore,
I had sent my heroine straight down a rabbit-hole, to begin with,
without the least idea what was to happen afterwards. And so, to
please a child I loved (I don't remember any other motive), I printed
in manuscript, and illustrated with my own crude designs—designs
that rebelled against every law of Anatomy or Art (for I had never
had a lesson in drawing)— the book which I have just had published
in facsimile.[1] In writing it out, I added many fresh ideas, which
seemed to grow to themselves upon the original stock; and many
more added themselves when, years afterwards, I wrote it all over
again for publication: but (this may interest some readers of "Alice"
to know) every such idea and nearly every word of the dialogue,
came of itself. Sometimes an idea comes at night, when I have had
to get up and strike a light to note it down—sometimes when out
on a lonely winter walk, when I have had to stop, and with half-
frozen fingers jot down a few words which should keep the new-
born idea from perishing—but whenever or however it comes, *it
comes of itself.* I cannot set invention going like a clock, by any
voluntary winding up: nor do I believe that any *original* writing (and

† First printed in *The Theatre* in 1887; reprinted in *The Lewis Carroll Picture Book,* ed.
Stuart Dodgson Collingwood (London, 1899)
163–70. *Alice in Wonderland,* a musical play
using episodes from both *Alice's Adventures in
Wonderland* and *Through the Looking-Glass,*
was created by H. Savile Clark, a popular writer
of burlesque and operetta. It was first performed
in London in December 1886 [*Editor*].
1. *Alice's Adventures Under Ground,* published by Macmillan in 1886 [*Editor*].

what other writing is worth preserving?) was ever so produced. If you sit down, unimpassioned and uninspired, and *tell* yourself to write for so many hours, you will merely produce (at least I am sure I should merely produce) some of that article which fills, so far as I can judge, two-thirds of most magazines—most easy to write, most weary to read—men call it "padding," and it is to my mind one of the most detestable things in modern literature. "Alice" and the "Looking-Glass" are made up almost wholly of bits and scraps, single ideas which came of themselves. Poor they may have been; but at least they were the best I had to offer: and I can desire no higher praise to be written of me than the words of a Poet, written of a Poet,

> "He gave the people of his best:
> The worst he ever kept, the best he gave."[2]

I have wandered from my subject, I know: yet grant me another minute to relate a little incident of my own experience. I was walking on a hill-side, alone, one bright summer day, when suddenly there came into my head one line of verse—one solitary line— "For the *Snark* was a Boojum, you see." I knew not what it meant, then: I know not what it means, now; but I wrote it down: and some times afterwards, the rest of the stanza occurred to me, that being its last line: and so by degrees, at odd moments during the next year or two, the rest of the poem pieced itself together, that being its last stanza. And since then, periodically I have received courteous letters from strangers, begging to know whether "The Hunting of the Snark" is an allegory, or contains some hidden moral, or is a political satire: and for all such questions I have but one answer, "*I don't know!*" And now I return to my text, and will wander no more.

Stand forth, then, from the shadowy past, "Alice," the child of my dreams. Full many a year has slipped away, since that "golden afternoon" that gave thee birth, but I can call it up almost as clearly as if it were yesterday—the cloudless blue above, the watery mirror below, the boat drifting idly on its way, the tinkle of the drops that fell from the oars, as they waved so sleepily to and fro, and (the one bright gleam of life in all the slumberous scene) the three eager faces, hungry for news of fairyland, and who would not be said "nay" to: from whose lips "Tell us a story, please," had all the stern immutability of Fate!

What wert thou, dream-Alice, in thy foster-father's eyes? How shall he picture thee? Loving, first, loving and gentle: loving as a dog (forgive the prosaic smile, but I know no earthly love so pure and perfect), and gentle as a fawn: then courteous—courteous to all,

2. Alfred Tennyson, "To———, After Reading a Life and Letters" (1840). Tennyson's line reads, "His worst he kept, his best he gave" [*Editor*].

high or low, grand or grotesque, King or Caterpillar, even as though she were herself a King's daughter, and her clothing wrought gold: then trustful, ready to accept the wildest impossibilities with all that utter trust that only dreamers know; and lastly, curious—wildly curious, and with the eager enjoyment of Life that comes only in the happy hours of childhood, when all is new and fair, and when Sin and Sorrow are but names—empty words signifying nothing!

And the White Rabbit, what of *him?* Was *he* framed on the "Alice" lines, or meant as a contrast? As a contrast, distinctly. For *her* "youth," "audacity," "vigour," and "swift directness of purpose," read "elderly," "timid," "feeble," and "nervously shilly-shallying," and you will get *something* of what I meant him to be. I *think* the White Rabbit should wear spectacles. I am sure his voice should quaver, and his knees quiver, and his whole air suggest a total inability to say "Bo" to a goose!

But I cannot hope to be allowed, even by the courteous Editor of *The Theatre,* half the space I should need (even if my *reader's* patience would hold out) to discuss each of my puppets one by one. Let me cull from the two books a Royal Trio—the Queen of Hearts, the Red Queen, and the White Queen. It was certainly hard on my Muse, to expect her to sing of *three* Queens, within such brief compass, and yet to give to each her own individuality. Each, of course, had to preserve, through all her eccentricities, a certain queenly *dignity. That* was essential. And for distinguishing traits, I pictured to myself the Queen of Hearts as a sort of embodiment of ungovernable passion—a blind and aimless Fury. The Red Queen I pictured as a Fury, but of another type; *her* passion must be cold and calm; she must be formal and strict, yet not unkindly; pedantic to the tenth degree, the concentrated essence of all governesses! Lastly, the White Queen seemed, to my dreaming fancy, gentle, stupid, fat and pale; helpless as an infant; and her just *suggesting* imbecility, but never quite pasing into it; that would be, I think, fatal to any comic effect she might otherwise produce.

※　※　※

Later Life

HELMUT GERNSHEIM

Lewis Carroll—Photographer†

*   *   *

Apart from some early photographs of his family and of members of Christ Church Common Room, Lewis Carroll's portraits fall into two clearly defined categories—distinguished people, and children.

His hobby reveals him as an indefatigable lion-hunter—which is the more suprising since Lewis Carroll strongly resented being lionised himself. At first it may seem difficult to reconcile this trait with his well-known shyness and reserved manner, but it is only one of the many contradictions in his character. The effort it must have cost him to overcome this shyness in his determination to track down eminent men and women is a measure of his keenness on photography.

*   *   *

In his constant desire to meet children, Lewis Carroll pressed his friends for introductions to families with good-looking daughters—though by no means all his friendships started in this conventional way. He went to archery meetings and Freemasons' fêtes to find subjects and was always ready with stories and games to amuse little girls whom he met on a journey, in a park, and, above all, at the seaside, where he habitually spent part of the Long Vacation[1] because the beach afforded especially good opportunities for such chance encounters. Lewis Carroll delighted in watching children at play, would make them paper boats or show them puzzles, and always came to the rescue with safety-pins if he saw a little girl hesitating to paddle in the sea for fear of spoiling her frock. When he had won the parents' confidence by presenting the child with a copy of *Alice* "From the Author", such acquaintanceships often ripened into friendships. *   *   *

Sometimes Lewis Carroll enjoyed posing his little sitters in fancy

---

† From *Lewis Carroll—Photographer* (London: Max Parrish & Co., Ltd., 1950; New York, Dover, 1969) 16, 18–19, 20–21, 28. Reprinted by permission of Dover Publications, Inc.

1. The Long Vacation occurred in August and September, between the last term of one academic year and the first of the next [*Editor*].

dress. He had a cupboard full of costumes: some had been used in pantomimes at Drury Lane, some had been borrowed from friends or, on occasion, even from the Ashmolean Museum; others were mere rags to pose them as beggar-children. As early as 1857 he dressed up a little girl as "Little Red Riding-hood", but it is not until many years later, chiefly in the 1870's, that we find this burst of costume pictures—"Chinamen", "Turks", "Greeks," "Romans", "Danes", and a whole string of "Beggar-girls" and "Dolly Vardens". * * *[2]

It goes without saying that most of these costumes pictures have to be condemned as errors of taste. Whereas Lewis Carroll's other photographic work shows a remarkable independence of contemporary photography, the sentiment of these pictures is a lamentable concession to Victorian taste. As a producer of costume pictures Lewis Carroll is almost always banal; as a photographer of children he achieves an excellence which in its way can find no peer.

* * *

Lewis Carroll considered children's simple nightdresses most becoming and quite a number of little girls were posed in them. He wrote to a mother, "If they have such things as flannel nightgowns, that makes as pretty a dress as you can desire. White does pretty well, but nothing like flannel"—the texture and colour of which are more photogenic than white cotton. In a letter to Harry Furniss, illustrator of *Sylvie and Bruno*, about dresses for the fairy children he goes a step further: "I *wish* I dared dispense with *all* costume. Naked children are so perfectly pure and lovely; but Mrs. Grundy would be furious—it would never do."[3]

Characteristically, his dislike of boys extended also to their nakedness. "I confess I do *not* admire naked boys. They always seem to me to need clothes—whereas one hardly sees why the lovely forms of girls should *ever* be covered up."

In his hobby there was no danger of outraging Mrs. Grundy provided he found little girls—and parents—who raised no objection. Lewis Carroll showed great consideration for the susceptibility of his young sitters, believing that if a girl had any scruple on the score of modesty, such feelings ought to be treated with "utmost reverence." A letter to Miss Gertrude Thomson, another of his illustrators, demonstrates his delicacy in this matter. "If I had the loveliest child in the world, to draw or photograph, and found she had a modest shrinking (however slight, and however easily overcome) from being

2. Dolly Varden is a character in Charles Dickens' *Barnaby Rudge* (1841), an urban, working-class coquette [*Editor*].
3. Characters in Tom Morton's play *Speed the Plough* (1800) worry about the opinions of Mrs. Grundy, a figure of strait-laced social morality. The letter from which Gernsheim quotes is not included in Cohen's edition [*Editor*].

taken nude, I should feel it was a solemn duty owed to God to drop the request *altogether."*

If Lewis Carroll's photographs of nude girls were as sentimental and devoid of artistry as Miss Thomson's drawings of fairies in *Three Sunsets*, we must be grateful to him for having stipulated that after his death they should be returned to the sitters or their parents, or else be destroyed. Naturally none of them were pasted in his albums, and as far as I know, none have survived.[4]

*   *   *

With his meticulous love of order, Lewis Carroll numbered every negative and print, but these numbers unfortunately do not give an exact indication of his total output. A true artist, he would from time to time go through his stock of negatives and erase a good many of them, filling the gaps in the numbers with new negatives, which he prefixed with the sign ℙ , meaning "second". In 1875 particularly, he had a thorough clean-up, numbering and cataloguing negatives for a month, often working at it for ten hours a day. Occasionally he also used fractions (e.g. 907½ and 200⅔), which still further increases our difficulty in arriving at a proper estimate of the number of photographs he took. The highest negative number I have seen—2641, referring to a picture taken the year he gave up his hobby—hardly conveys, therefore, a true idea of the extent of Lewis Carroll's photographic activity.

Apart from some rudimentary instruction in practical manipulation from his uncle, Skeffington Lutwidge, and from Reginald Southey, a fellow Student at Christ Church, Lewis Carroll was more or less self-taught. This fact is in itself not particularly noteworthy. Considering, however, Lewis Carroll's many other activities, his photographic achievements are truly astonishing: he must not only rank as a pioneer of British amateur photography, but I would also unhesitatingly acclaim him as the most outstanding photographer of children in the nineteenth century. After Julia Margaret Cameron he is probably the most distinguished amateur portraitist of the mid-Victorian era.

---

4. In 1979 Morton Cohen published *Lewis Carroll: Photographs of Children*, which contained four photographic nude studies of children.

LEWIS CARROLL

Letters to Children †

To Hallam Tennyson[1]

Christ Church, Oxford
January 23, 1862

My dear Hallam,

Thank you for your nice little note. I am glad you liked the knife, and I think it a pity you should not be allowed to use it "till you are older." However, as you *are* older now, perhaps you have begun to use it by this time: if you were allowed to cut your finger with it, once a week, just a little, you know, till it began to bleed, and a good deep cut every birthday, I should think that would be enough, and it would last a long time so. Only I hope that if Lionel ever wants to have *his* fingers cut with it, you will be kind to your brother, and hurt him as much as he likes.

If you will send me word, some day, when your two birthdays are, perhaps I may send *him* a birthday present, if I can only find something that will hurt him as much as your knife: perhaps a blister, or a leech, or something of that sort.

Give him half my love, and take the rest yourself.

Your affectionate friend,
Charles L. Dodgson

To Margaret Cunnyngham[2]

Christ Church, Oxford
January 30, 1868

Dear Maggie,

I found that the "friend," that the little girl asked me to write to, lived at Ripon, and *not* at Land's End—a nice sort of place to invite to! It looked rather suspicious to me—and soon after, by dint of incessant enquiries, I found out that she was called "Maggie," and lived in a "Crescent"! Of course I declared "after *that*" (the language I used doesn't matter), "I will *not* address her, that's flat! So do not expect me to flatter."

† From *The Letters of Lewis Carroll*, ed. Morton Cohen, 1: 53, 112–13, 276–77.
1. Hallam was the older son of Alfred Tennyson, whom Dodgson met and photographed in 1857. Hallam was ten when he received this letter; his brother Lionel was eight [*Editor*].
2. Margaret Cunnynghame was the daughter of a family whom Dodgson met when he visited his family at Croft rectory. She was thirteen when she received this letter, the first two paragraphs of which are written in rhyme ("write to," "invite to"; "to me," "Maggie"). John ("Jack") was her older brother; "Haly" her older sister; and the "small, fat, impertinent, ignorant brother" was Hugh, then aged eight [*Editor*].

Well, I hope you soon will see your beloved Pa come back—for consider, should you be *quite* content with only Jack? Just suppose they made a blunder! (Such things happen now and then.) Really, now, I shouldn't wonder if your "John" came home again, and your father staid at school! A most awkward thing, no doubt. How would you receive him? You'll say perhaps "you'd turn him out." That would answer well, so far as concerns the *boy*, you know—but consider your Papa, learning lessons in a row of great inky school-boys! This (though unlikely) *might* occur: "Haly" would be grieved to miss him (don't mention it to *her*).

No carte[3] has yet been done of me that does real justice to my *smile*; and so I hardly like, you see, to send you one—however, I'll consider if I will or not—meanwhile, I send a little thing to give you an idea of what I look like when I'm lecturing. The merest sketch, you will allow—yet still I think there's something grand in the expression of the brow and in the action of the hand.

Have you read my fairy-tale in *Aunt Judy's Magazine*?[4] If you have, you will not fail to discover what I mean when I say "Bruno yesterday came to remind me that *he* was my godson!" On the ground that I "gave him a name"!

Your affectionate friend,
C.L. Dodgson

P.S. I would send, if I were not too shy, the same message to "Haly" that she (thought I do not deserve it, not I!) has sent through her sister to me. My best love to yourself—to your Mother my kindest

3. Photograph [*Editor*].
4. "Bruno's Revenge," published in the December 1867 issue of *Aunt Judy's Magazine* for *Young People*. The sketch became part of *Sylvie and Bruno*, published more than twenty years later (1889) [*Editor*].

regards—to your small, fat, impertinent, ignorant brother my hatred.
I think that is all.

To Bert Coote[5]

The Chestnuts, Guildfold
June 9 [?1877]

My dear Bertie,

I would have been very glad to write to you as you wish, only
there are several objections. I think, when you have heard them,
you will see that I am right in saying "No."

The first objection is, I've got no ink. You don't believe it? Ah,
you should have seen the ink there was in *my* days! (About the time
of the battle of Waterloo: I was a soldier in that battle.) Why, you
had only to pour a little of it on the paper, and it went on by itself!
This ink is so stupid, if you begin a word for it, it can't even finish
it by itself.

The next objection is, I've no time. You don't believe *that*, you
say? Well, who cares? You should have seen the time there was in
my days! (At the time of the battle of Waterloo, where I led a
regiment.) There were always 25 hours in the day—sometimes 30
or 40.

The third and greatest objection is, my *great* dislike for children.
I don't know why, I'm sure: but I *hate* them—just as one hates arm-
chairs and plum-pudding! You don't believe *that*, don't you? Did I
ever say you would? Ah, you should have seen the children there
were in my days! (Battle of Waterloo, where I commanded the
English army. I was called "the Duke of Wellington" then, but I
found it a great bother having such a long name, so I changed it to
"Mr. Dodgson." I chose that name because it begins with the same
letter as "Duke.") So you see it would never do to write to you.

Have you any sisters? I forget. If you have, give them my love. I
am much obliged to your Uncle and Aunt for letting me keep the
photograph.

I hope you won't be much disappointed at not getting a letter from
Your affectionate friend,
C. L. Dodgson

5. Bertie Coote was an actor whom Dodgson saw in a pantomime in 1877. He was about nine
years old when Dodgson met him [*Editor*].

LEWIS CARROLL

From the Diaries [1868–71]†

Jan: 16. (Th). [1868]. * * * During my stay at Ripon, I have written almost all of the pamphlet on *Euclid* V by algebra, with notes, and have gone on with the MS. on Geometric Conic Sections. I have also added a few pages to the second volume of *Alice*.[1]

April 8. (W). [1868]. * * * I went down to Hammersmith, and spent a very pleasant evening with Mrs. MacDonald and the children. I left a message for Mr. MacDonald, begging him to apply to Sir Noel Paton for me about the pictures for *Looking-Glass House*.[2]

May 19. (Tu). [1868]. Heard from Mrs. MacDonald, enclosing Sir Noel Paton's letter to Mr. MacDonald. He is too ill to undertake the pictures for *Looking-Glass House*, and also urges that Tenniel is *the* man. I wrote to Tenniel again, suggesting that I should pay his publishers for his time for the next five months. Unless he will undertake it, I am quite at a loss.[3]

June 21. (Sun). [1868]. * * * On the 18th I wrote to *Tenniel*, finally accepting his kind offer to do the pictures (at such spare time as he can find) for the second volume of *Alice*. He thinks it *possible* (but not likely) that we might get it out by Christmas 1869. It will now be best, I think, to reserve the volume of verses[4] for this Christmas and not publish it, as I had intended, in September.

Aug: 17. (M). [1868]. Left Albury for town, and took my luggage to Uncle Skeffington's. He is out of town, so we (Fanny, Aunt Lucy and myself) are quietly taking possession of his house.[5]

† From *The Diaries of Lewis Carroll*, ed. Roger Lancelyn Green, 2: 265, 267, 269–70, 272, 273, 279, 294, 295–96, 297–98, 306–7.
1. Dodgson's father, who died in this year, was canon of the cathedral at Ripon. *The Fifth Book of Euclid Treated Algebraically* was published in 1868 by James Parker of Oxford [*Editor*].
2. Joseph Noel Paton was a painter and illustrator, also well known for his treatments of fanciful subjects [*Editor*].
3. The difficulty in getting Tenniel to agree to illustrate the sequel to *Alice's Adventures in Wonderland* was both that he was busy, and that he had found Dodgson a trying and demanding collaborator. After he completed the

illustrations for *Through the Looking-Glass*, more than a year after he had begun them, he undertook no more commissions to illustrate books [*Editor*].
4. The volume of verse is *Phantasmagoria*, which was published early in 1869. The volume is a collection of comic and sentimental poems and prose sketches, many of which Dodgson had previously published in his domestic magazines or in the *Comic Times*, *The Train*, and other periodicals [*Editor*].
5. It was probably during this stay in the house at Onslow Square that a chance meeting with his little cousin Alice Raikes helped Dodgson to the additional realization of the peculiarities

Aug: 24. (M). [1868]. The following seems a fair statement of the pecuniary result of *Alice*: I have already calculated the balance for Jan: 1869 (without allowing for the account of June '68, which will be paid then) to be £52 against me. Now by the account just received I find £136 due to me, and 2,000 copies in hand; which will cost to board £101 and bring me £412, thus clearing £311.

Hence adding£136 cash
311 value of books

£447
and deducting 52 balance against me,

we have 395 in my favour (besides paying for pictures) as

the ultimate result of the sale of the 13,000 copies now printed.
N.B. The first 2,000 brought no profit, and the next 2,000 only about £80, so that the *rate*, adding £185 for pictures, thus making £580, is about £55 per 1,000. i.e. a sale of 9,000 gave £500 profit.

Jan: 8. (F). [1869]. Another visit to Macmillan. * * * He tells me that *Alice* has had a great sale this Christmas, more than 3000 having been sold since June!

Jan: 12. (Tu). [1869]. Finished and sent off to Macmillan the first chapter of *Behind the Looking-glass, and What Alice Saw There.*

Jan: 4. (W). [1871]. Finished the M.S. of *Through the Looking-glass.* It was begun before /69.

---

of 'Looking-Glass House,' which gave still greater verismilitude to the new 'Wonderland' which he was then inventing for his own dream-child.

'As children', wrote Alice Raikes (Mrs. Wilson Fox) in *The Times*, January 22, 1932, 'we lived in Onslow Square and used to play in the garden behind the houses. Charles Dodgson used to stay with an old uncle there, and walk up and down, his hands behind him, on the strip of lawn. One day, hearing my name, he called me to him saying, "So you are another Alice. I'm very fond of Alices. Would you like to come and see something which is rather puzzling?" We followed him into his house which opened, as ours did, upon the garden, into a room full of furniture with a tall mirror standing across one corner.'

' "Now", he said, giving me an orange, "first tell me which hand you have got that in." "The right," I said. "Now", he said "go and stand before that glass, and tell me which hand the little girl you see there has got it in." After some perplexed contemplation, I said, "The left hand," "Exactly," he said, "and how do you explain that?" I couldn't explain it, but seeing that some solution was expected, I ventured, "If I was on the *other* side of the glass, wouldn't the orange still be in my right hand?" I can remember his laugh. "Well done, little Alice," he said. "The best answer I've had yet."

'I heard no more then, but in after years was told that he said that had given him his first idea for *The Looking-Glass*, a copy of which, together with each of his other books, he regularly sent me' [*Green's note*].

Jan: 13. (F). [1871]. Received from Clay slips[6] reaching to the end of the text of the *Looking-glass*. Nothing now remains to be printed but the verses at the end. The volume has cost me, I think, more trouble than the first, and *ought* to be equal to it in every way.

[*Letter on the Jabberwock*][7]

[*Early* 1871]. I am sending you, with this, a print of the proposed frontispiece for *Through the Looking-glass*. It has been suggested to me that it is too terrible a monster, and likely to alarm nervous and imaginative children; and that at any rate we had better begin the book with a pleasanter subject.

So I am submitting the question to a number of friends, for which purpose I have had copies of the frontispiece printed off.

We have three courses open to us:

(1) To retain it as the frontispiece.
(2) To transfer it to its proper place in the book (where the ballad occurs which it is intended to illustrate) and substitute a new frontispiece.
(3) To omit it altogether.

The last named course would be a great sacrifice of the time and trouble which the picture cost, and it would be a pity to adopt it unless it is really necessary.

I should be grateful to have your opinion, (tested by exhibiting the picture to any children you think fit) as to which of these courses is best.

May 4. (*Th*). [1871]. On this day, 'Alice's' birthday, I sit down to record the events of the day, partly as a specimen of my life now, and partly because they include *one* new experience. Went to breakfast with Thompson to meet Blore. Then lecturing from 10 till 2.15. Then I went (by request of King, vicar of St. Peter's in the East) to visit Quartermain, who used to work for me as carpenter, and who is dying of consumption. I visited him more as a friend than as a clergyman—though I *did* read him, at his own wish, two psalms and his favourite hymn 'Sun of my Soul'. I *hope* that my visit may have been of some comfort to him, though I feel terribly unfit to comfort anyone in such a time. After leaving him I fell in with George Jelf, and walked with him; and after that with Fowler. Then I took to the University Press the proof, finally corrected, of my *Suggestions for the Committee appointed to consider Senior Stu-*

6. Galley-proof [*Editor*].
7. Dodgson sent this circular letter to various friends. It is reprinted in *The Diaries of Lewis Carroll*, ed. Roger Lancelyn Green, 2: 295–

96. The proposed frontispiece was Tenniel's drawing of the Jabberwock; it was replaced as the frontispiece, although retained in the book, by his drawing of the White Knight [*Editor*].

dentships. Then strolled into a few College gardens. The evening went partly in work for Lecture, and partly in a talk with Bayne on College matters, etc.

I heard from Tenneil the other day, the welcome news that he hopes to have all the pictures done by the end of July at latest.

Nov: 30. (Th).[1871]. Heard from Macmillan that they already have orders for 7500 *Looking-glasses* (they printed 9,000), and are at once going to print 6000 more!

Dec: 8. (F). [1871]. Received from Macmillan three *Looking-glasses* in morocco, and a hundred in cloth.

I first sent three to the Deanery (the one for Alice being in morocco) and then sent to friends in Christ Church and to Parkers to be packed for book-post, ninety-five in cloth, and two in morocco (for Florence Terry[8] and Tennyson)—making a total of ninety-nine given away in one day.

Dec: 31. (Sun).[1871]. Nearly midnight. The past year has made little change in the position of myself, or the family, except that Edwin has given up accountancy, and has now had one term at the Chichester Theological College. Wilfred and Alice are staying at the Chestnuts and all the party are south, except Fanny and Elizabeth, who are nursing Mary with her second boy.

LEWIS CARROLL

Letter to Mrs. A. L. Mayhew†

Christ Church, Oxford
May 26, 1879

Dear Mrs. Mayhew,[1]

Two, out of the three negatives which I did on Saturday, are decidedly good: the one of Ruth alone as "Comte de Brissac,"[2] standing: and the one of Ethel in the same dress, seated: the group

---

8. Florence Terry, the sister of the actress Ellen Terry. Dodgson had met the Terry family in 1867, and continued a warm friendship with them, especially Ellen, the rest of his life [*Editor*].
† From Cohen, *Letters* 1: 337–39.
1. Mrs. Mayhew was the wife of an Oxford chaplain and lecturer. Ruth Mayhew was about twelve when Dodgson wrote this letter; her sister Ethel was a year younger, and Janet was about six or seven. Mrs. Mayhew's insistence on being present during the photographing sessions offended Dodgson (it is "the same as saying 'I cannot trust you' " [*Letters*, 1: 343]) and led to an estrangement [*Editor*].
2. The Comte de Brissac is a character in a comedy by John Madison Morton that Dodgson saw in 1856 [*Editor*].

is not so good, as Ethel moved a little. I would have liked to have done Ethel in Jersey and bathing-drawers (the dress worn by the children at Sandown) but did not like to do it without first getting leave.

If Saturday afternoon is fine, I shall be glad to have Janet as soon after 2 as she can be got here. If you cannot come yourself, Ruth and Ethel might bring her—or, if you have other places you wish to go to, and like to leave her for an hour or two, I shall be most happy to take charge of her: but in either of these cases I should like to know *exactly* what is the minimum of dress I may take her in, and I will strictly observe the limits. I hope that, at any rate, we may go as far as a pair of bathing-drawers, though for *my* part I should much prefer doing without them, and shall be very glad if you say she may be done "in any way she likes herself."

But I have a much more alarming request to make than *that*, and I hope you and Mr. Mayhew will kindly consider it, and not hastily refuse it. It is that the same permission may be extended to Ethel. Please consider my reasons for asking the favour. Here am I, an amateur-photographer, with a deep sense of admiration for *form*, especially the human form, and one who believes it to be the most beautiful thing God has made on this earth—and who hardly ever gets a chance of photographing it! Did I ever show you those drawings Mr. Holiday[3] did for me, in order to supply me with some graceful and unobjectionable groupings for children without drapery? He drew them from life, from 2 children of 12 and 6—but I thought sadly, "I shall never get 2 children of those ages who will consent to be subjects!" and now at last I seem to have a *chance* of it. I could no doubt hire *professional* models in town: but, first, they would be ugly, and, secondly, they would *not* be pleasant to deal with: so my only hope is with *friends*. Now your Ethel is beautiful, both in face and form; and is also a perfectly simple-minded child of Nature, who would have no sort of objection to serving as model for a friend she knows as well as she does me. So my humble petition is, that you will bring the 3 girls, and that you will allow me to try some groupings of Ethel and Janet (I fear there is no use naming Ruth as well, at her age, though *I* should have no objection!) without any drapery or suggestion of it.

I need hardly say that the pictures should be such as you might if you liked frame and hang up in your drawing-room. On no account would I do a picture which I should be unwilling to show to all the world—or at least all the artistic world.

If I did not believe I could take such pictures without any lower

3. Henry Holiday was a painter and illustrator; he did the illustrations for *The Hunting of the Snark* (1876) [*Editor*].

motive than a pure love of Art, I would not ask it: and if I thought there was any fear of its lessening *their* beautiful simplicity of character, I would not ask it.

I print all such pictures *myself*, and of course would not let any one see them without your permission.

I fear you will reply that the one *insuperable* objection is "Mrs. Grundy"—that people will be sure to hear that such pictures have been done, and that they will *talk*. As to their *hearing* of it, I say "of course. All the world are welcome to hear of it, and I would not on any account suggest to the children not to mention it—which would at once introduce an objectionable element"—but as to people *talking* about it, I will only quote the grand old monkish(?) legend:

> They say:
> Quhat do they say?
> Lat them say!⁴

It only remains for me to add that, though my *theories* are so out-of-the-way (as you may perhaps think them), my *practice* shall be strictly in accordance with whatever rules you like to lay down—so you may at any time send the children by themselves, in perfect confidence that I will try *no* experiments you have not previously sanctioned.

I write all this, as a better course than coming to say it. *I* can be more sure of saying exactly what I mean—and you will have more leisure to think it over.

Sincerely yours,
C. L. Dodgson

TONY BEALE

C. L. Dodgson: Mathematician†

"I only took the regular course".

Charles Lutwidge Dodgson obtained First Class Honours in the Final Mathematical School in 1854. He took his B.A. on December 18th of the same year. Although by modern standards the breadth of topics studied was narrow, the depth and necessary discipline was very exacting indeed. His examination results, by any standards, were no mean achievement. Dodgson was a mathematician, but he cer-

---

4. Cohen in the *Letters* identifies this motto as an inscription over the doors of houses in Scotland in the sixteenth century [*Editor*].
† From *Mr. Dodgson*, ed. Denis Crutch (London: Lewis Carroll Society, 1973) 26–33. Re-printed by permission of Tony Beale and the Lewis Carroll Society. The epigraph is from the Mock Turtle's Story (chapter 9) in *Alice's Adventures in Wonderland*.

tainly did not achieve the stature that many who know him as the author of *Alice* would believe.

It was inevitable that once Lewis Carroll had been identified as the quiet unassuming Oxford mathematical don, his work should have been subjected to analysis as an elaborate parody burdened with carefully thought out mathematical and logical arguments. It may be possible to work out the multiplication table that Alice recites down the Rabbit Hole as an example of multibase numbers, but to suggest that the exercise was contrived, is as lunatic as the suggestion that fortunes may be told from the numbers on bus tickets. Similarly to argue that *Through the Looking-Glass* was a dramatic preview of Einstein's Theory of Special Relativity, and that the author had some inkling of the theory, only distorts the peculiar genius of the man. One might with equal conviction suggest that when Shakespeare made Hamlet say: "I could be bounded in a nutshell, and count myself a king of infinite space", the author was on the verge of discovering hyperbolic geometry.

However seriously one takes these arguments, it often seems to be forgotten that Dodgson told his immortal story for the benefit of a *child*. The fact that generations of children of all ages have enjoyed its inimitable magic, only emphasises how sensitive he was to the needs of children. His immortal genius manifests itself in the world of *Alice*. It appears again and again in many other facets of the man, but let us not look for genius where none exists.

What was Dodgson like as a mathematician? To understand his true stature, it is necessary to look at the world he lived in and the quality of his professional work. Mathematics is a subject that often requires greater minds to stimulate the spirit of scholarship, and, truth to tell, very few existed in England at this time, particularly at Oxford. There was a revolution in mathematical thought but its centre was more likely to be found on the continent. The giants of the English mathematical world such as Cayley, Babbage and Hamilton,[1] were to be found at Cambridge, and there is no evidence to suggest that Dodgson read or had any interest in their work.

Mathematics also requires a certain single mindedness which Dodgson did not have. His interests were wide and although his mathematical training is evident in all his work, his application was always at an elementary level. His determination to understand every step of an argument and go from the beginning to the end with strict logical precision, often left him with a walnut size problem which he had cracked with a sledgehammer. Also his training was unimaginative. In the nineteenth century, Mathematics was bedeviled by subject barriers. Geometry was geometry, analysis was analysis

---

1. Arthur Cayley, Charles Babbage, and William Rowan Hamilton published their mathematical work during the early and middle decades of the nineteenth century [*Editor*].

and never the twain should meet. Euclid loomed as a kind of in-fallible Pope. Far too many English mathematicians were content to live in the past and dismiss the work of their continental coun-terparts as lacking in rigour, and ignore the imaginative ideas which so richly abounded in nineteenth-century mathematics.

It would be difficult to imagine what would have happened to Dodgson had his mathematical energies been given the right stimulus and he had devoted them to more serious pursuits. In later life he studied logic, and he did so at a time when it was beginning to be accepted as an essential part of mathematics. However he still walked the narrow path of the Classical Aristotelian Logic which had severe limitations for mathematics.

Dodgson was essentially a teacher. He had a natural love of teach-ing but he did not have a natural gift of communication in the formal classroom situation. He developed an interest in presenting his sub-ject in the simplest and most palatable form that he could devise. He started with text books for his students at Oxford, and in later life he tried to bring logic into the school curriculum. Throughout his life he took great delight in puzzles and paradoxes and presented them to his child friends and many adult ones as well. With the paradoxes, he did not always supply a solution and it gave him enormous pleasure to see great minds struggling to resolve them. It would be interesting to speculate how he would have reacted to the so called New Mathematics in schools today. He would have wel-comed the introduction of all the games and puzzles but he might have rejected the ruthless pruning of extraneous subject matter. He certainly would have objected to the lack of rigour and the apparently aimless manner in which children learn their basic arithmetic rules.

Dodgson's greatest love was the paradox, or the kind of question that starts with "what happens if?" After all this was how *Wonderland* began, and indeed *Through the Looking-Glass*. This was his way of stimulating thought and this was the way his mathematical energies were directed. Most of the problems were trivial but they were de-signed to amuse, or to quote his own words, "they were for the much larger class of *ordinary* mathematicians". He was rightly modest about his own mathematical ability but he enjoyed his subject, and in the manner of a good teacher, he wanted everyone else to enjoy it just as much.

Many references have been made to his alleged split personality: in his professional life he was Dodgson, and as a writer of children's books he was Lewis Carroll. Personally I do not believe in this. It was certainly true that he kept the names separate, but in his more serious work there are many flashes of Wonderland. In his earlier text books the cobbler stuck to his last, but these were intended for adults; the young teacher was establishing his reputation. Later in life, he did not seem to worry, and more and more of his books, including a serious book on logic, were written under his pseudonym. I do not draw any particular inference, other than to suggest that, had his pattern of life been reversed, we might have been treated to some entertaining treatise on determinants! Here was one man who wanted to teach; in mathematics and logic, within the limits of his own age, he knew what he was about.

* * *

Dodgson was very familiar with the Elements of Euclid. It is recorded by Collingwood in his *Life and Letters* that: "He would sometimes go through a whole book of Euclid in bed; he was so familiar with the bookwork that he could actually see the figures before him in the dark, and did not confuse the letters, which is perhaps even more remarkable". He produced his own edition of the first two books in 1882. It must have been an acceptable and successful text book since it ran into eight editions, the last one appearing in 1889. He acknowledges Isaac Todhunter the doyen of Victorian mathematics text book writers, but Dodgson's book is nowhere near as conservative. In many ways it acts as an introductory text for the more classical Todhunter version, first published in 1862. Dodgson's aims in producing this book were to present Euclid in a simpler form by stripping the traditional translations of, to quote his own words, "all accidental verbiage and repetition". In this he succeeded and his own version resembles in style many of the later text books in use in the earlier part of this century.

Dodgson's conservatism in things mathematical was not unshakeable. What he was reluctant to accept, was any change in the logical sequence of theorems or in the methods of proof. For him Euclid remained the only authority on geometry, and any alteration other than a minor one was verging on sacrilege. In Dodgson's mind the 47th Proposition (more generally known today as the Theorem of Pythagoras) had to be, "as clear a reference as if one were to quote the enunciation in full". He rejected, not without some thought, all the rival systems, including many of the findings of the Association for the Improvement of Geometrical Teaching. His contention was that there was nothing wrong in editing Euclid, or omitting many of the propositions, but the logically arranged sequence should be maintained. This does not detract from his value as a teacher. He wanted to improve the methods, but he was tilting at windmills. For example he records in his diary how all algebraical signs were forbidden in Cambridge examinations, and that he proposed deleting them in the second edition of his Euclid. This he did, although he recognised that his exposition was less useful.

Non-Euclidean geometry did not exist in Dodgson's thinking but then, in the nineteenth century, many far better mathematicians had been slow to recognise that other geometries were possible. The growth of these other geometries stemmed from the reluctance to accept Euclid's 12th Axiom involving parallel lines. An indication of the stranglehold which Euclid had on the world of mathematics can be seen by the reluctance of such eminent mathematicians as [Karl Friedrich] Gauss to propound any theories that might bring down scorn.

So Dodgson can hardly be blamed if he was timid in his geometrical thinking. It is also doubtful whether he had the kind of mind for really original mathematics. In all his work he pursued the solution of the problem with relentless logic, starting always from premisses which could be shown to be true. As he later wrote in a letter: "I shall not venture to assert 'some boots are made of brass' till I have found a pair!" What hope for the imaginative alternatives to Euclid's 12th Axiom!

In 1879 he wrote *Euclid and his Modern Rivals*. The "Modern Rivals" consisted of mathematics teachers of varying stature who had dared to rewrite Euclid. The book, which is in dramatic form, consists of a dialogue between Minos, an examiner, and the ghost of Euclid, who argue over the relative merits of each author's contribution. There are other characters, notably Professor Niemand, another ghost, who claims to have "read all books, and is ready to defend any thesis, true or untrue". This gentleman, a German, proved to be a rather incompetent Devil's Advocate, since Euclid wins the day. It is not recorded what the "Modern Rivals" thought of the criticism levelled against them.

The arguments are amusing but totally unscientific. To quote one on the subject of points taken from the 2nd edition:

Min.—'A point, in changing its position on a curve, passes, in moving from one position to another, through all intermediate positions. It does not move by jumps'.
Nie. That is quite true.
Min. Tell me, then—is every centre of gravity a point?
Nie. Certainly.
Min. Let us now consider the centre of gravity of a flea. Does it—
Nie. (*indignantly*) Another word, and I shall vanish! I cannot waste a night on such trivialities.

* * *

Dodgson resigned his Mathematical Lectureship at the end of 1881. He wrote in his diary on October 18th: "I shall now have my whole time at my own disposal, and, if God gives me life and continued health and strength, may hope, before my powers fail, to do some worthy work in writing—partly in the cause of Mathematical education, partly in the cause of innocent recreation for children, and partly, I hope (though so utterly unworthy of being allowed to take up such work) in the cause of religious thought". There is no doubt that he felt deeply that he could offer more from his teaching, if he were freed from the routine of University Lecturing. It was not a job he greatly enjoyed. He wrote in his diary as early as 1856 that "he was weary of lecturing and discouraged . . . It is thankless, uphill work, goading unwilling men to learning they have no taste for".

He employed his mathematical talents in a novel way from April 1880 until March 1885 when he wrote a series of ten short stories for Charlotte Yonge's magazine *The Monthly Packet*. The stories were mathematical problems and they were eventually collected in one volume and published in 1885 as A *Tangled Tale*. Some of the readers of the magazine had sent in their solutions to the author as they were published and, in the final version of the book, Dodgson used these attempted solutions to illustrate the mathematical difficulties of each problem, and of course, added his own correct solution. Contributors, often only recognisable by initials or a nom-de-plume, were assigned to "class lists", according to how skillfully they tackled the problem. The problems are all well within the reach of lay mathematicians, although some are better solved with a knowledge of elementary algebra. The writing is quite brilliant and the subtle balance of mathematics and logic make it a book of unrivalled quality.

* * *

Mention has already been made of Dodgson's love of the paradox. One was known as "The Monkey and Weight", in which a monkey, and a weight equal to that of the monkey, are supposed to be on opposite ends of a weightless rope hung over a weightless friction-free pulley. Initially, the system is in a state of perfect balance and the problem is, what happens to the weight, when the monkey begins to climb the rope?

Two other examples involve Time, and were originally included in *The Rectory Umbrella*, an early manuscript magazine which he wrote for his family. The first was the problem as to which clock to choose as being the most accurate, supposing one to lose a minute each day, and the other not to go at all? The second, later developed into a lecture entitled, "When does the Day begin?" asks, if a man walks westward around the earth at the same speed as the sun, at what point will the day change its name? The answer, to a certain extent, was resolved when the International Date Line was established in 1884.

And here lies the weakness of Dodgson's scholarship. The problems that interested him were fascinating but trivial; they amused him, and he liked to see others share his enjoyment by having pamphlets printed and circulated among his friends.

The paradoxes mentioned above were not original to Dodgson. His own ideas were often imaginative, although of little practical use. For example, it occurred to him, that in a Lawn Tennis Tournament, a player who was beaten in the first round might find that the losing finalist was inferior to himself. As a result of his deliberations, he produced in 1883, a pamphlet, *Lawn Tennis Tournaments*, which set out to prove first the inadequacies of the accepted system, and then to devise an alternative. Needless to say the alternative was far too elaborate and not adopted at Wimbledon. On another occasion, he noted what he thought was an ambiguity in the Post Office Guide, relating to the commission payable when a Postal Order has not been cashed within three months. He produced a sheet of 16 questions which he called "A *Postal Problem*", and promptly circulated it to his friends. It is not recorded what he did with the answers, but it is certain that the respondents found many logic pitfalls.

From games and puzzles all the way to the relative prices of port and chablis in the Senior Common Room, he managed to introduce mathematics, logic and fun in the most unexpected ways. Even his satire took on mathematical form. Living as we do in a society where the ability to pass examinations matters so much, one might consider the following example proposed by Dodgson in *Dynamics of a Particle*, in 1865:

> "A takes 10 books in the Final Examination, and gets a 3d Class: B takes in the Examiners, and gets a 2nd. Find the value of the Examiners in terms of books. Find also their value in terms in which no Examination is held".

The *Game of Logic* is not, as the name would suggest, a children's book; nor do I think that the author intended it to be anything more than his idea of a textbook for young adults. He had been giving a series of lectures on logic at Lady Margaret Hall. From an entry in his diary on July 24th 1886, it was clear that he intended to write a text book; he wrote: "The idea occurred to me this morning of beginning my 'Logic' publication, not with 'Book I' of the full work, *Logic for Ladies*, but with a small pamphlet and a cardboard diagram to be, called *The Game of Logic*."

The pamphlet was extended to a book and he received the first bound copy on November 23rd 1886. He did not like the printing and so the book suffered a similar fate to the 1865 *Alice*. The first 500 copies were sent to America, and a new edition came out on

February 21st 1887. The deductive logic is complete Wonderland, although of course the book had the serious message of propounding the basic rules of Classical Logic. The game aspect is found by using the accompanying card and counters. The diagram on the card produces a kind of Venn diagram,[2] and the use of the counters indicated whether the set is empty (grey), or occupied (red). Dodgson used the book as a basis for his logic lectures and the examples must have been a delight to his students.

* * *

It was some years later that he produced his other text book on Logic. *Symbolic Logic, Part I* was a development of *The Game of Logic* and is a much more satisfying introduction to the subject. It was published in 1896 and within a year had gone into four editions. The subject matter is still at an elementary level, but there are many more examples. It is possible to discover that "no grey ducks in a village wear lace collars", that "babies cannot manage crocodiles", "that donkeys are not easy to swallow", and that "no badger can guess a conundrum." Some of the examples are quite formidable. Even so they *can* be solved, given plenty of time, patience, concentration and of course an elementary knowledge of logic. The book's importance cannot be fairly judged; interest in Classical Logic was waning, Modern Logic was beginning to take shape, and the inadequacies of the old theory were being widely discussed.

Both *The Game of Logic* and *Symbolic Logic* were elementary textbooks. They reveal Dodgson's potential as a mathematical logician, but one can only conjecture how much he would have contributed to modern logic, had he lived longer, or started his work earlier in life. Recently the second part of *Symbolic Logic* has been discovered in manuscript form by Professor W. W. Bartley of the University of Pittsburgh. In an article published in *Scientific American* [see Selected Bibliography] he discusses some of the contents of the manuscript and comments on Dodgson's ability as a logician. He outlines several achievements which clearly show that he was very much in the twentieth century with his logical thinking.

For some years, Dodgson had been engaged in a series of arguments with Professor John Cook Wilson, a traditionalist, who probably offered little encouragement to new or improved theories. One such argument was *A Disputed Point in Logic*, which Dodgson had printed and circulated in 1894 in two editions. The paradox was a variation of an old theme: three men in a shop who may go in or out as they please, providing the shop is never left empty and that

---

2. Venn diagrams are graphic illustrations, usually using intersecting circles, of the logical relationships among classes or categories [*Editor*].

one of them never goes out without the second. The problem posed is whether the third can ever go out? The resolution of the paradox is not easy and the argument continues.

There is no evidence to suggest that Dodgson knew what depths he was stirring. As with many of his puzzles, he seemed more interested in the debate it provoked, rather than committing himself to any one answer. In this he was probably a better logician than he was a mathematician. The pity of it was that he lived in an age where the two subjects were so compartmentalized. The world was not exactly ready for Whitehead and Russell.[3]

* * *

DEREK HUDSON

[Rooms at Christ Church][†]

At the same time that his sisters went into "The Chestnuts", Dodgson took possession of new rooms at Christ Church which were to be his for the rest of his life. He first occupied this spacious apartment, which had formerly belonged to Lord Bute, at the end of October, 1868. The rooms, in the north-west corner of Tom Quad, are unusually imposing among the quarters of Oxford dons and have an interior staircase communicating to an upper floor. The entrance is into a dark passage, with doors leading to a diningroom, a pantry and a small bedroom (bleakly equipped in Dodgson's day with a "japanned[1] sponge bath"). The passage leads on into a large high sitting-room—cold in winter—with windows looking out over St Aldate's and the Archdeacon's garden. The sitting-room has a further amenity in the shape of two small turret-rooms on the St Aldate's front—more curious, perhaps, than valuable, but useful for amusing young visitors.

Upstairs (these are the arrangements of 1953) we find another bedroom, a box-room, a bath-room, and a cubby-hole which Dodgson turned into a photographic dark-room. Even here was not his furthest; for he eventually obtained permission to build a studio on the roof—an erection that can hardly have been sightly and has long been removed; he first used it in October, 1871.

Although he became increasingly abstemious and eventually almost gave up eating lunch altogether, it would be a mistake to

---

3. Alfred North Whitehead and Bertrand Russell collaborated to write *Principia Mathematica* (1910–13), a revolutionary work in mathematical logic [*Editor*].

† From *Lewis Carroll*, 145–47.
1. Treated with a hard, glossy varnish or lacquer [*Editor*].

suppose that Dodgson possessed no interest in food. It will be remembered that the contents of the bottle which Alice drank had "a sort of mixed flavour of cherry-tart, custard, pineapple, roast turkey, toffy, and hot buttered toast", and that the taste of a Snark was "meagre and hollow, but crisp: Like a coat that is rather too tight in the waist, with a flavour of Will-o-the-wisp"—all evidence, surely, of a discriminating palate? His little dining-room at Christ Church holds memories of many dinner-parties, some of them quite elaborate, though the dishes were always placed on squares of cardboard, as he considered mats an unnecessary extravagance. In his diary, luncheons and dinners were recorded by a small diagram, showing the names of the guests and the places they occupied; he also kept a *menu* book, so that the same people should not be given the same dishes too often. After a dinner-party of eight in May, 1871, he wrote promptly to his publisher, Macmillan, to report "an invention of mine" (which does not seem to have been proceeded with). This was a plan of the table with the names of the guests in the order in which they were to sit, and brackets to show who was to take in whom; one to be given to each guest. He tabulated its advantages.

(1) It saves the host the worry of going round and telling every gentleman what lady to take in.
(2) It prevents confusion when the reach the dining-room (the system of putting names round on the plates simply increases the confusion, though it would work well *with* this plan).
(3) It enables everybody at table to know who the other guests are—often a very desirable thing.
(4) By keeping the cards one gets materials for making-up other dinner-parties, by observing what people harmonise well together.[2]

Dodgson's study was simply but comfortably furnished with a large Turkey carpet, one or two arm-chairs, a crimson-covered couch and settee, and a dining-table and writing-table of mahogany. No visitor could fail to detect that its occupant was diligent and methodical. Manuscript boxes abounded, more than twenty of them—neatly labelled—being assembled in a special stand. The room also contained what was described after Dodgson's death as a "pine nest" of twelve drawers, as well as a pine reading stand with a cloth cover— this presumably being the "standing desk" at which he often liked to write. Letter scales and weights, quantities of stationery, shelves full of books, and a terrestrial globe filled much of the remaining space. When he was correcting exam papers at midnight, the scene must have been all too reminiscent of that described by Dodgson at

2. The entire letter, and Dodgson's sketch of his table arrangement, is reprinted in *Lewis Carroll and the House of Macmillan*, ed. Morton N. Cohen and Anita Gandolfo (see Selected Bibliography) 95–96 [*Editor*].

the opening of *Euclid and his Modern Rivals*. Minos is there discovered "seated between two gigantic piles of manuscripts. Ever and
anon he takes a paper from one heap, reads it, makes an entry in a
book, and with a weary sigh transfers it to the other heap. His hair,
from much running of fingers through it, radiates in all directions,
and surrounds his head like a halo of glory, or like the second
Corollary of Euc. I.32."

The pictures that hung in Dodgson's rooms were mostly of little
girls, and usually had some personal association for him, either with
the subject or the painter. There was a sprinkling of religious and
fairy pictures, a plaster bust of a child, and one or two stock Victorian
engravings, such as "Samuel" and "The Order of Release". (If we
could accept Reynold's dictum that "the virtuous man alone has true
taste", we should be quite satisfied.) Perhaps the most interesting of
the *objets d'art* in the sitting-room was a set of William de Morgan's
famous tiles, which Collingwood says that Dodgson liked to explain
by reference to *Alice in Wonderland* and *The Hunting of the Snark*.

The tiles, which figure largely in recollections of his later years,
made their appearance only a decade before Dodgson's death. They
were set around the fireplace and depicted a large ship (in three
sections) and a number of more or less fabulous creatures, some of
which Dodgson interpreted for the benefit of his child-friends as the
Lory, the Dodo, the Fawn, the Eaglet, the Gryphon and the Beaver.
In the intervals between these subjects, a tile showing a group of
weird birds was repeated.

"Called on Mr. William de Morgan and chose a set of red tiles
for the large fire-place", Dodgson wrote in his diary of March 4th,
1887. This indicates that the tiles were not made to his order but
were taken from de Morgan's stock, Dodgson making what he considered an appropriate selection. They did not, of course, play any
part in inspiring the "Alice" books or *The Hunting of the Snark*,
but—as one of Dodgson's child-friends, Enid Stevens, believes—the
intermediate tiles may have suggested the "Little birds are dining"
verses in *Sylvie and Bruno Concluded*. The tiles remained in position
until about twenty years ago when they were swept away, rather
unnecessarily, to reveal the original fireplace; and with them went
a plain green paper on canvas which covered the walls in Dodgson's
time.

ANNE CLARK

[Friendships with Women]†

†

* * *

Of her friendship with Dodgson, Ellen Terry wrote, 'He was as fond of me as he could be of anyone over the age of ten,'[1] and this in many ways sums up Dodgson's problem. All the indications, and these increase as his life progresses, are that Dodgson would have been perfectly able to form a normal marrigeable relationship with a mature woman, had he only known where to begin. Although his shyness did not prevent his enjoying the society of other people, including women, it inhibited him from embarking on a relationship of intimacy with a marriageable and desirable young woman. His only hope was of growing into such a relationship as an automatic development of a friendship with a child. Ironically, the older he got, the older the children were with whom he spent his leisure hours. But the more he developed, the greater was the age-gap between himself and his young protégées. At the same time, the older he grew, the more he fostered that extreme protectiveness that is the role of the father rather than that of lover, with the result that he became almost incapable of treating his childhood friends as adults with a mind of their own. It is remotely possible that he could have married Ellen Terry, had she been free, for he had known her from afar in childhood, and easily slipped into friendship with her. Children, and ultimately grandchildren of his own would have satisfied his urgent need for someone to protect and shelter. But had he attained that goal, the world might never have had Lewis Carroll.

By his standards, though separated, Ellen Terry was strictly unavailable, and remained so even after her divorce in 1877. For Dodgson's personal code of conduct was so strict that, while sympathetic to those who felt otherwise, he himself considered widowers were wrong to remarry. This being the case, marriage with a woman whose first husband was still living would be even worse. He was certainly never likely to allow his emotions to sway his judgment in matters of the heart. Once, when discussing the question of insurance with his father, he put forward the view that insurance policies were of no advantage to those without concrete intentions of matrimony. The only disadvantage of failing to insure was the risk that 'a life

---

† From *Lewis Carroll: A Biography*, 146–47.
1. Ellen Terry (1847–1928) was a successful actress and recently married to the painter G. F. Watts when Dodgson met her in 1864. She later left Watts, lived with a man with whom she had two children, and married again in 1878. The quotation is from Ellen Terry's *The Story of My Life* (London: Hutchinson, 1908) 184 [*Editor*].

which might have been insured at 20, may be precarious at 30 from disease or accident, and so it may be impossible then to insure it, but I do not give much weight to this because I think that the very fact of life having become precarious would render it inadvisable to marry.' Duty, with Dodgson, was always after all bound to prevail.

Ellen Terry was not only beautiful, talented, and representative of a great romantic ideal, but she and indeed her entire family shared Dodgson's love of the theatre. Dodgson was interested in the entire range of dramatic art, but his greatest interest was in child performers. Having been brought up to the theatre, Ellen Terry was an invaluable adviser on all aspects of the drama, and had a special sympathy for the feelings of little actresses, or would-be actresses. In January 1866 Dodgson decided to try his hand at writing a play for Ellen Terry and Percy Roselle, then aged about eighteen years, but able to pass himself off as a boy of eight. A week after seeing Roselle in *Little King Pippin*, Dodgson devoted several hours to writing out an extended synposis of his play, which he decided to call *Morning Clouds*. The hero (Percy Roselle) was to be stolen from his widowed mother (Ellen Terry) by his father's younger brother. On a cold winter's night the boy passes the house where his mother lives. She hears him singing outside, and opens the window, but too late. Finally the villain dies miserably, and the boy is reunited with his family. The play ends with the boy singing his old grandfather to sleep. It seems almost incredible that, while Dodgson was engaged in writing his timeless classic, he could sink to producing this maudlin Victorian plot.

Dodgson sent his synopsis to Tom Taylor,[2] who reacted favourably and promised to find out if Percy Roselle was likely to be available. He also undertook to show it to Ellen Terry; but finally their joint opinion was that the play would be impracticable, and lacked the sensationalism that public taste demanded. The final obstacle was the fact that Percy Roselle was not to be had. Dodgson thereupon decided to abandon the project.

*   *   *

---

2. Playwright and editor of *Punch* (1874–80) [*Editor*].

E. M. ROWELL

[To Me He Was Mr. Dodgson]†

When I first saw Lewis Carroll I was a sixth-form girl[1] at the Oxford High School. One morning at school the word went around that 'Mr Dodgson' was coming to give some lectures to the sixth on symbolic logic. To me the name 'Mr Dodgson' meant nothing, and when someone said casually, 'Lewis Carroll, you know,' I acquiesced in the synonym but my mind was blank as before.

I had of course always known *Alice in Wonderland*, but to me Alice and the White Rabbit and the Red Queen—and the Dormouse and the Mad Hatter and the Cheshire Cat—were endowed with all the vitality and reality and being of an age-old myth; and how they had managed to get into a book was really neither here nor there. In short, at the age of fifteen I was quite oblivious of the fact that Lewis Carroll had written *Alice in Wonderland*, and neither 'Lewis Carroll' nor 'Mr Dodgson' had any associations for me.

When Mr Dodgson stood at the desk in the sixth-form room and prepared to address the class I thought he looked very tall and seemed very serious and rather formidable, beyond that I did not go and, with the ready docility of a schoolgirl of the nineties, I soon settled down to the subject in hand and forgot the lecturer in his own fascinating 'Game of Logic'.

* * *

The day after Mr. Dodgson gave us his last lecture, I received from him this letter:

> Ch. Ch., Oxford
> April 18. /94.

My dear Ethel,

(I would gladly write "Miss Rowell" if I thought you would prefer it, but, with more than forty years' interval of age, the other way seems more natural.)

You did your logic so *very* well, that it occurs to me to ask whether you would like, and could spare the time, to have some more lessons during the vacation. If so, I will come and speak to your Mother, and see if any such arrangement can be made.

I should be very glad to do it; and it would be a real help in the book I am at work on.

yours very sincerely
C. L. Dodgson.

† From *Harpers* 186 (1943): 319–23. A somewhat shorter version is reprinted in *Lewis Carroll: Interviews and Recollections*, ed. Morton Cohen (Iowa City: U of Iowa P, 1989) 129–34.

1. Ethel Rowell was seventeen years old when Dodgson met her. She became a lecturer in mathematics at the Royal Holloway College [*Editor*].

The lessons began almost at once, and in those summer holidays I went to and fro to Mr Dodgson's rooms in Christ Church; we worked through the first proofs of the book, and as the subject opened out I found great delight in this my first real experience of the patterned intricacies of abstract thought.

In the beginning my inveterate docility got in the way; I could find nothing to comment on and my response was limited to a repetitive 'Yes, yes . . . yes, I see.' I was ready to accept everything that was put before me. One day after a long series of such feeble affirmatives Mr Dodgson put down his pen and, looking at me with his rather crooked smile, 'You do make the lion and the lamb consort together in your caravanserai, don't you?' he said. I did not understand and thought he was paying me a compliment, so I hastened to say deprecatingly 'Oh! but I'm afraid I don't get on easily with everybody.' He looked at me with his kindest smile and said: 'Well, my dear, let us leave the lamb to fend for itself, and get back to our muttons, shall we?'

His words were Greek to me, but in their very strangeness they lingered in my memory, and much later I understood both his criticism of me and the patience with which he so gently withdrew it in the face of my ignorance.

I did not understand, but I realized that he found my shallow receptivity disappointing. And presently I managed to face the thing more squarely, to halt the flow of passive response, to tell myself and to tell my teacher what I found difficult or obscure in his reasoning. By his own real wish to know what I was thinking Mr Dodgson compelled me to that independence of thought I had never before tried to exercise. I had always learned very easily, and such ready assimilation of all and sundry had filled my mind with a company of somnolent ideas which, awake, must surely have been at odds with one another. Mr Dodgson's protest of the lion and the lamb was indeed justified. But gradually under his stimulating tuition I felt myself able in some measure to judge for myself, to select, and, if need be, to reject.

But while he was urging me to exercise my critical faculties Mr Dodgson at the same time bestowed on me another gift of aspect more gracious. He gave me a sense of my own personal dignity. He was so punctilious, so courteous, so considerate, so scrupulous not to embarrass or offend, that he made me feel that I counted—counted not as much as anyone else, and certainly not more than anyone else, but just in and as myself. There was nothing competitive or precarious in this counting, and thus my own keen awareness of awkwardness, ignorance, and inadequacy could not inhibit this new sense of the freedom of selfhood.

In Mr Dodgson's presence I felt proud and humble, with the pride and humility which are the grace and personality, grace conferred thus upon an ignorant schoolgirl by the magnanimity of a proud and very humble and very great and good man. And then Mr Dodgson gave me his affection—the reflection, in our own particular relation, of his great-hearted concern for all children. He was so patient of all one's limitations, so understanding, so infinitely kind.

*   *   *

I became a student at the Royal Holloway College in October, 1895, and after that I saw Mr Dodgson very rarely; but I was sure of his friendly interest, and I never felt out of touch with him.

When it was suggested that I should go on from Honors Moderations to work for the Final Honors School Examination in Mathematics at Oxford he was gently concerned and made an urgent protest to my mother on the grounds that the proposed course was altogether unsuitable for a girl, that the work was far too exacting and would impose a strain which might even upset my mental balance! My brother remembers vividly how his distressful apprehensions and vehement opposition reduced my mother to tears. I think he was always very conscious both of the qualities and of the disabilities of women, and perhaps he overemphasized the differences in temperament and in capacity between men and women. But he was never for a moment patronizing to women or to children; he "consulted" one about this or that and took careful and serious account of any opinion given. He was always completely at ease with women and children, and I fancy he was happier with them than in the company of men.

Throughout my college course he always answered my letters, and he kept me in touch with the work he was doing.

ISA BOWMAN

[A Visit to Christ Church]†

*   *   *

In the morning I was awakened by the deep reverberations of "Great Tom" calling Oxford to wake and begin the new day. Those times were very pleasant, and the rememberance of them lingers with me still. Lewis Carroll at the time of which I am speaking had

† From *The Story of Lewis Carroll* (London: J. M. Dent & Sons Ltd., 1899) 20–23, 18–19. Isa Bowman was a child actress whom Dodgson had seen in the company of the theatrical version of the Alice books. He met her in 1887 [*Editor*].

two tiny turret rooms, one on each side of his staircase in Christ Church. He always used to tell me that when I grew up and became married he would give me the two little rooms, so that if I ever disagreed with my husband we could each of us retire to a turret till we had made up our quarrel!

And those rooms of his! I do not think there was ever such a fairy-land for children. I am sure they must have contained one of the finest collections of musical-boxes to be found anywhere in the world. There were big black ebony boxes with glass tops, through which you could see all the works. There was a big box with a handle, which it was quite hard exercise for a little girl to turn, and there must have been twenty or thirty little ones which could only play one tune. Sometimes one of the musical-boxes would not play properly, and then I always got tremendously excited. Uncle [Dodgson] used to go to a drawer in the table and produce a box of little screw-drivers and punches, and while I sat on his knee he would unscrew the lid and take out the wheels to see what was the matter. He must have been a clever mechanist, for the result was always the same—after a longer or shorter period the music began again. Sometimes when the musical-boxes had played all their tunes he used to put them in the box backwards, and was as pleased as I at the comic effect of the music "standing on its head," as he phrased it.

There was another and very wonderful toy which he sometimes produced for me, and this was known as "The Bat." The ceilings of the rooms in which he lived at the time were very high indeed, and admirably suited for the purposes of "The Bat." It was an ingeniously constructed toy of gauze and wire, which actually flew about the room like a bat. It was worked by a piece of twisted elastic, and it could fly for about half a minute.

I was always a little afraid of this toy because it was too lifelike, but there was a fearful joy in it. When the music-boxes began to pall he would get up from his chair and look at me with a knowing smile. I always knew what was coming even before he began to speak, and I used to dance up and down in tremulous anticipation.

"Isa, my darling," he would say, "once upon a time there was some one called Bob the Bat! and he lived in the top left-hand drawer of the writing-table. What could he do when uncle wound him up?"

And then I would speak out breathlessly, "He could really FLY!"

Bob the Bat had many adventures. There was no way of controlling the direction of its flight, and one morning, a hot summer's morning, when the window was wide open, Bob flew out into the garden and alighted in a bowl of salad which a scout[1] was taking to some one's rooms. The poor fellow was so startled by the sudden flapping ap-

---

1. A servant [*Editor*].

parition that he dropped the bowl, and it was broken into a thousand pieces.

* * *

I remember that [his] shyness was the only occasion of anything approaching a quarrel between us.

I had an idle trick of drawing caricatures when I was a child, and one day when he was writing some letters I began to make a picture of him on the back of an envelope. I quite forget what the drawing was like—probably it was an abominable libel—but suddenly he turned round and saw what I was doing. He got up from his seat and turned very red, frightening me very much. Then he took my poor little drawing, and tearing it into small pieces threw it into the fire without a word. Afterwards he came suddenly to me, and saying nothing, caught me up in his arms and kissed me passionately. I was only some ten or eleven years of age at the time, but now the incident comes back to me very clearly, and I can see it as if it happened but yesterday—the sudden snatching of my picture, the hurried striding across the room, and then the tender light in his face as he caught me up to him and kissed me.

* * *

LEWIS CARROLL

From the Diaries [1879–85]†

May 15. *(Th).* [1879]. Last night I had a dream which I record as a curiosity, as containing *the same person at two different periods of* life, a feature entirely unique, so far as I know, in the literature of dream. I was staying with my sisters in some suburb of London, and had heard that the Terrys were staying near us, so went to call and found Mrs. Terry at home, who told me that Marion and Florence were at the theatre, 'the Walter House,' where they had good engagement. 'In that case,' I said, 'I'll go on there at once, and see the performance. And may I take Polly with me?' 'Certainly,' said Mrs. Terry. And there was Polly, the child, seated in the room and looking about nine or ten years old: and I was distinctly conscious of the fact, yet without any feeling of surprise at its incongruity, that I was going to take the *child* Polly with me to the theatre to see the *grownup* Polly act! Both figures, Polly as a child and Polly as a woman, are I suppose equally clear in my ordinary waking memory: and it seems

† From *The Diaries of Lewis Carroll*, ed. Roger Lancelyn Green, 2: 379, 400, 433–34.

that in sleep I had contrived to give to the two pictures separate individualities.

Oct: 18. (Tu). [1881]. 6 p.m. I have just taken an important step in life, by sending to the Dean a proposal to resign the Mathematical Lectureship at the end of this year. I shall now have my whole time at my own disposal, and, if God gives me life and continued health and strength, may hope, before my powers fail, to do some worthy work in writing—partly in the cause of Mathematical education, partly in the cause of innocent recreation for children, and partly, I hope (though so utterly unworthy of being allowed to take up such work) in the cause of religious thought. May God bless the new form of life that lies before me, that I may use it according to His holy will!

March 29. (Sun). [1885]. Never before have I had so many literary projects on hand at once. For curiosity I will here make a list of them:—

(1) Supplement to *Euclid and his Modern Rivals*, now being set up in pages. (Pub. April '85).

(2) Second edition of *Euclid and his Modern Rivals*, this I am correcting for the press, and shall embody the above in it. (Pub. Nov: '85).

(3) A book of Mathematical curiosities, which I think of calling *Pillow Problems, and other Mathematical Trifles*. This will contain problems worked out in the dark, Logarithms without tables, sines and angles, etc., a paper I am now writing on 'Infinities and Infinitesimals', condensed long Multiplication, and perhaps others. [Published 1893.]

(4) *Euclid* V, treating Incommensurables by a method of Limits, which I have nearly completed.

(5) *Plain Facts for Circle-Squarers* which is nearly complete, and give actual proof of limits 3.14158, 3.14160.

(6) A Symbolical Logic, treated by my algebraic method (see 23/12/84). [Part I published 1896.]

(7) A *Tangled Tale*—with answers and perhaps illustrations by Mr. Frost.[1] (Pub. Dec. '85).

(8) A collection of Games and Puzzles of my devising, with fairy pictures by Miss E. G. Thomson.[2] This might also contain my 'Memoria

1. Arthur Burdett Frost, an American artist, had illustrated some of the poems in *Rhyme? or Reason?* (1883), a collection made up mostly comic poems Dodgson had published previously. Frost did illustrate *A Tangled Tale*, which was published in 1885 [*Editor*].
2. E. Gertrude Thomson, whose fanciful designs for a set of Christmas cards had attracted Dodgson's interest in 1878, met him in 1879, helped him with his own drawing, and illustrated some of the poems in *Three Sunsets* (1898), a collection in which Dodgson's serious poems were reprinted [*Editor*].

Technica' for dates, etc., my 'cipher-writing,' scheme for Letter-registration, etc. etc.

(9) *Nursery Alice*—for which twenty pictures are now being coloured by Mr. Tenniel. [Published 1889.]

(10) Serious poems in *Phantasmagoria*. I think of calling it *Reason and Rhyme*, and hope to get Mr. Furniss[3] to draw for it.

(11) *Alice's Adventures Underground*, a facsimile of the MS. book lent me by 'Alice' (Mrs. Hargreaves). I am now in correspondence with Dalziel [the engraver] about it. [Published 1886.]

(12) *Girls' Own Shakespeare.*[4] I have begun on *The Tempest*.

(13) New edition of *Parliamentary Representation*,[5] embodying supplement, etc. [Published 1885.]

(14) New edition of *Euclid I, II*, for which I am now correcting edition four.

(15) The new child's book, which Mr. Furniss is to illustrate: he now has 'Peter and Paul' to begin on. I have settled on no name as yet, but it will perhaps be *Sylvie and Bruno*.

I have also other shadowy ideas, e.g. a Geometry for Boys, a volume of Essays on theological points freely and plainly treated, and a drama on *Alice* (for which Mr. Mackenzie[6] would write music): but the above is a fair example of 'too many irons in the fire'!

STUART DODGSON COLLINGWOOD

[An Old Bachelor]†

* * *

An old bachelor is generally very precise and exact in his habits. He has no one but himself to look after, nothing to distract his attention from his own affairs; and Mr. Dodgson was the most precise and exact of old bachelors. He made a précis of every letter he wrote or received from the 1st of January, 1861, to the 8th of the same month, 1898. These précis were all numbered and entered in reference-books, and by an ingenious system of cross-numbering he was able to trace a whole correspondence, which might extend

3. Harry Furniss was one of *Punch's* cartoonists when he drew the illustration for *Sylvie and Bruno* (1889) and *Sylvie and Bruno Concluded* (1893). He did not illustrate the poems Dodgson mentions here [*Editor*].
4. Dodgson did not complete this project of a bowdlerized Shakespeare [*Editor*].
5. *Principles of Parliamentary Representation*, a pamphlet first published in 1884 [*Editor*].
6. Alexander Campbell Mackenzie (1847–

1935) was especially well-known as a composer and conductor of choral and operatic works. Dodgson records in his diary in August 1883 that Mackenzie had agreed "to undertake the Alice operetta—at the end of '84 or beginning of '85: *Diaries* 2: 419) [*Editor*].
† From *The Life and Letters of Lewis Carroll* (Rev. C. L. Dodgson) 265–74, 389–91, 329–31.

through several volumes. The last number entered in his book is 98,721.

He had scores of green cardboard boxes, all neatly labelled in which he kept his various papers. These boxes formed quite a feature of his study at Oxford, a large number of them being arranged upon a revolving bookstand. The lists, of various sorts, which he kept were innumerable; one of them, that of unanswered correspondents, generally held seventy or eighty names at a time, exclusive of autograph-hunters whom he did not answer on principle. He seemed to delight in being arithmetically accurate about every detail of life.

He always rose at the same hour, and, if he was in residence at Christ Church, attended College Service. He spent the day according to a prescribed routine, which usually included a long walk into the country, very often alone, but sometimes with another Don, or perhaps, if the walk was not to be as long as usual, with some little girl-friend at his side. When he had a companion with him, he would talk the whole time, telling delightful stories or explaining some new logical problem; if he was alone, he used to think out his books, as probably many another author has done and will do, in the course of a lonely walk. The only irregularity noticeable in his mode of life was the hour of retiring, which varied from 11 p.m. to four o'clock in the morning, according to the amount of work which he felt himself in the mood for.

He had a wonderfully good memory, except for faces and dates. The former were always a stumbling-block to him, and people used to say (most unjustly) that he was intentionally short-sighted. One night he went up to London to dine with a friend, whom he had only recently met. The next morning a gentleman greeted him as he was walking. "I beg your pardon," said Mr. Dodgson, "but you have the advantage of me. I have no remembrance of having ever seen you before this moment." "That is very strange," the other replied. "for I was your host last night!" Such little incidents as this happened more than once. * * *

He was modest in the true sense of the term, neither overestimating nor underrating his own mental powers, and preferring to follow his own course without regarding outside criticism. "I never read anything about myself or my books," he writes in a letter to a friend; and the reason he used to give was that if the critics praised him he might become conceited, while, if they found fault, he would only feel hurt and angry. On October 25, 1888, he wrote in his Diary: "I see there is a leader in to-day's *Standard* on myself as a writer; but I do not mean to read it. It is not healthy reading, I think."

He hated publicity, and tried to avoid it in every way. "Do not tell any one, if you see me in the theatre," he wrote once to Miss Marion Terry. On another occasion, when he was dining out at

Oxford, and some one, who did not know that it was a forbidden subject, turned the conversation on "Alice in Wonderland," he rose suddenly and fled from the house. I could multiply instances of this sort, but it would be unjust to his memory to insist upon the morbid way in which he regarded personal popularity. As compared with self-advertisement, it is certainly the lesser evil; but that it *is* an evil, and a very painful one to its possessor, Mr. Dodgson fully saw. Of course it had its humorous side, for instance, when he was brought into contact with lion-hunters, autograph-collectors, *et hoc genus omne.* He was very suspicious of unknown correspondents who addressed questions to him; in later years he either did not answer them at all, or used a typewriter. Before he bought his typewriter, he would get some friend to write to him, and even to sign "Lewis Carroll" at the end of the letter. It used to give him great amusement to picture the astonishment of the recipients of these letters, if by any chance they ever came to compare his "autographs."

On one occasion the secretary of a "Young Ladies' Academy" in the United States asked him to present some of his works to the School Library. The envelope was addressed to "Lewis Carroll, Christ Church," an incongruity which always annoyed him intensely. He replied to the Secretary, "As Mr. Dodgson's books are all on Mathematical subjects, he fears that they would not be very acceptable in a school library."

* * *

It was only to those who had but few personal dealings with him that he seemed stiff and "donnish"; to his more intimate acquaintances, who really understood him, each little eccentricity of manner or of habits was a delightful addition to his charming and interesting personality. That he was, in some respects, eccentric cannot be denied; for instance he hardly ever wore an overcoat, and always wore a tall hat, whatever might be the climatic conditions. At dinner in his rooms small pieces of cardboard took the place of table-mats; they answered the purpose perfectly well, he said, and to buy anything else would be a mere waste of money. On the other hand, when purchasing books for himself, or giving treats to the children he loved, he never seemed to consider expense at all.

He very seldom sat down to write, preferring to stand while thus engaged. When making tea for his friends, he used, in order, I suppose, to expedite the process, to walk up and down the room waving the teapot about, and telling meanwhile those delightful ancedotes of which he had an inexhaustible supply.

Great were his preparations before going a journey; each separate article used to be carefully wrapped up in a piece of paper all to itself so that his trunks contained nearly as much paper as of the more useful things. The bulk of the luggage was sent on a day or two before by goods train, while he himself followed on the appointed day, laden only with his well-known little black bag, which he always insisted on carrying himself.

He had a strong objection to staring colours in dress, his favourite combination being pink and grey. One little girl who came to stay with him was absolutely forbidden to wear a red frock, of a somewhat pronounced hue, while out in his company.

At meals he was very abstemious always, while he took nothing in the middle of the day except a glass of wine and a biscuit. Under these circumstances it is not very surprising that the healthy appetites of his little friends filled him with wonder, and even with alarm. When he took a certain one of them out with him to a friend's house to dinner, he used to give the host or hostess a gentle warning, to the mixed amazement and indignation of the child, "Please be careful, because she eats a good deal too much."

Another peculiarity, which I have already referred to, was his objection to being invited to dinners or any other social gatherings; he made a rule of never accepting invitations. "Because you have invited me, therefore I cannot come," was the usual form of his refusal. I suppose the reason of this was his hatred of the interference with work which engagements of this sort occasion.

He had an extreme horror of infection, as will appear from the following illustration. Miss Isa Bowman and her sister, Nellie, were at one time staying with him at Eastbourne, when news came from home that their youngest sister had caught the scarlet fever. From that day every letter which came from Mrs. Bowman to the children was held up by Mr. Dodgson, while the two little girls, standing at the opposite end of the room, had to read it as best they could. Mr. Dodgson, who was the soul of honour, used always to turn his head to one side during these readings, lest he might inadvertently see some words that were not meant for his eyes.

* * *

The following is an extract from a letter written in 1896 to one of his sisters, in allusion to a death which had recently occurred in the family:—

> It is getting increasingly difficult now to remember *which* of one's friends remain alive, and *which* have gone "into the land of the great departed, into the silent land." Also, such news comes less and less as a shock, and more and more one realises that it is an experience each of *us* has to face before long. That fact is getting *less* dreamlike to me now, and I sometimes think what a grand thing it will be to be able to say to oneself, "Death is *over* now; there is not *that* experience to be faced again."

I am beginning to think that, if the *books* I am still hoping to write are to be done at *all*, they must be done *now*, and that I am *meant* thus to utilise the splendid health I have had, unbroken, for the last year and a half, and the working powers that are fully as great as, if not greater, than I have ever had. I brought with me here the MS., such as it is (very fragmentary and unarranged) for the book about religious difficulties,[1] and I meant, when I came here, to devote myself to that, but I have changed my plan. It seems to me that *that* subject is one that hundreds of living men could do, if they would only try, *much* better than I could, whereas there is no living man who could (or at any rate who would take the trouble to) arrange and finish and publish the second part of the "Logic." Also, I *have* the Logic book in my head; it will only need three or four months to write out, and I have *not* got the other book in my head, and it might take years to think it out. So I have decided to get Part ii. finished *first*, and I am working at it day and night. I have taken to early rising, and sometimes sit down to my work before seven, and have one an a half hours at it before breakfast. The book will be a great novelty, and will help, I fully believe, to make the study of Logic far *easier* than it now is. And it will, I also believe, be a help to religious thought by giving *clearness* of conception and of expression, which may enable many people to face, and conquer, many religious difficulties for themselves. So I do really regard it as work for God.

Another letter, written a few months later to Miss Dora Abdy, deals with the subject of "Reverence," which Mr. Dodgson considered a virtue not held in sufficient esteem nowadays:—

My dear Dora,—In correcting the proofs of "Through the Looking-Glass"[2] (which is to have "An Easter Greeting" inserted at the end), I am reminded that in that letter (I enclose a copy), I had tried to express my thoughts on the very subject we talked about last night—the relation of *laughter* to religious thought. One of the hardest things in the world is to convey a meaning accurately from one mind to another, but the *sort* of meaning I want to convey to other minds is that while the laughter of *joy* is in full harmony with our deeper life, the laughter of amusement should be kept apart from it. The danger is too great of thus learning to look at solemn things in a spirit of *mockery*, and to seek in them opportunities for exercising *wit*. That is the spirit which has spoiled, for me, the beauty of some of the Bible. Surely there is a deep meaning in our

1. This book was to be a series of essays on difficult questions of religious belief. Dodgson wrote at least one essay (on eternal punishment). He wrote to a nephew to whom he sent a draft of this essay that he would discuss only those religious difficulties which affected conduct, and which did not conflict with certain principles he called axioms: for example, that men possess free will, that they are responsible for choosing wrong, that they are responsible to a person, and that "This person is perfectly good." "I call them axioms, because I have no

proofs to offer for them" (quoted in Collingwood, 326–27). Dodgson did not publish the book on logic mentioned in this letter. It has been reconstructed, from manuscript and galley sheets, and published as the second part of *Lewis Carroll's Symbolic Logic*, edited by William Warren Bartley II (see Selected Bibliography) [*Editor*].
2. The proofs to which Dodgson refers are presumably those of the 1897 edition, for which Dodgson wrote a preface (see p. 105 of this edition) [*Editor*].

prayer, "Give us an heart to love and *dread* Thee." We do not mean *terror*: but a dread that will harmonise with love; "respect" we should call it as towards a human being, "reverence" as towards God and all religious things.

Yours affectionately,
C. L. Dodgson

Essays in Criticism

GILLIAN AVERY

Fairy Tales with a Purpose†

Instruction when conveyed through the medium of some beautiful story or pleasant tale, more easily insinuates itself into the youthful mind than any thing of a drier nature; yet the greatest care is necessary that the kind of instruction thus conveyed should be perfectly agreeable to the Christian dispensation. Fairy-tales therefore are in general an improper medium of instruction because it would be absurd in such tales to introduce Christian principles as motives of action. . . . On this account such tales should be very sparingly used, it being extremely difficult, if not impossible, from the reason I have specified, to render them really useful.

—Mrs. Sherwood, in editing *The Governess, or The Little Female Academy* (1820).

In the nineteenth century there was prevalent a strong element of distrust toward fairy tales. Moralists, educationalists and those concerned with the religious teaching of children found it hard to reconcile their consciences to offering such fictitious enormities as two-headed giants, seven-league boots and all the stock-in-trade of fantasy to innocent boys and girls. They pondered chiefly over two problems, whether children who read fairy tales would ever learn to distinguish between truth and fiction, and whether it was not an iniquitous waste of time to study the kingdoms of fairyland instead of learning the latitude and longitude of Otaheite, and the main products of Peru. The first of these problems was debated throughout the century, although it diminished in importance as time passed. Harvey Darton diagnosed this opposition as "a manifestation . . . of a deep-rooted sin-complex. It involves the belief that anything fantastic on the one hand, or anything primitive on the other, is inherently noxious; or at least so void of good as to be actively dangerous."[1] The second objection, that fairy tales did not teach anything specific, provided a strong motive for opposition in the first thirty years of the nineteenth century, when children's books were almost uniformly educational. An anonymous writer in *The Ladies Museum* for September 1831 boasted joyfully—"The days of *Jack the Giant-Killer, Little Red Riding-Hood,* and such trashy productions are gone by, and the infant mind is now nourished by more able and efficient food." But with the growth and spread of children's literature after 1840 this issue was dropped.

* * *

The best defence against the educational critics comes in a trenchant article by Felix Summerly (the pseudonym for Sir Henry Cole),

† This essay and the one following are from *Nineteenth-Century Children: Heroes and Heroines in English Children's Stories*, 1780–1900 (London: Hodder and Stoughton, 1965) 41–48, 121–31. Reprinted by permission of the author, publisher and John Johnson, Ltd.

1. F. J. Harvey Darton, *Children's Books in England*, 3rd edition, revised by Brian Alderson (Cambridge, 1982) 99.

used as the prospectus to a new series of children's books, *The Home Treasury* [1841]. Like other children's books, these were published with a purpose; but the purpose was simply to revive the lost delights of childhood in volumes of nursery rhymes and fairy tales. Children's books in the last quarter of the century, he said, "have been addressed after a narrow fashion, almost entirely to the cultivation of the understanding of children. The many tales sung or said from time immemorial which appealed to other and certainly not less important elements of a little child's mind, its fancy, imagination, sympathies, affections, are almost gone out of memory, and are scarcely to be obtained."

* * *

The first great English collection, *Popular Fairy Tales; or, a Lilliputian Library; containing twenty-six choice pieces of fantasy and fiction, by those renowned personages King Oberon, Queen Mab, Mother Goose, Mother Bunch, Master Puck, and other distinguished personages at the court of the fairies. Now first collected and revised by Benjamin Tabart*. This book was published in 1818,[2] and had a decidedly moral slant. Previously, English fairy tales had occurred only in chap-books and oral versions, and they were frequently crude and vulgar, so that in order, as Tabart said, to please "every tender mother, and every intelligent tutor", the stories in the collection were pruned and refined, greatly to the detriment of the robust English ones, such as *Jack and the Beanstalk*, and *Jack the Giant-Killer*. In the former Jack's full-blooded roguery in tricking the giant is modified, following a debased chap-book version, where the giant is said to have robbed Jack's father, so that it appears that Jack is only reclaiming his own when he steals the giant's possessions. This travesty remained current until, in 1890, Joseph Jacobs published proof in his *English Fairy Tales* that it was not the original version. Thus Victorian children were protected against any possible incentive to theft.

Such was the state of affairs in 1840. Fairy tales were frowned upon, and only grudgingly admitted to the nursery shelves if their morals were impeccable. But a new attitude was creeping in, and during the decade 1840 to 1850 the literary fairy tale, as opposed to the rewriting of the traditional tale, was established. The earliest included *Uncle David's Nonsensical Story about Giants and Fairies*, a chapter in Catherine Sinclair's *Holiday House* (1839); Francis Paget's *The Hope of the Katzekopfs* (1844); Mme Clara de Chatelain's *The Silver Swan* (1847); Mark Lemon's *The Enchanted Doll* (1849);

2. The British Museum possesses one volume of an edition of 1809, apparently published in four volumes.

Margaret Gatty's *The Fairy Godmothers* (1851); and M. and E. Kirby's *The Talking Bird* (1856).

* * *

In most of these stories the chief character is reformed after indulging in the particular fault the book deprecates. Large sections are devoted to an exposition of the vice; we see Prince Eigenwillig's irresponsible selfishness towards his parents and companion; and in *The Enchanted Doll* Jacob Pout's mean-spirited envy of the prosperity of Tony Stubbs, the silversmith. This is often an advantage, as wicked behaviour usually excites a livelier style of writing than good, but it may also mean that the reformation is not accomplished very convincingly.

Enchantment, in all these books, is only in the nature of supernatural machinery. There is no highly imaginative writing, no strange fairy tale settings, no original characterisation. Invariably the supernatural is used to point the moral, not because the writers feel any intrinsic interest in it. Magic is a useful means of creating a situation, and bringing about the right denouement. The lessons are ordinary, and the fairies who enforce them are pallid and dull beside many creations of the nineteenth century.

* * *

Of all the fairy tales with a conspicuously moral purpose, none is so extraordinary as Christina Rossetti's *Speaking Likenesses* (1874). This is a particularly unpleasant little story, designed to illustrate the evils of anti-social behaviour. The heroine, Flora, ruins her own birthday party and, creeping away to sulk in a yew alley, finds a mysterious door leading to a great mirror-lined hall, where another party is being held. Instead of ordinary guests, Flora sees horrifyingly grotesque children. "One boy bristled with prickly quills like a porcupine, and raised or depressed them at pleasure; but he usually kept them pointed outwards. Another instead of being rounded like most people was facetted at very sharp angles. A third caught in everything he came near, for he was hung round with hooks like fish-hooks. One girl exuded a sticky fluid and came off on the fingers; another, rather smaller, was slimy and slipped through the hands." Flora is prevented from eating the delicious food by the domineering birthday queen, and victimized by the guests in a series of cruel games, until finally they all build glass towers round themselves. Insults and then missiles are hurled, and Flora wakes screaming to find herself back in the yew alley.

Throughout, the moral is thrust home with repellant intensity. As selfishness was the basis of Flora's naughtiness, Christina Rossetti

makes each loathsome dream child exercise its own deformity for
self-gratification, and the annoyance of others. There is the game
of Self Help, in which, for example, Flora is ironed and goffered[3]
by Angels; and the last game, when each encloses himself in a glass
tower, gives a final illustration of egotistical self-isolation. These
children can no more co-operate and play together than oil and water
can mix, and so their only pleasure is in tormenting each other, the
best means of asserting themselves. Finally Flora's experiences are
summed up for the benefit of the reader. "And I think if she lives
to be nine years old and gives another birthday party, she is likely
on that occasion to be even less like the birthday queen of her troubled
dream than was the Flora of eight years old; who, with dear friends
and playmates, and pretty presents, yet scarcely knew how to bear a
few trifling disappointments, or how to be obliging and good-
humoured under slight annoyances."

Speaking Likenesses illustrates two of the most unattractive features
of nineteenth-century fairy tales, the tendency to gloat over the
physically grotesque, and a determined insistence on punishment.
Throughout the history of the juvenile novel we find this preoccu-
pation with punishment. Nobody doubted its value. "Punishment
is as sure to do us good when we are naughty as physic when we
are ill," said Catherine Sinclair in *Holiday House*. The problem was
more how to devise suitable punishments, and much imagination
and, to modern taste, cruel ingenuity was brought to bear.

GILLIAN AVERY

Fairy Tales for Pleasure

It is hard to think of Felix Summerly's simple little book of fairy
tales[1] as in any way revolutionary in content. But it gave children
leave at last to enjoy themselves with their story books, and it suggested implicitly that fairy tales gave excellent entertainment value.
The appearance of this book coincided with a growing interest in
folk-lore and mythology, partly stemming from the work of the
Grimm brothers, whose tales had been taken down orally from German peasants; and from translations and collections of similar stories
of many countries. These were at hand just when they were needed,
so that Anthony Montalba's *Fairy Tales of all Nations* and C. B.
Burkhardt's *Fairy Tales and Legends of Many Nations* both appeared
in 1849, and the trend continued right on to the Coloured Fairy

3. Pressed into pleats [*Editor*].
1. Published in *The Home Treasury* (1841–49) [*Editor*].

Books of Andrew Lang in the 1890s and 1900s, which drew on innumerable sources.

* * *

1865—*Alice's Adventures in Wonderland* comes within the decade of [Frederic Farrar's] *Eric, or Little by Little* (1858), [Charles Kingsley's] *The Water Babies* (1863), and *Jessica's First Prayer* (1867) [by "Hesba Stretton," pseudonym of Sarah Smith], but the pious, the moralistic, and the didactic are as much absent from its pages as if they had never existed at all in children's literature. For some children the charm of the Alice books may rest on the sheer fantasy— Alice's extraordinary changes of size, the Cheshire Cat's grin, the pig baby; for others on the relentless logic with which Carroll works out his ideas, so that in Looking-Glass Country, where everything works backwards, Alice has to walk in the opposite direction to the place she wants to reach in order to arrive there, is given a dry biscuit by the Red Queen to quench her thirst after running, and learns to pass a cake round first and cut it up afterwards. Another amusing ingredient is the clever use of words—the puns of the Gnat, the Mock Turtle's verbal confusions, like the four branches of Arithmetic—Ambition, Distraction, Uglification, and Derision; of the use, in comparisons by the White Knight, of adjectives in the wrong sense—wind "as strong as soup", or, of himself struck upside down in his helmet, "as fast as lightning". But possibly the most refreshing thing of all about these books is the way the nonsense is set in sparkling contrast, against a background of dull, everyday, school-room life.

However far Alice wanders through Wonderland or Looking-Glass Country, she is constantly reminded of things she has learned, but always in a gloriously muddled way, which makes the real subjects seem equally nonsensical. For instance there are the parodies. Schoolroom poetry still consisted of pious, moralizing verses, like 'How doth the little busy bee', and ' 'Tis the voice of the sluggard', by Isaac Watts, and Jane Taylor's 'Twinkle, twinkle, little star'. These are triumphantly metamorphosed into 'How doth the little crocodile improve his shining tail', ' 'Tis the voice of the lobster', 'Twinkle, twinkle, little bat'. 'Star of the Evening', a song the Liddell children had learned, becomes the Mock Turtle's 'Soup of the Evening'. The difficult steps of the quadrille become the riotous romp of the lobster quadrille; historical facts about the Anglo-Saxons are repeated by the Mouse as the dryest things he knows, to restore Alice and the other creatures after their involuntary swim in the Pool of Tears; while morals to stories, always a bane of the nursery, are parodied by the Duchess's ridiculous habit of appending an utterly irrelevant 'moral' to every statement she makes—"Flamingoes and mustard both bite. And the moral of that is—'Birds of a feather flock together.' " The Red Queen is the concentrated essence of all governesses, giving rapid instructions on etiquette—"Look up, speak nicely, and don't twiddle your fingers all the time . . . Curtsey while you're thinking what to say. It saves time."

Through the Looking-Glass ends with the ridiculous examination of Alice by the two queens, rushing through schoolroom subjects, and turning them all upside down.

" 'Can you do Subtraction? Take nine from eight.'
" 'Nine from eight I can't, you know,' Alice replied very readily; 'but—'
" 'She can't do Subtraction,' said the White Queen. 'Can you do Division? Divide a loaf by a knife—what's the answer to *that*?'
" 'I suppose—' Alice was beginning, but the Red Queen answered for her. 'Bread and butter, of course.' . . .
" 'Do you know Languages? What's the French for fiddle-de-de?'
" 'Fiddle-de-de's not English,' Alice replied gravely.
" 'Whoever said it was?' said the Red Queen.
"Alice thought she saw a way out of the difficulty, this time. 'If you'll tell me what language fiddle-de-dee is, I'll tell you the French for it!' she exclaimed triumphantly.
"But the Red Queen drew herself up rather stiffly, and said, 'Queens never make bargains.' "

By treating the world of lessons and governesses with such play-fulness, Lewis Carroll reduces it from the terrifying place it must sometimes have seemed to a manageable absurdity. In this way the Alice books strike as strong a blow against didacticism and cramming as did Felix Summerly's manifesto against Peter Parleyism.[2] One of the best features of the books is that although in the course of her adventures Alice may be bullied and cross questioned by the creatures she meets (" 'I never was so ordered about before, in all my life, never!' "), she always takes final control, overcoming the hostility of the court of the Queen of Hearts with her cry—" 'Who cares for you? . . . You're nothing but a pack of cards!' "; and shaking the stiff, dictatorial, governessy Red Queen in *Through the Looking-Glass*, back to a soft, fat, round, black kitten. It is wishfulfilment of the most appealing kind.

On the whole *Alice's Adventures in Wonderland* was very well received. Children's magazines reviewed it favourably, for instance *Aunt Judy's Magazine*, where the critic, probably Mrs Gatty, de-

2. The pseudonym "Peter Parley" was invented by Samuel Goodrich, an American writer of children's books, and adopted by several British writers who exploited the popularity of the Peter Parley books in England. In the prospectus to *The Home Library*, Sir Henry Cole characterized "Peter Parleyism" as being hostile to fancy and tenderness in its emphasis on conveying information and moral instruction [*Editor*].

scribes is as an "exquisitely wild, fantastic, impossible, yet most natural history," and finishes with the revealing comment—"The above hints will probably make 'parents and guardians' aware that they must not look to *Alice's Adventures* for knowledge in disguise." *The Monthly Packet*, a serious Anglican magazine for young girls, edited by Charlotte Yonge, whose *Hints on Reading* usually covered only religious books, biographies, sermons, and improving novels, was enthusiastic: "We can figure to ourselves the shrieks of laughter with which it will be hailed. . . . It is one long dream of sheer nonsense." Its popularity remained undimmed, and at the end of the century the *Pall Mall Gazette*, which had been conducting a poll to find the twenty ideal books for a ten-year-old, found *Alice's Adventures in Wonderland* came easily first, with *Through the Looking-Glass* lower down, in eleventh place.

PETER COVENEY

Escape†

1

". . . the world of the adult made it hard to be an artist."
—William Empson: *Some Versions of Pastoral*

The purpose and strength of the romantic image of the child had been above all to establish a relation between childhood and adult consciousness, to assert the continuity, the unity of human experience. In their concern with childhood, Wordsworth and Coleridge were interested in growth and continuity, in tracing the organic development of the human consciousness, and, also, in lowering the psychic barriers between adult and child. For Blake, Wordsworth, and, for the most part, Dickens, the image of the child endows their writing with a sense of life, and the same is true of Mark Twain in *Huckleberry Finn*. In writing of the child, their interest was continuously adult; their children function within their total response to adult experience. In talking of the child, they were talking of life.

In the latter decades of the century, however, we are confronted with something entirely other, with a cult of the child wholly different from this. Writers begin to draw on the general sympathy for childhood that has been diffused; but, for patently subjective reasons, their interest in childhood serves not to integrate childhood and adult experience, but to create a barrier of nostalgia and regret between childhood and the potential responses of adult life. The child indeed

† From Peter Coveney, *The Image of Childhood*, revised edition (London, 1967) 240–49. Originally published as *Poor Monkey* (London: Barrie & Rockliff, 1957). Reprinted by permission of the author.

becomes a means of escape from the pressures of adult adjustment, a means of regression towards the irresponsibility of youth, childhood, infancy, and ultimately nescience itself. The children of Mrs Henry Wood and Marie Corelli, for whom it was better not to grow up, but die, were the commercial expression of something detectably sick in the sensitive roots of English child fiction at the end of the century. The aim of the great Romantics (and for that matter modern psychoanalysis; it is one of the main continuities between them), was to integrate the human personality by surmounting adult insensitivity to childhood. At the end of the century, the insensitivity is inverted. It become not so much a matter of adult sensibility barred from awareness of the significance of childhood, but of acute feelings for childhood which do not become integrated with a truly adult response to the significance of human experience as a whole. As Mr. Van Wyck Brooks said, very reasonably, of Mark Twain: the writer's consciousness "flows backward until it reaches a period in . . . memory when life still seemed . . . open and fluid with possibilities."[1]

But the "freedom" in question is of course entirely illusory. It is a regressive escape into the emotional prison of self-indulgent nostalgia. The justification of secular art is the responsibility it bears for the enrichment of human awareness, for the extension of the reader's consciousness. The cult of the child in certain authors at the end of the nineteenth century is a denial of this responsibility. Their awareness of childhood is no longer an interest in growth and integration, such as we found in *The Prelude*, but a means of detachment and retreat from the adult world. One feels their morbid withdrawl towards psychic death. The misery on the face of Carroll and Barrie was there because their response towards life had been subtly but irrevocably negated. Their photographs seem to look out at us from the nostalgic prisons they had created for themselves in the cult of Alice Liddell and Peter Pan.

Nostalgia can of course become too easily a blanket term of discredit. It can be as valid a part of human experience as any other. It is the expression and often the necessary solvent of the tension which inevitably exists between any individual and the society he is brought to adjust himself to. It is a product of sensitive adjustment in anyone. It is there in everybody. It is there in every artist. The recurrent nostalgia of romantic literature suggests forcibly enough the particular difficulties involved in that adjustment in the nineteenth century. The insistent nostalgia of the cult of the child at the end of the century suggests that for some the adjustment was unattainable. They indulged nostalgia because they refused or failed to

1. *The Ordeal of Mark Twain* (New York, 1920) 215–16.

come to sensitive terms with the cultural realities of the times. Regret for childhood takes on the same obsessive emotional quality as the exile's nostalgia for "home". Certain artists at the end of the century were clearly very much abroad in an alien world.

✻ ✻ ✻

Everything for Carroll pointed to disaster in his personal life. He was almost the case-book maladjusted neurotic. The tale of the stammering, awkward, spinsterish don, imprisoned within Christ Church, Oxford, from the age of nineteen till his death, has been often enough told, with its dinner-parties in college rooms for little girls, with his obsessive interest in that most nostalgic of all arts, photography. Children were, he confessed, three-fourths of his life. We have it from no less a safe authority than Collingwood that his features remained boyish; some with less interest in preserving a decent memory declare his face became girlish, and that he assumed the embarrassed mannerisms of a young girl. He led perhaps as uneventful a life as anyone possibly could. Everything led to his withdrawal.

As a young man of twenty-one he wrote:

> I'd give all wealth that years have piled,
> The slow result of life's decay,
> To be once more a little child
> For one bright summer-day.

At twenty-three, on seeing a performance of *Henry VIII*, he wrote: "It was like a delicious reverie, or the most beautiful poetry. This is the true end and object of acting—to raise the mind above itself, and out of its petty cares." The "one bright summer-day" became the fixated symbol of Dodgson's living fantasy, with its escape from "life's decay" and the "petty cares" of his mind.

The "cares" were, we suspect, not merely "petty". Tormented by insomnia, he wrote in the Preface to *Pillow Problems*:

> It is not possible . . . to carry out the resolution, 'I will *not* think of so-and-so'. . . . But it is possible . . . to carry out the resolution, 'I *will* think of so-and-so' . . . the worrying subject is practically annulled. It may recur, from time to time . . . there are unholy thoughts, which torture with their hateful presense, the fancy that would fain be pure. Against all these some real mental work is a most helpful ally.

In the Introduction to *Sylvie and Bruno* he declared his ambition to write a children's Bible, to compile a selection of Biblical quotations for children, and a selection or moralizing passages from other religious works: "These . . . will help to keep at bay many

330 · Peter Coveney

anxious thoughts, worrying thoughts, uncharitable thoughts, unholy thoughts."

This sense of sin recurs in his reminiscing account of what he had intended by the creation of Alice. She should have: "the eager enjoyment of Life that comes only in the happy hours of childhood, when all is new and fair, and when sin and sorrow are but names— empty words signifying nothing" ["Alice on the Stage"]. Alice was then the expression of the romantic pastoral child, the symbol of Blake's innocent Life, but also the expression of Dodgson's frustrated exclusion from Life, the means through which his sense of guilt and sorrow could become for him "empty words signifying nothing."

The fusion of the romantic tradition with his own personal nostalgia is so poignantly displayed in that Easter Greeting he composed in 1876 to "Every Child who Loves Alice". It is as sad an expression of a deeply troubled psyche as one could ever not wish to read. It opens with the middle-aged Dodgson so pathetically seeking the friendship of his child-readers:

> Please to fancy, if you, can that you are reading a real letter, from a real friend whom you have seen, and whose voice you can seem to yourself to hear wishing you, as I do now with all my heart, a happy Easter.

The rest is a fantasy of childhood created by the obsessive dreamer, by a psyche dreamily withdrawn from life:

> Do you know that delicous dreamy feeling when one first wakes on a summer morning, with the twitter of birds in the air, and the fresh breeze coming in at the open window—when . . . one sees as in a dream green boughs waving, or waters rippling in a golden light? . . . And is not that a Mother's gentle hand that undraws your curtains, and a Mother's sweet voice that summons you to rise? To rise and forget, in the bright sunlight, the ugly dreams that frightened you so when all was dark?

Were these, he says, strange sentiments to come from the writer of *Alice*? He, however, did not believe that:

> God means us thus to divide life into two halves. . . . Do you think He cares to see only kneeling figures . . . and that He does not also love to see the lambs leaping in the sunlight, and to hear the merry voices of the children, as they roll among the hay? . . . And if I have written anything to add to those stores of innocent and healthy amusement . . . it is surely something I may hope to look back upon without shame and sorrow (as how much of life must then be recalled!) when *my* turn comes to walk through the valley of shadows.

> The Easter sun will rise on you, dear child, feeling your 'life in every limb', and eager to rush out into the fresh morning air—and many an Easter-day will come and go, before it finds you feeble and gray-headed, creeping wearily out to bask once more in the sunlight.

The implied commentary on the Victorian Sabbatarians,[2] the reminiscence of Blake's *Innocence*, the evocation of the romantic symbol of 'life' in childhood, merge into Dodgson's own subjective regret. To grow up is no more than to become 'feeble and grayheaded, creeping wearily'. The 'fresh' innocence of the child is not something, as it was for Wordsworth and Coleridge, to conserve, in order to nourish the fulfilment of the adult; its evocation merely serves to create a sense of poignant contrast. There is no plea for continuity; but an insurmountable barrier of nostalgic regret for the 'eager enjoyment of Life that comes only in the happy hours of childhood', and the forlorn emphasis lies on that one word 'only'.

It was extraordinary that the artist, Carroll, could distinguish from all this, from the "delicious dreamy feeling", this "shame and sorrow", this self-apologia, the valid emotions which went to the creation of the *Alice* books. Every factor which made for weakness became focused into the astringent and intelligent art of *Alice in Wonderland*, so that, in a strange way indeed, the "dream", the reverie in Dodgson, becomes in *Alice in Wonderland* the means of setting the reader's senses more fully awake. Lewis Carroll is in fact one of the few cases where Lawrence's famous dictum of trusting the art and not the artist happens to be absolutely true. The *Easter Greeting* with its embarrassing sentimentalities reveals painfully enough all the weakness which the romantic child was heir to, if it subserved a personal regret. The romantic child could become a currency only too easily seized by the writer who had every good reason to seek its comfort in face of a sense of personal failure and shame.

The remarkable fact about Dodgson is that by using the very means of his weakness, by succumbing to his dream and fantasy, he should become so intelligently awake. *Alice in Wonderland* releases the vitality of an intelligent and sensitive commentary on life. It is precisely the opposite of withdrawn. The innocence of Alice casts its incisive, but delicately subtle intelligence upon Victorian society and upon life. But it is not simply that. It is not *simply* anything. Even in this first and greatest work, there is a content not far removed from nightmare. *Alice in Wonderland* has the claustrophobic atmosphere of a children's Kafka. It is the frustrated "quest" for the "Garden" which in the event is peopled with such unpleasant creatures. In those poignant lines of Alice's awakening, we feel the work turn towards unfulfilment, and very obviously towards death:

> At this the whole pack rose up into the air, and came flying down upon her: she gave a little scream, half of fright and half of anger, and tried to

---

2. Sabbatarianism was a nineteenth-century movement that tried, often successfully, to legislate that shops, parks, museums, and other entertainments be closed on Sundays [*Editor*].

beat them off, and found herself lying on the bank, with her head in the lap of her sister, who was gently brushing away some dead leaves that had fluttered down from the trees upon her face.

The juxtaposition of waking and the image of the dead leaves is no casual coincidence. Carroll's art was too carefully organized for it not to have some special reference of feeling. It has all the force of a poetic continuity, a felt development. With all the vitality and intelligence released within the dream, Carroll becomes very much Dodgson when he wakes. One feels a sense of shock at this sudden, waking reality, of the face of the girl's innocent life blighted with the "dead leaves". The whole tone of the work changes from this point. Alice's sister dreams:

> First, she dreamed of little Alice herself, and once again the tiny hands were clasped upon her knee, and the bright eager eyes were looking up into hers . . . Lastly, she pictured to herself how this same little sister of hers would, in the after-time, be herself a grown woman; and how she would keep, through all her riper years, the simple and loving heart of her childhood; and how she would gather about her other little children . . . remembering her own child-life, and the happy summer days.

This idealization introduces a note alien to the work as a whole. The Alice of the ending of the book is in fact not Carroll's Alice, in Wonderland, but Dodgson's Alice Liddell. Already in 1862 we are approaching the world of the *Easter Greeting* of 1876.

Returning to the fantasy of Alice seven years later, Carroll almost acheived the artistic triumph again. But the emotional pressures of seven years' further deterioration had their unmistakable effects. The mood of *Through the Looking-Glass* is ominously set by the introductory poem:

> A tale begun in other days,
> When summer suns were glowing—
> A simple chime, that served to time
> The rhythm of our rowing—
> Whose echoes live in memory yet,
> Though envious years would say "forget". . . .

> Without, the frost, the blinding snow
> The storm-wind's moody madness—
> Within, the firelight's ruddy glow,
> And childhood's nest of gladness.
> The magic words shall hold thee fast:
> Thou shalt not heed the raving blast.

> And though the shadow of a sigh
> May tremble through the story,
> For "happy summer days" gone by,
> A vanish'd summer glory—

It shall not touch with breath of bale
The pleasance of our fairy-tale.

Through the Looking-Glass is held between this and the dreaming
denial of the reality of life of the final poem:

> A boat beneath a sunny sky
> Lingering onward dreamily
> In an evening of July . . .
>
> Long has paled that sunny sky:
> Echoes fade and memories die.
> Autumn frosts have slain July.

Of his readers, he writes:

> In a Wonderland they lie,
> Dreaming as the days go by,
> Dreaming as the summers die.
>
> Ever drifting down the stream—
> Lingering in the golden gleam—
> Life, what is it but a dream?

Held within this frame, the book retains the intelligence of the
Adventures in Wonderland. Alice remains the vehicle for Carroll's
sensitive commentary. But the tone is perceptibly sharper. The humour is more sardonic. There is more merciless, embittered ridicule.
The dream takes on a quality of horror. The note of frustration is
struck more insistently; as in the episode in the shop:

> The shop seemed to be full of all manner of curious things—but the
> oddest part of it all was, that whenever she looked hard at any shelf, to
> make out exactly what it had on it, that particular shelf was always quite
> empty. . . . 'Things flow about so here!' she said at last in a plaintive
> tone, after she had spent a minute or so in vainly pursuing a large bright
> thing.

In the sequence among the rushes, the plaintive note makes its
meaning clear enough: Alice leaning out of the boat to gather the
beautiful rushes exclaims:

> 'Oh, *what* a lovely one! Only I couldn't quite reach it.' And it certainly
> *did* seem a little provoking ('almost as if it happened on purpose,' she
> thought) that, though she managed to pick plenty of beautiful rushes as
> the boat glided by, there was always a more lovely one that she couldn't
> reach. 'The prettiest are always further!' she said at last . . . as . . . she
> . . . began to arrange her newfound treasures.
>   What mattered it to her just then that the rushes had begun to fade,
> and to lose all their scent and beauty, from the very moment that she
> picked them? Even real scented rushes, you know, last only a very little

while—and these, being dream-rushes, melted away almost like snow, as they lay in heaps at her feet.

It is as if Carroll in a more self-conscious way than ever in *Wonderland* turns aside from his own fantasy; as if he remains regretfully and painfully awake in his own dream. This may perhaps account for the savagery of so much of the humour, such as in *The Walrus and the Carpenter*. Alice is subjected to a type of subtle cruelty in a way quite alien to the earlier book. The episode in the railway carriage has all the horror of a sadistic nightmare. If life for Carroll was indeed a "dream", the dream is evidently only too often in *Through the Looking-Glass* Dodgson's own personal nightmare. With only the slightest susceptibility to the analysis of literature in psychological terms, it would be difficult not to see both works as pyschological fantasies. They are clearly the works of neurotic genius. The initial rabbit-hole seems to serve as either a birth or copulative symbol. Dodgson's obsession with little girls was both sexual and sexually morbid. His own insistence on the purity of his interest has perhaps a telling, even a morbid undertone. But with Carroll's art, the neurosis is the irrelevance. Even in the clear references one feels to the neurosis, especially in *Through the Looking-Glass*, one senses the extraordinary power of artistic sublimation that Carroll brought to the achievement of the two books.

NINA AUERBACH

Alice in Wonderland: A Curious Child†

"What—is—this? he said at last.
"This is a child!" Haigha replied eagerly, coming in front of Alice to introduce her . . . "We only found it today. It's as large as life, and twice as natural!"
"I always thought they were fabulous monsters!" said the Unicorn. "Is it alive?"

For many of us Lewis Carroll's two *Alice* books may have provided the first glimpse into Victorian England. With their curious blend of literal-mindedness and dream, formal etiquette and the logic of insanity, they tell the adult reader a great deal about the Victorian mind. Alice herself, prim and earnest in pinafore and pumps, confronting a world out of control by looking for the rules and murmuring her lessons, stands as one image of the Victorian middle-class child. She sits in Tenniel's first illustration to *Through the Looking-Glass and What Alice Found There* in a snug, semi-foetal position, encircled by a protective armchair and encircling a plump kitten and a ball of yarn. She seems to be a beautiful child, but the

† From *Victorian Studies* 17 (1973): 31–47. Reprinted by permission of the author and *Victorian Studies*.

position of her head makes her look as though she had no face. She muses dreamily on the snowstorm raging outside, part of a series of circles within circles, enclosures within enclosures, suggesting the self-containment of innocence and eternity.

Behind the purity of this design lie two Victorian domestic myths: Wordsworth's "seer blessed," the child fresh from the Imperial Palace and still washed by his continuing contact with "that immortal sea," and the pure woman Alice will become, preserving an oasis for God and order in a dim and tangled world. Even Victorians who did not share Lewis Carroll's phobia about the ugliness and uncleanliness of little boys saw little girls as the purest members of a species of questionable origin, combining as they did the inherent spirituality of child and woman. Carroll's Alice seems sister to such famous figures as Dickens' Little Nell and George Eliot's Eppie,[1] who embody the poise of original innocence in a fallen, sooty world.

Long after he transported Alice Liddell to Wonderland, Carroll himself deified his dream-child's innocence in these terms:

> What wert thou, dream-Alice, in thy foster-father's eyes? How shall he picture thee? Loving, first, loving and gentle: loving as a dog (forgive the prosaic simile, but I know of no earthly love so pure and perfect), and gentle as a fawn: . . . and lastly, curious—wildly curious, and with the eager enjoyment of Life that comes only in the happy hours of childhood, when all is new and fair, and when Sin and Sorrow are but names— empty words, signifying nothing![2]

From this Alice, it is only a step to Walter de la Mare's mystic icon, defined in the following almost Shelleyan image: "She wends serenely on like a quiet moon in the chequered sky. Apart, too, from an occasional Carrollian comment, the sole medium of the stories is *her* pellucid consciousness."[3]

But when Dodgson wrote in 1887 of his gentle dream-child, the real Alice had receded into the distance of memory, where she had drowned in a pool of tears along with Lewis Carroll, her interpreter and creator. The paean quoted above stands at the end of a long series of progressive falsifications of Carroll's first conception, beginning with Alice's pale, attenuated presence in *Through the Looking-Glass*. For Lewis Carroll remembered what Charles Dodgson and many later commentators did not, that while *Looking-Glass* may have been the dream of the Red King, *Wonderland* is Alice's dream. Despite critical attempts to psychoanalyze Charles Dodgson through the writings of Lewis Carroll, the author of *Alice's Adventures in Wonderland* was too precise a logician and too controlled an artist

1. Little Nell is a character in *The Old Curiosity Shop* (1840–41); Eppie is in *Silas Marner* (1861) [*Editor*].

2. "Alice on the Stage," *The Theatre*, 9 (1 April 1887): 181.

3. Walter de la Mare, *Lewis Carroll* (London: 1932) 55.

to confuse his own dream with that of his character. The question "who dreamed it?" underlies all Carroll's dream tales, part of a pervasive Victorian quest for the origins of the self that culminates in the controlled regression of Freudian analysis.There is no equivocation in Carroll's first *Alice* book: the dainty child carries the threatening kingdom of Wonderland within her. A closer look at the character of Alice may reveal new complexities in the sentimentalized and attenuated Wordsworthianism many critics had assumed she represents, and may deepen through examination of a single example our vision of that "fabulous monster," the Victorian child.

Lewis Carroll once wrote to a child that while he forgot the story of *Alice*, "I think it was about 'malice.' "[4] Some Freudian critics would have us believe it was about phallus.[5] Alice herself seems aware of the implications of her shifting name when at the beginning of her adventures she asks herself the question that will weave through her story:

> "I wonder if I've been changed in the night? Let me think: *was* I the same when I got up this morning? I almost think I can remember feeling a little different. But if I'm not the same, the next question is, 'Who in the world am I?' Ah, *that's* the great puzzle!"

Other little girls traveling through fantastic countries, such as George Macdonald's Princess Irene and L. Frank Baum's Dorothy Gale, ask repeatedly "*where* am I?" rather than "*who* am I?" Only Alice turns her eyes inward from the beginning, sensing that the mystery of her surroundings is the mystery of her identity.

Even the above-ground Alice speaks in two voices, like many Victorians other than Dodgson-Carroll:

> She generally gave herself very good advice, (though she very seldom followed it), and sometimes she scolded herself so severely as to bring tears into her eyes; and once she remembered trying to box her own ears for having cheated herself in a game of croquet she was playing against herself, for this curious child was very fond of pretending to be two people.

The pun on "curious" defines Alice's fluctuating personality. Her eagerness to know and to be right, her compulsive reciting of her lessons ("I'm sure I can't be Mabel, for I know all sorts of things") turn inside out into the bizarre anarchy of her dream country, as the lessons themselves turn inside out into strange and savage tales of animals eating each other. In both senses of the word, Alice becomes "curiouser and curiouser" as she moves more deeply into Wonderland; she is both the croquet game without rules and its

4. Letter to Dolly Argles, 28 November 1867. Quoted in *A Selection From the Letters of Lewis Carroll (The Reverend Charles Lutwidge Dodgson) to His Child-Friends*, edited by Evelyn Hatch (London: 1933) 48–49.

5. See Martin Grotjahn, "About the Symbolization of *Alice's Adventures in Wonderland*," *American Imago*, 4 (1947): 34, for a discussion of Freud's "girl = phallus equation" in relation to Alice.

violent arbiter, the Queen of Hearts. The sea that almost drowns her is composed of her own tears, and the dream that nearly obliterates her is composed of fragments of her own personality.[6]

As Alice dissolves into her component parts to become Wonderland, so, if we examine the actual genesis of Carroll's dream child, the bold outlines of Tenniel's famous drawing dissolve into four separate figures. First, there was the real Alice Liddell, a baby belle dame, it seems, who bewitched Ruskin as well as Dodgson.[7] A small photograph of her concludes Carroll's manuscript of *Alice's Adventures under Ground*, the first draft of *Wonderland*. She is strikingly sensuous and otherworldly; her dark hair, bangs, and large inward-turned eyes give her face a haunting and a haunted quality which is missing from Tenniel's famous illustrations. Carroll's own illustrations for *Alice's Adventures under Ground* reproduce her eeriness perfectly. This Alice has a pre-Raphaelite langour and ambiguity about her which is reflected in the shifting colors of her hair.[8] In some illustrations, she is indisputably brunette like Alice Liddell; in others, she is decidedly blonde like Tenniel's model Mary Hilton Badcock; and in still others, light from an unknown source hits her hair so that she seems to be both at once.

Mary Hilton Badcock has little of the dream child about her.[9] She is blonde and pudgy, with squinting eyes, folded arms, and an intimidating frown. In Carroll's photograph of her, the famous starched pinafore and pumps appear for the first time—Alice Liddell seems to have been photographed in some sort of nightdress—and Mary moves easily into the clean, no-nonsense child of the Tenniel drawings. Austin Dobson wrote,[1]

> Enchanting Alice! Black-and-white
> Has made your charm perennial;
> And nought save "Chaos and old Night"
> Can part you now from Tenniel.

6. Edmund Wilson's penetrating essay, "C. L. Dodgson: The Poet Logician," is the only criticism of *Alice* to touch on the relationship between dream and dreamer in relation to Alice's covert brutality: "But the creatures that she meets, the whole dream, *are* Alice's personality and her waking life. . . . she . . . has a child's primitive cruelty. . . . But though Alice is sometimes brutal, she is always well-bred." Wilson cites as examples of brutality her innuendos about Dinah to the mouse and birds. *The Shores of Light*, 2nd ed. (1952; rpt. New York: 1967) 543–44.
7. See Florence Becker Lennon, *The Life of Lewis Carroll*, revised edition (New York: 1962) 151, for Ruskin's beatific description of a secret nocturnal tea party presided over by Alice Liddell.
8. Lewis Carroll knew the Rossetti family and

photographed them several times. Dante Gabriel Rossetti later claimed that Carroll's Dormouse was inspired by his own pet wombat. Perhaps his elongated, subtly threatening heroines had a deeper, if more indirect, impact on Carroll.
9. There is some debate as to whether Tenniel actually used the photograph of Mary Badcock as a model for his illustrations. Carroll, who was never fully satisfied with Tenniel's work, claimed he did not and so the head and feet of his drawing were sometimes out of proportion. But the resemblance between drawing and photograph is so great that I think we must assume he did.
1. "A Proem," *The Complete Poetical Works of Austin Dodson* (London: 1923) 420. First published in a 1907 edition of the Alice books [*Editor*].

But a bit of research can dissolve what has been in some ways a misleading identification of Tenniel's Alice with Carroll's, obscuring some of the darker shadings of the latter.[2] Carroll himself initiated the shift from the subtly disturbing Alice Liddell to the blonde and stolid Mary Badcock as "under ground" became the jollier-sounding "Wonderland," and the undiscovered country in his dream child became a nursery classic.

The demure propriety of Tenniel's Alice may have led readers to see her role in *Alice's Adventures in Wonderland* as more passive than it is. Although her size changes seem arbitrary and terrifying, she in fact directs them; only in the final courtroom scene does she change size without first wishing to, and there, her sudden growth gives her the power to break out of a dream that has become too dangerous. Most of Wonderland's savage songs come from Alice: the Caterpillar, Gryphon and Mock Turtle know that her cruel parodies of contemporary moralistic doggerel are "wrong from beginning to end."[3] She is almost always threatening to the animals of Wonderland. As the mouse and birds almost drown in her pool of tears, she eyes them with a strange hunger which suggests that of the *Looking-Glass* Walrus who weeps at the Oysters while devouring them behind his handkerchief. Her persistent allusions to her predatory cat Dinah and to a "nice little dog, near our house," who "kills all the rats" finally drive the animals away, leaving Alice to wonder forlornly—and disingenuously—why nobody in Wonderland likes Dinah.

Dinah is a strange figure. She is the only above-ground character whom Alice mentions repeatedly, almost always in terms of her eating some smaller animal. She seems finally to function as a personification of Alice's own subtly cannibalistic hunger, as Fury in the Mouse's tale is personified as a dog. At one point, Alice fantasizes her own identity actually blending into Dinah's:

> "How queer it seems," Alice said to herself, "to be going messages for a rabbit! I suppose Dinah'll be sending me on messages next!" And she began fancying the sort of thing that would happen: ' "Miss Alice! Come here directly, and get ready for your walk!" "Coming in a minute, nurse! But I've got to watch this mousehole till Dinah comes back, and see that the mouse doesn't get out."

While Dinah is always in a predatory attitude, most of the Wonderland animals are lugubrious victims; together, they encompass the two sides of animal nature that are in Alice as well. But as she

2. George Shelton Hubbell, "Triple Alice," *Sewanee Review*, 48 (1940): 174–196, discusses some of the differences between Tenniel's Alice and Carroll's.

3. It is significant that the Alice of *Looking-Glass*, a truly passive figure, is sung *at* more than she sings; the reverse is true in *Wonderland*. Tweedledum and Tweedledee sing the most savage song in *Looking-Glass*, "The Walrus and the Carpenter," which seems to bore Alice.

falls down the rabbit hole, Alice senses the complicity between eater and eaten, looking-glass versions of each other:

> "Dinah, my dear! I wish you were down here with me! There are no mice in the air, I'm afraid, but you might catch a bat, and that's very like a mouse, you know. But do cats eat bats, I wonder?" And here Alice began to get rather sleepy, and went on saying to herself, in a dreamy sort of way, "Do cats eat bats? Do cats eat bats?" and sometimes, "Do bats eat cats?" for, you see, as she couldn't answer either question, it didn't matter which way she put it.

We are already half-way to the final banquet of *Looking-Glass*, in which the food comes alive and begins to eat the guests.

Even when Dinah is not mentioned, Alice's attitude toward the animals she encounters is often one of casual cruelty. It is a measure of Dodgson's ability to flatten out Carroll's material that the prefatory poem could describe Alice "in friendly chat with bird or beast," or that he would later see Alice as "loving as a dog . . . gentle as a fawn." She pities Bill the Lizard and kicks him up the chimney, a state of mind that again looks forward to that of the Pecksniffian Walrus in *Looking-Glass*. When she meets the Mock Turtle, the weeping embodiment of a good Victorian dinner, she restrains herself twice when he mentions lobsters, but then distorts Isaac Watts's *Sluggard* into a song about a *baked* lobster surrounded by hungry sharks. In its second stanza, a Panther shares a pie with an Owl who then becomes dessert, as Dodgson's good table manners pass into typical Carrollian cannibalism. The more sinister and Darwinian aspects of animal nature are introduced into Wonderland by the gentle Alice, in part through projections of her hunger onto Dinah and the "nice little dog" (she meets a "dear little puppy" after she has grown small and is afraid he will eat her up) and in part through the semi-cannibalistic appetite her songs express. With the exception of the powerful Cheshire Cat, whom I shall discuss below, most of the Wonderland animals stand in some danger of being exploited or eaten. The Dormouse is their prototype: he is fussy and cantankerous, with the nastiness of a self-aware victim, and he is stuffed into a teapot as the Mock Turtle, sobbing out his own elegy, will be stuffed into a tureen.

Alice's courteously menacing relationship to these animals is more clearly brought out in *Alice's Adventures under Ground*, in which she encounters only animals until she meets the playing cards, who are lightly sketched-in versions of their later counterparts. When expanding the manuscript for publication, Carroll added the Frog Footman, Cook, Duchess, Pig-Baby, Cheshire Cat, Mad Hatter, March Hare, and Dormouse, as well as making the Queen of Hearts a more fully developed character than she was in the manuscript.[4] In other words, all the human or quasi-human characters were added in revision, and all develop aspects of Alice that exist only under the surface of her dialogue. The Duchess' household also turns inside out the domesticated Wordsworthian ideal: with baby and pepper flung about indiscriminately, pastoral tranquillity is inverted into a whirlwind of savage sexuality. The furious Cook embodies the equation between eating and killing that underlies Alice's apparently innocent remarks about Dinah. The violent Duchess' unctuous search for "the moral" of things echoes Alice's own violence and search for "the rules."[5] At the Mad Tea Party, the Hatter extends Alice's "great interest in questions of eating and drinking" into an insane *modus vivendi*; like Alice, the Hatter and the Duchess sing savage songs about eating that embody the underside of Victorian literary treacle. The Queen's croquet game magnifies Alice's own desire to cheat at croquet and to punish herself violently for doing so. Its use of live animals may be a subtler extension of Alice's own desire to twist the animal kingdom to the absurd rules of civilization, which seem to revolve largely around eating and being eaten. Alice is able to appreciate the Queen's savagery so quickly because her size changes have made her increasingly aware of who she, herself, is from the point of view of a Caterpillar, a Mouse, a Pigeon, and, especially, a Cheshire Cat.

The Cheshire Cat, also a late addition to the book, is the only figure other than Alice who encompasses all the others. William Empson discusses at length the spiritual kinship between Alice and the Cat, the only creature in Wonderland whom she calls her "friend."[6] Florence Becker Lennon refers to the Cheshire Cat as "Dinah's dream-self," and we have noticed the subtle shift of identities between Alice and Dinah throughout the story. The Cat shares Alice's equivocal placidity: "The Cat only grinned when it saw Alice. It looked good-natured, she thought: still it had *very* long claws and a great many teeth, so she felt it ought to be treated with respect." The Cat is the only creature to make explicit the identification between Alice and the madness of Wonderland: " ' . . . we're all mad here. I'm mad. You're mad.' 'How do you know I'm mad?' said Alice. 'You must be,' said the Cat, 'or you wouldn't have come here.' Alice didn't think that proved it at all." Although Alice cannot accept it and closes into silence, the Cat's remark may be the answer

---

4. In *Alice's Adventures under Ground*, Queen and Duchess are a single figure, the Queen of Hearts and Marchioness of Mock Turtles.
5. Donald Rackin makes the same point in "Alice's Journey to the End of Night," *PMLA* 81 (1966): 323.

6. In *Looking-Glass*, the pathetic White Knight replaces the Cheshire Cat as Alice's only friend, another indication of the increasing softness of the later Alice. William Empson, *Some Versions of Pastoral*, 2nd ed. (London: 1950).

she has been groping toward in her incessant question, "who am I?"[7] As an alter ego, the Cat is wiser than Alice—and safer—because he is the only character in the book who is aware of his own madness. In his serene acceptance of the fury within and without, his total control over his appearance and disappearance, he almost suggests a post-analytic version of the puzzled Alice.

As Alice dissolves increasingly into Wonderland, so the Cat dissolves into his own head, and finally into his own grinning mouth. The core of Alice's nature, too, seems to lie in her mouth: the eating and drinking that direct her size changes and motivate much of her behavior, the songs and verses that pop out of her inadvertently, are all involved with things entering and leaving her mouth.[8] Alice's first song introduces a sinister image of a grinning mouth. Our memory of the Crocodile's grin hovers over the later description of the Cat's "grin without a Cat," and colors our sense of Alice's infallible good manners:

> How cheerfully he seems to grin,
> How neatly spreads his claws,
> And welcomes little fishes in,
> With gently smiling jaws!

Walter de la Mare associates Alice with "a quiet moon" which is by implication a full moon. I think it is more appropriate to associate her with the grinning crescent that seems to follow her throughout her adventures, choosing to become visible only at particular moments, and teaching her the one lesson she must learn in order to arrive at a definition of who she is.

*   *   *

Presented from the point of view of her older sister's sentimental pietism, the world to which Alice awakens seems far more dreamlike and hazy than the sharp contours of Wonderland. Alice's lesson about her own identity has never been stated explicitly, for the stammerer Dodgson was able to talk freely only in his private language of puns and nonsense, but a Wonderland pigeon points us toward it:

> "You're a serpent; and there's no use denying it. I suppose you'll be telling me next that you never tasted an egg!"

7. Jan B. Gordon, "The *Alice* Books and the Metaphors of Victorian Childhood," relates the *Alice* books to Michel Foucault's argument that in the nineteenth century, madness came to be regarded as allied to childhood rather than to animality, as it had been in the eighteenth century. *Aspects of Alice*, edited by Robert Phillips (New York: 1971) 101.

8. Does it go too far to connect the mouth that presides over Alice's story to a looking-glass vagina? Carroll's focus on the organ of the mouth seems to have been consistent throughout his life: it is allied to both his interest in eating and the prodigious number of kisses that run through his letters to his child-friends. Kissing and cats seem often to have been linked together in his mind.

"I have tasted eggs, certainly," said Alice, who was a very truthful child; "but little girls eat eggs quite as much as serpents do, you know."

"I don't believe it," said the Pigeon; "but if they do, why, then they're a kind of serpent: that's all I can say."

This was such a new idea to Alice, that she was quite silent for a minute or two. [9]

Like so many of her silences throughout the book, Alice's silence here is charged with significance, reminding us again that an important technique in learning to read Carroll is our ability to interpret his private system of symbols and signals and to appreciate the many meanings of silence. In this scene, the golden child herself becomes the serpent in childhood's Eden. The eggs she eats suggest the woman she will become, the unconscious cannibalism involved in the very fact of eating and desire to eat, and finally, the charmed circle of childhood itself. Only in *Alice's Adventures in Wonderland* was Carroll able to fall all the way through the rabbit hole to the point where top and bottom become one, bats and cats melt into each other, and the vessel of innocence and purity is also the source of inescapable corruption.

Alice's adventures in Wonderland foreshadow Lewis Carroll's subsequent literary career, which was a progressive dissolution into his component parts. Florence Baker Lennon defines well the schism that came with the later books: "Nothing in *Wonderland* parallels the complete severance of the Reds and Whites in *Through the Looking-Glass*. In *Sylvie and Bruno*, author and story have begun to disintegrate. The archness and sweetness of parts, the utter cruelty and loathsomeness of others, predict literal decomposition into his elements" (156). The Alice of *Through the Looking-Glass*, which was published six years after *Wonderland*, represents still another Alice, Alice Raikes; the character is so thinned out that the vapid, passive Tenniel drawing is an adequate illustration of her. *Wonderland* ends with Alice playing all the parts in an ambiguous trial which concludes without a verdict. *Looking-Glass* begins with an unequivocal verdict: "One thing was certain, that the *white* kitten had nothing to do with it—it was the black kitten's fault entirely." Poor Dinah, relegated to the role of face-washer-in-the-background, has also dissolved into her component parts.

Throughout the books, the schism between Blacks (later Reds) and Whites is developed. Alice's greater innocence and passivity are stressed by her identification with Lily, the white pawn. The dominant metaphor of a chess game whose movements are determined by invisible players spreads her sense of helplessness and predestination over the book. The nursery rhymes of which most of the

9. Empson (270) refers to this passage as the Pigeon of the Annunciation denouncing the serpent of the knowledge of good and evil.

characters form a part also make their movements seem predestined; the characters in *Wonderland* tend more to create their own nursery rhymes. The question that weaves through the book is no longer "who am I?" but "which dreamed it?" If the story is the dream of the Red King (the sleeping embodiment of passion and masculinity), then Alice, the White Pawn (or pure female child), is exonerated from its violence, although in another sense, as she herself perceives, she is also in greater danger of extinction. Her increasing sweetness and innocence in the second book make her more ghost-like as well, and it is appropriate that more death jokes surround her in the second *Alice* book than in the first.

* * *

Victorian concepts of the child tended to swing back and forth between extremes of original innocence and original sin; Rousseau and Calvin stood side by side in the nursery. Since actual children were the focus of such an extreme conflict of attitudes, they tended to be a source of pain and embarrassment to adults, and were therefore told they should be "seen and not heard." Literature dealt more freely with children than life did, so adult conflicts about them were allowed to emerge more openly in books. As Jan Gordon puts it:

> The most amazing feature of, say, Dickens' treatment of children, is how quickly they are transformed into monsters. Even Oliver Twist's surname forces the reader to appreciate the twisting condition normally associated with creatures more closely akin to the devil! One effect of this identification with evil adults . . . is that the only way of approaching childhood is by way of the opposite of satanic monstrosities—namely, the golden world of an edenic wonderland whose pastoral dimension gives it the status of a primal scene.[1]

In its continual quest for origins and sources of being, Victorian literature repeatedly explores the ambiguous figure of the child, in whom it attempts to resolve the contradictions it perceives much as *Sylvie and Bruno* does: by an extreme sexual division.

* * *

We return once more to the anomaly of Carroll's Alice, who explodes out of Wonderland hungry and unregenerate. By a subtle dramatization of Alice's attitude toward animals and toward the animal in herself, by his final resting on the symbol of her mouth, Carroll probed in all its complexity the underground world within the little girl's pinafore. The ambiguity of the concluding trial finally,

1. "The *Alice* Books and the Metaphors of Victorian Childhood," *Aspects of Alice*, 109. Peter Coveney, *The Image of Childhood*, revised edition (Baltimore: 1967) is the most famous and comprehensive survey of Victorian attitudes to childhood. See especially pp. 291–292 for a discussion of these two conflicting currents.

and wisely, waives questions of original guilt or innocence. The ultimate effect of Alice's adventures implicates her, female child though she is, in the troubled human condition; most Victorians refused to grant women and children this respect. The sympathetic delicacy and precision with which Carroll traced the chaos of a little girl's psyche seems equalled and surpassed only later in such explorations as D. H. Lawrence's of the young Ursula Brangwen in *The Rainbow*, the chaos of whose growth encompasses her hunger for violence, sexuality, liberty, and beatitude. In the imaginative literature of its century, *Alice's Adventures in Wonderland* stands alone.

WILLIAM EMPSON

The Child as Swain†

* * *

It must seem a curious thing that there has been so little serious criticism of the Alices, and that so many critics, with so militant and eager an air of good taste, have explained that they would not think of attempting it. Even Mr. De La Mare's book [*Lewis Carroll*], which made many good points, is queerly evasive in tone. There seems to be a feeling that real criticism would involve psycho-analysis, and that the results would be so improper as to destroy the atmosphere of the books altogether. Dodgson was too conscious a writer to be caught out so easily. For instance it is an obvious bit of interpretation to say that the Queen of Hearts is a symbol of 'uncontrolled animal passion' seen through the clear but blank eyes of sexlessness; obvious, and the sort of thing critics are now so sure would be in bad taste; Dodgson said it himself, to the actress who took the part when the thing was acted.[1] The books are so frankly about growing up that there is no great discovery in translating them into Freudian terms; it seems only the proper exegesis of a classic even where it would be a shock to the author. On the whole the results of the analysis, when put into drawing-room language, are his conscious opinions; and if there was no other satisfactory outlet for his feelings but the special one fixed in his books the same is true in a degree of any original artist. I shall use psycho-analysis where it seems relevant, and feel I had better begin by saying what use it is supposed to be. Its business here is not to discover a neurosis

† From *Some Versions of Pastoral* (London: Chatto and Windus; New York: New Directions, 1935) 246–55, 262–64, 269–77. Reprinted by permission of Lady Empson, Chatto and Windus/The Hogarth Press, and New Directions Publishing Corporation. Copyright © 1974 by William Empson.
1. Dodgson wrote in "*Alice* on the Stage" that the Queen of Hearts is "a sort of embodiment of ungovernable passion." See p. 282 of this edition [*Editor*].

peculiar to Dodgson. The essential idea behind the books is a shift onto the child, which Dodgson did not invent, of the obscure tradition of pastoral. The formula is now '*child*-become-judge,' and if Dodgson identifies himself with the child so does the writer of the primary sort of pastoral with his magnified verson of the swain.[2] (He took an excellent photograph, much admired by Tennyson, of Alice Liddell as a ragged beggar-girl, which seems a sort of example of the connection.) I should say indeed that this version was more open to neurosis than the older ones; it is less hopeful and more a return into oneself. The analysis should show how this works in general. But there are other things to be said about such a version of pastoral; its use of the device prior to irony lets it make covert judgments about any matter the author was interested in.

There is a tantalising one about Darwinism. The first Neanderthal skull was found in 1856. *The Origin of Species* (1859) came out six years before *Wonderland*, three before its conception, and was very much in the air, a pervading bad smell. It is hard to say how far Dodgson under cover of nonsense was using ideas of which his set disapproved; he wrote some hysterical passages against vivisection and has a curious remark to the effect that chemistry professors had better not have laboratories, but was open to new ideas and doubted the eternity of hell. The 1860 meeting of the British Association, at which Huxley started his career as publicist and gave that resounding snub to Bishop Wilberforce,[3] was held at Oxford where Dodgson was already in residence. He had met Tennyson in '56, and we hear of Tennyson lecturing him later on the likeness of monkeys' and men's skulls.

The only passage that I feel sure involves evolution comes at the beginning of *Wonderland* (the most spontaneous and 'subconscious' part of the books) when Alice gets out of the bath of tears that has magically released her from the underground chamber; it is made clear (for instance about watering-places) that the salt water is the sea from which life arose; as a bodily product it is also the amniotic fluid (there are other forces at work here); ontogeny then repeats phylogeny, and a whole Noah's Ark gets out of the sea with her. In Dodgson's own illustration as well as Tenniel's there is the disturbing head of a monkey and in the text there is an extinct bird. Our minds

2. Empson may be referring here to the tradition of pastoral poetry in which the swain—the countryman, often a shepherd, who speaks the poem—implicitly and sometimes explicitly contrasts the desirable simplicity of his life with the complex corruptions of life at court or in the cities. Pastoral poetry, which is conventionally a celebration of country life and simple loves and disappointments, thus also becomes a vehicle for ironic and satiric attacks on less wholesome and more anxious ways to live and love [*Editor*].

3. During his attack on Darwin's explanation of species, Samuel Wilberforce, then bishop of Oxford, turned to Thomas Huxley and asked whether it was through his maternal or paternal line that he was descended from a monkey. Huxley, in his reply, said that he would not be ashamed to be descended from a monkey, but that he would be ashamed to be connected with a man who used great gifts to obscure truth [*Editor*].

having thus been forced back onto the history of species there is a reading of history from the period when the Mouse 'came over' with the Conqueror; questions of race turn into the questions of breeding in which Dodgson was more frankly interested, and there are obscure snubs for people who boast about their ancestors. We then have the Caucus Race (the word had associations for Dodgson with local politics; he says somewhere, 'I never go to a Caucus without reluctance'), in which you begin running when you like and leave off when you like, and all win. The subtlety of this is that it supports Natural Selection (in the offensive way the nineteenth century did) to show the absurdity of democracy, and supports democracy (or at any rate liberty) to show the absurdity of Natural Selection.[4] The race is not to the swift because idealism will not let it be to the swift, and because life, as we are told in the final poem, is at random and a dream. But there is no weakening of human values in this generosity; all the animals win, and Alice because she is Man has therefore to give them comfits, but though they demand this they do not fail to recognise that she is superior. They give her her own elegant thimble, the symbol of her labour, because she too has won, and because the highest among you shall be the servant of all. This is a solid piece of symbolism; the politically minded scientists preaching progress through 'selection' and *laissez-faire* are confronted with the full anarchy of Christ. And the pretence of infantilism allows it a certain grim honesty; Alice is a little ridiculous and discomfited, under cover of charm, and would prefer a more aristocratic system.

In the *Looking-Glass* too there are ideas about progress at an early stage of the journey of growing up. Alice goes quickly through the first square by railway, in a carriage full of animals in a state of excitement about the progress of business and machinery; the only man is Disraeli dressed in newspapers—the new man who gets on by self-advertisement, the newspaper-fed man who believes in progress, possibly even the rational dress of the future.

> . . . to her great surprise, they all *thought* in chorus (I hope you understand what *thinking in chorus* means—for I must confess that I don't), 'Better say nothing at all. Language is worth a thousand pounds a word.'
> 'I shall dream of a thousand pounds to-night, I know I shall,' thought Alice.
> All this time the Guard was looking at her, first through a telescope, then through a microscope, and then through an operaglass. At last he

---

4. Natural selection is the name Darwin gave to the process by which evolution occurs: those organisms survive that develop and transmit characteristics that enable them and their progeny to adapt to an environment, and those organisms disappear that fail to develop such characteristics. In the vocabulary of social Darwinians later in the century, natural selection was translated into the idea of the "survival of the fittest," which in turn supported ideas about the benefits of unbridled competition and the inevitablity of rule by the strong [*Editor*].

said, 'You're travelling the wrong way,' and shut up the window and went away.

This seems to be a prophecy; Huxley in the Romanes lecture of 1893, and less clearly beforehand, said that the human sense of right must judge and often be opposed to the progress imposed by Nature, but at this time he was still looking through the glasses.

> But the gentleman dressed in white paper leaned forwards and whispered in her ear, 'Never mind what they all say, my dear, but take a return ticket every time the train stops.'

In 1861 'many Tory members considered that the prime minister was a better representative of conservative opinions than the leader of the opposition' [*Dictionary of National Biography*]. This seems to be the double outlook of Disraeli's convervatism, too subtle to inspire action. I think he turns up again as the unicorn when the Lion and the Unicorn are fighting for the Crown; they make a great dust and nuisance, treat the commonsense Alice as entirely mythical, and are very frightening to the poor king to whom the Crown really belongs.

> 'Indeed I shan't,' Alice said rather impatiently. 'I don't belong to this railway journey at all—I was in a wood just now—and I wish I could get back there!'

When she gets back to the wood it is different; it is Nature in the raw, with no names, and she is afraid of it. She still thinks the animals are right to stay there; even when they know their names "they wouldn't answer at all, if they were wise." (They might do well to write nonsense books under an assumed name, and refuse to answer even to that.) All this is a very Kafka piece of symbolism, less at ease than the preceding one; *Wonderland* is a dream, but the *Looking-Glass* is self-consciousness. But both are topical; whether you call the result allegory or 'pure nonsense' it depends on ideas about progress and industrialisation, and there is room for exegesis on the matter.

* * *

Both books also keep to the topic of death—the first two jokes about death in *Wonderland* come on pages 3 and 4—and for the child this may be a natural connection; I remember believing I should have to die before I grew up, and thinking the prospect very disagreeable. There seems to be a connection in Dodgson's mind between the death of childhood and the development of sex, which might be pursued into many of the details of the books. Alice will die if the Red King wakes up, partly because she is a dream-product of the author and partly because the pawn is put back in its box at the end of the game. He is the absent husband of the Red Queen who is a governess, and the end of the book comes when Alice defeats the Red Queen and 'mates' the King. Everything seems to break up because she arrives at a piece of *knowledge*, that all the poems are about fish. I should say the idea was somehow at work at the end of *Wonderland* too. The trial is meant to be a mystery; Alice is told to leave the court, as if a child ought not to hear the evidence, and yet they expect her to give evidence herself.

> 'What do you know about this business?' the King said to Alice.
> 'Nothing,' said Alice.
> 'Nothing *whatever*?' persisted the King.
> 'Nothing whatever,' said Alice.
> " 'That's very important,' the King said, turning to the jury. They were just beginning to write this down on their slates, when the White Rabbit interrupted: '*Un*important, your Majesty means, of course,' he said in a very respectful tone, but frowning and making faces as he spoke.
> '*Un*important, of course, I meant,' the King hastily said, and went on to himself in an undertone, 'important—unimportant—unimportant—important—' as if he were trying which word sounded best.

There is no such stress in the passage as would make one feel there must be something behind it, and certainly it is funny enough as it stands. But I think Dodgson felt it was important that Alice should be innocent of all knowledge of what the Knave of Hearts (a flashy-looking lady's-man in the picture) is likely to have been doing, and also important that she should not be told she is innocent. That is why the king, always a well-intentioned man, is embarrassed. At the same time Dodgson feels that Alice is right in thinking 'it doesn't matter a bit' which word the jury write down; she is too stable in her detachment to be embarrassed, these things will not interest her, and in a way she includes them all in herself. And it is the refusal to let her stay that makes her revolt and break the dream. It is tempting to read an example of this idea into the poem that introduces the *Looking-Glass*.

> Come, hearken then, ere voice of dread,
>   With bitter summons laden,
> Shall summon to unwelcome bed
>   A melancholy maiden.

After all the marriage-bed was more likely to be the end of the maiden than the grave, and the metaphor firmly implied treats them as identical.

The last example is obviously more a joke against Dodgson than anything else, and though the connection between death and the development of sex is I think at work it is not the main point of the conflict about growing up. Alice is given a magical control over her growth by the traditionally symbolic caterpillar, a creature which has to go through a sort of death to become grown-up, and then seems a more spiritual creature. It refuses to agree with Alice that this process is not all that peculiar, and clearly her own life will be somehow like it, but the main idea is not its development of sex. The butterfly implied may be the girl when she is 'out' or her soul when in heaven, to which she is now nearer than she will be when she is 'out'; she must walk to it by walking away from it. Alice knows several reasons why she should object to growing up, and does not at all like being an obvious angel, a head out of contact with its body that has to come down from the sky, and gets mistaken for the Paradisal serpent of the knowledge of good and evil, and by the pigeon of the Annunciation, too. But she only makes herself smaller for reasons of tact or proportion; the triumphant close of *Wonderland* is that she has outgrown her fancies and can afford to wake and despise them. The *Looking-Glass* is less of a dream-product, less concentrated on the child's situation, and (once started) less full of changes of size; but it has the same end; the governess shrinks to a kitten when Alice has grown from a pawn to a queen, and can shake her. Both these clearly stand for becoming grown-up and yet in part are a revolt against grown-up behaviour; there is the same ambivalence as about the talking animals. Whether children often find this symbolism is as interesting as Carroll did is another thing; there are recorded cases of tears at such a betrayal of the reality of the story. I remember feeling that the ends of the books were a sort of necessary assertion that the grown-up world was after all the proper one; one did not object to that in principle, but would no more turn to those parts from preference than to the 'Easter Greeting to Every Child that Loves Alice' (Gothic type).

To make this dream-story from which *Wonderland* was elaborated seem Freudian one has only to tell it. A fall through a deep hole into the secrets of Mother Earth produces a new enclosed soul wondering who it is, what will be its position in the world, and how it can get out. It *is* in a long low hall, part of the palace of the Queen of Hearts (a neat touch), from which it can only get out to the fresh air and the fountains through a hole frighteningly too small. Strange changes, caused by the way it is nourished there, happen to it in this place, but always when it is big it cannot get out and when it is small it is not allowed to; for one thing, being a little girl, it has no key. The nightmare theme of the birth-trauma, that she grows too big for the room and is almost crushed by it, is not only used here but repeated more painfully after she seems to have got out; the rabbit sends her sternly into its house and some food there makes her grow again. In Dodgson's own drawing of Alice when cramped into the room with one foot up the chimney, kicking out the hateful thing that tries to come down (she takes away its pencil when it is a juror), she is much more obviously in the foetus position than in Tenniel's. The White Rabbit is Mr. Spooner to whom the spoonerisms happened,[5] an undergraduate in 1862, but its business here is as a pet for children which they may be allowed to breed. Not that the clearness of the framework makes the interpretation simple; Alice peering through the hole into the garden may be wanting a return to the womb as well as an escape from it; she is fond, we are told, of taking both sides of an argument when talking to herself, and the whole book balances between the luscious nonsense-world of fantasy and the ironic nonsense-world of fact.

I said that the sea of tears she swims in was the amniotic fluid, which is much too simple. You may take it as Lethe in which the souls were bathed before re-birth (and it is their own tears; they forget, as we forget our childhood, through the repression of pain) or as the 'solution' of an intellectual contradiction through Intuition and a return to the Unconscious. Anyway it is a sordid image made pretty; one need not read Dodgson's satirical verses against babies to see how much he would dislike a child wallowing in its tears in real life. The fondness of small girls for doing this has to be faced early in attempting to prefer them, possibly to small boys, certainly to grown-ups; to a man idealising children as free from the falsity of a rich emotional life their displays of emotion must be particularly disconcerting. The celibate may be forced to observe them, on the floor of a railway carriage for example, after a storm of fury, dabbling in their ooze; covertly snuggling against mamma while each still pretends to ignore the other. The symbolic pleasure of dabbling seems based on an idea that the liquid itself is the bad temper which they have got rid of by the storm and yet are still hugging, or that they are not quite impotent since they have at least 'done' this much about the situation. The acid quality of the style shows that Dodgson does not entirely like having to love creatures whose narcissim takes this form, but he does not want simply to forget it as he too would like a relief from 'ill-temper'; he sterilises it from the start by giving it a charming myth. The love for narcissists itself seems mainly based on a desire to keep oneself safely detached, which is the essential notion here.

The symbolic completeness of Alice's experience is I think important. She runs the whole gamut; she is a father in getting down the hole, a foetus at the bottom, and can only be born by becoming a mother and producing her own amniotic fluid. Whether his mind played the trick of putting this into the story or not he has the feelings that would correspond to it. A desire to include all sexuality in the

5. William Archibald Spooner, who became warden of New College, was at Oxford in 1862, and he suffered from albinism. But there is no persuasive reason to think that he was the original of the White Rabbit [*Editor*].

girl child, the least obviously sexed of human creatures, the one that keeps its sex in the safest place, was an important part of their fascination for him. He is partly imagining himself as the girl-child (with these comforting characteristics) partly as its father (these together make *it* a father) partly as its lover—so it might be a mother—but then of course it is clever and detached enough to do everything for itself. He told one of his little girls a story about cats wearing gloves over their claws: 'For you see, "gloves" have got "love" inside them—there's none outside, you know.' So far from its dependence, the child's independence is the important thing, and the theme behind that is the self-centered emotional life imposed by the detached intelligence.

The famous cat is a very direct symbol of this idea of intellectual detachment; all cats are detached, and since this one grins it is the amused observer. It can disappear because it can abstract itself from its surroundings into a more interesting inner world; it appears only as a head because it is almost a disembodied intelligence, and only as a grin because it can impose an atmosphere without being present. In frightening the king by the allowable act of looking at him it displays the soul-force of Mr. Gandhi; it is unbeheadable because its soul cannot be killed; and its influence brings about a short amnesty in the divided nature of the Queen and Duchess. Its cleverness makes it formidable—it has very long claws and a great many teeth—but Alice is particularly at home with it; she is the same sort of thing.

* * *

This sort of 'analysis' is a peep at machinery; the question for criticism is what is done with the machine. The purpose of a dream on the Freudian theory is simply to keep you in an undisturbed state so that you can go on sleeping; in the course of this practical work you may produce something of more general value, but not only of one sort. Alice has, I understand, become a patron saint of the Surrealists, but they do not go in for Comic Primness, a sort of reserve of force, which is her chief charm. Wyndham Lewis avoided putting her beside Proust and Lorelei to be danced on as a debilitating child-cult (though she is a bit of pragmatist too); the present-day reader is more likely to complain of her complacence. In this sort of child-cult the child, though a means of imaginative escape, becomes the critic; Alice is the most reasonable and responsible person in the book. This is meant as charmingly pathetic about her as well as satire about her elders, and there is some implication that the sane man can take no other view of the world, even for controlling it, than the child does; but this is kept a good distance from sentimental infantilism. There is always some doubt about the meaning of a man who says he wants to be like a child, because he may want to be like it in having fresh and vivid feelings and senses, in not knowing, expecting, or desiring evil, in not having an analytical mind, in having no sexual desires recognisable as such, or out of a desire to be mothered and evade responsibility. He is usually mixing them up—Christ's praise of children, given perhaps for reasons I have failed to list, has made it a respected thing to say, and it has been said often and loosely—but he can make his own mixture; Lewis's invective hardly shows which he is attacking. The praise of the child in the Alices mainly depends on a distaste not only for sexuality but for all the distortions of vision that go with a rich emotional life; the opposite idea needs to be set against this, that you can only understand people or even things by having such a life in yourself to be their mirror; but the idea itself is very respectable. So far as it is typical of the scientist the books are an expression of the scientific attitude (*e.g.* the bread-and-butter fly) or a sort of satire on it that treats it as inevitable.

The most obvious aspect of the complacence is the snobbery. It is clear that Alice is not only a very well-brought-up but a very well-to-do little girl; if she has grown into Mabel, so that she will have to go and live in that poky little house and have next to no toys to play with, she will refuse to come out of her rabbit-hole at all. One is only surprised that she is allowed to meet Mabel. All through the books odd objects of luxury are viewed rather as Wordsworth viewed mountains; meaningless, but grand and irremovable; objects of myth. The whiting, the talking leg of mutton, the soup-tureen, the tea-tray in the sky, are obvious examples. The shift from the idea of the child's unity with nature is amusingly complete; a mere change in the objects viewed makes it at one with the conventions. But this is still not far from Wordsworth, who made his mountains into symbols of the stable and moral society living among them. In part the joke of this stands for the sincerity of the child that criticises the folly of convention, but Alice is very respectful to conventions and interested to learn new ones; indeed the discussions about the rules of the game of conversation, those stern comments on the isolation of humanity, put the tone so strongly in favour of the conventions that one feels there is nothing else in the world. There is a strange clash on this topic about the three little sisters discussed at the Mad Tea-party, who lived on treacle. 'They couldn't have done that, you know,' Alice gently remarked, 'they'd have been ill.' 'So they were,' said the Dormouse, '*very* ill.' The creatures are always self-centred and argumentative, to stand for the detachment of the intellect from emotion, which is necessary to it and yet makes it childish. Then the remark stands both for the danger of taking as one's guide the natural desires ('this is the sort of thing little girls would do if they were left alone') and for a pathetic example of a martyrdom to the conventions; the little girls did not mind *how* ill they were made by living on treacle, because it was their rule, and they knew it was expected of them. (That they are refined girls is clear from the fact that they do allegorical sketches.) There is an obscure connection here with the belief of the period that a really nice girl is 'delicate' (the profound sentences implied by the combination of meanings in this word are (*a*) 'you cannot get a woman to be refined unless you make her ill' and more darkly (*b*) 'she is desirable because corpse-like'); Dodgson was always shocked to find that his little girls had appetites, because it made them seem less pure. The passage about the bread-and-butter fly brings this out more frankly, with something of the wilful grimness of Webster.[6] It was a creature of such high refinement that it could only live on weak tea with cream in it (tea being the caller's meal, sacred to the fair, with nothing gross about it).

A new difficulty came into Alice's head.

'Supposing it couldn't find any?' she suggested.
'Then it would die, of course.'
'But that must happen very often,' Alice remarked thoughtfully.
'It always happens,' said the Gnat.
After this, Alice was silent for a minute or two, pondering.

There need be no gloating over the child's innocence here, as in Barrie; anybody might ponder. Alice has just suggested that flies burn themselves to death in candles out of a martyr's ambition to become Snapdragon flies. The talk goes on to losing one's name, which is the next stage on her journey, and brings freedom but is like death; the girl may lose her personality by growing up into the life of convention, and her virginity (like her surname) by marriage; or she may lose her 'good name' when she loses the conventions 'in the woods'—the animals, etc., there have no names because they are out of reach of the controlling reason; or when she develops sex she must neither understand nor name her feelings. The Gnat is weeping and Alice is afraid of the wood but determined to go on. 'It always dies of thirst' or 'it always dies in the end, as do we all'; 'the life of highest refinement is the most deathly, yet what else is one to aim at when life is so brief, and when there is so little in it of any value.' A certain ghoulishness in the atmosphere of this, of which the tight-lacing may have been a product or partial cause, comes out very strongly in Henry James; the decadents pounced on it for their own

6. John Webster (1580?–1625?), playwright [*Editor*].

purposes but could not put more death-wishes into it than these respectables had done already.

* * *

Once at least in each book a cry of loneliness goes up from Alice at the oddity beyond sympathy or communication of the world she has entered—whether that in which the child is shut by weakness, or the adult by the renunciations necessary for the ideal and the worldly way of life (the strength of the snobbery is to imply that these are the same). It seems strangely terrible that the answers of the White Queen, on the second of these occasions, should be so unanswerable.

> By this time it was getting light. 'The crow must have flown away, I think,' said Alice: 'I'm so glad it's gone. I thought it was the night coming on.'

Even in the rhyme the crow may be fear of death. The rhymes, like those other main structural materials, chess and cards, are useful because, being fixed, trivial, odd, and stirring to the imagination, they affect one as conventions of the dream world, and this sets the tone about conventions.

> 'I wish I could manage to be glad!' the Queen said. 'Only I never can remember the rule. You must be very happy, living in this wood, and being glad whenever you like.'

So another wood has turned out to be Nature. This use of 'that's a rule' is [Richard Brinsley] Sheridan's in *The Critic* [1781]; the pathos of its futility is that it is an attempt of reason to do the work of emotion and escape the dangers of the emotional approach to life. There may be a glance at the Oxford Movement and dogma. Perhaps chiefly a satire on the complacence of the fashion of slumming, the remark seems to spread out into the whole beauty and pathos of the ideas of pastoral; by its very universality her vague sympathy becomes an obscure self-indulgence.

> 'Only it is so very lonely here!' Alice said in a melancholy voice; and at the thought of her loneliness two large tears came rolling down her cheeks.
> 'Oh, don't go on like that,' cried the poor Queen, wringing her hands in despair. 'Consider what a great girl you are. Consider what a long way you've come to-day. Consider what o'clock it is. Consider anything, only don't cry!'
> Alice could not help laughing at this, even in the midst of her tears. 'Can you keep from crying by considering things?' she asked.
> 'That's the way it's done,' the Queen said with great decision; 'nobody can do two things at once, you know. Let's consider your age to begin with—how old are you?'

We are back at once to the crucial topic of age and the fear of death, and pass to the effectiveness of practice in helping one to believe the impossible; for example that the ageing Queen is so old that she would be dead. The helplessness of the intellect, which claims to rule so much, is granted under cover of the counter-claim that since it makes you impersonal you can forget pain with it; we do not believe this about the queen chiefly because she has not enough understanding of other people. The jerk of the return to age, and the assumption that this is a field for polite lying, make the work of the intellect only the game of conversation. Humpty Dumpty has the same embarrassing trick for arguing away a suggestion of loneliness. Indeed about all the rationalism of Alice and her acquaintances there hangs a suggestion that there are after all questions of pure thought, academic thought whose altruism is recognised and paid for, thought meant only for the upper classes to whom the conventions are in any case natural habit; like that suggestion that the scientist is sure to be a gentleman and has plenty of space which is the fascination of Kew Gardens.

The Queen is a very inclusive figure. 'Looking before and after' with the plaintive tone of universal altruism she lives chiefly backwards, in history; the necessary darkness of growth, the mysteries of self-knowledge, the self-contradictions of the will, the antinomies of philosophy, the very Looking-Glass itself, impose this; nor is it mere weakness to attempt to resolve them only in the direct impulse of the child. Gathering the more dream-rushes her love for man becomes the more universal, herself the more like a porcupine. Knitting with more and more needles she tries to control life by a more and more complex intellectual apparatus—the 'progress' of Herbert Spencer;[7] any one shelf of the shop is empty, but there is always something very interesting—the 'atmosphere' of the place is so interesting— which moves up as you look at it from shelf to shelf; there is jam only in the future and our traditional past, and the test made by Alice, who sent value through the ceiling as if it were quite used to it, shows that progress can never reach value, because its habitation and name is heaven. The Queen's scheme of social reform, which is to punish those who are not respectable before their crimes are committed, seems to be another of these jokes about progress:

> 'But if you *hadn't* done them,' the Queen said, 'that would have been better still; better, and better, and better!' Her voice went higher with each 'better' till it got to quite a squeak at last.

---

7. In his many studies in science, philosophy, history, politics, education, sociology, and yet other disciplines, Herbert Spencer (1820–1903) argued that a rational systematizing of experience was the source of a comfortable and happy existence in it [*Editor*].

356 · *William Empson*

There is a similar attack in the Walrus and the Carpenter, who are depressed by the spectacle of unimproved nature and engage in charitable work among oysters. The Carpenter is a Castle and the Walrus, who could eat so many more because he was crying behind his handkerchief, was a Bishop, in the scheme at the beginning of the book. But in saying so one must be struck by the depth at which the satire is hidden; the queerness of the incident and the characters takes on a Wordsworthian grandeur and aridity, and the landscape defined by the tricks of facetiousness takes on the remote and staring beauty of the ideas of the insane. It is odd to find that Tenniel went on to illustrate Poe in the same manner; Dodgson is often doing what Poe wanted to do, and can do it the more easily because he can safely introduce the absurd. The Idiot Boy of Wordsworth is too milky a moonlit creature to be at home with Nature as she was deplored by the Carpenter, and much more of the technique of the rudeness of the Mad Hatter has been learned from Hamlet. It is the ground-bass of this kinship with insanity, I think, that makes it so clear that the books are not trifling, and the cool courage with which Alice accepts the madmen that gives them their strength.

This talk about the snobbery of the Alices may seem a mere attack, but a little acid may help to remove the slime with which they have been encrusted. The two main ideas behind the snobbery, that virtue and intelligence are alike lonely, and that good manners are therefore important though an absurd confession of human limitations, do not depend on a local class system; they would be recognised in a degree by any tolerable society. And if in a degree their opposites must also be recognised, so they are here; there are solid enough statements of the shams of altruism and convention and their horrors when genuine; it is the forces of this conflict that make a clash violent enough to end both the dreams. In *Wonderland* this is mysteriously mixed up with the trial of the Knave of Hearts, the thief of love, but at the end of the second book the symbolism is franker and more simple. She is a grown queen and has acquired the conventional dignities of her insane world; suddenly she admits their insanity, refuses to be a grown queen, and destroys them.

> 'I can't stand this any longer!' she cried, as she seized the table-cloth in both hands: one good pull, and plates, dishes, guests, and candles came crashing down together in a heap on the floor.

The guests are inanimate and the crawling self-stultifying machinery of luxury has taken on a hideous life of its own. It is the High Table of Christ Church that we must think of here. The gentleman is not the slave of his conventions because at need he could destroy them;

and yet, even if he did this, and all the more because he does not, he must adopt while despising it the attitude to them of the child.

*   *   *

ROGER HENKLE

Comedy from Inside†

"I seem to see some meaning in them after all."—*The King of Hearts*

Alice in Wonderland and *Through the Looking-Glass* present explorations of the cultural anxieties that concentrate within the mid-century sensibility. They have traditionally, of course, invited multiple interpretations—as retreats into childhood, as mythic excursions into the unconscious, as thinly disguised expressions of black humor, and as paradigms of games and sport. The coy intellectuality of Carroll's inversions of sophisticated ideas has prompted critics to consider the Alice books as paradigmatic works of self-contained logic (or illogic) that bear no resemblance to the outer social world. Such interpretations, though valid with respect to one dimension of Carroll's writing, cannot account for the remarkable impact that the Alice books have had upon adult readers for over a hundred years. They are explorations of an adult life that ventures as far as Carroll could risk going toward freedom from the duties, responsibilities, and arid self-limitations of modern society.

What a pleasant change the caucus-race would be from the completion of most "games" and adult occupations: "they began running when they liked and left off when they liked," and at the end of the race *"everybody* has won and *all* must have prizes." How nice it would be to sit, as the Mock Turtle does, on a shingle by the sea and sentimentally ruminate on one's experiences, to surrender to all the self-indulgence that seems too rarely possible in modern life. It is always teatime for the Mad Hatter, the March Hare, and the Dormouse, and people they don't like just aren't invited; "No room! No room!," says the Hare. And when Humpty Dumpty uses a word it means what *he* chooses it to mean, neither more nor less.

We cannot say exactly what was included in the original, oral version of *Wonderland* that Carroll spun for the Liddell sisters while boating on the Thames, but we do know that many of the additions that he made to the tale when writing it out for publication were those episodes of comic indulgence, such as the Mad Tea Party and

† From *Comedy and Culture: England 1820–1900* (Princeton: Princeton UP, 1980) 201–11. Reprinted with permission of Princeton University Press. Copyright © 1980 by Princeton University Press.

the reminiscences of the Mock Turtle.[1] Common to these additions is the sense of a poignant need to retreat to personal patterns of play and whim, as if to escape from the narrowing pressures of a life in society. In the years just before *Wonderland* was published, Carroll himself chafed and despaired under what seemed to him the onerous burdens and anxieties of adult life. At the end of each year, he sadly assessed himself and recorded in his diaries his failures to live up to his responsibilities as a scholar, teacher, and man of religion. "Great mercies, great failings," he wrote at year's end in 1855, "time lost, talents misapplied—such has been the past year" [I: 70]. * * *

Characteristically, in February 1863, he bemoaned, "This year has given no promise as yet of being better than its predecessors: my habits of life need much amendment"; he then listed four ways (including "denying myself indulgence of sleep in the evening") by which they could be improved [I: 191]. Distracted by his amusements, unambitious, eyed suspiciously by the parents of his little girls, and nagged by a sense of failure for forsaking a religious vocation, Carroll looked for life possibilities in which these concerns and burdens did not exist. In his own life, he found respite in his many hobbies and avocations; he was an inveterate riddler, gamemaker, rhymester. But in the Alice books, he could render through imagination the fragments, at least, of a desired life style, a life style that had the freedoms and satisfactions of adult play.

It was through play, in fact, that Carroll developed the talents for which he is most remembered. He began writing nonsense as a boy for his own amusement and that of his brothers and sisters. As he acquired a special, self-conscious skill at it, his play developed into an art—but an art that retained its child's play quality. Nonsense, to be successful, must keep that precarious balance between childlike whimsy and the capriccio of a trained artist showing off his skills. Like caricature, it is apparently casually rendered; but it is often swept up in the exuberance of comic creation, the writer improvising and piling on richer and wilder creations and scenes for his own delight in them (like Dickens indulging himself in more and more of Mrs. Gamp).

The exuberance of play, however, is often deliberately restrained by an arbitrary order of rules invented by the player, and this was especially important to Carroll. In this quality of personally devised order—the brief moments in the Alice books of creatures rehearsing their individual delights—one captures the pleasure of personal con-

---

1. Some of these were, of course, probably derived from separate stories made up by Carroll for little girls. The Mad Tea Party has such a source. Carroll himself, however, acknowledged that in writing down *Wonderland*, he added "many fresh ideas." *"Alice* on the Stage" [pp. 280–82 in this edition].

trol of one's life, and perhaps achieves the stasis that so many Victorians sought in a rapidly changing world.

Even more important is the relief that play brings from the officious moralizing of other people. The "moral" of *Wonderland* is drawn by the Duchess (although she doesn't practice it): "If everybody minded their own business, the world would go round a deal faster than it does." Victorian comic writers from Thackeray to Butler tried to fend off the ponderous forces that were bent on dictating ethical, social, and even psychological conformity. In moments of play, at least, one can operate, as Johan Huizinga has noted, "outside the antithesis of wisdom and folly . . . of good and evil."[2] In later years, Carroll could rhapsodize about his dream Alice because she was living in the happy hours "when Sin and Sorrow are but names— empty words signifying nothing! ["*Alice* on the Stage," p. 282]. The homiletic hymns and rhymes that Alice tries to recall in *Wonderland* but cannot—"The Old Man's Comforts," "Against Idleness and Mischief," "The Sluggard," and "Speak Gently"—all share three elements—an injunction to be industrious and responsible, the reminder that we shall all grow old, and an invocation of our religious duties. Significantly, these banished thoughts are those we try to forget in play.

Carroll could not forget them for long, however. *Wonderland's* imaginative projection as a possible variant life style was at the same time an opportunity to register and somehow work out the very anxieties that gave rise to the search for a new life style. In dreams we are often able to do all these things, and *Wonderland* is such a dream.

True to the realm of dreams, most things in Wonderland do not happen in a logical and chronological manner. There is no "plot" to the book; instead, dream thoughts pull seemingly disorganized elements together. Almost immediately the anxieties Carroll recorded so often in his diaries come to the surface in the behavior of the White Rabbit, who's late, who's lost his glove, who'll lose his head if he doesn't get to the Duchess's house on time.[3] The Rabbit will later act for the Crown in the surrealistic trial of the knave at the book's end, thereby explicitly linking such social anxieties with the arbitrary punishment and the dread of fury that persistently flash along hidden circuits of Wonderland's dreaming brain and periodically seize Alice and the creatures. At the end of the innocuous caucus-race, the Mouse tells Alice his "tale"; it is about Fury and

2. Johan Huizinga, *Homo Ludens: A Study of the Play-Element in Culture* (Boston: 1950) 6.
3. Carroll wrote on May 18, 1856: "I am getting into habits of unpunctuality, and must try to make a fresh start in activity: I record this resolution as a test for the future;" and as a proposed improvement for the new year, he wrote, on December 31, 1857, that there must be "constant improvements of habits of activity, punctuality, etc." (*Diaries* I: 85, 136).

it prefigures the terrifying dissolution of the Wonderland dream itself. According to the tale, personified Fury, who this morning has "nothing to do," imperiously decides he'll prosecute the Mouse: " 'I'll be the judge, I'll be the jury,' said cunning old Fury; 'I'll try the whole cause and condemn you to death.' "[4]

Time and again the delights of play are cut off suddenly by such arbitrary violence, for we perceive that play by its nature cannot last. No wonder the Mad Hatter curtly changes the subject when Alice reminds him that he will soon run out of places at the tea table. Too soon he is dragged into Court by the Queen to be badgered and intimidated, despite his pathetic protest. "I hadn't quite finished my tea when I was sent for." Play can only temporarily remove us from outside reality, as Carroll himself repeatedly discovered, because authority (characterized in those adult women—Queens and Duchesses) will interfere and impose its angry will. This is why I believe it is inaccurate to assert, as Hugh Kenner and Elizabeth Sewell have, that Carroll's books are "closed" works of art, literary game structures that are deliberately isolated and fundamentally unrelated to the Victorian social world outside them.[5] On the contrary, they show Carroll's reluctant conclusion that totally independent life patterns were impossible and even dangerous; they are Carroll's paradigms of the way social power was achieved and how it operated in Victorian England.

Inherent in the very freedom of play is its weakness. Functioning by personal whim, it is potentially anarchic and thus vulnerable to the strongest, most brutal will. Halfway through the book, Alice unaccountably must enter Wonderland a second time and she finds its tenor radically different. Instead of the pleasantly free caucus race, she plays in a croquet game where "the players all played at once, quarrelling all the while." All order has collapsed; hedgehog balls scuttle through the grass, bodiless cats grin in the dusk. And the domineering Queen of Hearts imposes her angry will more and more as she exploits the anarchy of the hapless world of play.

The antics that the Mad Tea Party group, the Caterpillar, and the other free souls had been indulging in were, in a word, nonsense. Just as nonsense writing is a form of play activity, play itself—at least as Carroll conceived it—is nonsensical in the context of the "real world"; it has been deliberately deprived of meaning, of any overt social and moral significance. Alice noted at the tea party that "the

4. The mouse's tale is a late addition to the manuscript. In the original version of his tale, the mouse emphasized the Darwinian randomness of death in the animal kingdom; a dog and cat, in search of a rat, crushed several mice who had been "warm and snug." It mentioned nothing of a trial, or Fury. The trial itself is a late addition.

5. See Hugh Kenner, *Dublin's Joyce* (Bloomington: 1956) 276–300, and Elizabeth Sewell, *The Field of Nonsense* (London: 1952) 144.

Hatter's remark seemed to her to have no sort of meaning in it, and yet it was certainly English." At the trial of the knave, however, suddenly there *is* meaning that the autocratic Queen wants attached to the words so that they can be made to serve her lust for persecution. The most damning piece of evidence, according to the Crown, is a nonsensical letter purportedly written by the defendant. Alice argues, "*I* don't believe there's an atom of meaning in it," but the King of Hearts insists, "I seem to see some meaning in [the words] after all." The individuals who assert power in society, Carroll is suggesting, decide what things shall mean. *Their* whims, prompted and carried out by an irrational fury against people who would be free, dictate our responsibilities, our duties, our guilts, our sins, our punishment.

Here, the adult victim's view nicely corresponds to the child's view of grown-up authority. If a child is called to task, told to remember some rule or duty he has forgotten about or never fully realized he was responsible for, he feels like the Mad Hatter, who is told, "Don't be nervous, or I'll have you executed on the spot." Justice from a child's perspective often does seem to function like the Queen's—verdict first, guilt later.

This vision is surely familiar to post-Kafka readers and may be one of the reasons why *Wonderland* has such contemporary appeal. If there is a difference between Carroll's rendition of social power and the view of present writers, it probably lies in Carroll's attribution of the evils of that power to the ambitions of specific unscrupulous individuals. Social authority is frequently depicted in contemporary literature as a vague but pervasive *impersonal* force—monolithic, self-sustaining, its motives obscure, its constituents unidentified. Although *Looking-Glass* implies a social order close to this, *Wonderland* delineates—as much mid-Victorian literature does—an Establishment that is made up of greedy, insensitive individuals fulfilling selfish urges for power and disguising it with moral cant. This view reflects the rise to power in nineteenth-century England of the entrepeneurs, the exploiters, and the social climbers who are so vividly depicted in Dickens and Trollope. It also reflects the abundance and variety of self-appointed moral arbiters of the time— the Churchmen, earnest reformers, and busy, bustling middle-class matrons. As W. L. Burn puts it, "One of the cardinal differences between the mid-Victorians and ourselves lies not in their optimism and our pessimism but in the much greater faith they had in the power of the human will."[6] Yet in the final analysis, Carroll's particular depiction of the way society worked stemmed largely from his own psychological makeup, the unique mix in him of fear of

6. *The Age of Equipoise* (New York: 1964) 21.

anarchy, self-doubt, and of sad realism about the way things were.

In the second of the Alice books, *Through the Looking-Glass*, published in 1871, six years after *Wonderland*, we can detect a significant sombering of outlook. There is a remarkable difference in the mood and strategy of the two books. In *Looking-Glass*, Carroll sees the prospects for free activity in society much more pessimistically. We discover immediately that *Looking-Glass* is worked out as a chess game, in which Alice is propelled along toward a visible goal; she is no longer exploring on her own. A deterministic impulse underlies the Looking-Glass dream; indeed, it ends with the suggestion that we are all part of the dream of a godlike Red King whose own unconscious wishes predetermined our lives.

Alice's entry to Wonderland had been balked by problems of identity; she had to shed some false notions relating to size, rote-knowledge, and rules of behavior before she could participate in the dream world. On entering the looking-glass, she is confronted with difficulties in moving "forward," as if her need now is to move out, away from home and childhood and into the adult world of roles and responsibilty.

While *Wonderland* is set in a spring afternoon, *Looking-Glass* takes place in mid-winter; the first book's golden aura now seems only the yellowing of age. Alice is rudely told by the flowers that she is beginning to fade. Humpty Dumpty dwells on her age and the possibility of death, and in parting, as he offers her his finger to shake, he says that he very much doubts if he'd know her if they *did* meet again: "you're so exactly like other people." How chilling it is, Carroll seems to be saying, to contemplate a dry, unsatisfying maturity like that of the Queens in *Looking-Glass*, whom Carroll later describes this way:

> The Red Queen I pictured as a Fury, but of another type from the Queen of Hearts in Wonderland; *her* passion must be cold and calm; she must be formal and strict, yet not unkindly; pedantic to the tenth degree; the concentrated essence of all governesses! Lastly, the White Queen seemed, to my dreaming fancy, gentle, stupid, fat and pale; . . . just *suggesting* imbecility, but never quite passing into it. [See "*Alice* on the Stage," p. 282 of this edition.]

The poems that frame *Looking-Glass* echo the plaint and seem to be spooned up from Carroll's deepest, stickiest treacle well:

> Come, harken then, ere voice of dread
>   With bitter tidings laden,
> Shall summon to unwelcome bed
>   A melancholy maiden!
> We are but older children, dear,
> Who fret to find our bedtime near.

Long has paled that sunny sky:
Echoes fade and memories die:
Autumn frosts have slain July.

Toward the end of *Looking-Glass*, the White Knight—whose resemblance to Caroll himself has often been noted—invents for Alice
a nonsense verse that is a Looking-Glass distortion of *Wonderland*.
This one, too, is set in a summer, now "long ago," not about a
child, however, but about a pathetically aged man "who seemed
distracted with his woe." Growing old, we recall, was banished from
Wonderland; it is in the poems that Alice "forgot." In *Looking-Glass*,
it is omnipresent.

Adult play, which was so vividly real early in *Wonderland*, is not
seriously offered again. Humpty Dumpty, the Lion and the Unicorn,
and the Tweedles carry on a bit, but their careers are predetermined
by the nursery rhymes about them. By wishing for the crow of the
Tweedle rhyme to come, Alice makes it come; and we uneasily
suspect that if she willed it, Alice could make Humpty Dumpty fall
off the wall immediately. If the Cheshire Cat of *Wonderland* is the
comic spirit of play, able to go where he wishes, do as he wishes,
and remain—sometimes literally—detached, the gnat that Alice
meets in *Looking-Glass* is the comic spirit of that book: he can barely
be heard, his humor is forced and restricted in range, and he himself
is miserable.

The mood in *Looking-Glass* is close to that of the humor tradition
in English letters that we have traced earlier. Although the tones of
adult play and eccentricity admittedly shade into each other, it is
apparent from the manner and structure of *Looking-Glass* that Carroll felt he could not go back again to an exploration of the possibilities of a free life style. As he grew older, he settled for a
conventional, if less joyful, accommodation to the societal patterns
of his time. The White Knight, for example, has all the characteristics
of the humor tradition's amiable eccentric: he is melancholy, lovable,
laughable, and very obviously modeled after Don Quixote, who, to
early nineteenth-century readers, seemed a perfect specimen of the
amiable humorist.[7] And he is very much part of the chessboard
social pattern. Contrast the White Knight to the waspish Hare and
Hatter who have no part in army larger social order. The creatures
in *Looking-Glass* spend much of their time perched on walls or
upside down in ditches idly contemplating—like [Fielding's] Parson
Adams or Sterne's Walter Shandy. At one point in *Looking-Glass*
when Alice burst into tears because it is so very *lonely* there, the
White Queen tries to comfort her by telling her to "consider what

7. Stuart Tave, *The Amiable Humorist: A Study in the Comic Theory and Criticism of the 18th
and Early 19th Centuries* (Chicago: 1960) 151–163.

a great girl you are. Consider what a long way you've come today."
"Can *you* keep from crying by considering things?" Alice asks. "That's
the way it's done," the Queen says.

Consider what a long way you've come: *Looking-Glass*, unlike
Wonderland, had the speeded up tempo and brassy talk of the ac-
quisitive, industrial society. Alice is flung onto a rushing train and
asked where her ticket is. "Don't keep him waiting, child," a chorus
of voices demands, "his time is worth a thousand pounds a minute."
The land is worth a thousand pounds an inch, the smoke from the
engine a thousand pounds a puff. Alice is haplessly driven on toward
womanhood as an underlying anxiety constricts the dream's action
tighter and tighter toward the breaking point, until at last life becomes
unbearable and rapacious.

The last moments in the Looking-Glass, with the banquet guests
wallowing in the gravy, are a hideous analogue of the life of an
indulgent society. Just as the characters are less joyful and independent than those of Wonderland, so the society here is faster, harder,
more manipulative. The Darwinian motif of survival of the fittest
and of cannibalism that had shot randomly through Alice's first
dream have now become almost the governing principle in a world
where people are figuratively "consuming" others.

The half a dozen years between the two books had resigned Lewis
Carroll to an even more muted expression of rebellion. They were
years in which Victorian England grew more affluent, more wasteful,
perhaps a bit more frenetic. And Carroll's own life, as the diary
entries from 1866 to 1870 reflect, was more demanding, and his
interests had turned more to politics and affairs of the world. Ever
sensitive to changes in the quality of life, Carroll may have sensed
the disillusionment that was to beset the late Victorians when the
promise of a more satisfying life through progress proved empty. For
all the vigor of the 1860s, "doubts and fears there were," says G.
M. Young. "The roaring slapdash prosperity of a decade had worked
itself out to its appointed end: overtrading, speculation, fraud, and
collapse."[8] Already feeling like a man hopelessly out of tune with
his time, Carroll, in his oblique and highly personal way, registered
these nuances of change in English culture and, sadly, in his own
prospects for happiness and freedom.

8. G. M. Young, *Victorian England: Portrait of an Age*, 2nd ed. (London: 1953) 114.

ROBERT POLHEMUS

The Comedy of Regression†

Lewis Carroll's words and images are to the formulation of a comic faith what Jesus's parables are to Christian doctrine: they create a fiction so radical that it can bring its audience to look with fresh wonder at the structure and meaning of experience. Ultimately, they point to the necessity of faith in humanity's potential. But, unlike Scripture, they also proclaim and make up laugh at the inescapable absurdity of the world.

Carroll's way is the way of regression. By befriending small girls, identifying with them, projecting himself back into childhood, and writing tales explicitly for children, he managed to create two texts that have been, and are, as widely read and quoted, and as influential, as any imaginative literature of the past century. The Alice books do not address our serious, responsible, moral selves; Carroll turns his back on the adult world. Nevertheless, this man who retreats into juvenility and dream states, reverts to play and nonsense, toys with language, avoids any overtly didactic or practical purpose, and escapes from society, history, and "reality" into the fantasy of his own mind appears before us as a comic prophet and a father of modernism in art and literature. From out of the rabbit-hole and looking-glass world come not only such major figures as Joyce, Waugh, Nabokov, Beckett, and Borges but also much of the character and mood of twentieth-century humor and life.

*   *   *

*   *   * In all comedy there is something regressive that takes us back to the world of play that we first knew as children. And if all comic literature somehow involves regression, many will naturally find it frivolous. But I see the comic regression in *Through the Looking-Glass* as profound. Regression means a going or coming back; it can be defined as a reverting to earlier behavior patterns so as to change or escape from unpleasant situations. It is both radical and conservative: radical in rejecting the present and in juxtaposing material from both our conscious and unconscious minds; conservative in holding on to time past. In Freudian dream psychology, regression means the translation of thoughts and emotions into visual images and speech when the process of idea-content on its normal way to consciousness is blocked. It is a way of expressing and elab-

† This essay and the one following are from *Comic Faith: The Great Tradition from Austen to Joyce* (Chicago: U of Chicago P, 1980) 245– 46, 258–260, 288–93. Reprinted by permission of the author and the University of Chicago Press.

orating suppressed memories and daring psychic formations from infancy and childhood and letting them play on present realities. Regression can thus be a means of seeing the world anew. The child's fantasy can be father to the adult's changing civilization.

The way to go forward in looking-glass land is to go backward—back to origins, first principles, early years, early pleasures, and premoral states—in order to see with fresh clarity what, through habit and social repression, we have come to accept as absolutely the truth and to find in a place of make-believe that *make-believe* is the essence of our fate and being. The way to freedom and curious wonder is to recognize and comprehend the arbitrary, predetermined, and artificial structures that order our lives. The way to knowledge of culture and society is to explore one's inner fantasy life. The way to honor intelligence is to know and laugh at its limitations. The way to celebrate creation is to play with its silly mysteries. The intention that comes through in *Through the Looking-Glass* is, in effect, the meaning of mankind's comic capacity, and it is this: I will play with and make ridiculous fear, loneliness, smallness, ignorance, authority, chaos, nihilism, and death; I will transform, for a time, woe to joy.

* * *

* * * The child often experiences authority as a kind of abrupt rudeness. Carroll subverts it by making it look petty; he knew that the exercise of power can simply be the childishness of big beings. The Red Queen is his principal explicit authority figure in the book, and he uses her for satire. He called her "pedantic to the tenth degree, the concentrated essence of all governesses," which means she must be the essence of government and authority as a Victorian upper-class child first knew it. In the way of most perceived authority, she has a personality but no depth of self; all her being goes into telling others what to do. She has no self-doubt, no disinterested wonder, no hesitancy that might humanize her. Contradictory and rude, like so many of the cocksure characters Alice meets, she asks questions but then gives orders before they can be answered. "Where do you come from? . . . And where are you going? Look up, speak nicely, and don't twiddle your fingers all the time." That may simply caricature the authoritarian type; but her next command, "Curtsey while you're thinking what to say. It saves time," provides a whole comic disquisition on the role of manners as well as a blueprint for success. Her pronouncements come out as a mad strategy for facing the mystery of things. When Alice sets out through the unknown countryside, the Red Queen says, "Speak in French when you can't think of the English for a thing—turn out your toes as you walk—and remember who you are!" As words to live by, nothing could make clearer the capricious and ridiculously inadequate nature of authority and the tragicomic fragility of people who must face their fate without proper knowledge. Yet the Queen's advice makes as much sense as most rules of conduct. Humanity must rely on simplistic formulas, internalized slogans, and funny little gestures as it moves about in its unfathomable game.

Carroll is the don of comic reduction: shrink the essence of authority to a child's scale, diminish the threatening urgencies of society, make jokes of them, show up their triviality—those are his imperatives. Fleeting impressions and images stand for and mock great patterns and manifestations of power. In chapter 3, he manages to fit the mighty clamor of capitalism and industrialism into a single square, through which Alice is rushed—by railway, naturally. A chorus dins at her:

> "Don't keep him waiting, child! Why, his time is worth a thousand pounds a minute!" . . . "The land there is worth a thousand pounds an inch!" . . .
> "Why, the smoke alone is worth a thousand pounds a puff!" . . .
> "Better say nothing at all. Language is worth a thousand pounds a word!"
> "I shall dream about a thousand pounds tonight, I know I shall!" thought Alice.

We have the assault of the capitalistic system, the canting hustle of steam and price, as it might be felt by a child with whom we sympathize, but Carroll reduces this financial mania "to child's play, the very thing to jest about."[1]

Chapter 4, the great Tweedledee and Tweedledum chapter, treats in the same fashion such matters as fratricide, contradictions in human nature, power struggles, war, and political controversy. Here we have Cain and Abel reduced to puerility: "Tweedledum and Tweedledee / Agreed to have a battle; / For Tweedledum said Tweedledee / Had spoiled his nice new rattle":

> "Of course you agree to have a battle?" Tweedledum said. . . .
> So the two brothers went off hand-in-hand into the wood, and returned in a minute with their arms full of things—such as bolsters, blankets, hearth-rugs, tablecloths, dish-covers, and coal-scuttles. . . .
> Alice said afterwards she had never seen such a fuss made about anything in all her life . . . she arranged a bolster round the neck of Tweedledee, "to keep his head from being cut off," as he said.
> "You know," he added very gravely, "it's one of the most serious things that can possibly happen to one in a battle—to get one's head cut off."
> Alice laughed loud: . . .

1. Sigmund Freud, "Humour," in *The Complete Works of Sigmund Freud*, Standard Edition (London, 1953) 21: 166.

"We *must* have a bit of a fight. . . . What's the time now?"
Tweedledee looked at his watch, and said "Half-past four."
"Let's fight until six, and then have dinner," said Tweedledum.
"Very well," the other said. . . .
Tweedledum looked round him with a satisfied smile. "I don't suppose,"
he said, "there'll be a tree left standing, for ever so far round, by the time
we've finished!"
"And all about a rattle!" said Alice, still hoping to make them a *little*
ashamed of fighting for such a trifle.

Such an excerpt shows the error of those who dismiss the profound
seriousness of Carroll's humor. In a way almost unparalleled in
literature, he treats comically and succinctly the most momentous
subjects and the most terrible problems of humanity. Here his topic
and target are, in fact, war and its perpetrators. The comedy controls
for the moment the potential horror of battle by putting it in a context
of play and asserting that from a certain dispassionate point of view,
which we have the power to assume, war means the ridiculous
behavior of Tweedledee and Tweedledum. Ridiculing the twins,
Carroll withdraws dignity from those who make the highest claim
to it but do not deserve it—namely, fighters and force-worshipers of
any sort. All our sympathy and our respect in this scene go to Alice.

In "Tweedledum and Tweedledee," Carroll, as usual, reverses
roles: Alice, the child, has the maturity and wise judgment that a
parent was supposed to have. She does not, however, have the parent's authority or influence. She knows what's right, but she is pow-
erless to stop the inevitable charade of inanity. She cannot control
her world, but she can know it, and she survives. At the end of
nearly every chapter, including this one, she moves on, away from
violence, futility, death, disaster, emerging as an image of the child
as refugee and survivor, a figure with a future.

ROBERT POLHEMUS

Play, Nonsense, and Games: Comic Diversion

Carroll stands by the pervasiveness and humanity of play.
—Kathleen Blake[1]

The spirit of play predominates in Carroll's comedy. He is *Homo
ludens* asserting his right to divert himself and seek pleasure for its
own sake. *Through the Looking-Glass* presents a strategy for mastering
experience through play, nonsense, and games. They are modes for
temporarily changing and controlling reality, but they also become
ways of reflecting and criticizing the arbitrariness and absurdities of

1. Kathleen Blake, *Play, Games, and Sport, The Literary Works of Lewis Carroll* (Ithaca: 1974)
19.

life. Something in Carroll and in much of modern comedy says that life is so absurd that only play can illuminate it or make it mean anything worthwhile. Needing to disarm to get a hearing, he offers comic play as harmless interlude; but, as it does in so many modern writers, it defies the inhibiting social and natural order and flouts the opressive work of others. Comic play asserts the personal freedom to change mood and perspective. It incorporates time and space into elaborate and shifting games.

Diversion, with its sense of pleasing distraction, seems the perfect word for Carroll's play. He begins by offering to divert us from the summons of death—"Come, harken then, ere voice of dread / With bitter tidings laden, / Shall summon"—and then goes on to subordinate death, pride, madness, power, language, chaos, himself, his characters, his readers, "reality," and even his God to his play. He manipulates, for his own amusement, whatever seems threatening. Continually improvising, he makes a comic game of anything, and by doing so he exposes the games of others that set limits on human liberty.

His verbal play and nonsense are full of rebelliousness. "Jabberwocky," as we have seen, expresses a longing to break through conventional language and get to a state of free utterance. One impulse behind it is the implied protest: "I do not have to make sense; I can say anything I like, any way I like." Another is, "I can construct my own language and style for others to decipher." The test for artistic success in nonsense language is whether it suggests pleasing connotations that an audience will be motivated to discover and itself manipulate. That means that it must maintain a poise between mere gibberish and common usage.[2] Carroll's nonsense generally manages to let us experience language as something full of opportunities for play and exhilarating freedom. "O frabjous day! Callooh! Callay!" "Then fill up the glasses as quick as you can, / And sprinkle the table with buttons and bran: / Put cats in the coffee, and mice in the tea —/ And welcome Queen Alice with thirty-times-three!" That sort of thing diverts us by breaking down our conventional expectations and drawing our attention, for many reasons, to the joy that we can find in words. We, like the author, play with his language.

But there is an equally strong hostile impulse in nonsense—the desire to satirize the senselessness of the world. The Red Queen sums it up: "You may call it 'nonsense' if you like . . . but *I've* heard nonsense, compared with which that would be as sensible a a dictionary!" As usual in Carroll, what at first seems self-enclosed is, in another light, mimetic and referential. The nonsense poem "A-sitting on a Gate" says in effect that there are things in Wordsworth's

2. See Elizabeth Sewell, *The Field of Nonsense* (London: 1952) for a provocative discussion of nonsense. [See pp. 380–88 of this edition.]

"Resolution and Independence" just as absurd as anything the White
Knight can devise. Look at these lines:

> His accents mild took up the tale:
> He said "I go my ways,
> And when I find a mountain-rill,
> I set it in a blaze;
> And thence they make a stuff they call
> Rowland's Macassar-Oil—
> Yet twopence-halfpenny is all
> They give me for my toil."
>
> But I was thinking of a way
> To feed oneself on batter,
> And so go on from day to day
> Getting a little fatter.
> I shook him well from side to side,
> Until his face was blue:
> "Come, tell me how you live," I cried,
> "And what it is you do!"

The verse works in two ways: Its vision is so crazy that we don't
have to take it seriously, and it frees us of the pressures and responsibilities of our usual mental life. Nothing can keep the poem's
speaker (the White Knight) from trying to invent schemes that no
one would have any reason to conceive, and just this motiveless
originality taps some source of anarchic sympathy in us. That is the
nontendentious side of nonsense. On the other hand, the "aged man"
plans and acts in ways just as zany as the Knight's, even if he does
so to get paid. Macassar oil really did exist—for greasing hair; and
a world that used it must have been as nonsensical as any that could
be devised by an author. And the parody of Wordsworth's leech-
gatherer seems even more powerful now than in the nineteenth
century: what could be more foolish than paying money for leeches
to suck sick people's blood? Carroll plays here with literature and
language: with himself, in the guise of the nonsense-loving solipsistic
White Knight, with the farce of mutually misunderstanding minds,
with vocation, and with the queer arbitrariness that calls Rowland's
Macassar Oil and leeches sensible and "The Jabberwocky" nonsense.
Therefore, the lines also imply: "I write nonsense because nonsense
is reality."

The way of the *Looking-Glass* world is constant diversion. It turns
all sorts of subjects into games that can be played, often simultaneously, and mastered through comedy—e.g., philosophy, semantics, and religion. One of the most important is the mirror game,
whose main rule is reversal, i.e., literally considering things from
the very opposite of the conventional point of view. All of Carroll's

games, however, tend to be fluid, as befits a dream game, rather than fixed and rigid.

He structures the book on the model of a chess sequence, which he controls, and the implications of the game matter a great deal. In his parody of Huxley's universal game, he is the sole player.[3] He accepts the analogy of life to chess but makes it clear that his game, though it usually conforms to chess rules, is a loose, sliding contest ("The *alternation* of Red and White is perhaps not so strictly observed as it might be," says Carroll; and some of the characters move like chessmen, but some do not). This fussy man of exactitude and logic always notices and insists on the innate sloppiness and imprecision of being. A game, however, does serve nicely to point up the inscrutable, arbitrary nature of things. Carroll's play and game contribute to the insights of modern game theory, which, as Kathleen Blake says, "helps to reveal the literally artificial nature of our mental universe"(93). Games, like language, depend on agreed-upon conventions; but conventions do shift, and people may not be playing the same game by the same rules: in Huxley's chess match, the game of life is being played between each person and a supreme being who enforces the fixed laws of nature. In *Through the Looking-Glass*, with the authoritarian, Huxley-like Red (the Red Queen) versus mild-mannered Carrollian White (Alice as White pawn; the White Knight), Carroll rigs it so that White wins. He moves his characters about as if he were omnipotent and makes the game subservient to himself, the player. It provides the framework for the action, but he ignores its status when he wishes; for example, when the Red Queen puts the White King in check, nothing happens.

The chess game is diversion—one more element of Carroll's play, but not usually the primary focus of attention. Its climax, however, *is* crucial and makes for Carroll's version of a happy ending. According to the chess plan, Alice actually wins the match for her side: her sudden move, upsetting the Queen's banquet, eliminates the Red Queen and put the Red King in checkmate. *The child takes the power.* All these pieces are counters in their author's game. If the Red King in some sense stands for God, as the Tweedles' discussion with Alice indicates, and if Carroll identifies with Alice, then the structure of the game and the plot, as well as the thought and humor of the book, show the child winning out over God, Carroll winning out over the Reverend Mr. Dodgson, and comic regression and reversal winning out over orthodox religion.

The business about the Red King in the Tweedle chapter makes us see the kind of game Carroll was capable of playing with us and, oddly enough, with himself. When Tweedledum and Dee talk of

3. In his essay "A Liberal Education and Where to Find It" (1868), the scientist and writer Thomas Henry Huxley compares life to a chess game played against nature in which success depends on knowing the rules of the game, which are the laws of nature [*Editor*].

the Red King's dream, they parody Bishop Berkeley's view that all material objects are only " 'sorts of things' in the mind of God." In fact, I think Carroll means to associate the Tweedles particularly with Berkeley, who, after all, wrote *Siris*, a tract that began as a disquisition on "tar-water." The monstrous crow of the nursery rhyme, "as black as a tar-barrel," along with the Tweedle travesty of idealism, makes the identification likely. I think, also, that the Tweedles may represent bishops in the chess game; bishops are the only pieces that Carroll fails to mention directly or put on the board, and their absence would be glaring to a gamesman like himself.

It is all very strange but revealing: the author fears to put the word "bishop" in his story, rails elsewhere at looking "at solemn things in a spirit of mockery," yet somehow manages to make God a shabby plaything, whose defeat ends the game happily. To understand the Carroll of *Looking-Glass*, we must see that he not only could and would play with what a part of him held to be most serious and sacred, he would also play with the side of his own consciousness that made a subject taboo for comedy. He will sacrifice anything to his own play here—even the Reverend Charles Dodgson and God— because only the ability to play, in this text, can subject the chaos of reality and the disappointments of life to personal will.

Play, as such games-playing modern authors as Joyce, Nabokov, Borges, and Garcia Marquez attest, is a way of establishing order for the self in the midst of an absurd universe and of asserting one's own unconquered free spirit. Elizabeth Sewell, looking at Carroll from the point of view of an orthodox believer in God, writes: "If Carroll is to play with the whole of . . . life, always to be in control of it as a player must be, and as none other can, then he must be his own God" (180). He usurps the right of deity to play with all creation, and his desperate faith is that he can game and jest with anything, even his doubts.

For upon doubt Carroll builds his *Looking-Glass* house. One important difference between *Wonderland* and this book is that *Through the Looking-Glass* ends with questions rather than assertions: "Which do *you* think it was?" and "Life, what is it but a dream?" In this world, nothing is sure. Such doubt requires diversion and sets the wild comic imagination loose to play with senselessness and folly, which seem to be everywhere. "You might make a joke on *that*" and "Consider anything, only don't cry" are the humble twin commandments of Carroll's comic faith.

A. L. TAYLOR

[Chess and Theology in the Alice Books]†

*   *   *

Alice when she is a pawn is continually meeting chess-men, red and white, and according to the key, they are always on the square next to her on one side or the other. To the right, she meets the Red Queen, the Red King, the Red Knight, the White Knight and, at the end of the board, the Red Queen again. To the left, she meets the White Queen, the White King and, at the end of the board, the White Queen again. Of what is happening in the other parts of the board she has no knowledge. She sweeps a narrow track, and events more than one square distant to either side, or behind, or ahead of her, are out of her world. A certain lack of coherence in her picture of the game is understandable, particularly as it is in an advanced stage when she begins to move.

In the *Lewis Carroll Handbook*, Falconer Madan regrets that 'the chess framework is full of absurdities and impossibilities' and considers it a pity that Dodgson did not bring the game, as a game, up to chess standard, as, says Mr Madan, he could easily have done. He points out that among other absurdities the white side is allowed to make nine consecutive moves, the White King to be checked unnoticed; Queens castle, and the White Queen flies from the Red Knight when she could take it. 'Hardly a move,' he says, 'had a sane purpose, from the point of view of chess' (48–49). There is also a mate for White at the fourth move (Dodgson's reckoning): W.Q. to K.'s 3rd instead of Q.B.'s 4th. Alice and the Red Queen are both out of the way and the Red King could not move out of check.

Dodgson's own words, in a preface written in 1887, in reply to criticism of this kind, are as follows:

> As the chess problem given on the previous page has puzzled some of my readers, it may be well to explain that it is correctly worked out so far as the *moves* are concerned. The alternation of Red and White is perhaps not so strictly observed as it might be, and the 'castling' of the three Queens is merely a way of saying that they entered the palace; but the 'check' of the White King at move 6, the capture of the Red Knight at move 7, and the final 'checkmate' of the Red King, will be found, by any one who will take the trouble to set the pieces and play the moves as directed, to be strictly in accordance with the laws of the game.

He was not interested in the game as a game, but in the implications of the moves. Dodgson could easily have 'worked out a

† From *The White Knight* (Edinburgh: Oliver and Boyd, 1952) 100–110. Reprinted by permission of the author.

problem'. He spent a considerable part of his life doing that kind of thing. But in *Through the Looking-glass* he was otherwise engaged. In the first place it would be illogical to expect logic in a game of chess dreamed by a child. It would be still more illogical to expect a pawn which can see only a small patch of board to understand the meaning of its experiences. And there is a moral in that. This is a pawn's impression of chess, which is like a human being's impression of life.

Alice never grasps the purpose of the game at all and when she reaches the Eighth Square tries to find out from the two Queens if it is over. None of the pieces has the least idea what it is all about. The Red King is asleep. The White King has long ago abandoned any attempt to intervene. 'You might as well try to catch a Bandersnatch.' The Red Knight is quite justified in his battle-cry of 'Ahoy! Ahoy! Check!' but the White Knight, too, leaps out of the wood, shouting 'Ahoy! Ahoy! Check!' and he is not giving check at all but capturing the Red Knight. Neither of them has any control over the square on which Alice is situated, yet the Red Knight thinks he has captured her and the White Knight that he has rescued her. Alice cannot argue with either of them but is simply relieved to have the matter settled in a manner favourable to herself.

As for the Queens, they "see" so much of the board that they might be expected to know what is happening fairly well. But, as will appear, their manner of 'seeing' is so peculiar that they know less about it than anybody. To understand one's part in a game of chess, one would have to be aware of the room and the unseen intelligence which is combining the pieces. Deprived of any such knowledge, the chess-men have to explain things as best they can. Nor is this a game between two players. To have made it that would have been tantamount to a confession that he believed in two separate and opposite Powers above us. Dodgson deliberately avoided any such implication.

He based his story, not on a game of chess, but on a chess lesson or demonstration of the moves such as he gave to Alice Liddell, a carefully worked-out sequence of moves designed to illustrate the queening of a pawn, the relative powers of the pieces—the feeble king, the eccentric knight and the formidable queen whose powers include those of rook and bishop—and finally a checkmate. That is to say, he abstracted from the game exactly what he wanted for his design, and expressed that as a game between a child of seven-and-a-half who was to 'be' a White Pawn and an older player (himself) who was to manipulate the other pieces.

Only the other day, it will be remembered, Alice had had a long argument with her sister about playing kings and queens. Alice had been reduced at last to saying, 'Well, *you* can be one of them, then, and *I'll* be all the rest.' Through the Looking-glass she was 'one of

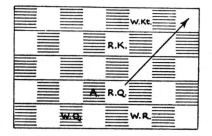

them' and the Other Player 'all the rest'. Perhaps that is how things are. Dodgson certainly hoped so.

Observe the Red Queen about to do her disappearing-trick:

> 'At the end of two yards,' she said, putting in a peg to mark the distance, 'I shall give you your directions—have another biscuit?'

The biscuit is deliberately used to distract our attention from the fact that these pegs mark out the stages of Alice's pawn-life.

> 'At the end of *three* yards I shall repeat them—for fear of your forgetting them. At the end of *four*, I shall say good-bye. And at the end of *five*, I shall go!'
> She had got all the pegs put in by this time, and Alice looked on with great interest as she returned to the tree, and then began slowly walking down the row.
> At the two-yard peg she faced round, and said, 'A pawn goes two squares in its first move.''

To demonstrate that, she had walked two yards. As a pawn starts from the second square, that takes us to the fourth square on the board. The third peg marks the fifth square, the fourth the sixth and the fifth the seventh. There is still another square, the eighth, but on that Alice will no longer be a pawn. ' "In the Eighth Square we shall be Queens together, and it's all feasting and fun!" '

The Red Queen had begun 'slowly walking down the row'. At the two-yard peg she paused to give Alice her instructions. Alice got up and curtseyed, and sat down again. At the next peg the Queen jerked out some staccato remarks. She did not wait for Alive to curtsey this time, but 'walked on quickly' to the next peg, where she turned to say goodbye and then 'hurried' on to the last. She was getting up speed. 'How it happened, Alive never knew, but exactly as she came to the last peg, she was gone.'

What happened we can represent but not really imagine. According to the key, the Red Queen moved away from Alive at an angle across the board (R. Q. to K. R.'s 4th). [See diagram above.] So long as the Red Queen was in the square next to her, Alice could

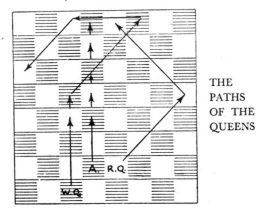

THE
PATHS
OF THE
QUEENS

see her and hear her, but when she steamed off in a direction which did not as yet exist for Alice, she simply vanished.

> Whether she vanished into the air, or ran quickly into the wood ('and she *can* run very fast!' thought Alice), there was no way of guessing, but she was gone, and Alice began to remember that she was a pawn, and that it would soon be time to move.

The moves of the two Queens are inexplicable to Alice because of a limitation in her powers. She is unable to conceive of such moves as R.Q. to K.R.'s 4th or W.Q. to Q.B.'s 4th. They can zigzag about the board, sweep from end to end of it if they like, or from side to side. She must laboriously crawl from square to square, always in one direction, with a half-remembered promise to spur her on: ' "In the Eighth Square we shall be Queens together, and it's all feasting and fun!" '

But if the length of the board is time, the breadth of the board must be time also, a kind of time known only to mathematicians and mystics: the kind of time we call eternity.

> For was and is, and will be are but is;
> And all creation is one act at once,
> The birth of light: but we that are not all
> As parts, can see but parts, now this now that,
> And live, perforce from thought to thought and make
> One act a phantom of succession; thus
> Our weakness somehow shapes the Shadow, Time.[1]

What Tennyson puts in poetry, Dodgson represented on his chessboard. [See diagram above.] Alice as she trotted along could see but

---

1. Alfred Lord Tennyson, *The Princess*, Part III: 307–13 [*Editor*].

parts, now the Red King to her right, now the White Queen to her left, but once she became a Queen there was a change:

> Everything was happening so oddly that she didn't feel a bit surprised at finding the Red Queen and the White Queen sitting close to her, one on each side: she would have liked very much to ask them how they came there,

(we can follow their moves by the key)

> but she feared it would not be quite civil.

She could see them both at once; in the language of psychology, she could attend to a plurality of impressions to which formerly she would have attended in succession.

However, she was by no means sure of herself or her crown as yet, and the Queens put her through her paces:

> 'In *our* country,' Alice remarked, 'there's only one day at a time.'
> The Red Queen said, 'That's a poor thin way of doing things. Now *here*, we mostly have days and nights two or three at a time, and sometimes in the winter we take as many as five nights together—for warmth, you know.'
> 'Are five nights warmer than one night, then?' Alice ventured to ask.
> 'Five times as warm, of course.'
> 'But they should be five times as *cold*, by the same rule—'
> 'Just so!' said the Red Queen. 'Five times as warm, *and* five times as cold—just as I'm five times as rich as you are, *and* five times as clever!'

(Note clever and rich as opposites here.)

> Alice sighed and gave it up. 'It's exactly like a riddle with no answer!' she thought.

It is, however, the answer to the 'chess-problem', or at any rate, one part of it, the checkmate which, Dodgson said in the 1887 Preface, was strictly in accordance with the laws of the game, while Mr Madan in the *Handbook* gives him the lie direct: 'whereas there is no attempt at one'.

According to the key, the position would appear to be: [see diagram on p. 378]. There is therefore something very like a checkmate and a fairly complicated one. The only objection is that the White King must have been in check while the White Queen moved to Q.R. 6th (soup) at Move 10. On the other hand, when Alice was on the Seventh Square she was still a pawn. The White King was behind her and if he had moved to Q.B. 5th she would not have known and he would not have been in check.

As to the succession of the moves, Dodgson admitted that was 'perhaps not so strictly observed as it might be'. When Alice reached the Eighth Square and became a Queen she naturally acquired new

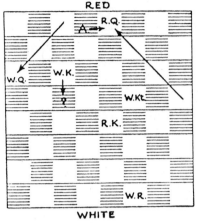

RED

'All sorts of things happened in a moment.'

WHITE

powers, but not all at once. She could now see from end to end of the board, but her sweep of vision from side to side was limited by the presence of the White Queen on one side and the Red Queen on the other. Whenever the White Queen moved to Q.R. 6th Alice had to wake up. ' "I can't stand this any longer!" she cried', and as the chess world collapsed in ruins she seized the Red Queen and accomplished the checkmate.

In the *New Method of Evaluation* Dodgson had shown that the University, like the Church of England and, in a still wider sense, the whole country, was broken up into two 'partial factions'. One of these, the Rationalist faction, had as its locus a superficies, and the other, the extreme High Church party, had as its locus a catenary 'known as the Patristic Catenary', which he defined as 'passing through Origen and containing many multiple points'. A Catenary is a curve formed by a cord or chain suspended at each end and acted upon only by gravity.

No doubt these notions, working in his mind, helped him towards the idea of the two Queens, those mighty opposites in chess, living on a surface which was actually curved and representing once more two partial factions in the University, the Church or the human mind.

'The Red Queen,' said Dodgson, in his *Theatre* article of 1887, 'I pictured as a Fury, but of another type: her passion must be cold and calm; she must be formal and strict, yet not unkindly; pedantic to the tenth degree' (I suspect that he wrote n-th here), 'the concentrated essence of all governesses!' Clearly, she is on the Dogmatic side. She lays down the law to Alice, stresses her title (Apostolic Succession), claims that all the walks belong to her, demands the use of French (Latin services?), the curtseying (genuflection). She is condescending, pats Alice on the head, and has 'heard nonsense, compared with which that would be as sensible as a dictionary'.

The biscuit which the Red Queen offered Alice as a thirst-quencher might be dry on the Looking-glass principle, simply as the opposite of a refreshing drink, or might partake of the woody nature of visible, tangible chess-pieces and be made of sawdust; but over and above these meanings, its dryness must be similar to that of the passage read by the mouse in *Alice*. ('This is the driest thing I know. Silence all round, if you please!') Shane Leslie suggests that the biscuits were sermons and it is true that the High Church sermons, regarded as of less importance than sacrament, were often perfunctory.

* * *

'Lastly,' said Dodgson in *The Theatre* of 1887, 'the White Queen seemed to my dreaming fancy, gentle, stupid, fat and pale; helpless as an infant; and with a slow maundering, bewildered air about her just suggesting imbecility, but never quite passing into it; that would be, I think, fatal to any comic effect she might otherwise produce.'
* * *

The White Queen has trouble with her shawl, and Alice has to help her to put it on again while the White Queen looks at her in a helpless, frightened sort of way and whispers something that sounds like 'bread-and-butter, bread-and-butter'. Compare this with Jowett singing the Articles for the sake of his tum-tum.[2]

Again, she had been 'a-dressing' herself. 'Every single thing's crooked,' Alice thought to herself, 'and she's all over pins!' These pins are no doubt the counterpart of the Red Queen's thorns. The latter was wearing a crown of thorns when Alice met her, only the thorns were turned outward. ' "She's one of the thorny kind," said the Rose.' Because she was a-dressing herself, because every single thing was crooked and she was all over pins, the White Queen must represent the side of the Church which argued, protested and tried to re-interpret religious ideas by the light of reason—the Protestant side of the Church of England and in particular the Rationalist 'mode of thinking'.

Alice herself does duty in the allegory for * * * the Church of England, though she certainly does not represent the Church of England as it was in Dodgson's day. Rather she is the essential quality of the Christian religion—the one all the sects seemed to have forgotten—love.

She took the place of Lily, the White Queen's Imperial Kitten—no doubt the Imperial Church of England which might be expected

2. When Benjamin Jowett, a classical scholar who later became master of Balliol College, Oxford, was named regius professor of Greek at Oxford in 1855, his appointment was protested on the ground that certain of his commentaries on some of the writings of Paul were doctrinally doubtful. Jowett agreed to re-subscribe to the Thirty-Nine Articles, the formulations of the doctrines of the established English church; at this time, subscription to the articles was a condition of receiving degrees from and holding appointments in Oxford or Cambridge [*Editor*].

to result from the first 'Pan-Anglican' Conference at Lambeth in 1867. That was why Lily was too young to play and also why she was the child of the King and Queen of Controversy. Alice was the True Church, hoping all things, believing all things, suffering long. In the *Theatre* article, she was to be 'loving as a dog' and 'gentle as a fawn', courteous

> even as though she were herself a King's daughter and her clothing of wrought gold: then trustful, ready to accept the wildest impossibilities with all that utter trust that only dreamers know; and lastly curious—and with the eager enjoyment of Life that comes only in the happy hours of childhood.

To have used a real chess-problem would have been fatal to the allegory, for it was by no means Dodgson's view that the opposition of the two sides Red and White, two aspects of the same Church, sprang from the operations of two Hostile Players. On the contrary, the two Queens are really two kittens who come from one cat, Dinah, and Dinah in Tenniel's final illustration is both black and white.

ELIZABETH SEWELL

The Balance of Brillig†

*   *   *

It is important to take a fairly wide field, because the authoritarian Humpty Dumpty, backed up later by Carroll himself, has suggested an over-simple explanation. Humpty Dumpty undertakes to interpret the hard words, says that *brillig* is four o'clock in the afternoon, when you start broiling things for dinner, and then goes on to *slithy* which he maintains is a combination of lithe and slimy: 'You see— it's like a portmanteau—there are two meanings packed up into one word.' To this Carroll adds in the Snark Preface: 'Humpty Dumpty's theory, of two meanings packed into one word like a portmanteau, seems to me the right explanation of all.' As Mr. Partridge[1] points out, this is no explanation of genuine inventions such as the *Jubjub*,

† From *The Field of Nonsense* (London: Chatto and Windus Ltd., 1952) 116–29. Reprinted by permission of the author and Chatto and Windus and The Hogarth Press.

In her study of the nonsense of Lewis Carroll and Edward Lear, Elizabeth Sewell describes the practices and purposes of nonsense as those of a game. A game she defines as "the active manipulation, serving no useful purpose, of a certain object or class of objects, concrete or mental, within a limited field of space and time and according to fixed rules, with the aim of producing a given result despite the opposition of chance and/or opponents" (27). The objects manipulated in the game of nonsense are

words, and in nonsense the mind uses words so that "its tendency towards order [will] engage its contrary tendency towards disorder, keeping the latter perpetually in play and so in check" (48). In the section of her book reprinted here, Sewell considers how nonsense uses language so that words and syntax maintain a balance between a disorder of discrete objects entirely without relation to one another, and the coherence and similitudes of dream or poetry.

1. Eric Partridge, "The Nonsense Words of Edward Lear and Lewis Carroll," in, *Here, There and Everywhere* (London: 1950) 162–88 [*Editor*].

or Lear's *Moppsikon-Floppsikon*. Alice herself seems reassuringly sceptical, for to Humpty's suggestion about *brillig* she replies, 'Yes, that will do very well,' which implies a good deal of reserve or at least the understanding that a number of other interpretations would do equally well. There is a more interesting remark earlier in the conversation, and it may be as well to start here rather than with the portmanteau theory. Alice and Humpty have been having a difference of opinion about the noun 'glory', to which Humpty attributes an entirely personal meaning. When Alice complains, Humpty says that he intends to be master of his own house, and continues with the remark that adjectives are pliable and verbs tough. 'They've a temper, some of them—particularly verbs: they're the proudest—adjectives you can do anything with, but not verbs.' It is certain that in Nonsense vocabulary nouns and adjectives play by far the biggest part. Mr. Partridge in his classification of the vocabulary of *Jabberwocky* gives four new verbs, *gimble, outgrabe, galumphing* and *chortled*, to ten new adjectives and eight new nouns. In the list of Lear's neologisms the proportions are even more marked, with over two pages of new nouns and a page of adjectives to six verbs and one adverb.

It is worth noticing at the beginning that it is possible to classify Nonsense words into the normal grammatical categories. This is something we take very much for granted with Lear and Carroll, but it need not necessarily be so. For example, no classification is possible in this bit of Lear gibberish:—

> There was an old man of Spithead,
> Who opened the window, and said—
> 'Fil-jomble, fil-jumble, Fil-rumble-come-tumble!'
> That doubtful old man of Spithead.

any more than in the ballad refrain 'Hi diddle inkum feedle!' Nonsense inventions which are to serve as nouns and which might be hard to identify in isolation, *dong* for instance, or *rath*, are given their context carefully, either by a definite or indefinite article, or by means of adjectives or other attributes: 'the dong with a luminous nose', or 'the mome raths'. Very often, too, they are given capital letters. The adjectives are nearly always recognizable by a typical adjectival suffix: *tulgey, uffish, manxome,* or Lear's *scroobious* and *borascible*. The verbs follow the same lines, and where form alone would be insufficient indication, syntax makes the word's function clear.

We can assume that the writers wanted their sentences containing Nonsense words to look like genuine sentences bearing reference, and that they found nouns and adjectives better for their purpose than verbs. If Nonsense words are to appear to be one of a class, it must be in order that they should carry conviction as words rather than gibberish. *Brillig, Cloxam, Willeby-Wat* have no more reference than *Hey nonny no* or *Hi diddle diddle*, but they seem to have, because they are presented to us as nouns or adjectives, and remind us of other words which have reference. As regards the preference for nouns and adjectives over verbs, it is interesting that Mallarmé, that most logical of poets, should have shared it to a marked degree. (*Vide* Jacques Scherer, *L'Expression Littéraire dans l'Œuvre de Mallarmé*, Droz, Paris, 1947, pp. 87–113). In logic, a verb expresses a relation, and this suggests two reasons for the few invented verbs in Nonsense. The first is the impossibility of inventing new relations in logic. The second is that a verb is an expressed relation, and relations in logic have to be simple and exact. If a Nonsense verb is invented, the mind can only deal with it as it deals with Nonsense words in general: it will produce from its memory all the other words the neologism resembles, and this will multiply relationships and associations in a manner quite alien to the operation of logic. The latter is concerned with implied relations between certain data, and it is well, therefore, to keep the expressed relations as simple as possible, since they are the groundwork. The verbs have to be simple because they are important. The terms and the nature of them, i.e. in this case nouns and adjectives, are, as we have seen, much less important to the working of the system, and so they can be played with to a much greater degree. An example from Carroll's *Symbolic Logic* will illustrate the point:—

(1) No kitten, that loves fish, is unteachable;
(2) No kitten without a tail will play with a gorilla;
(3) Kittens with whiskers always love fish;
(4) No teachable kitten has green eyes;
(5) No kittens have tails unless they have whiskers.

We can move on now to an example of Nonsense wording; a very short one will do to start with:—

> . . . and shun
> The frumious Bandersnatch.

The verb is simple and familiar; we are left with a noun and an adjective. Humpty Dumpty's commentary on the poem does not go beyond the first verse, but the similar phrase, 'the slithy toves' is dealt with as follows: 'Well "*slithy*" means "lithe and slimy" . . . "*toves*" are something like badgers—they're something like lizards— and they're something like corkscrews." The noun is treated as if it were a technical term, a label and no more, and is invested at once with Nonsense properties of the kind we have observed in the last few chapters. The adjective is an example of Humpty Dumpty's portmanteau, and *frumious* is of the same type. Carroll says of it in the Snark Preface that it is a combination of 'fuming' and 'furious'.

To take the adjectives first, *slithy* and *frumious*, it seems curious that Humpty Dumpty should have got by so easily on his portmanteau theory, for when one looks at it, it becomes very unsatisfactory. It would fit a pun well enough, in which there are precisely that—two meanings (or more than two) packed up in one word. But *frumious*, for instance, is not a word, and does not have two meanings packed up in it; it is a group of letters without any meaning at all. What Humpty Dumpty may have meant, but fails to say, is that it looks like two words, 'furious' and 'fuming', reminding us of both simultaneously. It is not a word, but it looks like other words, and almost certainly more than two. In the examples given below one can see the sort of thing that happens, for each mind will vary in the particular words recalled by these Nonsense formations. I give Mr. Partridge's, from *Here, There and Everywhere*, and my own.

FRUMIOUS:
> *Carroll*: furious, fuming.
> *Partridge*: frumpish, gloomy.
> *Myself*: fume, with a connection with French *brume* and English *brumous*, frumenty, rheumy.

BANDERSNATCH:
> *Partridge*: bandog, (?) *Bandar*, from Hindustani, snatching proclivities.
> *Myself*: Banshee and bandbox.

BORASCIBLE:
> *Partridge*: irascible, boring.
> *Myself*: Boreas, boracic, connection with Eastern Europe, through, I think, the prefix 'Bor', as in General BorKomorowski.

STAR-BESPRINGLED:
> *Partridge*: bespangled and besprinkled.
> *Myself*: connection with 'tingled', through the Tennysonian line: 'A cry that shivered to the tingling stars'; the name 'Pringle', connecting with dress-making (? through a story), also perhaps 'pin-prick'.

MOPPISIKON-FLOPPSIKON BEAR:
> *Partridge*: 'with a great *mop* of hair and a *floppy* gait?'
> *Myself*: Connection with Russia, through the 'ikon' ending. (Cf. Partridge's comment on 'Soffsky-Poffsky trees': 'of Siberian habitat?')

These are not intended as interpretations. They merely show that these words, though possessing no meaning themselves, remind the reader of many words which have reference. Nonsense words which do not act in this way, *Jubjub*, for instance, must have their function as technical terms made clear at once, and this in fact is what happens:

Beware the Jubjub bird . . .

Should we meet with a Jubjub, that desperate bird,
We shall need all our strength for the job!

On the whole, however, the first of these two forms is the commoner, a Nonsense word reminding the mind of other words which it resembles. It is important, for if a word does not look like a word, so to speak, the mind will not play with it. Carroll coins examples of this sort, *Mhruxian* and *grurmstipths* from *Tangled Tales* or the 'occasional exclamation' of the Gryphon, *Hjckrrh* from *The Mock Turtle's Story*. Words such as these do not interest the mind; but dongs and toves look strangely familiar, and the mind can enjoy itself with them. Mr. Partridge has some delightful examples, making Lear's *Gramblamble* into *Grand Lama? grand brambles?* or Carroll's *Ipwergis* pudding from *Sylvie and Bruno* into *Walpurgis* and *haggis*. We are left with a half-conscious perception of verbal likenesses, and, in consequence, the evocation of a series of words.

It looks as if Nonsense were running on to dangerous ground here, for two of its rules are (*a*) no likenesses are to be observed, and (*b*) no trains of association are to be set up. At this point we shall have to go back to the Snark Preface for a moment, for, although we have rejected Carroll's suggestion that Humpty Dumpty's theory will cover all the Nonsense words, making the portmanteau into an umbrella, there is an interesting remark a little later on. Discussing the alternative of saying 'fuming-furious' or 'furious-fuming', Carroll says, 'but if you have that rarest of gifts, a perfectly balanced mind, you will say "frumious".' It is a hint that here as elsewhere Nonsense is maintaining some kind of balance in its language.[2] After all, Humpty Dumpty who is the chief language expert in the Alices is himself in such a state; Carroll could have made any of his characters discourse upon words, and it is interesting that the one who in fact does so was 'sitting, with his legs crossed like a Turk, on the top of a high wall—such a narrow one that Alice quite wondered how he could keep his balance.' * * *

Nonsense has a fear of nothingness quite as great as its fear of everythingness. Mr. Empson says in *Some Versions of the Pastoral* that the fear of death is one of the crucial topics of the Alices, but it will be simpler for us at present to think of it as a fear of nothingness.

. . . 'for it might end, you know," said Alice to herself, "in my going out altogether, like a candle. I wonder what I should be like then?' "

'You know very well you're not real.'
'I *am* real!' said Alice, and began to cry.

---

2. Belle Moses in *Lewis Carroll in Wonderland and at Home* (New York: 1910) quotes him as saying of his Nonsense language, 'A perfectly balanced mind could understand it' (6).

The Snark breaks the rules here, for in Fit the Seventh someone has 'softly and suddenly vanished away', that is, has become nothingness. Nonsense does not deal in any kind of physical or metaphysical nothingness, one needs to remember. It deals in words. Where these are normal and are acting normally, there cannot be a nothingness in so far as they are concerned, for words have reference to experience. 'Word implies relation to creatures' (Aquinas, *Summa* [*Theological*], Pt. I, Q. 34, Art. 4). The only way in which nothingness could set in might be by some sort of separation between words and things, by things having no words attached to them or by words without reference to things. It comes down to a question of names.

Names come in for a good deal of attention in the Alices. 'What's your name, child?' is the first remark of the Queen of Hearts to Alice. Humpty Dumpty also enquires what her name is, but makes the rather interesting remark that it is unsatisfactory because it does not mean anything. Alice questions the need for names to mean anything, but Humpty insists on the point, as if he were trying to set up a closer connection between the name and the thing, in the case of proper nouns. Generally, we use proper nouns as pointers and nothing more. Poetry makes much use of this, using them where possible as series of lovely sounds but not entirely devoid of reference or at least of connections, since they have associational power if not much in the way of content. * * *

Nonsense, as we have seen, eschews beauty, but its proper nouns work in the same way as these, though the associations are verbal, the isles of Boshen recalling the Biblical land of Goshen, Chankly Bore seeming a metamorphosis of Branksome Chine, Tinniskoop of Tinnevelly and so on. The names in Nonsense are not nothingness; they work by association, as the names in poetry do, but their associations are with words. Here, too, in its own way, Nonsense preserves the connection between these names and things, and we are given details:—

> Landing at eve near the Zemmery Fidd
> Where the Oblong Oysters grow
> (Lear, *The Dong with a Luminous Nose*)

. . . the Soffsky-Poffsky trees,—which were . . . covered with blue leaves . . .

> (Lear, *The Seven Families*)

Of the Jubjub:—

> Its flavour when cooked is more exquisite far
> Than mutton, or oysters, or eggs:
> (Some think it keeps best in an ivory jar,
> And some, in mahogany kegs).

Nothingness in all these cases is successfully defeated by the number of the verbal reminiscences called up by the Nonsense words, by their close association with things, and by illustrations. The Jabberwock is pictured for us, and so are the Pobble and the Dong and the Jumblies and nearly all of Lear's inventions. The Nonsense words are sufficiently protected from nothingness; but what happens if the reverse process takes place, and things are separated from words in some way, becoming nameless?

It is interesting that such a case is dealt with explicitly in *Through the Looking-Glass*, in Alice's entry into the wood where things have no name. This is at the end of Chapter III, *Looking-Glass Insects*, a very significant chapter despite its rather limited title, for it is all about words and names. It starts with Alice trying to make a survey of the country and attempting to name, as one might do in geography, the mountains and rivers and towns. Then comes the scene in the railway carriage * * * with [its] remark, 'Language is worth a thousand pounds a word!' Soon after this, two remarks are made to Alice about knowing her own name and knowing the alphabet, and then begins a series of puns, made by the Gnat. It is as if, having got words and references put together at this point (as they were not at the beginning of the chapter, where Alice says, 'Principal mountains—I'm on the only one, but I don't think it's got any name') and having realized the value of it—worth a thousand pounds a word—one can start playing with it. Puns, as we have seen, are a safe enough game for Nonsense, because they are real portmanteaux, where the two meanings are distinct but are incongruously connected by an accident of language formation. After the puns, Alice and the Gnat discuss the purpose of names, and whether they have any use. Then follows another game with words: Alice's horse-fly becomes a rocking-horse-fly, the butterfly a bread-and-butter-fly. A piece of each word is allowed to develop, rather as Lear's people develop enormous noses, all out of proportion. Images in Nonsense are not allowed to develop, to turn into or mingle with other images as happens in dreams and poetry; but words may do so, provided they merely develop into another word, and by their development accentuate an incongruity. Here again, circumstantial details are given at once: 'Its wings are thin slices of bread-and-butter, its body is a crust, and its head is a lump of sugar.' Looking-Glass Insects, in fact, are not insects at all but compounds of words to which are added lists of properties in the best Nonsense manner.

The next stage is a further discussion on names. 'I suppose you don't want to lose your name? . . . only think how convenient it would be if you could manage to go home without it!' Alice is a little nervous about such an idea, and the Wood where things have no names, to which she proceeds immediately after this conversation, is frighteningly dark. Once in it, she cannot remember her own name or give a name to any of the objects round her. This is a terrifying situation, but Carroll preserves the readers from it by subjecting Alice alone to the experiment; the passage in the book makes no attempt to forgo the use of names. It is at this point that Alice meets the Fawn, a pretty creature 'with its large gentle eyes . . . Such a sweet soft voice it had!' It asks her name, and she makes a similar enquiry, but neither can remember, and they proceed lovingly—the word is Carroll's own—till they emerge from the wood. There each remembers its name and identity, and in a flash they are parted.

This passage is one of the most interesting in the Alices. There is a suggestion here that to lose your name is to gain freedom in some way, since the nameless one would no longer be under control: 'There wouldn't by any name for her to call, and of course you wouldn't have to go, you know.' It also suggests that the loss of language brings with it an increase in loving unity with living things. It is words that separate the fawn and the child, just as they separate the Yonghy-Bonghy-Bò and his love in that wood of Bong-trees where we began:—

> 'Though you're such a Hoddy Doddy,
> Yet I wish that I could modi-
>   fy the words I needs must say!
> Will you please to go away?'

Nonsense is a game with words. Its own inventions wander safely between the respective pitfalls of o and 1, nothingness and everythingness; but where words without things are safe enough, things without words are far more dangerous. To have no name is to be a kind of nothing:—

> 'What do you call yourself?' the Fawn said . . .
> She answered rather sadly, 'Nothing just now.'

But it is also to have unexpected opportunities for unity and that is a step towards everythingness. We are safe with *brillig* and the *Jabberwock* because that is a fight, a dialectic and an equilibrium; but despite the Yonghy-Bonghy-Bò and the Bong-trees—words which as we have seen play the Nonsense game in the usual way—and despite the early pumpkins and the jug without a handle, something has crept in here which words cannot cover, cannot split up and control. There is a nostalgia in each of these scenes:—

> Alice stood looking after it, almost ready to cry with vexation at having lost her dear little fellow-traveller so suddenly.

> On that coast of Coromandel,
> In his jug without a handle
>   Still she weeps, and daily moans;

On that little heap of stones
To her Dorking hens she moans . . .

But Nonsense can admit of no emotion—that gate to everythingness
and nothingness where ultimately words fail completely. It is a game
to which emotion is alien, and it will allow none to its playthings,
which are words and those wielders of words, human beings. Its
humans, like its words and things and Nonsense vocabulary, have
to be one, and one, and one. There is nothing more inexorable than
a game.

MICHAEL HOLQUIST

What Is a Boojum? Nonsense and Modernism†

The other project was a scheme for entirely abolishing all words whatsoever; and this was
urged as a great advantage in point of health as well as brevity. . . . An expedient was therefore
offered, that since words are only names for things, it would be more convenient for all men
to carry about them such things as were necessary to express the particular business they are
to discourse on.
—Swift, *Gulliver's Travels*

What am I to do, what shall I do, what should I do, in my situation, how proceed? By aporia
pure and simple? Or by affirmations and negations invalidated as uttered?
—Samuel Beckett, *The Unnamable*

Because the question "What is a Boojum," may appear strange
or whimsical, I would like to begin by giving some reasons for posing
it. Like many other readers, I have been intrigued and perplexed by
a body of literature often called modern or post-modern, but which
is probably most efficiently expressed in a list of authors: Joyce, Kafka,
Beckett, Nabokov, Borges, Genet, Robbe-Grillet[1]—the list could be
extended, but these names will probably suffice to suggest, if very
roughly, the tradition I have in mind. The works of these men are all
very dissimilar to each other. However, they seem to have something
in common when compared not to themselves as a class, but to past
literature. In casting about for specific terms which might define this
vaguely felt sense of what was distinctive and yet shared in these
works, two things constantly inhibited any progress. The first was
one's sense of the ridiculous: aware of other attempts to define the
modern, one knew that it was difficult to do so without becoming
shrill or unduly chiliastic. There is a group of critics, of whom Ihab
Hassan and Nathan Scott might be considered representative, who
insist on an absolute cut-off between all of previous history and the

† From *Yale French Studies* 43 (1969): 145–
64. Reprinted by permission of the publisher
and the author.
1. Jorge Luis Borges is an Argentine poet and
writer of fiction; Jean Genet is a dramatist; and
Alain Robbe-Grillet is a novelist and writer of screenplays. Like that of Joyce, Kafka, Beckett,
and Nabokov their work is frequently charac-
terized by themes and devices that emphasize
that literature is a fabrication, a created reality
in a world in which illusion and reality are
difficult to distinguish [*Editor*].

modern experience. They have in their characteristically humorless way taken seriously Virginia Woolf's remark that "on or about December, 1910 human nature changed."[2] The work of these critics is easily recognized in the apocalyptic rhetoric which distinguishes their writing, and in the irresponsible application they make of terms derived from modern German philosophy. Some rather thick books on the subject of recent literature could easily be reduced in size through the simple expedient of excising any mention of *Heimweh, Geworfenheit*, and that incantory word, *Angst*.[3] So one thing which made it difficult to get at distinctive features in recent literature was the sense that it was very different from previous literature; and at the same time to recognize that it was not the end of history.

Another stumbling block, much less serious, was the constant recurrence of a phrase, which continually passed through my mind as I would read new works. I would read that Gregor Samsa woke up one morning to discover that he was an *Ungeziefer*,[4] and immediately a ghostly refrain would be heard in my inner ear: "Aha, for the Snark *was* a Boojum, you see!" The same thing would happen when in [Vladimir Nabokov's] *Lolita*, one discovered that all those strange men following Humbert were Quilty; or when reading in Gombrowicz that there was nothing to identity but the grimace [geba];[5] and so on and on—one kept hearing "The Snark *was* a Boojum, you see." Pausing to reflect on this, the association of Lewis Carroll with modern literature seemed natural enough: his name figures in the first Surrealist manifesto (1924); Louis Aragon and André Breton write essays on Carroll; the former attempts a translation of *The Snark* (1920), the latter includes selections from Carroll in his *Anthologie de l'humour noir* (1939). Henri Parisot publishes a study of Carroll in 1952, in a series called, significantly, *Poetes d'aujourd hui*; Antonin Artaud tried to translate the Jabberwocky song; Joyce's use of portmanteau words, without which there would be no *Finnegans Wake*, is only one index of his high regard for Carroll; Borges admires Carroll, and Nabokov translates all of *Alice in Wonderland* into Russian (*Anja v strane chudes*, 1932).[6] But such

---

2. Virginia Woolf's remark is in her essay "Mr. Bennett and Mrs. Brown," first published in 1923 and collected in *The Captain's Death Bed and Other Essays* (1950). Ihab Hassan and Nathan Scott are critics of twentieth-century literature who have emphasized how modern writers begin in isolation from the past and work in their books to their own structures of belief [*Editor*].

3. *Heimweh*: a longing for home, or for the certainty of the past; *Geworfenheit*: a sense of exile, of having been cast out; *Angst*: fearful anxiety [*Editor*].

4. Gregor Samsa is the central character in Franz Kafka's *Metamorphosis* (1916); he turns into an insect [*Editor*].

5. Witold Gombrowicz (1904–69) wrote his novels and plays in Polish, although he lived much of his life in South America, Berlin, and Paris; probably his best-known novel, *Ferdydurke* (1937), was translated into English in 1961 [*Editor*].

6. Louis Aragon and André Breton were among the founders of the surrealist movement in France; Aragon later broke with the movement and became a Marxist. Henri Parisot has edited several volumes of fantastic and hallucinatory poetry. Antonin Artaud was a director and playwright who advocated the use of starkly violent and primitive image and action, a "theater of cruelty," in one of the best-known formulations of his ideas [*Editor*].

obvious associations of Carroll with modern authors were not, it turned out, the reason why the *Boojum* kept raising its head as I read these men.

Finally I picked up again, after many years, *The Hunting of the Snark*, and it soon became apparent why its final line kept popping up in connection with modern literature: Lewis Carroll's "agony in eight fits" was not only among the first to exemplify what is perhaps the most distinctive feature of modern literature, it did so more openly, more paradigmatically than almost any other text one knew. That is, it best dramatized the attempt of an author to insure through the structure of his work that the work could be perceived only as what it was, and not some other thing; the attempt to create an immaculate fiction, a fiction that resists the attempts of readers, and especially those readers who write criticism, to turn it into an allegory, a system equatable with already existing systems in the non-fictive world * * *

The *Snark* is the most perfect nonsense which Carroll created in that it best exemplifies what all his career and all his books sought to do: achieve pure order. For nonsense, in the writings of Lewis Carroll, at any rate, does not mean gibberish; it is not chaos, but the opposite of chaos. It is a closed field of language in which the meaning of any single unit is dependent on its relationship to the system of the other constituents. Nonsense is "a collection of words or events which in their arrangement do not fit into some recognized system" [Elizabeth Sewell, *The Field of Nonsense*, 25], but which constitute a new system of their own. As has recently been said, "what we have learned from Saussure is that, taken singly, signs do not signify anything, and that each one of them does not so much express a meaning as mark a divergence of meaning between itself and other signs . . . The prior whole which Saussure is talking about cannot be the explicit and articulate whole of a complete language as it is recorded in grammars and dictionaries . . . the unity he is talking about is a unity of coexistence, like that of the sections of an arch which shoulder one another. In a unified whole of this kind, the learned parts of a language have an immediate value as a whole, and progress is made less by addition and juxtaposition than by the internal articulation of a function which in its own way is already complete."[7] My argument here is that *The Hunting of the Snark* constitutes such a whole; it is its own system of signs which gain their meaning by constantly dramatizing their differences from signs in other systems. The poem is, in a small way, its own language. This is difficult to grasp because its elements are bound up so closely

7. Maurice Merleau-Ponty, "Indirect Language and the Voices of Silence," *Signs*, tr. Richard C. McCleary (Evanston: Northwestern UP, 1964) 39–40. [Ferdinand de Saussure (1857–1913) was a linguist whose best-known work was translated into English as *A Course in General Linguistics* [*Editor*].

with the syntax, morphology, and, fleetingly, the semantics of the English language.

Some illustrations, taken from Carroll, may help us here. In the book which most closely approximates the completeness of the system in the *Snark*, *Through the Looking-Glass*, Humpty Dumpty says in a famous passage: " 'When *I* use a word . . . it means just what I choose it to mean—neither more nor less.' 'The question is,' said Alice, 'whether you *can* make words mean so many different things.' 'The question is,' said Humpty Dumpty, 'which is to be master— that's all.' " This last remark is a rebuke to Alice, who has not understood the problem: it is not, as she says, to "make words mean so many *different* things." It is to make a word mean just *one* thing, the thing which its user intends and nothing else. Which is to be master—the system of language which says " 'glory' doesn't mean 'a nice knockdown argument' " or Humpty who says it does mean that, and in his system, only that. Nonsense is a system in which, at its purest, words mean only one thing, and they get that meaning through divergence from the system of the nonsense itself, as well as through divergence from an existing language system. This raises, of course, the question of how one understands nonsense. It is a point to which I will return later; for the moment suffice it to say that if meaning in nonsense is dependent on the field it constructs, then the difference between nonsense and gibberish is that nonsense is a system which can be learned, as languages are learned. Thus the elements of the system can be perceived relationally, and therefore meaningfully, within it. Gibberish, on the other hand, is unsystematic.

What this suggests is that nonsense, among other things, is highly abstract. It is very much like the pure relations which obtain in mathematics, where ten remains ten, whether ten apples, ten horses, ten men or ten Bandersnarks. This is an important point, and helps to define one relationship of nonsense to modernism. For it suggests a crucial difference between nonsense and the absurd. The absurd points to a discrepancy between purely human values and purely logical values. When a computer announces that the best cure for brain cancer is to amputate the patient's head, it is, according its system, being logical.[8] But such a conclusion is unsettling to the patient and absurd to less involved observers. The absurd is a contrast between systems of human belief which may lack all logic, and the extremes of a logic unfettered by human disorder. Thus the absurd is basically play with order and disorder. Nonsense is play with order only. It achieves its effects not from contrasting order and confusion, but rather by contrasting one system of order against another system

---

8. For raising the problems of the relationship between nonsense and the absurd, and for the computer example, I am grateful to my friend Jan Kott.

of order, each of which is logical in itself, but which cannot find a place in the other. This distinction may help to account for the two dominant modes of depersonalization in recent literature. The absurd operates in the theater, where the contrast of human/non-human serves to exploit the presence of living actors on the stage. Nonsense, understood as defined above, dominates in prose fictions, where the book may become its own hermetic world, its own laboratory for systematic play, without the anthropomorphizing presence of actors. * * *

The best argument against the *Snark*'s allegorization remains, of course, the poem itself. The interpretation which follows is based not only on the poem itself, but on the various ways in which it *is* itself. That is, the poem is best understood as a structure of resistances to other structures of meaning which might be brought to it. The meaning of the poem consists in the several strategies which hedge it off as itself, which insure its hermetic nature against the herme-neutic impulse. Below are six of the many ways by which the poem gains coherence through inherence.

1. The dedication poem to Gertrude Chataway appears at first glance to be simply another of those treacly Victorian set pieces Dodgson would compose when he abandoned nonsense for what he sometimes thought was serious literature. But a second reading re-veals that the poem contains an acrostic: the first letter of each line spells out Gertrude Chataway; a third reading will show that the initial word in the first line of each of the four quatrains constitute another acrostic, Girt, Rude, Chat, Away. This is the first indication in the poem that the words in it exist less for what they denote in the system of English then they do for the system Carroll will erect. That is, the initial four words of each stanza are there less to indicate the four meanings present in them before they were deployed by Carroll they at first convey (clothed, wild, speak, begone) than they are to articulate a purely idiosyncratic pattern of Carroll's own devising.

2. Another index of the systematic arbitrariness of the poem is found in the second quatrain of the first Fit: "Just the place for a Snark! I have said it twice: / That alone should encourage the crew. / Just the place for a Snark! I have said it thrice: / What I tell you three times is true." The rule of three operates in two ways. First of all it is a system for determining a truth that is absolutely unique to this poem. When in Fit 5 the Butcher wishes to prove that the scream he had heard belongs to a Jubjub bird, he succeeds in doing so by repeating three times, "Tis the voice of the Jubbub!" Now, there will be those who say that there is no such thing as a Jubjub bird. But in fact, in the system of the Snark poem, there is—and

his existence is definitively confirmed through the proof which that system *itself* provides in the rule of 3. In the game of nonsense that rule, and only that rule, works. The system itself provides the assurance that only it can give meaning to itself.

The rule of three also operates as a marker, indicating that the intrinsic logic of the poem is *not* that of extrinsic logic which operates in systems outside the construct of the poem. In other words, it is a parody of the three components of that core element in traditional logic, the syllogism. As an example of this, take an exercise from Dodgson's own book, *Symbolic Logic* (1896): "No one has read the letter but John; No one, who has *not* read it, knows what it is about." The answer is, of course, "No one but *John* knows what the letter is about." The third repetition "Tis the voice of the Jubjub," has the same effect in nonsense that the third part of the syllogistic progression has in logic. The *Oxford Universal Dictionary* defines a syllogism as a major and a minor premise, "with a third proposition called the conclusion, *resulting necessarily from the other two.*" If you begin with nonsense, and its conclusion, like the syllogism, results necessarily from the beginning, you also end with nonsense. The progression is closed to other systems. It is not, incidentally, without significance for Carroll's play with words that the etymology of syllogism is a portmanteau from the Greek *syllogizesthai* (to reckon together) and *logizesthai* (to reason) which has its root, *logos.*

3. The same effect of an arbitrariness whose sense can be gleaned only from the poem itself is to be found in the various names of the crew members: Bellman, Boots, Bonnet-maker, Barrister, Broker, Billiard-marker, Banker, Beaver, Baker, and Butcher. They all begin with a B. And much ink has been spilled in trying to explain (from the point of view of the allegory a given critic has tried to read into the *Snark*) why this should be so. The obvious answer, if one resists the impulse to substitute something else for the text, is that they all begin with B *because they all begin with B.* The fact that they all have the same initial sound is a parallel that draws attention to itself because it is a parallel. But it is only a parallel at the level where all the crew members on this voyage will be referred to by nouns which have an initial voiced bilabial plosive. In other words, it is a parallel that is rigidly observed, which dramatizes itself, but only as a dynamic *process* of parellelism, and nothing else.

4. Another way in which the poem sets up resistances which frustrate allegory is to be found in the fifth Fit. The butcher sets out to prove that two can be added to one. "Taking three as the subject to reason about— / A convenient number to state— / We add seven and ten, and then multiply out / By one thousand dimished by eight.

The result we proceed to divide, as you see, / By nine hundred and ninety and two: / Then subtract seventeen, and the answer must be / Exactly and perfectly true."

And in fact the answer is perfectly true—but it is also what you begin with. The equation begins with 3—the number the Butcher is trying to establish—and it ends with 3. The math of the equation looks like this:

$$\frac{(X + 7 + 10)(1000 - 8)}{992} - 17 = X; \text{which simplifies to x, or a pure integer.}$$

The equation is a process which begins with no content and ends with no content. It is a pure process which has no end other than itself. It is thus perhaps the best paradigm of the process of the whole poem: it does what it is about. It is pure surface, but as Oscar Wilde once observed, "there is nothing more profound than surface."

5. A fifth way in which the poem maintains its structural integrity is found in the many coinages it contains, words which Humpty Dumpty defines as portmanteau words, two meanings packed into one word like a portmanteau; words which Giles Deleuze, in the most comprehensive study of Carroll's significance for language, *Logique du Sens*, has so charmingly translated as "les mots-valies" [Paris: 1969, 59, 268–78]. Carroll, in the introduction to the *Snark* writes, ". . . take the two words 'fuming' and 'furious.' Make up your mind that you will say both words, but have it unsettled which you will say first. Now open your mouth and speak. If your thoughts incline ever so little towards 'fuming' you will say 'fuming-furious;' if they turn by even a hair's breadth towards 'furious,' you will say 'furious-fuming;' but if you have that rarest of gifts, a perfectly balanced mind, you will say 'frumious.' "

"If you have that rarest of gifts, a balanced mind . . . ," in other words, you will find just the right word, and not some approximation. In the seventh Fit, when the Banker is attacked by the Bandersnatch, the bird is described as having "frumious jaws." And the Banker, utterly shaken, chants "in the mimsiest tones," a combination of miserable and flimsy. For a bird which exists only in the system of nonsense, adjectives used to describe objects in other systems will not do; they are not precise enough, and so the system itself provides its own adjective for its own substantive. Since only the Banker has ever been attacked by a Bandersnatch, it is necessary to find a unique adjective adequate to this unique experience: thus "mimsiest." This attempt to find just the right word, and no other, resulting finally in coinages, is another way in which Carroll's search for precision, order, relates him to language as an innovative process in modern literature. Carroll speaks of "that rarest of gifts, a balanced mind" as the source of his experiment. In our own century it was a man remarkable for *not* possessing that gift who has best expressed the pathos of its absense in the face of language. In one of his fragments Antonin Artaud says "there's no correlation for me between *words* and the exact states of my being . . . I'm the man who's best felt the astounding disorder of his language in its relation to his thought."[9] Carroll's portmanteau words are revealing not only for the way they participate in the self-insuring autonomy of the poem. They also provide an illustration of how Carroll's nonsense is grounded in a logic of surface. The portmanteau word is not only a combination of two definitions, it is a combination of two systems, language and logic. Mention was made earlier of Saussure's insight into the way language *means* through *divergence*. The portmanteau word creates a new meaning by phonologically exploiting the divergence between two old meanings. It thus provides one of the most economical proofs of Saussure's insight into language. But the portmanteau word is also the third element of a three part progression, from one, furious, to two, fuming, to three, frumious. Like the rule of three it results in a new "truth," and like the rule of three it is a unique kind of syllogism. In order to get a logical conclusion to the syllogism, it must grow out of a divergence between two prior parallel statements.

This is an important point if one is to see the logic which determines that Carroll's system is a *language* and not gibberish. * * * Carroll's nonsense is just such an extrapolation, it is the transcendence of the post hoc, ergo propter hoc principle into an aesthetic. Carroll's portmanteaux are *words* and not gibberish because they operate according to the rule which says that all coinages in the poem will grow out of the collapse of two known words into a new one. Carroll can deploy words he invents and still communicate because he does so according to rules. Whereas an expression of gibberish would be a sound pattern whose meaning could not be gleaned from its *use* according to rules: an expression of gibberish would be a sound pattern whose meaning could not be gleaned either from the syntactic or morphological principles provided by its use, or which would be deducible according to such principles in a known language system. Nonsense, like gibberish, is a violence practiced on semantics. But since it is systematic, the sense of nonsense can be learned. And that is the value of it: it calls attention to language. Carroll's nonsense keeps us honest; through the process of disorientation and learning which reading him entails, we are made aware again that language is not something we know, but something alive, in process—something to be discovered.

9. *Artaud Anthology*, ed. Jack Hirshman (San Francisco, 1965) 37.

6. The final structure of resistance I'd like to mention is contained in perhaps the most obvious feature of the poem, its rhyme. William K. Wimsatt, in a well-known essay, makes the point that in a poem the rhyme imposes "upon the logical pattern of expressed argument a kind of fixative counterpattern of alogical implication." He goes on to say that "rhyme is commonly recognized as a binder in verse structure. But where there is need for binding there must be some difference or separation between the things to be bound. If they are already close together, it is supererogatory to emphasize this by the maneuver of rhyme. So we may say that the greater the difference in meaning between rhyme words the more marked and the more appropriate will be the binding effect."[1] This important insight into verse is contained in a piece entitled "One Relation of Rhyme to Reason." Now, Lewis Carroll wrote a book entitled *Rhyme? and Reason?* (1883), and I suggest that the distinctive role which rhyme plays in the *Snark* is best caught by means of a titular portmanteau here. That is, it is precisely that one relation of rhyme to reason which Professor Wimsatt evokes in *his* title, which is put into question marks not only by *Carroll's* title of 1883, but which is also put into question in the function rhyme serves in *The Hunting of the Snark*.

Professor Wimsatt suggests that "the words of a rhyme, with their curious harmony of sound and distinction of sense, are an amalgam of the sensory and the logical, or an arrest and precipitation of the logical in sensory form; they are the icon in which the idea is caught" (165). I read this to mean that two words which are disparate in meaning result, when bound by rhyme, in a new meaning which was not contained in either of them alone. In other words, you get a kind of rule of three at work. Like the syllogism, two disparate but related elements originate a third. Thus understood, the rhyme of traditional verse has the effect of meaningful surprise; two rhymes will constitute a syllogism resulting in a new association.[2]

But this is not true of nonsense verse. "They sought it with thimbles, they sought it with care; / They pursued it with forks and hope; / They threatened its life with a railway-share; / They charmed it with smiles and soap." This stanza begins each of the last four Fits, and may stand as an example for what rhyme does throughout the poem. The rhyme words, "care, railway-share," and "hope, soap" would be very different from each other in traditional verse, and binding effects of the sort Professor Wimsatt has demonstrated in Pope or Byron would be possible. Because the language of most verse is simply a more efficiently organized means of making sense of the sort that language *outside* verse provides. Thus, while very different,

1. *The Verbal Icon*, 3rd edition (New York: 1963) 153.
2. For a detailed study of sound/sense patterns
in verse see: A. Kibedi Varga, *Les Constantes du poème* (The Hague, 1963) 39–42, 91–121.

some kind of meaningful association could be made of them capable of catching an idea.

But "care," "railway-share," "hope" and "soap" in this quatrain have as their ambiance *not* the semantic field of the English language, but the field of Carroll's nonsense. In traditional verse "rhyme words . . can scarcely appear in a context without showing some difference of meaning" [Wimsatt 156]. But if the whole context of a poem is *without* meaning, its separate parts will also lack it. There can be no differences in meaning between words because they are all equally meaningless in this context. So the reader who attempts to relate rhyme to meaning in Carroll's poem will be frustrated. The syllogism of rhyme, which in other verse has a new meaning as its conclusion, ends, in Carroll's verse, where it began. Instead of aiding meaning, it is another strategy to defeat it. Language in nonsense is thus a seamless garment, a pure cover, absolute surface.

But if *The Hunting of the Snark* is an absolute metaphor, if it means only itself, why read it? There are several answers, but the one I have chosen to give here is that it may help us to understand other, more complex attempts to do the same thing in modern literature. It is easy to laugh at the various casuistries by which readers have sought to make an allegory, something else, out of the *Snark*. But the same sort of thing is being done every day to Kafka or Nabokov. Possibly the example of Lewis Carroll may suggest how far we must go, how much we must forget, how much we must learn in order to see fiction as fiction.

For the moral of the *Snark* is that it has no moral. It is a fiction, a thing which does not seek to be "real" or "true." The nineteenth-century was a great age of system building and myth makers. We are the heirs of Marx and Freud, and many other prophets as well, all of whom seek to explain *everything*, to make sense out of *everything* in terms of one system or another. In the homogenized world which resulted, it could be seen that art was nothing more than another—and not necessarily privileged—way for economic or psychological forces to express themselves. As Robbe-Grillet says, "Cultural fringes (bits of psychology, ethics, metaphysics, etc.) are all the time being attached to things and making them seem less strange, more comprehensible, more reassuring."[3]

Aware of this danger, authors have fought back, experimenting with new ways to insure the inviolability of their own systems, to invite abrasion, insist on strangeness, create fictions. Lewis Carroll is in some small degree a forerunner of this saving effort. To see his nonsense as a logic is thus far from being an exercise in bloodless formalism. That logic insures the fictionality of his art, and as human

---

3. "A Path for the Future of the Novel," in Maurice Nadeau, *The French Novel Since the War*, tr. A. M. Sheridan Smith (London, 1967) 185.

beings we need fictions. As is so often the case, Nietzsche said it best: "we have art in order not to die of the truth."[4]

After having stressed at such length that everything in the *Snark* means what it means according to its own system, it is no doubt unnecessary, but in conclusion I would like to answer the question with which we began. What is a Boojum? A Boojum is a Boojum.

DONALD RACKIN

Blessed Rage: Lewis Carroll and the Modern Quest for Order†

What should we make of a man who for fifty years kept a meticulous register of the contents of every letter he wrote or received— summaries of well over 100,000 letters? Of a man who maintained a record of the many luncheons and dinners he gave throughout a sociable lifetime, with diagrams showing where each guest sat and lists of just what dishes were served? Of a man who threatened to break off relations with his publisher of thirty years' standing because he found slight imperfections in the eighty-four thousandth copy of one of his popular children's books, then in print for twenty years? These are a few of the curious facts that shape our understanding of Charles Lutwidge Dodgson, that religious Oxford don, obsessive and conservative, who denied publicly throughout his life that he had anything to do with those masterpieces of mad, nonsensical disorder signed by a comic genius called Lewis Carroll.

Wherever we look, the biographical evidence indicates that Dodgson was passionately devoted to order in his everyday affairs and that his rage for order sometimes even bordered on the pathological. But he was by no means unique: We recognize the type all around us. People like Dodgson, people who manifest their extraordinary need for order by obsessively regulating their everyday lives, seem also to manifest through this behavior a deep-seated anxiety about the messiness that surrounds us, an anxiety about the morally random nature of existence. On guard against this apparently mindless chaos that threatens their beliefs and their very sanity, they fill their waking lives with artificial structure—with manufactured systems and rules their wills impose on all the disorderly matter and events they inevitably encounter.

Scientific studies demonstrating the strict mechanical order in nature, like Darwin's explanations of nature's puzzling randomness,

4. *The Will to Power* (1909–10), Book III, Section 822.
† From *Lewis Carroll: A Celebration*, ed. Edward Guiliano (New York: Clarkson Potter, 1982) 15–23. Copyright 1982 by Donald Rackin. Reprinted by permission of the author.

variation, and waste (*The Origin of Species*, by the way, was published less then two years before Dodgson told the first Alice story to his beloved Alice Liddell), cannot even begin to dispel such troubled people's desperate sense of underlying anarchy. Indeed, these troubled souls are likely to find in theories like Darwin's further evidence of ultimate moral chaos; for such strict mechanical order in nature offers little human comfort, little or no power to resolve the anxieties we can suffer in contemplating the morally meaningless process that is nature and our only home. Instead of finding in Darwinian and post-Darwinian science some solution to the metaphysical problems of apparently random natural variety, these obsessively orderly people—and by no means are they always scientifically naive—might very well find their objective, daytime corroborations of their worst nightmares: a chilling panorama of the pointless, mindless, amoral, and inescapable mechanisms in which science has now placed them firmly and forever. And they might easily find themselves—in their need for a corresponding moral pattern, for individual or collective human significance—alone, terrifyingly alone in a careless, indifferent, absurd universe. When Alice in her Wonderland cries because she is, as she says, "so *very* tired of being all alone here!" she pines not only for the human companionship she has lost, but also for some familiar signposts of intelligible order that her fellow humans dream or construct for themselves in their darkness above nature's ultimate emptiness. The religious and metaphysical assumptions that once answered the basic human need for orderly and permanent explanations and reasons beyond the reach of reason had thinned out and vanished for many Victorians during their very lifetimes, destroyed by a natural childlike curiosity like Darwin's— and like Alice's. The resulting void was terrifying.

Thus, the broadly operative teleological vision that found or mythologized an orderly metaphysical structure within nature's bewildering mulitplicity, fecundity, and waste was swept away in the nineteenth century by modern science hitting its full stride, an inescapable science that now began to demonstrate conclusively the true cold order of nature. Like religion, natural history could not longer serve as a refuge for those who searched for the warm comforts of an intelligible moral pattern in their physical environment. The deep need for such order that Dodsgon expressed overtly in this life and covertly in his imaginative works could no longer be satisfied by those genial forays into shapely nature and natural history in which genteel English amateurs had indulged before Darwin. It might therefore be symbolically important that Dodgson's hobbies were usually ordered not naturally, but mechanically—photography, music boxes, mechanical toys, cerebral puzzles and games. In his conscious pastimes at least, Dodgson was wise enough to avoid what his own Cheshire Cat feels is unavoidable—going among mad people—wise enough to avoid journeys to the natural substratum, to that threatening underground beneath his orderly, civilized, conventionally religious existence.

But in Carroll's great and honest literary fantasies, games and toys will not suffice: The ends of his *Alice* games are arbitrary and forced, the search for the Shark is doomed for failure, the Riddle of the Raven and the Writing Desk—that is, the connection between predatory, amoral nature and polite civilization, between Nature and the Word—has no answer. His human and animal creatures, aside perhaps from Alice, symoblize a *permanent* confusion—not the merely physical, and thus solvable, puzzles of something like Darwin's Galapagos Islands creatures. The explanations that Carroll's fantasies seem to call for from within nature will *never* be found. There can be no *telos*, no final goal or ultimate "meaning" within Alice's biological nature or her natural surroundings: Her natural curiosity and her human need for what she calls "the meaning of it all" make her, like us, a permanent stranger to her natural environment. She will never attain that Eden she calls "the loveliest garden you ever saw." The creatures she meets will always go round and round their mad tea tables and pointless caucus rings, with no possible rationale or goal, no final end to their circles—graphic metaphors for the Darwinian model of nature's instinctual, unthinking, amoral, and endless round of self-preservation and of the permanent schism between the workings of nature and the human mind's need for final meaning. Such comic vignettes epitomize and focus the chaos that pervades the *Alices* and *The Snark*: Their games are essentially ruleless, circular, and without end—games undoubtedly, for "mad people."

The fault here lies, of course, in life itself. When Alice complains to the Cheshire Cat that the croquet game seems to have no rules, she couples this with "and you've no idea how confusing it is all the things being alive." A cat literally has no idea of this confusion, but we humans certainly do. For after Darwin, life itself becomes almost by definition a maddening moral confusion. The lovable imp Bruno in Carroll's *Sylvie and Bruno Concluded* (1893), seeing the letters "E-V-I-L" arranged by Sylvie on a board as one of his "lessons" and asked by Sylvie what they spell, exclaims, "Why it's 'LIVE,' backwards!" The narrator sympathetically adds, "(I thought it was, indeed)." Carroll critics often cite this passage as a clue to Dodgson's psychology; but they generally miss its more direct and crucial relationship to Carroll's "backwards" literary fantasies—to the evil confusion in all the living things being alive, to the darkness and the old chaos inherent in living and dying nature after Darwin's simple biological vision has settled on the world, after innocent, childish Darwinian curiosity has enticed us down the rabbit-hole and behind our manufactured, anthropomorphic looking-glass.

* * *

Indeed, in Wonderland the sort of progressive evolutionism voiced at the end of *In Memoriam* and echoed in much conventional Victorian literature is treated with particular scorn: For example, a baby can devolve into a pig as easily as a pig can evolve into a baby. In Carroll's comic vision, motion is mere motion without first cause or final goal. And despite Alice's queening and the checkmate in looking-glass chess, no one really wins by progressing logically and by deliberately reaching some known and desired end¹—or everyone wins, as in the endlessly circular Caucus Race, which in itself nonsensically destroys the very grounds of all teleology. Alice, of course, does progress, but only toward a recognition that she must deny her frighteningly vivid perceptions of nature's endless, careless, amoral, and unprogressive dance. The final chapter of *Wonderland* is called appropriately "Alice's Evidence," and the subtitle of all *Looking-Glass* is *and what Alice found there*. Both titles underscore the fact that Alice gains the evidence necessary to impel her to end her threatening dreams.²

In order to survive, Alice—like the orderly Charles Dodgson—must create a meaningful world out of the morally unintelligible void, and often in opposition to clear evidence from the natural world of which we are an inseparable part. Such order is thus made *in spite*; and the spiteful element in Dodgson's rejections of disorder (like his spiteful rejections of babies and little boys because of their natural messiness) remains never far from the surface of his fantasies. Alice's own spitefulness ("Who cares for *you*. . . . You're nothing

---

1. Ivor Davies—in "Looking-Glass Chess," *The Anglo Welsh Review*, 15 (1970): 189–91—points out that the apparently ruleless chess of *Through the Looking-Glass* can be made intelligible if the game is played according to the rules of the original ancient Indian chess from which modern chess developed. "At the remote period of its birth in India," writes Davies, chess "belonged to the widespread family of human games based on chance and 'the moves were governed by the casts of dice.'" These significant words occur in the very first sentence" of Howard Staunton's *The Chess-Player's Companion; Comprising a new Treatise on Odds, and a Collection of Games* (1849), and Carroll owned a copy of Staunton's treatise. "Not only does the chess become intelligible," writes Davies, "it reveals something fresh and disturbing about the meaning of the looking-glass world." Davies concludes his article with this paragraph:

"They don't keep this room so tidy as the other," thought Alice when she arrived behind the looking-glass and discovered a world beyond the care of providence or the decrees of fate. How disturbing if Carroll is suggesting that this "other world" is, after all, the real one and that it is ruled by the principle of uncertainty! A pawn's progress toward the eighth rank is hazardous in the hands of a skilled chess player.

In looking-glass chess its survival depends on the casting of unseen dice by an invisible master. No wonder Alice cried as she threw herself down on the last square. "Oh, how glad I am to get here!"

2. A Victorian churchman with Dodgson's Broad Church views would, whether consciously or unconsciously, naturally associate the title "Alice's Evidence" with William Paley's celebrated *Evidences (Natural Theology, or Evidence of the Existence and Attributes of the Deity Collected from the Appearances of Nature*, 1802). Paley's work—usually referred to simply as "Paley's *Evidences*"—served during much of the earlier nineteenth century as one of the principal sources for a logical proof of God's existence based on the argument of orderly design in natural phenomena. Among later Victorian intellectuals, Paley's *Evidences* suffered an almost fatal blow from the "evidences" presented by modern geology and particularly by modern evolutionary theory. Carroll's play on Paley's *Evidences* vs. "Alice's Evidence" constitutes, like much of his comedy, a little joke with cosmic applications. Moreover, the fact that Alice is a little girl operating with the laughable logic of a normal naive child and that Paley was a grown man operating with the formidable but finally laughable logic of a brilliant adult theologian adds several degrees of irony to the jest.

but a pack of cards!", for example) is one of Carroll's principal means to make her characterization believably human. It also helps explain why modern readers frequently admire what they see as her "heroism." Like many spiteful heroines and heroes of failed causes in stage tragedies, Alice is a not altogether attractive figure. But we still admire her because she unwittingly learns to act heroically when she fails to find the order she seeks in the surrounding natural chaos. She thus becomes for many modern readers what she undoubtedly was for Dodgson: a naive champion of the doomed human quest for ultimate meaning and Edenic order. In the *Alices*, as in modern existential theory, human meaning is made in spite of the void; and, in making her order and meaning out of, essentially, *nothing*, the child Alice spitefully makes—for herself and for us, her elders—sense out of nonsense.

But this is not to say that the *Alice* books are little *King Lears*. For all their tragic implications, they are basically comic. Accordingly, their heroine, besides persevering and fighting back, has the practical good sense of a comic, rather than a tragic, heroine. At the end of each book, she has the good sense to do another necessary human thing, to run away, to deny and suppress her own true nightmares.

In any case, to a certain extent Alice's imposed order becomes all the more admirable and precious because of its seriocomic fragility (the way the *Alice* books have become the cherished, sometimes sacrosanct, possession of troubled adults). The comic tone at the end of *Wonderland*, for example, like the customary tone of Carroll's adult narrator, is so sure of itself because it is ultimately so unsure of itself, because it is forged in shaky anxiety, emerging suddenly and full-blown from the rejection of an orderly person's nightmare of disorder. Like the total rejection of any bad dream we have just broken off, Carroll's concluding pages seem to deny completely the validity of adventures that have all the luminosity of our truest experiences, whose creatures and insanities will continue, we sense, indefinitely after we reject them and wake to our fragile veneer, our dreams of cosmic order. Therefore, the endings of both *Alice* books, contrived and sentimental as they are, are paradoxically appropriate and paradoxically true to our ordinary ambiguous experience. Brazen (and frightened) Alice heroically rejects all her evidence as nonsense and dream; chaos and old night are ironically dispelled by mere teatime and a little kitty cat (both, by the way, fine and delicate symbols of insouciant high civilization); and the final narratives seem to explain away sensibly whatever residual conviction of the adventures' relevance and validity might persist—in dreamers, readers, or writers whose waking moments are shaped by and dedicated to humanly constructed order.

*   *   *

* * * Carroll's comic fantasies of the 1860s and 70s stand in curious contrast to the attitudes toward ultimate order found in most Victorian literature (Pater is the notable exception). And on this contrast rests, perhaps, Carroll's strongest claim to a place in the rise of modernism. The order that is restored at the ends of both *Alices* in no "Victorian compromise" between a horror vision of nature's moral disorder and a consoling assertion of some traditional moral order within nature. Missing in Carroll is even that nostalgic sadness, that vain longing, that hopeless but "blessed Hope" Hardy half senses in darkening nature, a spirit that might revive some corresponding, if ephemeral, hope in us. Instead, Carroll's final, above-ground order stands fully isolated, discontinuous with the literal anarchy of Alice's adventures and the metaphysical and moral anarchy they encapsulate. Instead of the typical Victorian compromise, here at the ends of both *Alice* books is a defiant, spiteful, total, and uncompromising rejection of one vision and a complacent, comic reassertion of another—one that, significantly, no longer appears to retain a shred of philosophical validity, even within its own field of play, the adventures themselves.

Like a haughty member of the upper classes staring down an incontrovertible but class-threatening fact, the frame story of each *Alice* book stands in direct, defiant opposition to the body of the book, the adventures themselves. When Humpty Dumpty tells Alice "the question is . . . which is to be master—that's all," he refers to many things. Like Alice's assertion that the "great puzzle" is "Who in the world am I?" Humpty's remark has deep existential, linguistic, political, social, and even economic significance. He is master of his world because he *chooses* to be in spite of the actual circumstances and because in his class-ordered, hierarchical, cash-nexus world, he has the power (words and money) and the elevated position (class and proper diction) to pay for and command obedience—and thus a kind of existence and order. Who "in the world" we are (and who we are "in the world") is a function of how we order (master, boss about, bully, verbalize, and force into a coherent order) our essentially unorderable worlds. Never mind that our mastery over members of lower classes or over the intransigent moral chaos underlying all classes and systems is as fragile as Humpty Dumpty's eggshell and as precarious as Humpty Dumpty's perch. At the end of her Looking-Glass adventures, Alice says of their "dreadful confusion," "I can't stand this any longer!" Similarly, at the end of her Wonderland adventures she finally decides she will have no more of their even more dreadful confusion. Like Humpty Dumpty, she decides for herself what to call this dreaded and uncontrollable chaos—and she calls it mere "curious dream," mere "nonsense" (sense though it most certainly seems to be). So too do the ends of both fantasies define as wonderful "nonsense" what we and Alice have just experienced vividly as frightening reality—asserting through their form as well as their content that they too will have none of it. For at this point in the adventures and the narratives there appears no sane choice for humans but to seize power, to impose the fragile, artificial order of above-ground human law and social convention, using their shaky *words* as their primary means of mastery—calling, for example, Alice's ominous "under Ground" a sunny "Wonderland."

Of course, like the White Knight (a most probable candidate for Dodgson's persona behind the looking-glass)—who says of his silly upside-down box "it's my own invention"—we sometimes allow ourselves to recognize that such order and such power are merely our own silly, upside-down inventions of a whole world. But generally we keep up our guard, and such chilling recognitions come to us indirectly and disguised in fantasies, jest, nonsense, and dreams—not straight and not in that daylight we choose to call sober, unadorned everyday life. Besides, we are also well aware, at some level of comprehension, of the final danger: If our eggshell, invented, but coherent waking world falls and is shattered, we too, like that imperious but fragile Humpty Dumpty, may be shattered forever.

Thus, like the aesthetic order of much modern art, the final order of the *Alice* books and *The Snark* is not an order discovered in objective nature, but an order openly imposed upon nature—a human meaning and coherence that frames and shapes a morally shapeless void. Like Wallace Stevens' singer whose song "mastered the night and portioned out the sea," Alice, with her naive declaration of that all the assembled disorderly creatures of her disorganized adventures are "nothing but a pack of cards," masters them with language, to satisfy what Stevens calls our "blessed rage . . . to order the words . . . of ourselves and of our origins" ["The Idea of Order at Key West"]. Like Stevens' shapely but simple jar, simply placed in the wild nature of Tennessee, Alice's simple final declarations make the forever "slovenly wilderness" of her underground adventures in raw nature take on *her* order, shape, and meaning. Like Stevens' plain jar, her childish declarations of mastery not only take dominion over her particular nightmares of chaos; in a sense, they also take, as Stevens puts it, "dominion everywhere." And for this, many of Carroll's modern readers bless him unaware. For the question is not whether Alice's ordering of night and sea, of herself and her origins, is ultimately valid in terms of physical nature as we post-Darwinians now know it. The question is much more pressing and pragmatic: It has to do with Alice's capability to fulfill her human potential despite her own nature and that nature of which she remains a permanent part.

Selected Bibliography

Works excerpted for this volume are not listed here.

WORKS, LETTERS, AND DIARIES

The Annotated Alice, Ed. Martin Gardner. New York, 1960. Supplemented by *More Annotated Alice*. Ed. Martin Gardner. New York, 1990. The latter book includes interesting early twentieth-century illustrations by the American artist Peter Newell.
The Annotated Snark. Ed. Martin Gardner. New York, 1962.
The Complete Works of Lewis Carroll, London, 1939. The Nonesuch edition, reprinted in the United States in the Modern Library.
The Complete Illustrated Works of Lewis Carroll.Ed. Edward Guiliano. New York, 1982. Includes the Alice books and *Alice's Adventures Under Ground*, *The Hunting of the Snark*, *Sylvie and Bruno* (1889, 1893), the comic poems of *Rhyme? and Reason?* (1883), the sentimental poems of *Three Sunsets* (1898), and *A Tangled Tale* (1885).
Lewis Carroll and the House of Macmillan. Ed. Morton N. Cohen and Anita Gandolfo. London, 1987. Letters to publisher.
Lewis Carroll: Photos and Letters to His Child Friends. Ed. Guido Almansi. Parma, 1975. Excellent reproduction of photographs.
Lewis Carroll's Alice's Adventures in Wonderland, Lewis Carroll's Through the Looking-Glass, and *Lewis Carroll's The Hunting of the Snark*. Berkeley, 1982, 1983. Text by Selwyn H. Goodacre. Illustrations by Barry Moser. Introduction and notes by James R. Kincaid.
Lewis Carroll's Symbolic Logic. Ed. William Warren Bartley III. New ed. New York, 1986. Excellent introduction makes a good case for Dodgson's innovative thinking as a mathematical logician.
The Mathematical Recreations of Lewis Carroll. Two volumes. New York, 1958. Includes *Symbolic Logic* (1896), *The Game of Logic* (1886), *Pillow-Problems* (1893), and *A Tangled Tale* (1885).
The Rectory Umbrella and Mischmasch. Ed. Florence Milner. Cambridge, 1932. Two of Carroll's youthful domestic magazines.
The Russian Journal and Other Selections from the Works of Lewis Carroll. Ed. John Francis McDermott. New York, 1935.
Useful and Instructive Poetry. London, 1954. Carroll's earliest poems.

BIBLIOGRAPHY

Crutch, Denis. *The Lewis Carroll Handbook. Being a New Version of A Handbook of the Literature of the Rev. C. L. Dodgson, by Sidney Herbert Williams and Falconer Madan [1931], revised and augmented by Roger Lancelyn Green [1962], now further revised*. Folkstone and Hampden, 1979.
Guiliano, Edward, ed. *Lewis Carroll: An Annotated International Bibliography, 1960–1977*. Charlottesville, 1980.
———. "Lewis Carroll: A Sesquicentennial Guide to Research." *Dickens Studies Annual* 1982: 263–310.
Fordyce, Rachel, ed. *Lewis Carroll: A Reference Guide*. Boston, 1988.
Godman, Stanley. "Lewis Carroll's Final Corrections to 'Alice.'" *Times Literary Supplement* 2 May 1958: 248.
Goodacre, Selwyn H. "Lewis Carroll's 1897 Corrections to *Alice*." *Library*, 5th series, 28.2 (June 1973): 131–46.
Preston, Michael J. *A KWIC Concordance to Lewis Carroll's* Alice's Adventures in Wonderland *and* Through the Looking-Glass, *and* A Concordance to the Verse of Lewis Carroll. New York, 1986, 1985.
Weaver, Warren. "The Mathematical Manuscripts of Lewis Carroll." *Princeton Library Chronicle* 16 (1955): 4–9.
———. *Alice in Many Tongues: The Translations of* Alice in Wonderland. Madison, 1964.

BIOGRAPHY

Clark, Anne. *The Real Alice: Lewis Carroll's Dream Child*. London, 1981. Biography of Alice Liddell.
Cohen, Morton, ed. *Lewis Carroll: Interviews and Recollections*. New York, 1989.

Furniss, Harry. "Recollections of 'Lewis Carroll.' " *Strand* 35 (1908): 48–52. Furniss illustrated both parts of *Sylvie and Bruno.*
Gordon, Colin. *Beyond the Looking Glass: Reflections of Alice and Her Family.* New York, 1982.
Green, Roger Lancelyn. *Lewis Carroll.* London, 1960.
Lennon, Florence Becker. *Victoria Through the Looking Glass: A Life of Lewis Carroll.* Rev. ed. New York, 1962.
Moses, Belle. *Lewis Carroll in Wonderland and At Home.* London, 1910.
Ovenden, Graham. *Lewis Carroll.* London, 1984. In Masters of Photography series.
Pudney, John. *Lewis Carroll and His World.* New York, 1976.

COLLECTIONS OF ESSAYS

Bloom, Harold, ed. *Modern Critical Views on Lewis Carroll.* New York, 1987. Includes essays by Jan Gordon ("The *Alice* Books and the Metaphors of Victorian Childhood"), John Hollander ("Carroll's Quest Romance"), and Judith Crews on Carroll's word games.
Crutch, Denis, ed. *Mr. Dodgson: Nine Studies.* London, 1973.
Guiliano, Edward, ed. *Lewis Carroll Observed: A Collection of Unpublished Photographs, Drawings, Poetry, and New Essays.* New York, 1976. Includes essays by Roger Henkle ("High Art and Low Amusements"), Morton Cohen on contemporary reviews of *The Hunting of the Snark,* and Jeffrey Stern ("Lewis Carroll the Pre-Raphaelite").
————, ed. *Lewis Carroll: A Celebration.* New York, 1982. Includes essays by Michael Hancher ("*Punch* and Alice"), Roger Henkle ("Carroll's Narratives Underground: 'Modernism' and Form"), and Edward Guiliano ("A Time for Humor: Lewis Carroll, Laughter and Despair, and *The Hunting of the Snark*").
————, and James R. Kincaid, eds. *Soaring with the Dodo: Essays on Lewis Carroll's Life and Art.* New York, 1982. Includes essays by Nina Auerbach ("Falling Alice, Fallen Women, and Dream Children"), Joyce Carol Oates on *The Hunting of the Snark,* Jan B. Gordon and Edward Guiliano on Dodgson's photography, and Kathleen Blake on recent commentary on Carroll.
Philips, Robert, ed. *Aspects of Alice.* New York, 1971. Includes essays by Woolf, Hinz, and Grotjahn cited below, and an essay by Patricia Meyer Spacks.

HISTORICAL STUDIES

Cripps, Elizabeth A. "*Alice* and the Reviewers." *Children's Literature* 11 (1983): 32–48. Contemporary reviews. See also *Jabberwocky* 9 (1980): 3–8, 27–39, 55–58.
Darton, F. J. Harvey, *Children's Books in England: Five Centuries of Social Life.* 3rd ed. rev. by Brian Alderson. Cambridge, 1982.
Gray, Donald J. "The Uses of Victorian Laughter." *Victorian Studies* 10 (1966): 147–76.
Higbie, Robert. "Lewis Carroll and the Victorian Reaction against Doubt." *Thalia* 3 (1980): 21–28.
Inglis, Fred. *The Promise of Happiness: Value and Meaning in Children's Literature.* Cambridge, 1981. 101–14.
Jackson, Rosemary. "Victorian Fantasies." *Fantasy: The Literature of Subversion.* New York, 1981. 141–56.
Knoepflmacher, U. C. "Little Girls Without Their Curls: Female Aggression in Victorian Children's Literature." *Children's Literature* 11 (1983): 14–31.
Leach, Elsie. "Alice in Wonderland in Perspective." *Victorian News Letter,* no. 25 (1964): 9–11. The Alice books as mid-Victorian children's literature.
Leslie, Shane. "Lewis Carroll and the Oxford Movement." *London Mercury* 28 (1933): 233–39.
Lovett, Charles C. *Alice on Stage: A History of Early Theatrical Productions of Alice in Wonderland.* Westport, London, 1990.
Moss, Anita. "Lewis Carroll." *Writers for Children.* Ed. Jane Bingham. New York, 1988. 117–27.
Mulderig, Gerald P. "Alice in Wonderland: Subversive Elements in the World of Victorian Children's Fiction." *Journal of Popular Culture* 11 (1977): 320–29.
Pattison, Robert. *The Child Figure in Victorian Literature.* Athens, 1978.
Prickett, Stephen. *Victorian Fantasy.* Bloomington, 1979.
Rackin, Donald. "Corrective Laughter: Carroll's Alice and Popular Children's Literature of the Nineteenth Century." *Journal of Popular Culture* 1 (1967): 243–55.
Reinstein, Phyllis Giles. *Alice in Context.* New York, 1988. Context is children's literature of Victorian period.
Sale, Roger. *Fairy Tales and After.* Cambridge, 1978. 101–26.
Zipes, Jack. *Victorian Fairy Tales: The Revolt of the Fairies and Elves.* New York, 1987.

LITERARY AND LINGUISTIC STUDIES

Atherton, J. S. "Carroll, the Unforeseen Precursor." *Books at the Wake: A Study of Literary Allusions in James Joyce's Finnegan's Wake.* New York, 1960. 124–36.
Auden, W. H. "The Man Who Wrote Alice." *New York Times Book Review* 28 Feb. 1954: 4.

Bivona, Daniel. "Alice the Child Imperialist and the Games of Wonderland." *Nineteenth-Century Literature* 41 (1986–87): 143–71.

Blake, Kathleen. *Play, Games, and Sport: The Literary Works of Lewis Carroll*. Ithaca, 1974.

Cammaerts, Emile. *The Poetry of Nonsense*. London, 1926. Study of Carroll, Edward Lear, and other nineteenth-century comic writers.

Cixous, Helene and Marie Maclean (tr.). "Introduction to Lewis Carroll's *Through the Looking-Glass* and *The Hunting of the Snark*." *New Literary History* 13 (1982): 231–51.

Clark, Beverly Lyon. *Reflections of Fantasy: The Mirror-Worlds of Carroll, Nabokov, and Pynchon*. New York, 1986.

Cohen, Morton N. "Another Wonderland: Lewis Carroll's *The Nursery Alice*." *Lion and Unicorn* 7 (1983): 120–26.

Deleuze, Gilles. "The Schizophrenic and Language: Surface and Depth in Lewis Carroll and Antonin Artaud." *Textual Strategies*. Ed. Josue V. Harari. Ithaca, 1979. 277–95.

Flescher, Jacqueline. "The Language of Nonsense in *Alice*." *Yale French Studies* 43 (1969–70): 128–44.

Gattegno, Jean. *Lewis Carroll*. Tr. Rosemary Sheed. New York, 1976.

Green, Roger Lancelyn. "The Real Lewis Carroll." *Quarterly Review* 292 (1954): 85–97. Review of biographies and criticism.

Gregory, Andre. "Alice in Wonderland." *The Drama Review* 14 (1970): 94–104. Description of a theatrical adaptation of the Alice books in New York City in the 1960s.

Gregory, Horace. "Lewis Carroll's Alice and Her White Knight and Wordsworth's Ode on Immortality." *The Shield of Achilles*. New York, 1944. 90–105.

Hancher, Michael. "Humpty Dumpty and Verbal Meaning." *Journal of Aesthetics and Art Criticism* 40 (1981): 49–58.

Henkle, Roger. "The Mad Hatter's World." *Virginia Quarterly Review* 49 (1973): 99–117.

Hinz, John. "Alice Meets the Don." *South Atlantic Quarterly* 52 (1953): 253–66. The Alice books and *Don Quixote*.

Hubbell, George Shelton. "Triple Alice." *Sewanee Review* 48 (1940): 174–95.

Kelly, Richard. *Lewis Carroll*. Rev. ed. New York, 1990.

Kenner, Hugh. "Alice in Chapelizod." *Dublin's Joyce*. Boston, 1956. 276–300. The Alice books and *Finnegan's Wake*.

Kincaid, James R. "Alice's Invasion of Wonderland." *PMLA* 88 (1973): 92–99.

Kirk, Daniel F. *Charles Dodgson, Semiotician*. Gainesville, 1962.

Lecercle, Jean-Jacques. *Philosophy Through the Looking-Glass: Language, Nonsense, and Desire*. LaSalle, 1985. 74–79.

Levin, Harry. "Wonderland Revisited." *Kenyon Review* 27 (1965): 591–616.

Little, Judith. "Liberated Alice: Dodgson's Female Hero as Domestic Rebel." *Women's Studies* 3 (1976): 195–205.

Luchinsky, Ellen. "Alice: Child or Adult." *Jabberwocky* 6 (1977): 63–71. Considers appeal of Alice books to adults.

Madden, William A. "Framing the Alices." *PMLA* 101 (1986): 362–73.

Matthews, Charles. "Satire in the Alice Books." *Criticism* 21 (1970): 105–19.

Mellor, Anne. "Fear and Trembling: From Lewis Carroll to Existentialism." *English Romantic Irony*. Cambridge, 1980. 165–80.

Muskat-Tabakowska, E. "General Semantics Behind the Looking-Glass." *ETC*. 27 (1970): 483–92.

Partridge, Eric. "The Nonsense Words of Edward Lear and Lewis Carroll." *Here, There, and Everywhere*. London, 1950. 162–88.

Rackin, Donald. "Alice's Journey to the End of Night." *PMLA* 81 (1966): 313–26.

Shire, Linda. "Fantasy, Nonsense, Parody, and the Status of the Real: The Example of Carroll." *Victorian Poetry* 26 (1988): 267–83.

Sutherland, Robert D. *Language and Lewis Carroll*. The Hague, 1970. What Dodgson knew about language and how he used his knowledge in the Alice books.

Thody, Philip. "Lewis Carroll and the Surrealists." *Twentieth Century* 163 (1958): 427–34.

Watson, George. "Tory Alice." *American Scholar* 55 (1986): 543–52.

White, Alison. "Alice After a Hundred Years." *Michigan Quarterly Review* 4 (1965): 261–64.

Wilson, Edmund. "C. L. Dodgson: The Poet-Logician." *The Shores of Light*. New York, 1952. 540–50.

Woolf, Virginia. "Lewis Carroll." *The Moment and Other Essays*. New York, 1948. 81–83.

PSYCHOANALYTICAL STUDIES

Faimberg, Haydée. "The Snark Was a Boojum." *International Review of Psychoanalysis* 4 (1977): 243–49.

Greenacre, Phyllis. *Swift and Carroll*. New York, 1955.

Grotjahn, Martin. "About the Symbolization of *Alice in Wonderland*." *American Imago* 4 (1947): 32–41.

Hirsch, Gordon. "Double Binds and Schizophrenic Conversations." *Denver Quarterly* 19:2 (1984): 85–106.

Schilder, Paul. "Psychoanalytical Remarks on *Alice in Wonderland* and Lewis Carroll." *Journal of Nervous and Mental Diseases* 87 (1938): 159–68.

MATHEMATICAL AND PHILOSOPHICAL STUDIES

Alexander, Peter. *Logic and the Humour of Lewis Carroll.* Leeds, 1951.
Bartley, William Warren III. "Lewis Carroll's Lost Book on Logic." *Scientific American* 227 (1972): 38–46.
Braithwaite, R. B. "Lewis Carroll as Logician." *Mathematical Gazette* 16 (1932): 174–78.
Garnett, William. "Alice Through the (Convex) Looking Glass." *Mathematical Gazette* 9 (1918–19): 237–41, 293–98. Non-Euclidean space and relativity in the Alice books.
Heath, Peter, ed. *The Philosopher's Alice.* New York, 1974. Annotated to identify logical, mathematical, and linguistic references and problems.
Holmes, Roger W. "The Philosopher's Alice." *Antioch Review* 19 (1959): 133–49.
"Lewis Carroll as a Mathematician." *Nature* 57 (20 Jan. 1898): 279–80. Dodgson's obituary notice.
Pitcher, George. "Wittgenstein, Nonsense, and Lewis Carroll." *Massachusetts Review* 6 (1965): 591–611.
Pycior, Helena M. "At the Intersection of Mathematics and Humor: Lewis Carroll's *Alice in Wonderland* and Symbolical Algebra." *Victorian Studies* 28 (1985): 149–70.
Quine, W. V. "Lewis Carroll's Logic." *Theories and Things.* Cambridge, 1981.
Weaver, Warren. "Lewis Carroll, Mathematician." *Scientific American* 194 (1956): 116–28.

ILLUSTRATIONS

Hancher, Michael. *The Tenniel Illustrations to the 'Alice' Books.* Columbus, 1985.
———. *On the Writing, Illustration, and Publication of Lewis Carroll's Alice Books.* New York, 1984.
Mespoulet, Marguerite. *Creators of Wonderland.* New York, 1934. Study of nineteenth-century artists and illustrators of grotesque and fantastic subjects, including Tenniel and the French caricaturist Jean Grandville.
Mitchell, Charles. "The Designs for the Snark." *Lewis Carroll's* The Hunting of the Snark. Ed. James Tarris and John Dooley. Los Altos, 1981. 83–115.
Ovenden, Graham, and John Davis, eds. *The Illustrators of Alice.* Rev. ed. New York, 1979.